In the road ahead shimmered a gilt-edged portal like a ring around the sun. Swooping from the middle came a huge yellow glob only vaguely man-shaped. Its jellyfish arms had enfolded Ruellana and were dragging her toward the shining portal.

Unsheathing Harvester as he ran, Sunbright dove and grabbed Ruellana's boot with his free hand. He stabbed at the creature, but to no avail. The woman was hauled steadily into the glittering portal.

Greenwillow ran to the barbarian's side, grabbed his arm, and tugged. "Let go!" the elf shrilled. "You can't help her!"

"I can't desert her now! I didn't desert you!"

"But she's not what she seems!" the elf wailed. "Don't—"

"Get to Dalekeva!" Sunbright roared. "I'll meet you there!"

Then, hanging on to only a foot, the barbarian lunged headfirst at the portal, now no bigger than his hips. With a twinkle of golden light on his hobnailed boots, he was gone.

The Netheril Trilogy

Sword Play
Clayton Emery

Dangerous Games
(available November 1996)

Sword Play

Clayton Emery

SWORD PLAY

Random House and its affiliate companies have worldwide distribution rights in the book trade for English language products of TSR, Inc.

Distributed to the book and hobby trade in the United Kingdom by TSR Ltd.

Distributed to the toy and hobby trade by regional distributors.

Cover art by Alan Pollack.

First Printing: May 1996
Printed in the United States of America.
Library of Congress Catalog Card Number: 95-62204

9 8 7 6 5 4 3 2 1

ISBN: 0-7869-0492-5   8569XXX1501

TSR, Inc.   TSR Ltd.
201 Sheridan Springs Rd.   120 Church End, Cherry Hinton
Lake Geneva, WI 53147   Cambridge CB1 3LB
U.S.A.   United Kingdom

**Dedicated to
Hunter, My Best Bud**

Chapter 1

They'd seen him climbing, and he'd seen them following. He'd scaled as high and fast as he could, but they'd pursued, and now he was trapped.

Making the best of a bad situation, the young barbarian selected a pocket in the sheer wall of red-gray granite. The pocket curled around to his left, then broke off jaggedly. A trail trickling through the mountains kissed the jagged edge, but after that descended into a gorge full of shadows. The shadows he could have used to hide in, despite the midday sun, but he'd peered over the edge and seen the trail was too steep. He'd be tripping down it, wary of breaking his neck and unable to turn around, his back a perfect target when his enemies arrived. He settled for rolling a round boulder into the trail as a temporary barricade. Then he stayed put. They could attack only from the front and the left, and would have to mount a short slope to do it, so they couldn't flank him. As long as

they didn't have missile weapons—arrows or slings—
he could fight hand to hand to match any warrior.

The sunny cliff was warm against his back as he
waited—perhaps to die. It was coming on winter, especially here in the high country bordering the Barren Mountains. The thin wind that sighed and
soughed around his legs was cool, but would bite
after sundown—if he were still alive to feel it. Away
from the warm cliff, patches of snow hugged the
northern side of the rocks. It was all rocks here above
the tree line, which was a clean cut, as if by the knife
of a titan. Sunbright wondered if the gods were closer
up here, and if so, to whom he should pray. Garagos,
god of war, to give him strength in the fight to come?
Or Tyche, Lady Luck? Somehow neither seemed ap-
propriate, so he sent a common prayer for help and
guidance to Chauntea, the Earthmother. She was
laid out before his feet, miles and miles of scrubby
trees down a long sweeping valley over which red-
tailed hawks and vultures soared. Sunbright might
be visiting her soonest, after all. But if so, he
wouldn't go alone. A grunt from below brought his
sword up.

They skulked out of the tree line, seven of them.
Orcs, but not the usual variety. These had gray-
green skin, lank black hair, pug noses, and long
knotted arms. They moved warily, watching him and
not charging to crush his skull as the usual idiots
did.

But this lot, seen for the first time close up, were
oddly neat. They wore actual uniforms, almost like
human soldiers. Tunics of various leathers had been
dyed a consistent lichen gray, and painted on each
breast was a not-so-smeary red hand of five spread
fingers. Rather than go barefoot, and thus cripple
themselves on the scree, they wore sturdy, scuffed

boots that came to their knobby knees. And each orc soldier wore a rusty kettle helmet, round with a short brim. In their hands trailed clubs studded with black obsidian, which Sunbright knew to be sharper than his own steel blade, for the layered stone presented not one but a dozen razor edges.

Sunbright could have shot his few arrows, but didn't bother. Somehow it didn't seem right on this momentous, lonely day. He'd work with what the gods had given him, take the contest as it came.

Still, to die now seemed unfair when he'd been so careful to cover his tracks, stepping from stone to stone all morning. How had they discovered him? Were the orcs' gods favoring them?

The orcs grunted again and stopped, consulting about how to attack. They could see their prey, a young human male, tall and gangly, yet laid with ropy muscle. His hair was sun-bright blond, shaved at the temples, then gathered into a topknot from which dangled a short tail. He wore a faded linen shirt that fell to his knees, stout boots of many leather straps and iron rings, and a jerkin made of brown- and white-blotched goatskin, laced across his chest. A rolled blanket was carried over one shoulder, a longbow and quiver over the other, along with his scabbard.

But most curious was his sword. As long as his arm, the blade widened at the tip to make a graceful arc, its back face deeply cut into a hook. It looked more like an elongated brush cutter than a sword, and gave the orcs pause.

"You like this sword?" The young man shook his weapon, impatient to fight, to get the trial over. "Its name is Harvester of Blood. Come up, orcish offal, and hear it sing its name and that of its wielder, Sunbright Steelshanks!"

The ritual battle curses didn't seem to impress the orcs, who merely fanned out along the short slope below him, from the rock he'd propped in the trail to the cliff wall at his right elbow. Strangely, they said nothing until the captain, which had a red hand painted on a placard in the band of its helmet, bellowed, "Rag-faa!"

Then they charged, howling.

Careful not to lift his feet lest he slip on the scree and pebbles, Sunbright hoisted the long blade high over his right shoulder and simultaneously scooted his left foot forward for balance. Then he contracted like a coiled spring. The foot snapped back, and the sword came almost to meet it. Caught between was an orc that had scampered up quicker than its fellows. Keen-eyed, Sunbright avoided the steel helm that might nick his blade. He struck at the juncture of neck and shoulder, steel shaving the orc's collarbone and hunting a major vein. He struck hard, but not hard enough to fetch up the blade in bone. The blow was perfect. At the solid cut, the orc's blood squirted in three directions. The creature dropped more from shock than the actual blow, though the wound would kill within a minute.

Sunbright didn't linger to gloat, or even watch. Conserving every ounce of strength for the battle yet to come, he ripped the blade free and slung it backhand at the next encroaching orc.

Harvester lived up to its name. The deep hook in the blade lodged under an orc's upraised arm. Slashed in the armpit, the orc was knocked off-balance, away from Sunbright, then dragged back by the boy's twisting yank. The hook tore more flesh, skinning muscle from bone, throwing the orc onto its side to writhe in agony.

Normally Sunbright would have ripped out his opponent's throat, finishing it, but he could hear the voices of Thornwing and Blindhawk, who'd schooled the children in swordplay. "Don't focus on one enemy, but on all. Keep your vision wide, like the reindeer and snow wolf. Track movement, not details."

Good advice, for the orc captain had taken the rightmost wing of the attack. Counting on gaining the man's blind side, the creature came silently at a rush, club in its left hand to be out of sight, aiming to hit the human behind the knee.

Sunbright saw all of this, in a half second, as a gray, threatening blur. He didn't really understand the threat before he swung instinctively.

Slinging the long sword blade so fast and viciously it hissed in the thin mountain air, Sunbright aimed for the orc's head below its helmet. Harvester's tip sounded a *splotch* as it split the captain's face, then a *clang* as it struck and bounced off the red-gray granite. A well-struck blow and a mistake, dulling a spot on his blade. How would Blindhawk and Thornwing rate that?

Yet even the mistake he exploited. If the sword wanted to bounce off the cliff, so be it. Throwing his shoulders behind the flying steel, he sheared into an orc's arm as it swept for his head. The blow clipped off the wrist so club and hand flew in one direction and the orc's scarlet blood in another.

But so fast, so clean was the blow, the orc failed to notice it had lost a hand. The spurting hand chopped at the barbarian's head, spraying him with blood. Then the orc stumbled—and crashed full into Sunbright.

This is bad, screamed his two phantom instructors.

Stinking like a flyblown goat, the orc sagged against Sunbright's chest, bowling him back against the granite wall. Directly under the young man's nose was a dirty neck speckled with coarse black hairs and flea bites on gray skin. And over that ugly sight, a horde of orcs—How many? He hadn't counted his kills!—pressed him, howling in triumph. The dying orc hung on Sunbright's right arm, dragging it down, entangling Harvester's long blade. Before he could yank free or shove the orc off, a stone-studded club whipped at his head. Ducking, he felt the greasy smoke-stained wood brush his topknot, heard black obsidian teeth crunch on the cliff wall. Another orc punched at his face with a club, and Sunbright almost snapped his neck whipping the other way.

Use what you have, urged his teachers. Use what the gods have given you, Sunbright had told himself moments ago. But what was it?

"Ah!" he gasped aloud. Sensing more than seeing, he judged there was one orc crowding his left, two still alive on his right.

With hysterical strength, Sunbright hoisted the dead orc before him, pitched it, grunting, into the orc at his left. The orc's eyes flew wide as its dead comrade crashed into it like a sack of grain. The orc tumbled onto its back, its steel helmet striking sparks as it skidded down the short slope, its dead brethren atop it.

Still using the dead orc as cover, Sunbright followed. He scurried along the wall of the pocket, slammed his foot down alongside the tumblers, and skipped onto the round rock. It lurched, as did the man; then he vaulted over.

The trail dropped sharply, steep enough to give a goat pause. But Sunbright Steelshanks could outrun and outclimb goats, and with sure steps and reckless abandon he stabbed his feet here to this boulder, there on that flat spot, to that corner, and so on, hopping, skipping, dropping almost as fast as a stone could roll.

Within seconds he was far below the orcs, if they pursued at all. Gasping, laughing, he yipped with delight like a crazed snow wolf puppy. Gone, for the moment, were sullen black thoughts of death and revenge. He was exuberant.

He was alive!

* * * * *

"See? I told you so!"

"You liar! You had no more faith in him than I did!"

"He won; I won. That's all I care about."

A sniff replied.

Two wizards glared at one another, but not hard enough to kill. They had to get along, after all. In their own way.

The two were a study in contrasts. Candlemas was a small, podgy, balding, bearded man in an undyed smock of sackcloth tied with a rope. Sysquemalyn was a woman, taller, flame-haired, dressed in a green tunic that sparkled like fish scales, tight white breeches of soft leather, and pointed red boots that laced to the knee. At her breast hung a pendant sporting a gargoyle face whose expression shifted constantly, but which was always ugly and leering. Her clothes were a statement about her personality, as were those of Candlemas, though in a much different way.

Sysquemalyn touched a gold-painted fingernail to the palantir on the scarred worktable. In the smoky globe, Sunbright could be seen, still goat-skipping down the mountain's shoulder, but more cautiously now, aiming for the thorn and rhododendron tangle at the bottom of the gorge. "He won't last. He'll be full of himself, reveling in victory. He'll probably lie down out in the open and sing to himself and be eaten by wolves before dawn."

Candlemas nudged her finger off the globe and used the sleeve of his smock to polish off her fingerprint. "The way you're always denigrating humans, you'd think you weren't one yourself. That you'd ascended to godhood already."

"I have! Ascended!" The woman arched her back, raked and fluffed up her flaming red hair. "In my dreams, anyway. And what are dreams but portents of the future? I'll be grander than Lady Polaris someday!"

"I hope I live that long," sniped Candlemas. "I can watch the sun crash to earth."

"Oh, pooh! You're jealous because I'm a real wizard and you're a . . . a hedgehopper."

"Better than a bedhopper. Don't touch anything!"

Sysquemalyn slunk around the other mage's workshop idly, like a cat, but also like a cat, she watched her surroundings. The workshop was huge, big enough for a herd of musk-oxen, and high, wide windows all around made it seem larger, for nothing showed past the windows but winter-blue sky. The red-haired wizard had glided to a window and picked up an exquisite silver statue of a paladin on horseback. Candlemas had hundreds of such objects, all as beautiful as he was squat and plain, scattered around the vast workroom.

The woman turned the statue over as if admiring it, then chucked it out the window.

"Hey!" Candlemas ran to the opening, foolishly sticking his head out. When his head passed the spell shielding the window, cold air kissed his bald pate. The statue, of course, was long gone. And so was the wizard, almost, for Sysquemalyn playfully swatted his rump. If he hadn't grabbed the sill, he'd have followed the statue.

"You bitch!" The brown-clad wizard whirled, felt dizzy, and slumped against the stone wall. "I could have fallen!"

"So? You can fly, can't you?"

"Yes. But I'd fall a long way before I got the spell working! And why'd you chuck out my paladin? That was pilfered from the birthplace of Raliteff the Second!"

"I wanted to strike your barbarian on the head. I cheat, remember?" Idly, Sysquemalyn picked up a pliers and threw it at another window. This time Candlemas shot both hands into the air, first and final fingers erect. The shield spells on the windows, which kept heat in and wind out, thickened, and the pliers bounced off thin air and clanked on the floor. "Sys, you're a guest. Try to be civil, or I'll make you fly home."

"Piffle. I go where— Whoops! Company!"

She pointed a gold nail. The palantir shimmered, ethereal smoke inside clearing from the top downward. But that one glance was enough, for the caller had snow-white hair. Only one person they knew was so adorned.

The wizards waited quietly. Candlemas was high steward of Delia, this magical castle in which they stood, and Sysquemalyn was chamberlain. Their duties meshed, for the steward managed the grounds of the castle and the chamberlain the interior. When not engaged in the Work, the furtherance of their own magical might, Candlemas oversaw the lesser wizards who oversaw other humans who oversaw their brethren in the manuring of crops, culling of forest growth, diverting of streams and dams, and the maintaining of many lesser castles and barns and granaries, all mundane resources that kept the manor and lands thriving. Sysquemalyn oversaw her own staff of wizards who in turn supervised others who directed a staggering number of maids and footmen and cooks who kept the castle neat and its people fed; artisans who made furniture, clothing, and other goods; and entertainers and musicians who needed to be prepared at any moment in case the castle's owner dropped by.

Their methods, however, differed greatly. Candlemas felt he must oversee everything personally and drove his wizards and their clerics and farm stewards and huntsmen crazy with fussy details. Sysquemalyn most often waved a laconic hand, ordering her magical lackeys to "Do it however so." Then she would return in a day or two to scream and rant and order random folks flogged half to death for guessing wrongly about how to execute such vague orders. So the two, Candlemas and Sysquemalyn, worked together, more or less, and often squabbled, though there were weeks when, because of the castle's vast size, they never even met.

Now an image cleared, and the castle's owner could be seen. Lady Polaris was beautiful, her face calm and poised, her white hair setting off perfect golden skin. A groundling might think her a goddess, but despite staggering powers, she was human, though she'd never admit it. The lady was archmage of Delia, one of many small city-states that made up the Netherese Empire. In the pyramidal power of the empire, Lady Polaris ranked fairly high but was still under the thrall of the preeminent mages. Yet she had under her control many powerful mages of her own, as well as many normal humans.

Two of these mages were Candlemas and Sysquemalyn, who, despite their own awesome powers, were mere apprentices compared to Lady Polaris. So when she demanded their attention, the pair were as meek as schoolchildren caught squabbling on the playground.

Lady Polaris had vast holdings and vast powers—neither of which the two wizards knew much about—so she never wasted time with underlings. She spoke immediately. "Candlemas, and Sysquemalyn, this concerns you, too. There is something wrong with the wheat harvest. Everyone at court is talking about it, and I said I would take care of the problem, whatever it is. Fix it." The palantir went blank, a black glass globe again.

Candlemas shook his head. "What did she say? A problem with wheat?"

Sysquemalyn sniffed. "Who is she to treat us like peasants? What does she have that we don't?"

"Enough power to turn this castle into a volcano, if she wished it," muttered Candlemas. "But what's this foolishness about wheat?"

He stopped at a knock on the doorjamb. Two lesser mages from one of the bottommost workshops stood in the hall. Candlemas didn't even know their names. Timidly, one said, "Milord? This basket arrived for you."

Sysquemalyn sniffed, but Candlemas waved them forward with a sigh. Any delivery from Lady Polaris would almost certainly be bad news. "Yes, yes, bring it here; then get out." Almost dropping the basket in their haste, the lesser mages fled.

Candlemas approached the bushel of grain slowly, as if it might explode. Archmages were known to slaughter their thralls on short—or no—notice, and anything sent by one was suspect. But kneeling carefully beside the container, the steward found it contained only wheat, if oddly red-tinged.

Sysquemalyn sauntered over, sniffed again. "What does she expect us to do, bake coriander rolls?"

Candlemas gingerly rolled a wheat kernel between a stubby finger and thumb. "It's hollow. And red."

"So?"

Peering closely, Candlemas crushed another kernel. Instead of resisting, as would solid, food-rich seeds, it flattened like a milkweed pod. The red dust stained his fingers, and he wiped them fastidiously on his robe. "I've never seen this before, though I've heard of it. Rust, the peasants call it. It's a blight that eats the heart of the kernels."

"You're boring me, 'Mas."

"You don't understand." Candlemas dumped the contents of the basket out onto the floor. All the grain was afflicted with rust. "This is bad, and could mean disaster. There's nothing to these kernels but jackets, hulls. There's no food value here. If all the crops are like this, people will starve!"

"We won't starve. There's enough preserved food, dried and jarred and pickled, in the larders and pantries and cellars to last a year or more. Lady Polaris orders it so, in case we're besieged."

"No, no, the *peasants* will starve, or go hungry, anyway. Wheat makes bread and ale. Without it, they'll have only rye and barley. That means a third of our crops lost, a third fewer cattle and horses and pigs in the spring!"

"You're still boring—"

Agitated, Candlemas grabbed a handful of grain and shook it so some spattered onto Sysquemalyn. "Blatherbrain, listen! Less grain to sell. A third less revenue! Or worse, because we'll have to buy grain. Less money! Get it now? Do you want to explain to Lady Polaris that she'll have less money to gamble, to spend on magic, to squander on lavish presents for her friends? A woman who once bet ten thousand crowns on whether the next drop of candle wax would land inside a dish or without?"

"Oh." Sysquemalyn bit her lower lip. "No, I wouldn't want to tell her. Fortunately, you will, because she sent you the basket."

"She sent *us* the basket! She included you in the order, remember?"

"No," the woman lied. Then she shrugged. "Maybe it's not a real problem. Maybe it's just a local bug. Or it may be that it's a test she's sending you, hoping you'll find a cure for someone else's crops, someone to whom she owes a debt. We don't know what she thinks or really wants."

"No, that's true." Candlemas tossed down the grain. "Still, I'll have to find a cure. *We* will. Or she'll feed our livers to the peasants."

A shrug was his answer. Sysquemalyn returned to the palantir, traced an arcane pattern, first circles, then intersecting triangles, and brought up the image of Sunbright, who appeared to be scouting for a defensible hollow under thornbushes at the bottom of the gorge. "Let's get back to our bet."

"What? Oh, yes." Somehow their silly wager didn't seem so important now. They'd begun it this morning out of boredom. They were humans, after all, and had lived an incredible number of years. Not much happened in the castle or grounds, so boredom was their major enemy, and squabbling their main entertainment. Candlemas joined her at the palantir. "So, you still contend surface humans—"

"Mud men."

"Yes, mud men are no better than cows and horses?"

Lifting glittering eyes of green, Sysquemalyn laughed. "Worse, actually. Livestock are tractable.

These creatures are independent. When they think, they invariably think about hating us."

Candlemas watched the young man hunt for a campsite. He noticed that the barbarian rejected many spots, places with too many or not enough exits or that were too far from water or likely to flood if it rained. "You don't know humans like I do. Most of those under your command were born in this castle and have never set foot on real soil. I deal with humans all the time, and they're capable of accomplishing a great deal if given proper supervision."

"So are—what are they called?—prairie dogs. They burrow holes and connect them up, and make entire cities, someone told me. Clever things, digging holes in dirt so wolves have a hard time eating them." Scorn tinged her words.

Candlemas pointed at the room around him. "Our castles and cities are of stone, which is merely hardened dirt. And we use humans—mud men, as you call them—to maintain them. If we Netherese get any more decadent, the humans may take over someday and supplant us entirely."

Sysquemalyn laughed long and loud, a rippling trill that chilled the man's spine. "Ah, yes! I can see it now, groundlings sitting at table, eating with silverware, running Toril with brays and squeals and grunts! If you believe that, then by all means, let's firm our wager."

"Fine." Candlemas's eyes strayed to the dumped wheat, which his underwizard was already hurriedly cleaning off the workroom floor. Perhaps it wouldn't be such a nuisance, after all. He'd send his apprentices out with news of a reward, and perhaps someone would produce a cure. If that didn't work, he'd have to be more severe. Perhaps the threat of kidnapping firstborns would make the farmers produce better crops. "What's the bet?"

So far this morning, Sysquemalyn had idly steered the orcish patrol onto Sunbright's trail, and so precipitated their battle. Now the wizard continued, "Let's subject this gruntling to more tests. Increasingly exacting. Until he dies and I win, or he perseveres and you win. The loser loses a limb."

"Limb?" Candlemas looked at his own arms and legs. "I'm rather fond of the ones I have."

"I don't see why." Cattily, Sysquemalyn looked him up and down. "They're podgy and hairy and none too clean, I suspect. You could pass for human."

"Don't sweet-talk me, love," was the snide reply.

Smirking, Sysquemalyn pointed a finger at the man's rope belt. Candlemas jumped as his smock suddenly tilted upward below the knot. He grabbed it and pushed it flat. "That is not a limb!"

"No? Then perhaps you'll miss it less when it's gone. You're not using it overmuch now, according to my maids' gossip."

Candlemas huffed. "Obviously your maids don't tell you everything, like my stable hands tell me."

Sysquemalyn idly moved the toe of her boot to point at some grain that still lay on the floor. The underwizard hurried over and scooped it up into a small crock, which the redhead casually took from his hands. "So our bet is on?"

"Yes, yes." Candlemas agreed dismissively. Something was wrong with this wager. It never paid to let someone else set all the terms. But the reminder of the blight had distracted him. What should he do first?

"Fine. I won't be bored for a few days, anyway." Sysquemalyn walked toward the door. "I'll send up a maid with your midday meal. Bellstar, perhaps. She likes hairy men. You can eat the food or have the maid, for all I care."

As she passed the window, she pitched the crock of wheat out, as if dismissing the problem.

Candlemas's shout of dismay went unheard.

* * * * *

Sunbright jumped as a crash sounded a hundred feet down the gorge. He crouched, wary, but no more sounds followed.

Trying to watch everywhere at once, padding silently, nocked bow in his hand, sword at his back, the barbarian moved toward the sound. It took a while to locate the source, and it only confused him.

A redware crock had shattered on the rocks. Scattered among the shards were grains of blighted wheat.

Hunkering between two rhododendron bushes, he craned his neck upward. High overhead, half a league, was the squarish black blotch of Delia, the castle in the sky from whence Lady Polaris and her minions ruled. They dumped dishwater and sewage and garbage on the peasants below, Sunbright knew. But crocks of wheat he'd never heard of.

He watched the castle curiously, waiting for more. The huge structure drifted over the land much like a cloud, though often against the wind. Sometimes in summer it roamed so far north the tundra barbarians saw it. It was said, by old slaves returned from the castle, that the archmage of Delia ruled all she could see, and since the castle drifted a mile or more high, that was a lot of land. But it was still only a tiny fraction of the Netheril Empire, and Sunbright's people's land was the tiniest fragment of that fraction.

And now the young man didn't have even that, just a leaf-strewn hollow under thornbushes. But, more to be stubborn than for any other reason, he'd guard that patch of ground as boldly as a knight would his liege lord's castle.

And with that thought, he peered around at his surroundings once more, then crawled in for some sleep, reciting prayers to various gods, both thanks for deliverance and appeals for the future. He'd need all the help he could get, for he'd have more adventures tomorrow, if night beasts and fiends and dreams didn't carry him away.

Chapter 2

Sunbright dreamed, and in his dreams he relived his entire life.

He saw his clan, the Ravens, trekking across the vast and unending tundra, a herd of reindeer driven before them by dogs more savage than snow wolves. He saw their life as a vast circle, moving season by season from place to place by ancient routes and ancient tradition: cutting through ice for seals in winter, craning from weirs to spear salmon in spring, crawling across a plain of brown skull-like rocks to flush ptarmigan in summer, slipping through cedar forests to shoot moose and elk in fall. And then watching the first snow fall, and steering gradually for the ice that hadn't yet formed, but would, as it had for centuries.

He recalled his mother Monkberry, strong but silent and shamed, for she had borne only one child. And his father, Sevenhaunt, a mighty warrior and shaman, returning to the tribe with yellow scalps when the tribe made war.

He saw his mother splicing rawhide reins for dog sleds and braiding her own hair for arrow strings, heard his father discoursing to the men long into the night, citing the old wisdom and his shaman's visions that helped guide the tribe to safety year by year.

Then had come the bad times. His father collapsing, wheezing like a speared seal, so weak he had to be carried to his bed where he lay day after day, sweating and chilled under six musk-ox pelts, wasting away until he died from a curse no one could name. His mother, tamping down the moss on her husband's grave, then lifting his great sword Harvester of Blood in one hand to hang over the door of their yurt, so her husband's spirit might continue to guard his family. For Harvester was a steel sword, the only one among the tribe's arsenal of bronze and iron, won by Sunbright's father in the distant past from a source he would never reveal. And being a mighty sword, and well-nigh unbreakable, the boy could believe something of his father's spirit lived in it.

Sunbright saw himself in his dream, a skinny lad with hair so blond it looked white, reaching for the sword month by month, measuring his height until he was tall enough to cut his finger on the blade and so share his father's blood, then tall enough to take Harvester down and practice with it, though it hadn't yet been granted to him.

He saw himself besting the other boys and girls in combat with swords sheathed in reindeer hide, being first the best fighter in the Raven clan, then the best among all the youths of the Rengarth tribe. He relived the night by the ritual fire, the flames heaped with all his childhood possessions and clothes, and the scalp of an enemy, a hated Angardt tribesman killed by his own hand. At this final test of manhood his mother had granted him his father's sword, Harvester of Blood, and gave him a new name. No longer would he be called Mikkl, for "Scrawny One," but Sunbright Steelshanks, for his hair so bright and legs so sturdy that he could outrun everyone in the tribe, youths and adults alike.

That had been a year ago, but only seconds in dream time, for the past was always with him, as was the scowling face of Owldark, the tribe's new shaman, given to fits of rage when his head throbbed so mightily his eyes bulged and his face turned as red as a sunset. Owldark, who'd watched the boy with envy and hatred, who sensed the youth's shamanism, mighty like that of his father, Sevenhaunt. Owldark, who cried one night that he'd seen a vision of Sunbright standing over the tribe with a bloody sword in hand, fire and smoke filling the horizon, even the livestock slaughtered, and Sunbright the cause of the destruction. How the village elders had conferred then, smoking rank sumac leaves and red willow bark day and night, arguing whether Sunbright should be killed outright or sacrificed to the gods, for Owldark's prophecies always came true.

And so had come the night, only six past, when Monkberry had awakened him, hissing, "They come! Take this and depart!" She kissed him and pushed him out a hole cut in the yurt's leather side, while she remained to face the council and their wolf-masked executioners.

For days Sunbright had fled over the tundra and, coming to the mountains, had crossed them and entered the lowlands. Friendless, clanless, miserable, a burning thirst for revenge was now his only companion.

He tossed in his sleep and would have cried out had not the need for silence been beaten into him during his early years. The pictures, the sights and smells of his people's lonely encampment on the gray, flat, unending tundra, rose and swirled and blurred together. Sounds of shouting, or wood crackling, or bones splintering grated in his ears, came closer, louder . . .

Sensing an enemy, Sunbright jerked upright.

But it was only a murder of crows, nine or more, winging low over the gorge, cawing and croaking and carrying on.

But a flight of disturbed crows often meant something on the move, and so the barbarian, still sitting, nocked an arrow and waited. And more came. From the south, where the gorge followed a jut of the Barren Mountains and scrub forest continued, a badger scuttled to the top of a flat rock, boldly sniffed the air in front and behind it, then slid around the rock and out of sight. Two snakes, intertwining, spilled over the edge, into holes and out of them, still traveling, a very odd thing. Even an owl winged from the forest, silently, and sought another patch of shadow in which to hide.

What could be pursuing them? A forest fire? Sunbright covered his mouth and sniffed deeply, but sensed no tang of smoke. What else, then? Some magic? A wolf pack? Another orcish patrol?

Debating whether to stay and watch or go, Sunbright detected the faintest of footfalls up on the forest flat. That sound he knew. Leaning forward for a better shot, he drew his bow to half-nock, made sure he could draw fully . . .

Here they came, bounding over the edge like a river of tawny bodies: roe deer, shaggy and dappled white on their red backs. There were a dozen at least, leaping high but barely skipping as they landed, like stones across water, bouncing like heath hares.

Pulling to full nock, Sunbright instinctively aimed for the longest-bodied animal with the knobby horns. An elder male, past its prime. The gods would not begrudge him that. He aimed for the spot where the buck would land, loosing an arrow at nothing. The string kissed his cheek, the arrow vanished, and the deer leapt full into its path. With a *thunk* the arrow slapped through the stag's heart. Stalled in its leap, the animal banged its jaw on the earth as it somersaulted. By the time Sunbright was upright, the other deer had disappeared down the gorge.

Running, skidding to a halt, he did a dozen things at once. He whispered a prayer to Moander, beastlord, for sending him this bounty. He added a prayer to the deer, thanking it for giving old flesh to feed the young, and hoped in the spirit world it was young and healthy and fat, with good teeth and many does to mount. All the while, he was flipping the animal, awkward now in death, over by its long legs and plying his flaked-flint knife to slice out liver and kidneys and lungs, stuffing the bloody gobbets inside his jerkin. He only half-watched himself work, despite the danger of slashing his hands, for he also nervously observed the forest flat to see if whatever marauders had driven the beasts were still coming on.

Yet no one appeared at the lip, nor any more animals. The disturbance couldn't be far off, if only those few had been pushed. Knife in bloody hand, Sunbright crept up the rocky slope and peered over the edge, keeping a tuft of yellow-green grass before his face.

The forest was red pines, thick trees with scabby bark and round clusters of short green needles.

There was little undergrowth amidst the trunks. Only more rhododendron and granite ledge showed. No animals, no monsters, no men. What, then, was out there?

Whatever, Sunbright took advantage of the lull. Returning to the deer, he sliced the hide around the neck and legs, slit it where needed, and with strong fingers yanked the hide off like a sticky sock. Artfully, the tundra native, who'd grown up on reindeer and musk-ox meat, sliced off lean steaks and heaped them into the hide on the fatty white side. Making final slits, he tugged a handful of red hide through itself, forming a pouch and a loop to slide over his shoulder as a makeshift strap. He'd need his hands free for any fights to come.

For he meant to find out what haunted the forest.

Not wasting an opportunity to eat—for any minute he might be fighting or fleeing—Sunbright shaved slices from the deer liver as he set out across the forest floor. The deer had been old, and the liver was tough and shot with worms. He'd have preferred to light a fire and roast it but didn't dare, so he munched as he walked.

If there was one thing his barbarian upbringing had taught him, it was that no matter how bad things were, they could always grow worse, and so he should enjoy any good times. Right now Sunbright had food, was alive and healthy and free, and had mysteries to investigate, so he could have been much worse off. The only thing he really missed was not having someone to talk with. Rengarth tribesmen lived off their herds, which spent the day foraging, so the barbarians had plenty of time for talk and stories and gossip and jokes. Sunbright missed company, and for the first time wished he had at least a dog to talk to.

That he walked into danger made him wary but not particularly afraid. Life was full of hazards, some a man could flee, others he could not. And he had to admit that this time of loneliness and seeking would have come eventually anyway. Young men and women of his tribe went out alone after sixteen summers to seek wisdom, a totem animal, guidance from the gods, and whatever else they could learn. Sunbright, then Mikkl, had done all that, but for him there had always loomed more. Since his father had been a great shaman and medicine-healer, Sunbright would be expected to go forth on another solitary quest to find his own shamanistic powers, else he would never become a spirit warrior.

Perhaps, he realized, this adventure was his spirit journey, and the gods had simply propelled him into it earlier than he'd planned. If so, perhaps he'd learn some of the gods' secrets. Perhaps he could return to his tribe someday and prove Owldark's dream of destruction false, and so take his place among the elders, and be a healer and teacher. Perhaps not.

In either case, he recognized visions when he dreamed them, and signs when they overran his crude camp. Whatever had roused the animals to flee had roused Sunbright's curiosity.

Now, ahead, the forest growth parted. Bushes were ripped up, the pine needles scoured away so that dusty brown earth showed. Here was the disturbance, and he stowed away his bloody breakfast to skulk from tree trunk to tree trunk. Circling, watching both ahead and behind him, he spiraled in toward the spot of churned earth.

Finally, sure he was alone, he crept up on the spot. He found a hole.

An odd hole, to be sure. It was neat, an inverted cone dug into the earth, as if someone had twirled a great shovel. Dirt and rocks from the hole were scattered evenly around it, as neat as a dike. Earthworms still twitched on the churned soil. Whiskers twitching, a befuddled mouse scuttled along a tiny balcony where its burrow had been shorn in half.

Leaning over the dike, Sunbright laid his hand on the cut soil. It felt warm, but that might just have been the warmth of Earthmother. He sniffed, smelled only dirt. Obviously this was a magical hole, for he knew no beasts that could dig this way, and the hole ended seven feet down at a point. As if, his mind toyed, as if a giant icicle had fallen from the castle of Delia on high, then vanished. Could that be?

Then he started as dirt suddenly spilled down the side of the hole. Under his hand, the earth moved, not in a jump, but uneasily, roiling, like a beast turning in its sleep. Some great earth-spirit was stirring. Sunbright whispered a protection spell and the rumbling subsided, though he doubted he could credit himself for its dying down.

Waiting in the still, eerie forest from which all animals had fled, the boy felt the hairs on his arms and neck rise. Yet still he waited, to see if any guidance came.

He waited until he grew bored. The hole told him nothing, didn't seem to be part of his spirit journey.

To show he wasn't afraid, he checked around for enemies one more time, then pissed into the hole.

Then he pushed on through the forest.

* * * * *

Thousands of feet below, in the blackest cavern, yet only half in Sunbright's dimension, a clutch of strange creatures felt the human's footsteps recede. They returned to their conversation.

Bad, thought one. Words, for it, were useless. *Too bad. Dead.*

The magic storms come more and more frequently.

More and more the fault of the Above-World.

Neth, they call themselves. Wizards, toying with magic, squandering it. We starve for magic they waste.

We must tell them, warn them not to trifle. We learned long ago.

We cannot tell them. One of us just exploded trying to do so.

Adding its dweomer to the magic storms raging everywhere, and aggravating the problem.

The beings resembled animate tornados, upright cones with stinger tails formed of polished diamond. They were the phaerimm, the oldest race on Abeir-Toril. And as might be expected, there were few of them. A handful.

Men did not know the phaerimm existed, though some had been seen now and then, observers mistaking them for dust devils. Or upon discovering their true identity, being eaten. The phaerimm had slits all the way around their middles, slits lined with ridges harder than diamond, which could gape to suck in nourishment of a wide variety: tree roots, certain rocks, reptiles, insects, groundhogs, humans—all as easy to ingest as a bowl of mush. Phaerimm chose not to reveal themselves, for they feared slavery, though all were more powerful wizards than any humans that dwelt above ground.

Phaerimm could move through their own ancient passageways and chambers, or even through soil and rock almost as easily, for then they slipped into another dimension, leaving only a fragment of themselves behind for a toehold. Yet if one of the phaerimm blundered into a magic storm near the surface, it was immediately—and violently—shunted wholly into this dimension. Where soil and rock already existed, the phaerimm ceased to exist, and left only a cone-shaped crater.

Nothing works. We tried astral visitation and only drove wizards mad. They clawed out their eyes, tore out their hearts, killed their fellows until at last they killed themselves. We tried visions, we tried lifedrain. Now we've tried direct visitation.

And failed.

Maybe more than failed. Perhaps our efforts fuel the magic storms.

Impossible. We know magic. We invented it.

Untrue.

Cease to argue. Back to the reason for this conference. How next shall we experiment to stop the Neth from spinning magic into storms?

We cannot.

Then we will die.

And they.

And the whole world.

I have a suggestion.

Yes?

Let them squander more. Encourage them to squander.

Why?

Humans expending magic have generated magic storms, and the more humans working magic, the more storms, true? Were they to accelerate the pace of magic use, the humans might destroy themselves all the more rapidly.

And us, mushmouth.

Perhaps not. We can move humans hither and thither, we know. Already our lifedrain spells have caused their wheat to rot on the stalk. Starving them sets them moving, searching for food.

Too slow. The high wizards who fritter the magic are the last to suffer hunger.

Still, the spells work lifedrain. And the drain grows, feeding itself to spread and drain yet more life.

But not down here, one hopes.

As I was saying . . . If we can make the Neth squander magic faster, grow ever more reckless in pursuit of who-knows-what, perhaps only their immediate area will collapse. Perhaps they will destroy themselves in one final cataclysm, a hellfire to scour the earth and leave us masters again! Well?

It . . . is a thought.

No, it's foolishness.

It is fighting fire with fire, as humans say.

Human wisdom cannot save us.

What can, then?

Well . . .

Good. Think on my scheme. We have time. A little, anyway . . .

* * * * *

Candlemas's nose was red from breathing wheat rust. It clung to his skin and covered his robe with a fine coating. The stubby mage had supervised his underwizards all night long and most of the day, but they were still no closer to stopping the blight or finding its cause.

The door blew open and Sysquemalyn flounced in. Today she wore a red sheath from high collar to ankle that split all the way down the front. Much of her was revealed, but not all, for a purple mass, like a jellyfish, pulsed and writhed across her stomach and loins. Another of the grotesques she collected, Candlemas thought. A particularly ugly one, like the world's biggest bruise.

"What do you want?" he snapped.

"My, we're touchy. Solve your problem with rye blisters yet?"

"It's wheat blight. And no, I'm not even—"

"Too bad." She didn't listen, but sashayed around his workshop, touching a silver statue, an inlaid box, a glazed porcelain plate, a wreath of silver-gilt holly leaves.

"Don't touch my things!" Candlemas was touchy, not so much from loss of sleep as from frustration. A hurried query to his various substewards had confirmed his fears: wheat rust was everywhere throughout Lady Polaris's lands. There simply was no crop to speak of. "The last time, you threw one of my favorite pieces out the window—"

"And might again, if any of these trashy trinkets suit." Sysquemalyn stood with forefingers at the corners of her mouth, pouting prettily, but the spectacle was spoiled by the purple horror, which wriggled up her flesh and curled a tentacle around her breast. Idly, she scratched. "I've decided to up the stakes. Your mud man is too canny to stumble over the orcs."

"Those orcs bother me too." Candlemas arched his back, found it hurt, and stepped to a small, low table laden with jars and potions. He began to mix a soporific. "Those orcs are remarkably organized, for orcs. They wear uniforms, and all have that red hand painted on the front. I've never heard of—"

"Mud men, all of them." Sysquemalyn waggled purple fingernails in dismissal. "The antics of ants would concern me more, for they might get into the honey in the larder. Ah!"

From a table she plucked up a spun-glass ornament that resembled a crystalline praying mantis. "Since it's your mud man who must fight this, you won't mind sacrificing it."

"I *do* mind!" Candlemas took a slug of painkiller, grimaced at the taste, and added more blackberry brandy. "I don't come down to your kitchens and paw through your shelves!"

"No, you paw the scullery maids. There was one you stripped and smeared with raspberry vinegar, I'm told. Didn't that make your mouth pucker?" She stroked designs on the black palantir until she had a picture of Sunbright plodding through an icy mountain pass. The barbarian was bent double against an immense head wind. "Perfect!"

Stepping to a window on the western side, Sysquemalyn balanced the crystal on both palms, pushed past the mild shield on the windows, and puffed the glass creature into space. It zipped away from her hands as if launched by a crossbow.

Candlemas stood over the palantir. Ahead of Sunbright by perhaps a quarter mile, the glass object bounced off a wall and hit the icy ground. "Good shot. And it was raspberry jam, not vinegar. But your girls talk too much."

"Shall I have her rip out her own tongue?" Sysquemalyn asked sweetly as she dusted off her hands. "And smoke it for sandwich meat?"

Candlemas looked at her with a mix of disgust and pity. "You can't defame humans enough, can you? You think you're ready to move on to the next plane."

"Let's hope." A bright smile, a poke at the purple slime moving down over her flat stomach. "If I advance quickly enough, I plan to make Lady Polaris my personal chambermaid. She'll shine shoes and empty chamber pots, and no man will lust for her, for I'll slit her nose and slice off her eyelids. I'll make her feel like a lowly groundling."

Candlemas shook his head and tapped the palantir, making the snow scene within jiggle. "Care to watch? This lowly barbarian might surprise you."

"No, he won't. He'll die." Sysquemalyn stepped up beside him. The purple slime plucked a tentacle from her navel and tried to wrap itself around the man's wrist. He moved out of reach. "And I'll laugh, and then collect on the debt. Won't the maids be disappointed to hear of that tragedy?"

"You talk too much, too," Candlemas growled. "Look!"

* * * * *

Head down, Sunbright slipped and slid across lumpy glare ice.

The ice was old, he decided, probably old snowpack left from last winter. He found it hard to believe it had lasted the summer, but this granite-walled pass was deep and the bottom shadowed. And this evil unceasing wind had polished everything as smooth as glass.

He didn't mind the ice so much, for a tundra barbarian lived with it eight months a year. But the screaming wind he couldn't face for long. Thus he trudged, skidding every which way from high to hollow, paused to squint into the wind, seeing little with watery eyes, then moved on. He'd tied his blue blanket around his shoulders and face to better breathe. He kept both hands free in case he fell, so he could land lightly. It would be death to break an arm or even fingers.

Then he did slip, and it saved his life.

He'd been leaning into the gale when suddenly it lessened directly in front of him. Caught off-balance, he stumbled headlong, tried to correct himself, and lost his footing, crashing on his bottom as his long shirt rode up.

Skidding, swirling around like a top, Sunbright had a glimpse of twin columns of icicles flash by. Icicles thicker than his leg, and jointed.

And moving.

The young man fetched up against the second column of icicles, felt them twitch at his touch. Above him, he found, was an arched ceiling, starting at three feet and rising to . . .

. . . a round, flattened head as big as a musk-ox carcass, with a snarling mass of glittering icelike teeth and mandibles and whiskers.

And twin eyes like glowing blue lamps that craned down to see him, there under the creature's belly, trapped between columns of jointed legs like a wicker fence.

Remorhaz, the barbarian's mind flickered. Ice worm.

He'd never seen one, only heard adventurers speak of them. They infested ice plains in the far west and north, and crushed entire dog teams and musk-oxen in their clashing jaws. Not formed of ice, really, the stories went, but with a solid carapace like an ant's only white, with blue-white slush churning inside.

But no one had hinted that they moved so fast!

Fumbling his blanket off his head, Sunbright had barely snatched his sword from its back scabbard before the remorhaz drove a bushel of glittering, icy mandibles at his chest. The mandibles were as long as Sunbright's arms, backhooked and jagged so fiercely he could barely tell one end from another. Too, the wicked wind was still sizzling, keening a song of death, hissing between the forest of legs and around his head, making his eyes sting and impeding his vision. He saw no way to shear those mandibles or even deflect them, so he simply whipped the sword directly in front of him, locked his elbows, and hung on.

Harvester's hooked point lodged into that nest of shining evil and fetched tight with a *clunk*, as if he'd struck cordwood. The beast's immense head brushed the sword backward like a twig, and Sunbright went with it.

As the great jolt struck his arms, his head and back slammed a trio of the beast's legs. The tips resembled ski poles so much that part of Sunbright's brain wondered if man hadn't copied monster. The chitinous legs expanded to mushroom shapes, that the beast might cross snow, but underneath formed points as hard and sharp as ice axes, which they were. Two of these legs gave way before Sunbright's body, and he slid clear of them, out into the open, icy stretch of canyon.

The beast had retracted its head rather than tie itself into a knot. The boy half spun and thumped a granite wall. Instinctively Sunbright scrambled to rise and defend himself, but the ice might have been oiled. Paddling uselessly, he fought down panic, tried to think how to survive.

Use what you've got, screamed instructions burned into his brain.

Ideas flashed. The beast could maneuver; he couldn't. Why? Because it had ice axes for feet. So if he . . .

Acting, Sunbright juggled Harvester to one hand and with the other snatched out his flint knife. Striking hard, he stabbed the ice enough to gain hold. Gingerly, warily, he scooted his feet on either side of his hand. He might look foolish, he thought, but at least he wasn't sledding on his butt.

Chipping ice, swirling in a circle as gracefully as a dancing horse, the remorhaz turned to face its foe—

or meal. Sunbright marveled at the size of it, fully as long as a fourteen-dog team and sled and as many-legged, higher than he could reach with the tip of his long sword. How could he kill something like this? Or even strike it? Given a choice, he would have run, screaming if necessary, but he was a cripple on ice and the beast was at home.

Yet again, his mind shrilled, why was this monster so far from its native land? Were the gods playing with him again? Or was everything he'd heard of the beast wrong?

The one thing he did know was not to strike its back. The old tales agreed that the ice beast managed to funnel all its body heat out a vent behind its head, a slot as scorching as any natural hot springs, hot enough to melt a sword. So . . .

The warrior watched as the horror rippled, arched its long back like a rainbow, and lunged from on high. The slashing mandibles clashed for his head.

Yet keeping cool, Sunbright managed two things. He kicked at the granite wall behind him while hanging on to the steady flint knife, then released it. He couldn't have done it on earth or grass, but on the slick ice he fairly flew in a full circle. One second he was facing the creature; the next he was sprawled full length pointing toward it, sliding into it.

The great head smashed down where he'd been. Closing mandibles scarred the ice. But Sunbright was skidding on his side toward the first triplet of legs. His sword was ready, and as he closed on the columns he rolled and swung.

Before the keen steel, the sturdy but hollow legs snapped like thick reeds. Three of them were shorn; then Sunbright's feet rapped into the opposing column, which flinched. Clapping his feet around one woody leg, he reached high over his head—blinding himself with his own shoulders—and chopped chopped chopped wherever he felt resistance.

His efforts worked too well.

With half a dozen legs cut from under it, the undulating bulk of the ice worm, its belly as smooth and white as a snake's, sagged to the ice—pinning Sunbright underneath. At the same time, the foot he'd been clinging to lifted and slammed down on his belly.

Smothered by an icy insect carapace, Sunbright still screamed at the pain. The ice-axe foot ground into his guts like the club of a frost giant. And now the blistering cold of the monster's belly stuck to his warm skin, stuck and burned like fury, then ripped skin when it lurched. The barbarian was being suffocated and crushed at the same time, and despite the white-hot agony lancing through him, he knew it would only get worse as the beast settled.

He wasn't going to escape this trap.

Desperately thrashing his arms and legs yielded nothing, for there was nothing to strike but tough carapace. Somehow he retained his sword in a death grip, but could apply no leverage, hit nothing. And his vision was fading, swirling flashes like the northern lights exploding in his eyeballs.

The great weight of the creature settled further, and Sunbright heard his ribs snap, snap, snap, like pine trees freezing and splitting on the coldest winter days. His own screams were loud in his ears.

Then he heard nothing.

Chapter 3

Sysquemalyn slapped the top of the palantir smartly, making the image of the screaming Sunbright jiggle and fade.

Over Candlemas's chirps about his equipment, she cackled, "Done! He's dead! That was too easy!"

"He's not dead," protested the other wizard. "He appears to be dying, I'll grant you, but these barbarians are tough! He may yet live!"

Smug, the female wizard only smirked and backed away from the worktable. When she was six feet away, she laughed again and snapped the fingers of both hands, then pointed at Candlemas. "No, no, no. I win; you lose. Pay up."

The stocky man crossed his arms across his chest. He felt cold, seeing Sunbright die frostbitten and crushed to ice like that. "I still contend— Eh?"

Something had flicked at his sleeve. Something behind him.

Taking his eyes off Sysquemalyn, he turned to see what it was.

A vibrant hiss, like a steam geyser erupting, made him jump. Looming beside him was a monster as skinny as a coatrack, gray-skinned, with a tall head and elongated jaws sporting dripping fangs as long as Candlemas's fingers. Slanted yellow eyes bored into his from above that evil, gap-toothed grin—an evil smile much like Sysquemalyn's.

Gibbering, Candlemas backpedaled from the horror. Fiend, he identified. Lesser fiend, from the outermost rings of the Nine Hells. Not particularly dangerous to a wizard with personal shields in place, but they were known to bite . . .

Hopping, the fiend grabbed Candlemas, one scaly claw on the human's neck, one grasping his wrist. The wizard uttered a curse, a foolish waste of words. For a blast or banish spell was what he needed. Hurriedly he babbled, "Fiend, I name you, and command—"

Too late. The gaping jaws clamped down on his biceps, biting flesh to the bone. Candlemas screamed, then shrilled as the beast ripped down toward his elbow. Horror-stricken, the wizard saw muscle and arteries stripped from his arm bone like a peel wrenched off an orange. The fiend bit again, and he heard its harsh teeth grate on bone—his.

Then the bone snapped, parted, and the fiend fell back with Candlemas's right arm in its mouth. Far behind him, Sysquemalyn laughed and laughed, the sound a rising shriek of hysteria.

The wizard's vision went black, as black as he imagined Sunbright's had gone only minutes ago. Was this what it felt like, he wondered for a second, for the groundling to die?

It hurt!

Then the pain was everything and crowded out all thought, all feeling.

* * * * *

Again, Sunbright dreamed. If a dead man can dream.

He lay on a sheet of steel that ran to the horizon: the tundra turned metal, he supposed, with a steel-gray sky overhead. He tried to rise, but couldn't lift his arms or legs or head, or even roll over, so he must be bound. Then something dark flickered and filled the sky. Soft wisps of blackness brushed his cheeks.

"Sunbright . . ."

Someone called his name. He should open his eyes and see who. But his eyes were open, the dream insisted, else how could he see the sky?

"Sunbright, wake up."

He didn't want to wake up, despite being half frozen on his sheet of tundra steel. Oh, frozen! That was why he couldn't rise. Some enemy had come in the night and poured water over him, binding him with ice. Shar, perhaps, night goddess, winter goddess, in his land where nights were months long. Lady of loss, mistress of the night and cold. Would she have black hair?

He opened his dream eyes, saw it was indeed a beautiful woman with black hair who hovered over him. A silver circlet bound her hair at the brow, and her clothes were silver, or else shining black. He couldn't see that far down.

"Sunbright, get up!" she demanded.

The young man peered up at her. She seemed petulant for a goddess, he thought, but they were used to getting their way. Her face was longer and narrower than before, her nose almost pointed. Her eyes were now black on black. Human eyes weren't like that. With an icy white finger she jabbed his chest, again and again. "Wake up, fool! You're in danger!"

At this, the helpless, frozen barbarian chuckled softly, then laughed aloud. "No, no," he gasped, "I'm not in danger anymore. I'm dead now. There's no danger worse than that."

The figure continued to poke, poke at his chest, until the jabs hurt. "But there is! Danger not to your body, but to your spirit!"

"Oh, that." Sunbright gave up laughing, groaned instead. "Smolyn's eyes, there's always something! Who said the dead rest easy? Who wants my soul?"

"You do. You're not done with it."

"Eh?" He peered at the woman, but she was shrinking rapidly, to the size of a yearling pup, then a cat, then a— What was that sitting on his chest?

"Awake?" croaked the bird. "Good. Eat this."

The black bird banged his lip with a black beak that had an extra bend at the bridge. Sunbright yipped in pain, and the bird dropped a berry into his mouth. Instantly his mouth and nose flared at the bitter turpentine flavor. He tried to spit the berry out, but glucked and swallowed it instead.

"Juniper berries are poison!" he gargled.

"Nonsense, eat 'em all the time. Stay here." The raven flew away.

Sunbright watched it go, winging high along the canyon walls, then up into the late autumn sky. The sun was slanting long there, warming the cliffs. To be warm would be nice.

"Stay here?" the young man rasped. "Why should I? I'm cold! I—*aah!*"

Trying to pick up his head, he learned why he couldn't. Hair from his topknot ripped in a hundred places. The sharp pain made him wrench up his arms, but they too were frozen to the ice, and so lost hair and skin when he spasmed. And that made him gasp, which made his cracked ribs screech and his belly wound howl . . .

"I said to stay put," croaked a cranky voice.

Sunbright lay gasping on his side, hugging his ribs and gut and head with hands and arms rubbed raw and bleeding. It would take all the fat that could be rendered out of one ox to soothe all these frost blisters. Glumly he rolled over, hissing with pain, and heard rattles and crunches from behind him. Most of his tackle was broken and hung in tatters from his body, like porcupine quills. Head spinning, he saw the outline of his arms had stained the ice red, while a patch of golden hair, like misplaced grass, adorned the ice. Glop like thin ice milk coated him, had wet him and glued him to the ice. "What is this stuff— worm snot?"

"Remorhaz blood," rattled the bird, beak full. "The creature leaked all over you."

"I sheared off its legs. A bunch of legs. Oh." Now that his vision had cleared, he saw the legs lying not three feet off. They looked like hollow birch logs. "Uh, where is the— *Ouch!*" Turning his head too fast, moving anything in fact, hurt.

"Crawled off north, toward the cold lands. It's going pretty slow. Saw it just now, winging back. Open up."

This time, Sunbright dutifully opened his mouth. The bird hopped to his shoulder and dropped in a half dozen blood-red juniper berries. Their tangy sting set the barbarian's nose running, and he coughed, which racked him from sore head to tingling toes.

Careful not to move or cough, Sunbright munched slowly. The bird flew off and returned with more berries. The young man ate those too. Oddly, they made him hungry. A roast, he salivated at the thought, a roast would be mighty good right now. A roast of anything. With a fire to go under it, like the warmth up high.

"Now," pronounced the bird, standing on the ice before him with fat black toes. Built for arctic climates, even the feathers on its legs came down to brush the thick appendages. "Do you feel worthy?"

"Worthy?" the boy gulped. "Worthy of what?"

"My power."

"Your power?" Then, for the first time, the boy realized he was talking to an animal, and what the animal was. "You're a raven!"

"True. But are you worthy?"

"Worthy?" The questions were tiring Sunbright. He should have paid better attention, he knew. A raven was the totem of his clan. Even the name of the tribe, Rengarth, some said was simply a rendering of "raven" from an ancient tongue. So now, if he of the Raven clan in the "raven" tribe saw a raven, that should be triply lucky.

But really, he just wanted to sleep for a while. It would be night soon, and he could sleep the night away, here on the warm ice that had already sucked up so much of his blood.

The raven interrupted his thoughts. "If you're worthy, prove it. Or else lie here, pity yourself, and die." With a flap of wide wings, it took off toward the south.

"Prove what?" Sunbright groaned. "That I'm worthy of a raven's power? Easy for him to say: he can fly. I don't even have any blood left."

But this test is important, a voice urged. Follow the raven. Perhaps it was his mother's voice, off in the east, or perhaps his father's, speaking from the lands of the dead. Or perhaps it was his own. He was stubborn too, and made demands on himself. But could he follow the raven? He doubted he could walk.

Still, he could crawl. Maybe that would do.

Squinting, he located south, one of only two directions he could go in this narrow canyon. The ice worm had gone north, so south was better. He put out a hand, hissing as skinned flesh stuck to the ice. But the wounds continued to weep their salty tears and didn't stick as badly as healthy flesh might. He put down the other hand, grabbed ice . . .

No, he was forgetting something. Two hands empty wasn't right.

Sword. His father's sword.

Lurching in a circle on his hip, he found the long steel tool half embedded in the ice. He almost wept as he dug into the ice to free it with fingers that were already raw. But then he clutched it tight. And it worked well, helped him, for when he turned the arched blade down, it bit the polished ice of the canyon floor and gave him a brace to pull on.

He shoved the sword ahead, chunked the edge down, pushed lamely with his toes, pulled with his arms, caught up to it. Did it again. And again.

Hours later, he crawled from the ice shadows, then blinked, blinded. The morning sun, as big as a god's face, rose in the east and bathed him in glorious, life-giving warmth.

Laying his head on a steel pillow, Sunbright slept.

* * * * *

Candlemas limped down a long, long hall wide and high enough for a coach-and-six to run flat out. The floor was black onyx and white quartz, the two colors swirling and interlacing in complex patterns hand

cut and meshed by generations of artisans. The surface of the floor was so shiny it was almost invisible,
which made it difficult for the wizard to tell where to
place his feet. And further, he limped, because his
missing arm set him lurching off-balance.

At the far end of the corridor, he heard maids giggling and chiding one another over some sexual es-
capade, but when he appeared, they hushed and
scurried back to work. Each wore a white cap and
short white dress with a black apron: the colors of
Lady Polaris, which Candlemas found monotonous.
At one time, the maids would have been glad to see
him, a welcome distraction in their dull routines
here in Sysquemalyn's territory.

But after five months the wizard's arm was still
regenerating. It had done so bit by bit, from the inside out, needing to be left in the open air. First the
bones had grown, until he had a skeleton's arm rattling alongside, with no muscles to pick it up. Then
the arteries had stitched themselves, so he was bothered by the pulsing of his own heart's blood. Then
muscle, slowly knitting together. Now came the
worst part, the spinning of nerves, like a thousand
tiny spiderwebs, every one itching and burning yet
sending electric shrieks from his teeth to his toes if
he touched or bumped them. He prayed for the skin
to grow back soon, for now his tingling arm looked
like the work of a clumsy butcher. Maybe, with skin
on it, the girls could stand for him to touch them
again.

Snarling at the once friendly maids, he learned
Sysquemalyn was in the conservatory torturing
flowers. So he stumped that way, careful not to brush
his raw arm against any obstacles.

Sysquemalyn was deep into the conservatory, which
was longer and higher than some wizards' houses and

roofed entirely with tiny diamond panes of bull's-eye glass. Green plants poured forth a riot of red and white and purple and yellow flowers, and no less than nine human stoop-backed gardeners bustled about them. Their supervisor tended her own patch at the back of the conservatory. Here in the hot greenhouse, she wore nothing but a short chemise and a frilly apron that looked ludicrous. Especially since, as a collector of grotesques, Sysquemalyn had many weird and sinister plants concealed back where Lady Polaris wouldn't see them on her infrequent visits. The flowers resembled fleshy organs, bilious teardrops, lizards' tongues, finger bones, and more. The female wizard hummed as she snipped liver-colored blossoms and dropped them into a pail.

"Your damned barbarian is still alive!" Candlemas growled without preamble. "You owe me an arm!"

She pretended bemusement. "An arm, dear 'Mas? Why do you need three? A third to comb your beard? Certainly not to comb your head." She laughed gaily at her wit.

Exasperated, exhausted by his long walk—regenerating strained a body—Candlemas nevertheless ran his good hand over his bald pate, evoking another merry trill. "Don't change the subject! And don't mock me! Your barbarian—you started this stupid contest—is still alive! He's been healing in the forest south of the Barren Mountains! He didn't die when attacked by the remorhaz, damn it, and you owe me an arm!"

Sysquemalyn set down her snippers and pouted prettily, as if sympathetic. "Dear, dear Candlemas. You're all tuckered out by your little rebuilding project there. Barbarian? I don't . . . Oh, the yellow-haired fellow, skinny as a plucked chicken! I remember him!"

"I remember too!" In the greenhouse, the wizard was sweating heavily. Salty drops running down his healing arm stung like wasps. "You cheated, sicced a fiend on me too soon—*aargh!*" Pained, he lurched backward against a table, knocking a dozen potted flowers to the slate floor with a crash.

Sysquemalyn *tsked*, but clearly Candlemas wasn't about to go away. With a theatrical sigh, she perched her rump on a tall stool. "Very well, I may have been in error when I conjured the fiend. It could have happened to anyone. You should feel sorry for me, I'm so embarrassed."

"Sorry?" gasped the man. "Em-embarrassed?" He swooned, clawing sweat from his face.

Smirking, Sysquemalyn replied, "You know, this is great fun. I'm so glad we formed this little wager. It was dead boring around here."

Eyes bugging from his head at her audacity, Candlemas couldn't answer. Almost absently, Sysquemalyn picked up a lacquered bladder and gave an experimental squeeze. A thin green stream arced across the space between them and struck Candlemas's red-meat arm.

With a scream, the wizard leaped fully three feet in the air, crashed against a rack of potted flowers, and sent them smashing as he shrieked and clawed and ripped at his new arm as if to tear it off.

"By Tipald, am I careless!" Sysquemalyn tipped a crockery pot to sprinkle cool water over the writhing wizard. "That's liquid fertilizer. My, I'll bet that stings!"

As Candlemas ground his teeth and fought to regain his feet, Sysquemalyn jabbered on. "I'll tell you what, since you feel so put-upon. Let's continue the contest, and up the stakes even further. Let's see . . . If your barbarian is healthy, we'll dump some more tests on him, hard ones this time. If he survives, you win, as before. If he dies, I win. And the loser this time gets flayed alive!"

"Flayed . . ." croaked Candlemas. He felt flayed now.

"And just to be fair, *you* decide the test! I'll stay out of it."

Despite dire warnings and his own pain, Candlemas was intrigued. But one thought intruded that had bothered him for weeks. "No, wait, wait. There's a flaw in the argument, and I should have seen it when we made this bet. To win, you need the barbarian to die. And if we keep piling on tribulations, he *will* die. Then you'll have won. But for me to win, he must survive, which he won't if we keep—keep— Put that damned thing down!"

"But, dear, it makes things grow." She'd been toying with the bulb of fertilizer again. Now she squirted juice amidst the hanging fronds of a plant that looked like dead snakes wrenched inside out, as if she were giving them a loving kiss. "But I understand your dilemma, and that's why I've turned the contest over to you. Surely, if you control all the tests, and you're fair, your hero will win. Then you can braid a whip from whatever you like and get whichever slave you like, no matter how strong, to beat me until I'm a heap of hash. Now wouldn't that be fun?"

Candlemas groaned, but had to admit the idea gave him great pleasure. He tried to detect flaws in her new arguments, new tricks, but it was hard to think in this steamy den and through the fog of pain. Finally he snarled, "Agreed! And I hope you suffer as keenly as I have!"

"Me, too," came the prim answer. "It will serve me right."

Stumbling, brushing aside slithering greenery, Candlemas lurched down the long rows of plants toward the cool black-and-white halls. He tried not to think about what could go wrong. And its consequence.

* * * * *

Sunbright lay wrapped on a bower of spruce boughs under the tatters of a blanket and heaps of pine needles. The sun was just setting, its beams slanting long through the forest. His bed lay against a rock wall, and a merry but tiny fire banked with rocks reflected heat from the wall and kept him warm on both sides. He'd had a good day, killing a young brown bear in a deadfall, and he'd eaten his weight, almost, in bear fat and liver and steak. The skin would make him a new jerkin, for his goatskin one had long since been sliced into rawhide strips. And the jawbone he might fashion into a club, or at least sink the teeth into a wooden branch to make a jagged edge weapon such as the orcs carried.

Once more, as he did each night, the young man sent up prayers to Chauntea and Garagos and Shar, and marveled that he was still alive. He wasn't sure how he'd managed it, other than by simply waking up every morning and refusing to die. From the high icy pass five months back, he'd crawled into the deepest parts of the forest and set about surviving. At first he could only crawl, and ate grubs and crayfish and frogs and snakes and tree bark and ground nuts. Eventually he could stand and lurch from tree to tree, and had strung rawhide snares across rabbit tracks and eaten well. Gaining strength, he'd ambushed deer from rocky heights, hunted sleepy bears settling for winter, reached into hollow trees to strangle raccoons, and done a thousand other things too reckless to ponder. Then had come the snows, and he'd dug into a cave and piled up rocks to seal the entrance, and had hunkered down hugging himself and whiled away long, dark days whispering stories from the elder times.

The raven had helped. It had scouted from the treetops, located game, warned of approaching orcs, found water and food. Without the raven, he would have died the first week. Though there were times the bird was gone for days, and though it never said why it helped him, Sunbright accepted its help as one of life's mysteries.

He had shaved a new bow and strung it with his own braided hair, fletched three ash arrows with turkey feathers, beaten deer hides to stiff leather, and kept his sword polished bright. Oddly, he'd gained weight, had filled out in the chest and legs and arms. Sometimes he'd used simple healing spells on himself, but since they sapped a user's life-force, that was counterproductive. As a result, he bore scars on his forehead and hands from his battle with the remorhaz, and still ached in one shoulder, but overall he was healthier than he'd ever been.

He was tougher too. Before, young and headstrong, he'd thought he was formidable. Now he'd proven it by surviving what would have killed lesser men. And with this toughness of the body came a toughness of the spirit. No more would he boast of his strength and abilities, like a squeaky-voiced boy. He knew he was a warrior, and it showed, and that was enough.

One day, he promised himself, he'd stride into his tribe's camp and see his mother, older and grayer, and all his cousins and uncles and aunts, and old friends and enemies. He'd be a mighty, battle-scarred hero and would have a thousand wondrous stories to relate, but he'd tell none of them, no matter how much the people begged, would only drop veiled hints of fantastic and desperate struggles in the far reaches of the world.

Someday . . .

As he clung to life, so too did he cling to thoughts of his tribe, almost torturing himself with them. He loved his people and had been forced to flee because of Owldark's lies. So he thought of revenge and savored the day he'd return and even the score for his father's murder and his own banishment. He knew that time might be years away, for the strength needed to battle his enemies would be great. For now he'd continue to wander, and learn, and grow strong.

And dream.

They came often, these dreams, and confused the hell out of him. Pictures of himself walking black-and-white marbled halls, hearing weird noises and girls giggling and a man and woman squabbling like siblings, and smelling exotic flowers and queer spices or brimstone. There were visions of flying dragons, red against a blood-drenched sunset; white-haired women as cold as ice; talking tornadoes forming icicle-shaped holes; twisted, hellish halls like stone bowels where every step found a new and writhing surface; and glittering cities where unnatural beasts hauled brimming wagons and soldiers in seashell helmets tramped to foreign orders. And much more, even stranger than all this.

Sometimes he wondered if the visions were real, if he could see into the future or another part of Toril. Or if some god or goddess put the dreams in his head so he might . . . What? Act them out? Maybe someday, when he was a great shaman, he'd be able to interpret these dreams and put them to use. Unless, of course, he'd simply slammed his head too hard against rock walls and rock-hard ice and was fast becoming an idiot.

"Hello, the camp!"

In an eye-blink, Sunbright was out from under his blanket and hunkered down between two spruce trees, sword ready at hand. If his winter alone had taught him one thing, it was to move rapidly when threatened.

Yet the man who came to the camp seemed hardly a threat. He was not tall, but podgy, dressed in a simple sackcloth smock and rope belt and sandals. He was bearded and balding, well tanned except for one arm, which had strange, dead-white skin. The arm seemed whole enough, but hung as slack as a trout on a line and glowed ghostly pale by firelight, as if it weren't real. But the man was real enough, and he seemed friendly, though worried. Under his bald pate, his forehead was etched with deep wrinkles. In his one good arm he carried a lumpy bundle wrapped in red leather.

The chunky man came right into the firelight and squinted around, failing to see Sunbright hunkered nearby, which showed he was out of his element. Undaunted, the man set down the bundle and talked to the fire.

"I'm a friend. My name is Chandler. I'm steward of a castle nearby, east of here. The raven sent me. He said you needed supplies, so I've brought some."

One sign of intelligence was having a great curiosity, and Sunbright's was piqued. Warily, he rose and pushed out of the dark, cedar-fragrant trees. Chandler started when the groundling with the scowling, scarred face and long, shining sword that reflected yellow flames emerged from the shadows.

"Your kind give nothing for free." Sunbright kept

his voice flat, neither friendly nor hostile. "What's the price of your supplies?"

"I wish you to do me a favor. I need information and want you to fetch it."

"That's vague enough. Why not dig up this information yourself?"

"I can't." Chandler flapped his useless arm. "I can't travel like this, and I have duties at my master's castle. And it's dangerous on the roads these days. I need a runner who's capable and trustworthy. The raven mentioned you."

"How is it that you can speak to the raven?" Actually, Sunbright wasn't sure why he could himself. Either it was part of the totem magic, or else the raven conversed with every stranger it met.

"I'm a mage," came the simple answer. "Not much of one, just a hedge wizard. I can do simple healings and conjurings. That's why I'm a steward. Talking to animals comes in handy in my position."

That sounded like an unknown joke to Sunbright. All of it sounded queer, but then it was a queer world.

"What have you brought?"

Hiding a smile, knowing his fish was hooked, Chandler squatted with a grunt and, one-handed, untied the bundle. "Useful stuff such as warriors need. No trash." Indeed, the contents sparkled in the firelight and set Sunbright's mouth watering. A steel knife, iron arrowheads, copper rivets, thick needles, a waterskin on a leather strap, a new red shirt, a gray wool blanket, fishhooks, a razor, two candles, flint strikers, a blacksmith-forged file, a handful of silver and copper coins, and squares of rations in waxed paper: jerked meat, dried fruit, lard.

Sunbright would have attacked an army of orcs for even a small portion of such treasure. Still, he fought to stay wary and composed. "What's the information and when do you need it?"

Chandler sighed, held his bad right wrist in his left hand, then sat on a nearby rock. "Do you mind? I tire easily with this wound. To answer your question, I don't know yet. I'm waiting for news from the south before I seek news in the east, if that makes sense. My master wishes to know where best to market his excess crops. If I spend days questioning runners, I might make him a profit of two silver crowns per bushel." Another sigh. "Will you do it? You don't have any other plans, do you?"

Other than simply to survive? the young man thought. No. But work for a wizard? Sunbright tried to think why not, and came up blank. Although mages were uncommon among his people—shamans who could cure ills and find game were of more use in his harsh land than muttering wizards with crocks and stinkpots—they were not considered evil, only different. Sunbright himself had "wizardly" powers, or would have if he continued to seek them and practice. And wild dreams, lately, that might be visions.

Piling up arguments, Chandler went on, "For place, I wish you to trend east, whence come these rumors. You've been moving east, the raven says, albeit slowly, due to the snows and your needing to hunt."

Sunbright frowned. Talk of ravens blabbing his whereabouts sounded like more manipulation, such as he'd suffered from last fall. Now here came a stranger knowing much about him and offering strange pacts in return for remarkable gifts. Of course, Sunbright could merely slay this hedgehopper and take the gifts, as many in his tribe might do, but he wouldn't. Somehow the mage knew this and, oddly, that made Sunbright trust him. And too, the lonely barbarian found it pleasant just to talk to another human being.

And they were wonderful gifts.

"Very well. Leave those and tell me where to go."

Chandler stood up, smiling, but did not offer to shake hands. "Splendid. Why don't you salt away all these goodies and take your time, but hie to Augerbend on the River Ost. Thirteen leagues due east you'll strike the river, then turn south. My master's fief is not far from there. Check at the inn—there's only one—and I'll send word when I know more. Is that satisfactory? Good. I'll see you there."

And Chandler strode from the camp without a backward glance, to be swallowed up by the forest.

Sunbright watched him go, frowning more at himself than the stranger. If the castle was thirteen leagues distant, he wondered, four days' travel for a healthy man, how had a tired and wounded mage come here?

Clucking his tongue, Sunbright turned to the glittering loot. He'd reaped a fine bounty, but suspected he'd gotten a bad bargain.

Chapter 4

"Beg pardon, sir, but there's someone come."

A page, a girl not yet ten and dressed in the requisite black-and-white uniform, had rapped on the doorframe. Her blue eyes were big as she surveyed the forbidden workshop of Master Candlemas. Though she had to admit, it didn't look any more special than the crofter's workshop where he made barrels and horse furniture. Except for scores of beautiful, glittering objects scattered about, it looked rather drab.

So did Master Candlemas, as well as tired and pouchy-eyed. The wizard had instinctively slammed shut a wide, fat book at the knock. Reddish wheat was scattered over the worktable, and chaff clung to his clothes and beard. Now he snapped, "What? Company? Who?"

"The honored delegates of the Beneficent Traders' Guild of Dalekeva, master," she recited.

"What?" Candlemas seemed hard of hearing this morning. "A bunch of chintzy traders? How did they come to the castle? Did they fly?"

"No, milord. They came by the magic portal."

Candlemas grimaced. What did that mean? Who'd authorized a bunch of uppity moneygrubbers to penetrate the castle magically? Was this some convoluted purse-snatching deal of Lady Polaris's? Or some rival's trick? Or a plea for the gods knew what? Candlemas stood thinking and staring so long the girl began to fidget. Finally he decided, "I guess I'll have to see them. Seat them in the reception hall. I'll come." For the first time, he really noticed the girl, a sweet child with a black bowl haircut. Candlemas smiled tiredly. While he bore hearty lust for women both ripe and seasoned, he had a genuine affection for children, especially small, antsy girls. "What is your name, child? Were you born here in the castle?"

"I'm Ysgarda, sir." A small curtsey. "Yes. My father keeps the dovecotes."

"That's good," Candlemas sighed. "Tell him I admire him."

The fuddled girl departed, and Candlemas walked the length of the workshop. Beside a far table stood an upright mirror framed in polished wood. Both were dusty, the mirror blearily showing a short fat man with a shepherd's smock and mangled arm. With more sighs, Candlemas flipped through a small book until he found a portrait of a young nobleman with a pinched mouth and nose and splendid clothes. "Can't impress groundlings looking like a privymucker, I suppose. Let's see . . . Quantol's Changer."

A short while later, a nobleman with pinched mouth and nose and splendid clothes swept into the reception hall. It was the richest room in the high-flying castle, the walls hung in doubles and triples of tapestries, the floors thick with handwoven rugs, the furniture carved and gilt, the statues and bowls and crystal sparkling on a dozen small tables worth a king's ransom. It was a room meant to impress visitors, as were the magically augmented half-giant guards in black-and-white armor and tabards who guarded the doors with pikes whose edges crackled with electricity.

From the nobleman's pinched mouth came, "I am Candlemas, High Steward of Castle Delia, home to Lady Polaris, Noble of the Neth, High-born and Beloved of the Gods. What will you have?"

The party was large, almost twenty traders in their finest long robes and brocaded sleeves and tall, gaudy hats. With them were eight bodyguards, mostly scarred and hearty warriors, both male and female, but there was also a craggy dwarf lugging a warhammer. A big-bellied man with a flowing white beard and blue and silver finery stepped forward to wheeze, "We represent the Beneficent—"

"Yes, yes, I know who you are." With the young, petulant disguise came a fussy, whiny voice. "Why are you here? Don't waste my time."

The trader blinked and looked to his fellow delegates, who looked in turn at the ceiling. The man then abandoned his speeches and platitudes and stuttered to the point. "Good sir, we know you represent the might of Lady Polaris and all the Neth above her." At Candlemas's glare, he began to speak faster. "Uh, sir, as you know, Dalekeva is one of the Low Cities that lie on the eastern outskirts of Netheril. As such, we enjoy the love and protection of the empire."

Candlemas doubted that. The Netherese were so contemptuous of groundlings that Low Cities or cesspools were all the same to them.

"We in Dalekeva work for the good of the empire, as do you, sir," the man continued nervously, "and are privileged to trade our meager goods to the High Ones, the Netherese themselves. No army, no despicable wyrm dares come to humble Dalekeva while the High Ones protect us."

That was not quite true, thought Candlemas. Most armies and dragons were just smart enough to steer clear of Netheril. Robbing, raping, or gulping down peasants and horses wasn't worth the grief the empire could muster.

"Yet now, good sir, we find an army threatens on the horizon."

"Eh?" Candlemas lifted his pinched nose. His thoughts had begun to drift as he pondered the wheat rust problem again. Rumors said the rust had spread to the spring barley crop. If so, it meant famine. "What army?"

A middle-aged woman stepped forward, cleared her throat, and caroled, "The army of the One King, sire. That's what he calls himself. No one knows much about him, but he's managed to pull together an army of both orcs and men. They're cooperating, master, something unheard of."

Just to butterfly-brained groundlings, Candlemas thought. In his long life, he'd heard everything at least twice. But it did explain the presence of the oddly well-organized orcs in the forests and mountains below. To startle the man, he asked a question to which he'd already guessed the answer. "He flies the banner of the red splayed hand?"

The traders gasped. The woman answered, "Y-yes, sire. This One King's horde has overrun the city of Tinnainen, killed or enslaved the populace, and made it its headquarters. Tinnainen is only at the fringe of the empire, sire, and is not even a Low City.

But it lies not twenty leagues east of us, and we are the next city in its path. The One King has sworn to unite all the land, to the sea as well as the southern deserts. We fear . . ."

"Yes, of course you do. You fear your own shadows, I expect." Candlemas waved a hand for silence. What a crackbrained notion, sweeping to the sea, as if the empire would let him. And uniting the southern deserts? What for? To build sand castles and farm pit vipers? Poppycock. The Neth had seen hordes before, usually pushed out of the eastern steppes by other hordes pushed west by the growth of empires in distant Kara-Tur. Even the tribe of Sunbright's barbarians had been pushed to the wall of the Barren Mountains a few generations back. The Neth had endured forever, almost, and seen other empires come and go. Most times they didn't care. But any upstart foolish enough to gain the attention of the Netherese fizzled quickly.

". . . please, milord?" The woman was still blathering. "They say the most horrendous things about the One King. That he commands powerful magics of the most obscene kind. And that he's not even human, but a red dragon in disguise."

"Oh, balderdash!" Candlemas found himself actually divulging secret knowledge to a groundling. " 'Wyrm eats wyrm and so grows great!' Dragons consume only other dragons. No dragon walks out in the open in any guise!" His voice was a haughty squeak, because he himself was guised.

Disgusted with penny-ante clerks, Candlemas was ready to order them all out of the castle, out the nearest window if need be. What did he, and certainly Lady Polaris, care if their miserable city were overrun by a miserable army? It would be justice for their having skimped on building a defense and then squandering their money on lavish clothes. The wizard cared only to note the name of their potentially doomed city, that he might notify Lady Polaris in case one of her cronies owned the pisshole. Then . . .

"Wait." He pursed pouty lips. "What's the name of your pisshole? Uh, city?"

The sweating traders exchanged glances. "It's Dalekeva, your lordship."

"Dalekeva?" Candlemas unconsciously scratched his healing right arm, even though, guised, it looked fine. "That's not right. What was it formerly called?"

"Oh." One of the men had just recalled that wizards, human or not, lived a very long time. "Under the last dynasty, milord, it was called Oberon's Hold, after the great lord Ober—"

"Yes, yes. Hush. The blank region . . ." Candlemas talked to himself as his audience regarded him curiously. In the past, at various times, the wizard had tried to scry that area from afar, but could not. Perhaps there'd been a battle there—that was a safe guess for anyplace in the empire—and residual magic clouded scrying, ancient shields and glamours and hexes. There were several spots in Toril where Netherese magic could not penetrate, but this patch of blankness had moved! That was the intrigue. And lately, it had drifted. Where did these idiots say? East. Toward Tinnainen. A powerful lure that, to any real wizard interested in real study. If Candlemas had been a ferret, his nose would have twitched.

Very well then, he'd put these seeking fools to work. For only fools would run to wizards they hated to solve their piddling problems. He'd grant them wizardry, along with terror and mystery and great adventure. That would cure their bellyaching. And if they happened to waltz into the jaws of whatever monsters were moving magic blankets around, all the better.

"Very good. Remain here. And don't touch anything." Humans' hands were always sticky, and they'd mar the porcelain.

Striding from the room, favoring his right arm, Candlemas made the long trek to his workshop high in the centermost tower. Still disguised, he moved to the palantir and rapped it smartly. Instantly the black glass began to smoke; then a gray cloud at the top turned white and sank, revealing Lady Polaris.

The archmage took one look at the caller, curled her red lips, and spat, "*Stellmalagra!*"

Candlemas barely ducked his nobleman's head as a white-hot lightning bolt exploded from the palantir. Seeking iron and ground, it sizzled over his head and punished an iron hook hammered into a room beam. The force scorched the iron hook to a melted dollop, blackened and set fire to the wooden beam, and spattered hot metal over the cringing Candlemas. Red-hot drops pierced the guise, which included a head of curly black hair, so his bald pate was stung as if by hornets.

"Milady!" yelled the wizard. " 'Tis I, your faithful thrall, Candlemas! Please, cease!"

"Oh." The archmage framed in the black glass squinted. "I thought it was some servant playing with the palantir. Don't you know enough not to summon me while guised?"

Yes, Candlemas did know but, lost in thought, had forgotten. This wheat and corn rust thing was obsessing him. But he'd remember next time. "I beg forgiveness, your ladyship."

"Don't bother. It's nothing. What do you want?"

It occurred to Candlemas that these were the same imperious words he'd flung at the cowering delegates. Not that he felt any sympathy for them. The world was a hierarchy of lords ruling underlings. The trick was to ascend high and fast, and so have more underlings and fewer lords.

Mopping his guised brow, the wizard told of the advancing horde, the rape of Tinnainen, the threat to Dalekeva, the ambitions of an empire-building One King, and the rest, excepting the weird magic-blanketed area. Lady Polaris looked increasingly petulant, but at least she hurled no more bolts. At the end she said only, "Yes, yes. Handle it as you see fit. That's why I empowered you. Oh, and one more thing."

Uh-oh, thought the wizard.

"Somewhere in that neck of the woods, or so I'm told by someone who lusts for it, is a book. It's very big, they say, and has a ruby set into the cover. Or a pearl. It's chock-full of ancient lore from a race of nonhumans. Stone people or spirits, or some such. It might prove an amusing read. Fetch it."

The palantir went black.

Horror-stricken, Candlemas stared at the blank black ball. He muttered over and over, "Fetch it? A mystery book lost in hundreds of square leagues? Fetch it? Just like that?"

* * * * *

The delegates of the Beneficent Traders' Guild of Dalekeva had been waiting nervously, and now their unease got a huge boost. Whitefaced, the prissy noble-man stamped into the room hard enough to dent the marble floors.

There was no wasted time now. Candlemas planted his feet before the delegates and pronounced, "I have gained audience with Lady Polaris. You, all of you, will journey hence to Tinnainen, seek audience with this usurper, the One King, and demand he send word of his immediate submission to Netheril. Don't return without it."

That the delegates were stunned barely described their reaction. One screamed and fell to his knees. Another gargled until he clutched his chest and collapsed. Two swooned. The rest babbled like rabid weasels, pointing fingers and hurling blame, while the bodyguards hollered resignations or demands for higher pay.

Candlemas swung on his heel and strode from the room. To the guards, he ordered, "Drag this lot to the magic portal and shove them through. See they're dumped in the village of, uh, Augerbend on the River Ost. They can walk from there. Oh, I almost forgot."

He swung back to the room, where the delegates were still crying and gibbering, and shouted, "There's a young barbarian named Sunbright in the village! Take him with you!"

Striding away, Candlemas, as was his wont, reviewed that decision too. The hell with Sysquemalyn's foolish bet for now, and the hell with gathering rumors. There was no time for games. Candlemas had to get that damnable book with its pearl- or ruby-studded cover for Lady Polaris, and soon. She hated to be kept waiting—if she even remembered issuing the order later. That was another damnable quality of hers! But perhaps this would work out well. Rather than go alone, Sunbright could journey with this pack of cannon fodder as a buffer. When not slaying orcs or whatever, he could be easily shunted hither and yon to search for the book. The boob would do whatever the raven recommended, after all.

So it might work out fine, if all these clucks survived long enough.

And himself, Candlemas.

Briefly he thought of what he'd told that little girl,

how he admired her father, keeper of the dovecotes. Perhaps Candlemas could assume his disguise, if all failed. When Lady Polaris flew shrieking through the halls, Candlemas could happily shovel pigeon shit.

That's what it all was, he sighed. Shitting. Shit fell from the privies of the archmages onto him, and he in turn shit on the lowly groundlings. Somewhere was the lowliest groundling of all, he thought, who collected all the shit of the world on his or her head. He wondered if they were ever happy.

* * * * *

One day's walk from the village of Augerbend, Sunbright was settling onto his camp bed, blissfully unaware of the machinations happening high over his head. He knew only that he was pleasantly tired after walking a dozen miles that day and bringing down a brace of wood ducks for his dinner.

He had his usual small banked fire, reflecting off a fallen oak this time. This would be his last camp, he supposed, for tomorrow he would enter a real village. He'd never visited one before, had been only to markets erected in fields on the edge of the tundra, where his people traded meat and hides and beaten copper ornaments for salt and iron and cloth and other provisions. Rengarth warriors did not venture far into the lowlands except for cattle and spouse raids. So as for this place, he didn't know what to expect. For the thousandth time, he wished he had a companion, even a dog, to travel with him. Truth to tell, the brawny barbarian was a bit shy. And with everything so new . . .

A twig snapped, and as quick as thought Sunbright was off his blanket and behind the log with sword poised. He readied to spring, for he reckoned that the closer he got to civilization, the more dangerous the woods would be, not less. But this clumsy visitor would probably only be the podgy Chandler.

No, definitely not.

A woman tiptoed into his camp. Her hair was long and tawny red, the color of the fire. She wore nothing but a simple shift, the soft cloth washed and worn so much it had taken her shape, thin enough so Sunbright could see every curve as she stood by the fire.

Peering first at his empty bedroll, then at the darkness around her, she quavered, "Hello? Hello, is anyone here? I'm lost and need help."

It couldn't be true, thought Sunbright. Her plight had "trap" smeared all over it. So he surprised himself by calling, "Where you are from?"

"Oh!" The girl jumped, startled. She tiptoed, barefoot, to the fallen oak and peered over it. "Oh, there you are!"

Sunbright felt foolish aiming a sword at the girl. But his childhood had been filled with horror stories of mysterious women who accosted wandering men. Silkies, they were called, or dryads, water sprites, nymphs, succubi, and other names. Invariably they cozied up to a man, then visited him with some unspeakable death: turned him inside out, changed him to a frog, drowned and ate him, planted insect eggs into his paralyzed body.

As the girl leaned over him, the shift gaped open revealingly. She shivered. "I'm nearly frozen! I was bathing in the river, and some boys from the village stole my clothes. I had to wait until nightfall to return home, but I lost my way in the dark. Can you . . ." Her voice trailed off as he continued to stare at her.

A likely story, thought Sunbright. She had to be a

night hag, a harpy, a killer. He couldn't be this lucky. He kept his sword ready, but felt himself melting under her warm green gaze. He knew he should tell her to leave, but some traitorous part of himself replied, "I'm a stranger here and don't know the way to the village. But if you'd like to share my fire . . ."

She smiled gratefully and sank down on his camp bed of boughs and blanket.

Now what? Sunbright wondered, standing. Would she grow fangs and red eyes? Would he have to lop off her head?

"Would you sit beside me?" The girl looked up at him, her green eyes pleading. "I'm still cold."

Sunbright felt his knees turn to water. This was magic, for sure, but perhaps only normal man-woman magic. He tried to answer, but only croaked like a frog.

"What?" she breathed. Her eyes were soft, her lips moist. "I can't hear; you'll have to come closer."

Twisting a surprisingly strong hand into his bearskin jerkin, she pulled his face downward. His legs failed, and the rest of him followed, collapsing on the camp bed next to her. She bent over him and placed her mouth on his.

She's not cold, the barbarian thought groggily as he gave himself up to her eager ministrations. Not cold at all.

And this was bound to be better than dying in combat.

* * * * *

Sunlight stabbed into his eyes, and Sunbright sat bolt upright on his blanket. He'd overslept.

Rubbing his eyes, he simultaneously searched for his sword, his possessions, and the girl. The first two were where he'd dropped them, the last gone without a trace. No, there was one trace, for her delicate footprints showed in the scalped dirt around the dead campfire.

"But that doesn't make sense," he wondered aloud. "Either they suck your soul or lift your purse." But everything was here, including an ache at the base of his spine. It had been the most delightful night of his life.

So where was she? And *who* was she?

The name *Ruellana* tolled a bell in his mind. At some point in the evening, he'd remembered to ask her name. She'd gasped it at the time, and the memory set him to wondering.

Why would she love him half to death and depart? There were no stories where a man got boundless joy and didn't pay dearly for it. But that seemed to be the case. Standing, legs apart, sword in hand, he followed her tracks a ways, but they quit at a deer trail that pointed toward Augerbend. Had she gone that way? Or flown into the sky, or slid inside a tree? Would he ever see her again? He certainly hoped so. Maybe in the village, since it was the only human settlement around.

Whistling, eager now to get to Augerbend, the barbarian threw together his meager camp, hoisted his pack and bow, and swung off.

"Ruellana of Augerbend, here I come."

He was still whistling, and breaking every other rule about moving through enemy territory, as he left the deer trail for a rutted road, then passed the first farm. It was a fortified cabin with a double-barred door, thick log walls, and a slate roof that would not burn. The door stood open this bright spring morning, and from inside Sunbright heard a woman singing. Dogs ran up the road and barked furiously, but the young man only waved at them graciously and bid them good day. A girl chivvying geese with a switch looked up, saw the wanderer, and ran for the house. In a moment the woman came to the doorway. Sunbright waved, but she only jerked the girl inside and slammed the door.

Touchy folk, the young man thought. No doubt Ruellana lives elsewhere.

Before he knew it, he was threading cabins on both sides of the road, then came to a crossroads where four matched maples cast a green tint from early spring leaves filtering sunlight. The barbarian saw now that the village occupied land that jutted squarely into a small river. Hence its name, for the river made a bend like an auger brace used for drilling holes. A nice place, Sunbright thought, if Ruellana lived here.

There were few people about, for most were in the fields, tilling and planting. Another dog barked, but the barbarian spoke to it and it stilled. "Hush, you. Where's the inn? Ah!"

Facing a flattened stretch of earth and the river was a squat building that streamed smoke from a thatched roof. Above the low door hung a sign crudely drawn with a brimming mug. That, Sunbright understood.

Whistling again, the curious dog still trailing and sniffing along behind him, the warrior shifted his pack on his back and ducked through the low door. It was black inside, for there were no windows, but he heard voices and smelled meat and fruit pies that set his stomach growling. It was time, he thought, to test whether Chandler's coins were good.

As his eyes were adjusting to the dimness, something whizzed by his head like an angry bee, then shattered on the lintel. Crockery and ale splashed his shoulder.

"By the yellow god," roared a bleary voice. "A barbarian!"

"He's got a nerve!"

"Kill him!"

"Get his sword!"

Surprised by the hostility and unused to being indoors, Sunbright hesitated for a moment. Better to lurk in the dark, warned one teaching. Better to get outside in the clear, warned a contradiction.

And in that second, someone hammered his head into the young man's midriff.

Grunting, Sunbright cannoned backward into the doorjamb. The uneven threshold, worn by generations of feet, tricked his heel, and he stumbled. The man pressing him grappled clumsily, enfolding Sunbright in ale fumes. They probably wouldn't attack if they weren't drunk, the barbarian thought evenly. He dug an iron thumb into the man's neck to make him gasp and let go.

Meanwhile, a second man reared from the dark den and swung a meaty fist at the barbarian's face. Sunbright shifted his head coolly, but banged it against the jamb, and the roundhouse punch smashed his lips against his teeth. Damn it, he thought, he hated being indoors!

While being hugged around his middle, Sunbright avoided the next blow. The assailant's fist smashed into the jamb. He heard a knuckle snap. But a third man rose from the dark like a smoky wraith, and he had a knife that flashed in leaking sunlight.

"Enough!" the barbarian bellowed. But they didn't hear, for the men were shouting as if the pub were on fire.

Scooting a hair, he drove his knee straight up into the grappler's gut. The man oofed, relaxed his grip, then grabbed hold again. The puncher reached with two hands to drive thumbs into Sunbright's eyes, but the warrior flicked his head, caught a thumb in his mouth, and bit to the bone. The man howled. With the puncher trapped, the knife wielder couldn't close.

Seeking to disengage the grappler, Sunbright bent one knee, then smashed as hard as he could upward with the other. The grappler urped, then vomited hot, stinking ale and stomach juice all over the barbarian's shirt.

That made Sunbright furious. Spitting out the howler's thumb, he gave a battle shriek that raised hackles and set dogs barking all over the village.

Ten minutes later, his tackle torn from his shoulders, his topknot spilled down around his face, his knuckles skinned and bleeding, his shirt torn, Sunbright was bashing the head of the last man standing—actually, he'd found him cowering behind the short bar—against the bar, yelling in time with the thumping, "Never, never, treat me that way again! You hear me? Never—"

A sharp whistle cut him off. He squinted at the doorway. A lumpy shape filled it sideways, but left the top half full of sunlight. Not a man, the barbarian thought dazedly.

The squat shadow asked, "You Sunbright?"

"Aye." He let go of the barkeep's ears.

"Someone wishes to speak with you."

"Oh. Thank you." Creaking, groggy from battle lust and the following weakness, the warrior combed back his yellow hair, picked up his tackle, and ducked low under dark beams, heading for the door.

The squat shadow was gone.

Chapter 5

Outside, the sun had retreated behind some clouds, and Sunbright smelled rain coming. A party of traders ill-dressed for traveling milled awkwardly at the ferry crossing. A handful of capable-looking bodyguards were busily strapping bundles and bedrolls to a dozen pack animals. The squat figure who'd summoned him stumped in that direction: a dwarf, the first real one Sunbright had ever seen.

With the party was Chandler, the plain-dressed steward of the local castle, who'd sauntered into Sunbright's camp thirteen leagues hence with gifts and odd propositions. Now he left the party and walked over, but halted when he got a whiff of the barbarian's scent.

Looking at his jerkin and shirt, Sunbright found vomit, ale, candle wax, blood, and other fluids. He strode to the riverbank and, notwithstanding an audience, stripped and washed his shirt and himself. On his forearm he discovered a deep bite he didn't recall getting. Chandler stood nearby and talked.

"I've chosen a task for you," said the erstwhile steward. "I wish you to travel with this party. They seek audience with a would-be emperor in the east called the One King."

Sunbright wrung out his shirt, scattering curious minnows in the rippling water. He thought it over, knew the party would have directions and such, so asked only, "Then what?"

"Eh?" Chandler, really Candlemas, was startled by the barbarian's cutting to the heart of the matter. The groundling was not slow-witted. If he survived the journey and audience with the One King, which was unlikely, Candlemas hoped to send him for Lady Polaris's benighted book. "Uh, find out all you can about this One King and come back. Would I were one of those cloud-living wizards who can see down into the world at a snap of the fingers, but alas."

Shrugging on his shirt and lacing his jerkin, Sunbright squinted. "I thought your master, the lord of the castle, wanted information about local grain prices. What's a foreign ruler got to do with that?"

Chandler almost smiled. The barbarian wasn't that bright, and lying was a wizard's specialty. "Oh, quite a bit. People hoard food in times of trouble, so prices go up. If armies attack from the east, there'll be a greater demand there than locally. So it might profit to freight the grain down the river, for instance."

"I see." The barbarian didn't, really. His people lived by barter. Chandler's coins in his pouch were the first he'd ever owned, and he couldn't comprehend their value. How could disks of metal be worth a set price when everything was negotiable? Nor did he believe all Chandler wanted was information, but then wizards were supposed to be devious and mysterious. And dangerous, so it wouldn't do to rile this one with too many questions. It would be best to keep on his good side.

He shrugged as he whipped his hair through its top-knot. "Very well. What will I be paid when I return?"

That, Chandler thought, was not a worry. So he lied, "A twentieth part of the profits, perhaps? Or a flat fee? Or would you prefer some magical item?"

The words gave Sunbright pause. Seeing his piqued interest, Chandler pulled from a belt pouch a small corked vial. "I thought you'd welcome that idea. Give me your sword." Sunbright slapped his hand on the pommel so fast the wizard backstepped. "Uh, wait. This will make your weapon more potent! I'll just pour it on the blade, and then the sword can wound enchanted beings!"

The barbarian glared from under blond brows. "You'll spoil the temper."

What a moron, thought Chandler, as if he'd reforge the blade here by a riverside. "Look, may I demonstrate? Just ease the blade out a hair. Watch."

Fooling a peasant would be easy. Laying his left thumb on the sharp edge, Chandler pushed hard enough to dent the skin. "See there? I'm only a hedge wizard, but I've enough power to shield myself from harm." He pulled the cork and tipped the clear fluid onto the edge, then reapplied his thumb. Instantly, the razor edge split the skin. A tiny trickle of blood stained the steel. "See?"

Despite himself, Sunbright was impressed. Trying to hide his eagerness, he drew the sword and held it while Chandler poured the liquid from the vial all along the blade. The potion ran like water and dripped off. "Do I rub it in or let it dry?"

"Oh, just wipe it off. One touch is enough, as I showed you. Now your blade is enchanted and can rend the flesh of any magical creature: harpies,

liches, bugbears, anything."

"And I'll receive more enchantments when I return?" Carefully, Sunbright dried Harvester with a rag, then slowly slid it home in the sheath. "That's a promising reward. Thank you. I'll do my best to get your information on the One King."

"Please do." Chandler raised his left hand in farewell, his right hanging at his side.

Sunbright turned toward the party of traders, then suddenly whirled. "Oh, I almost forgot. You must know everyone here. Where lives a girl named Ruellana?"

Chandler frowned. He didn't know any of these peasants, but was supposed to command them. To stall, he asked, "Ruellana? There are so many young women here. How does she appear?"

"Curves like a walrus tusk. Green eyes, red hair." Lust dripped in his voice.

Red hair? A warning flag rose in the wizard's mind. Was Sysquemalyn sticking her oar into his machinations? "Uh, I'm not sure. I'll ask around, and see she's available when you return."

Thwarted, Sunbright frowned, but nodded curtly and, without another word, turned to go.

Chandler, or Candlemas, was glad to see him leave. The enchanting, of course, was a trick. He'd simply shielded his thumb from the first cut, relaxed it for the second. The "magic potion" had been river water this morning. Humans were easy to fool, and barbarians more so than most, it seemed. Still, the groundling was a fast learner. He wouldn't be tractable forever.

* * * * *

Right away, Sunbright saw problems.

The party milling by the ferry head didn't look or

sound right. Travelers would normally be busy, pre-occupied, a little nervous, giddy at the thought of adventure. This group milled like cattle in a slaughter pen: cursing each other and the packhorses, bickering with the bodyguards, screaming orders at locals fetching supplies, weeping openly and crying to the gods for protection. Many wore gaudy long robes, impossible for walking any distance, and slippers on their feet instead of shoes or boots. But these were lowlanders, the barbarian told himself, and so were soft in the arm, rump, *and* head.

He began to walk toward the dwarf, who was quietly organizing things, but a woman intercepted him with a glare as hard as glacier ice. "What do you want?"

The warrior lifted his chin. "I want nothing. I'm to join your party."

"You're not!"

Sunbright blinked, nonplussed by her rudeness—and the exotic looks of a half-elf. Her face was as pale as milk, with high arching brows and pointed ears, her hair jet black, drawn straight back into a braid intertwined with silver wire and rawhide. She wore a shirt of silk rife with white embroidery, boiled and molded leather armor of a glistening emerald green and breeches of the same color, with a wide black belt and boots. She looked like a brilliant banded lizard from the southlands that Sunbright had once seen at a market stall. An ornate sword with a basket hilt, very slim, jingled at her belt with a matching dagger, and on her back was a black bow as slender as a fox's rib.

She was beautiful but unfriendly, so Sunbright simply went around her. He hailed the dwarf. "I am Sunbright, Raven Clan of the Rengarth. I'm to join the party."

"Dorlas, son of Drigor. Welcome." They shook hands, the dwarf's like a sun-warmed rock. With a sigh, he pointed a craggy finger at a trader who'd dropped a bundle and then collapsed weeping atop it. "Cease your blubbering, Fendril! We've been over this. Consign your soul to the gods and get your sorry arse into motion!"

Sunbright gestured at the party. "Why are they so reluctant to depart?"

"Because it's a cock-up, that's why. Because they're idiots. Because I'm cursed," the dwarf rumbled. He wasn't that small, as the legends told, but came almost to the barbarian's breastbone, though he was twice as wide with arms like the rope hawsers restraining the ferry. His beard was strawberry-blond and braided, his hair the same under a simple steel helmet painted with a compass on the top. He wore all rough-out leather and a steel cuirass besides, easily toted a pack almost as big as himself and a fluted warhammer that Sunbright would have swung to kill an ox.

The half-elf interrupted. "This barbarian is *not* joining our party!"

The two males looked at her, querying. Green-gray eyes flashing, she snapped, "Barbarians can't be trusted! They're savages, not much risen above orcs! They've no sense of honor or decency, but pillage and rape and raid without mercy! And they're dirty and infested!"

Sunbright scratched his ear insolently. "Those traits are the same as I've heard attributed to elves. And I took a bath this morning." He held up his damp shirttail.

Dorlas rumbled again, a chuckle this time. "I've heard the same said of dwarves."

"I won't have him with us!" the elf went on. "Dorlas,

if you're responsible—"

"I am, and so's he, if his scars are any proof. And part of this disaster was to employ a barbarian named Sunbright, if you recall. And we need another sword. Tears of Jannath, we need a dozen! Hoy there, don't strike that animal or I'll tie you to its tail!"

Sweetly, Sunbright said, "You haven't introduced yourself, sister."

"Greenwillow of the Moon Elves, cousin to the High Elves of Cormanthyr! Too high-born to wallow in a trough with human barbarians!"

Still smiling, Sunbright bowed. "Then please, your ladyship, don't speak to me." Huffing and jingling, the elf swung away.

"Never mind her. She's joined us with some mission to somewhere, and paid to do it, so thinks she has a say in my doings." The dwarf hooked a calloused thumb down the road through the village, where a round-backed wizard plodded toward the forest. "Who's your friend?"

"Not a friend. That's Chandler, steward of the local castle."

"No, he isn't." At the barbarian's angry look, as if he'd been accused of lying, the dwarf explained, "We bunked at the local castle last night. The steward's a tall cob that lacks two front teeth."

Sunbright didn't argue, only pondered. If there was no reason for the dwarf to lie, then Chandler must be lying about his true identity. For sure, he was a wizard, but who was he really?

"What a mess." Dorlas interrupted his thoughts. "I can't believe I signed on with these clowns. They'll be dead in the first five miles. Help them strap on these provisions, or we won't even cross the river before nightfall."

"In a moment. First I must seek a girl."

Dorlas peered up at him from under bushy brows. "Night's the time for loving. Day's for working. But go and hurry up. And boy, you'd better be a fighter. We'll need that sword."

* * * * *

Sunbright had no luck finding Ruellana. None of the villagers knew a girl by that name. He supposed some might lie to keep a rapacious barbarian away from the local girls, but many answers seemed sincere. Strangely, the people he believed most were the lumpy, bruised men he'd brawled with. They were nursing their hurts while picking up the mess in the tavern, but gave grudging admiration to a stranger who could bring down the house. But no, there was no Ruellana living nearby. No redheads at all within a dozen miles, in fact. One old duffer rasped, "If you spent the night with a fire-faerie or whatever she be, think yourself lucky to escape still a man and not a gelding."

Sunbright did not feel lucky and, remembering her firm, ripe body under his hands, found it hard to believe her a phantom. He'd hoped to find her quickly and ask her to accompany him, or at least wait until he returned. But maybe she was, after all, only a dream: the shaman's double blessing and curse.

Reluctantly, he rejoined the party, strapped tents and leather cases and satchels of food and finally a few traders to the horses, and slapped and prodded and dragged beasts and men onto the wobbly ferry raft.

It was before nightfall, but well after noon, by the time they were assembled on the other side and blundering into the spring-leafy cathedral of a forest.

* * * * *

The party trended east, southeast, and east again. For weeks, as spring ripened to summer, they threaded forests, skirted hills, forded rivers, picked their way cautiously through swamps, passed villages and towns and fields and orchards. Names learned from locals blew by Sunbright like birds and butterflies: Red Lake, Hidden Lake, Shylock Mountains, Conifer City, Zweihaus River, High Ice, Fluvion, Frostypaw, Frothwater, Cede Run, Gillan River, Hatchet Mountains, Remembrance, Gods' Legion. The Dalekevans grumbled at every step. They had to walk all the way home, when earlier they'd been whisked by magic portals to Delia, the castle in the air. Yet even on that they couldn't agree, for some took a perverse pride in the lofty ways of the high wizards and were disdainful of those who had to travel afoot. Sunbright thought they should have been happy to be able to return home at all, but some lamented how the elder council would condemn their failed mission, while the rest fretted into the future, of their ongoing mission to meet the One King. By the evening campfires, snivelers delighted in tormenting one another about the hideous deaths they would no doubt reap. Then the bickering would flare up again, and accusations would make the air ring like crows fighting over a dead horse.

The way was sometimes easy, a saunter across open fields with new grass to the horses' hocks. Often it was hard, when rain was pounding them senseless yet they had to ford a river to their chins before it rose higher and blocked them for days, or on one stretch where there was no groundwater at all, and everyone plodded along with gasping, protruding tongues.

There were deaths. An elderly merchant, already

half dead with fear and fatigue, tripped over his now-tattered gown and landed in the campfire. Folks dragged him out and rolled him in dirt, but he died of burns two days later. One woman panicked and drowned while fording a river. One bodyguard left her bedroll one night, walked into the woods, and never returned, and even Sunbright couldn't track her.

The barbarian heard strange and wondrous stories, mostly of wizards and their stupendous spells, usually ending with some deserving trader gaining a fortune. The bodyguards, most of whom Sunbright liked, told tales of heroes and beasts, some new to him. He would have liked to hear other people's stories as well, but the dwarf had little to say unless it involved the caravan moving on, and Greenwillow was often gone by night, wandering the woods on strange errands of her own, for she never seemed to sleep.

Sunbright spent his nights uneasily, for by dusk and dawn he was haunted by memories of Ruellana. He relived his night with her over and over, savoring the details, then fretting over what had happened the next morning. Who was she? Why did she appear and disappear? Was she human, or even real? He half dreaded the thought she was enchanted, for then he'd probably never see her again. But by that token, he hoped she was, for a spirit might surprise him no matter how far he traveled. Often he felt her warm flesh under his calloused hands, the nibble of her teeth on his chest. Yet he always woke alone by a cold fire. So he was quiet in his own way, and pondered, and knew he'd eventually forget her. Yet every night's dreams possessed the same intensity as before, as if she brought her astral self to him but not her body. And what a body . . .

Occasionally, too, to his dreams would come the raven-haired woman. But that one, he knew, was just the raven in another form. Wasn't it? When he asked either the dream-woman or the raven, he got no answer. All in all, portents could be a pain.

The barbarian proved a valuable member of the party right off. His wilderness training, shaman abilities, and honed reflexes let him follow any sort of trail, warn of danger or changing terrain ahead, predict bad weather, identify poisonous plants, and more. He could heal minor wounds too, and often did, for all the traders were incompetent. None had been allowed to bring servants along with the delegation, and now the coin counters were stranded in the wilds having to learn the most basic camping and walking and survival skills. Sunbright swore he healed burns and cuts on every finger of every trader in the party at least once. Yet when they tried to haughtily order him to do so, he growled them into submission. The bodyguards all agreed they were not servants.

So they plodded on. The young man tried to learn from his surroundings, absorbing whatever the land and creatures might teach. Although many of these lowland animals were not denizens of the tundra, and thus were unfamiliar, he could usually read their behavior. He could tell whether an animal was calm and unworried or nervous, and if so, from what. An ambling bear too close to the road was pushed by wolves. Deer feeding in an open field near coyote scat told him one of their kind had died that morning, and the hunters were sated for the nonce. Beavers improving their dams warned of heavy rain to come. In some swamps and fens the barbarian even spotted some antique reptiles, the great long-necked honkers and screechers like giant lizards. But, caught up in their own clumsy struggles after food and life, they had little to teach him, for their time was fading away, their lands and numbers shrinking.

At every encounter, Sunbright tried to read the animals' thoughts, but all he drew were puzzled stares or no reaction at all. Men could speak to beasts, he knew. His father had been able to, but Owldark, who'd taken his father's place, could not. Nor could Sunbright, it seemed. Not without some secret knowledge, some key he lacked. But he would someday, he promised himself. He must to become a shaman like his father. He would return to his tribe a great man, or die trying. That was certain. But he made sure his animal-speaking attempts went unseen by the traders and bodyguards. He didn't need his traveling companions thinking him strange. Or stranger.

Sometimes Sunbright reflected that adventure could be damned tedious. Out of sheer boredom, he perversely tried to befriend Greenwillow, but she continued to snub him. Still, he used every opportunity to drift near her, if only to rattle her.

And one day in late summer, he actually got a compliment. . . .

* * * * *

Sunbright was ahead of the main party, scouting one of two roads from a fork. Willows lined a meadow cropped by woods bison, and small streams cut the hardpack. There was so much water he suspected a swamp lay ahead and the road would peter out. The sun was hot, for they'd drifted south, but the free flow of sweat was pleasant. And it was nice to escape the others' bickering for a while. Still, he would have to turn back soon.

Then the raven spiraled in on wide wings and plunked to the road. Sunbright bid it good day, received the same, and added, "What's the news?"

"You'll lose some hair soon," croaked the bird. Its black beak, with the thick bump near the nose, clacked open and shut a few times.

"*Hair?* That's a prophecy?"

"Death is in the air." The bird cocked its head at a tuft of grass, jabbed, and nailed an inchworm.

"Death is as common as life," Sunbright chided. "That's no news."

"Don't go into dragon caves, either."

"Wait! Back to the death part. Whose death? Where? When? Hey, wait!"

But the bird rabbit-hopped, beat the air with wide wings, and took off in the direction from which Sunbright had come.

The barbarian cursed. It was often thus. The winged bugger spiraled in, croaked something obscure and somber, and flew off. Not much help except to worry a man. The whiny Dalekevans prophesied doom all the time—

"The traders!"

Sunbright spun on his heel and ran. As he trotted, he strung his longbow and nocked an arrow. The bird passed on ahead, higher, obviously over the traders' band.

Even charging, Sunbright knew enough not to top a rise in plain view. Hopping over grass so as not to leave a break, panting and trying to listen at the same time, he pattered along behind interlaced willows, scurried along a ravine, then climbed the slope. Even a quick glance showed someone else had done the same recently.

Between tree trunks he saw the caravan and its attackers. A horse was down with an arrow in its neck, another kicked from a rump shot. A trader lay dead, shot through the back. More had hands in the air, one bleeding from a shoulder wound. A bodyguard rolled in agony while another lay dead. But for the moment there was silence and stillness. Dorlas held his warhammer ready; Greenwillow and the other bodyguards had swords out. The dwarf negotiated, at a distance, with the bandits' leader. There were a dozen or more, with two dead, a scruffy lot of men and women in rags and skins and hacked-off hair. But their swords and pikes were top-notch weapons, as were the crossbows some held leveled on the fighters. Four held captives from behind with knives to their throats.

Sunbright had the advantage of surprise and knew he'd best use it. Below the ravine's lip he tugged out four arrows, all he had, for it took hours to make one properly. He laid them on the leaves before him, then placed his great hooked sword Harvester beside them. Judging whom to shoot, he braced his toes lest they slip, nocked an arrow, and rose.

The first arrow caught the leader smack in his yapping mouth. He was knocked flying, grabbing the shaft in both hands even while dying.

Scanning, Sunbright ignored the bandits holding the hostages, who instinctively ducked behind the captives. He next killed a stout fellow with ritual scars down his arms, for he looked dangerous. He felled a woman scanning the woods with a crossbow, aimed for another man drawing a bead on him . . .

Something hissed by his face like a long black hornet. His bowstring snapped, and the longbow flicked open like a flapping fish. Dropping the useless weapon, the warrior grabbed his sword in two hands and charged down the slight slope. "Attack! Battleleaf, Sealkiller, Manslayer!"

Bandits started at the running fiend, scanned for more of the madmen. Many of them scattered for the willows on the other side of the road. Two robbers pushed their hostages away for running room; two strangled theirs by dragging them backward by their collars. Dorlas hollered, and Greenwillow shrilled and flashed into action. Fleet as a deer, she chased down a bandit and thrust a sword through her back. The woman fell screaming. Dorlas jumped to a halt and hurled his warhammer by the leather strap. It bowled a running man over, and the dwarf charged, caught up the weapon, and crushed the man's skull.

Sunbright rushed, screaming and slashing the air, but there were no bandits left by the time he arrived. Greenwillow, he saw, had run into trouble unknowingly, for she'd actually outrun some of the fleeing felons. Hunting a pair amidst the willows, she was unaware of two more coming up behind her. Sunbright's shouts went unheard in the uproar, so he put on a burst of speed and pelted after her.

Driving through willows that snagged on his face and arms and topknot, he bellowed just as a running bandit aimed a sword point at the half-elf's green lizard armor. Startled, the bandit half turned. The barbarian's sword chopped through his cheek, sheared off his jaw, and knocked him sprawling. Before he hit the ground, his face pouring red, a backswing punched the sword's hook through his throat.

Sunbright craned around, but saw no more enemies, only Greenwillow staring at her dead assailant. The barbarian wiped leaf flecks off his sweaty face and panted, "Well?"

Cool gray-green eyes rose to his. "Thank you."

"Doesn't hurt, does it?" He grinned and shouldered his sword. "You're welcome."

* * * * *

The traders, of course, were not properly grateful for their rescue. Of the four hostages who'd had knives at their throats, two were unharmed and one had been sliced across the cheek. The fourth had had his throat cut as the bandit shoved him away.

"I'm sorry," Dorlas told them, "but the boy did well." Sunbright had no idea how old the dwarf was, but Dorlas always referred to him as "the boy." "Bartering their lives would have yielded naught. They stalled only to make us lay down arms. More would have died in time, probably all of us, for these bandits would not let us go to warn others. It was the only way. You should reward the boy for his quick wits, good eye, and fast arm."

But the merchants groused among themselves, threatening to extract blood money from the bodyguards' eventual pay.

Sunbright basked in the fighters' compliments, until he went to pick up his fallen longbow from the ravine slope. He knew he'd kissed Death, for as he'd drawn the arrow to his cheek, a black crossbow bolt had severed the bowstring and almost split his face.

"I'll need my hair cut to braid a new string," he laughed in relief.

Then he stopped, recalling the raven's dark prophecy: that he'd "lose hair." And more. For the damned bird had flown right over the bandits' attack, but kept going. With no effort, it could have circled back to warn Sunbright, but hadn't.

The barbarian struck an imaginary chalk mark on the raven's slate: not to be trusted.

* * * * *

It was coming on autumn, almost a year since Sunbright had been banished and begun his adventures, when they came to the head of a vast valley. Far down, through miles of trees like giant steps, they saw open farmland, and in the distance along a broad river was their destination, the city of Dalekeva. Even the gloomy traders, the ones who'd survived, cheered when they saw the high walls of yellow stone, the onion-topped towers, and the colorful town that sprawled around the city and meandered along the many roads into yellow-grained farmland and beyond. Even the horses picked up their feet and plodded faster toward the last stretch of forest road, now that their destination was in sight.

But scouting ahead with Sunbright, Greenwillow lifted her nose, swiveling her head like a stork. Pointed black brows knit as she asked Sunbright, "Where is everyone?"

"Eh?" The warrior shifted his quiver and longbow at her tone. "Where should they be?"

"Look!" With her arm she swept the whole valley, the sky. "It's the harvest season, half the fields sport grain, the sun is high, there's no threat of rain, yet there's not a soul out working. No peasant would pass up this kind of day to get his crops in, not with the weather so changeable."

Stringing his bow, Sunbright squinted. He'd been staring at a long set of old gashes marring a red oak, gray-white gouges in red-gray bark. The gashes were as wide as his finger and as long as his bow, and occurred a dozen feet high on the tree. He tried to remember where he'd seen them before. Distracted, he mused, "Perhaps they're all inside those walls. A festival, perhaps, or—"

Greenwillow's answer was a shrill in the elven tongue. She, too, grabbed her bow while nodding back toward the woods behind them. "The Hunt! They come! The Hunt!"

Sunbright whirled around to see. From over the treetops, like dragons of silver and gold, soared a party of flying folk. Some skimmed on huge disks of metal; others rode clockwork wyverns. All were armored and armed and masked, with long lances whose points glinted in the afternoon sun.

With the shrill "halloo" of foxhunters, the flying folk swooped toward Sunbright's party.

Chapter 6

"Traders to the city!" roared Dorlas like a lion. "Guards to me!"

"What are they?" yelled Sunbright. He and Green-willow drew long arrows to their cheeks. Hers were slender, black, polished, fletched with exotic red and yellow feathers, while his were of plain ash and fletched with dark turkey.

"A Neth hunt!" she cried. "They hunt humans! Loose!"

Their arrows flashed from bowstrings. They'd automatically chosen foes at opposite sides of the attackers, squat men on flying disks, but the arrows spanked off armor or shattered. Sunbright was not surprised, but he cursed nonetheless.

Dorlas and the other bodyguards had cut some loads, grabbed whichever traders came to hand and plunked them on horses, then whacked the beasts, urging them toward the distant city. The traders left afoot were similarly whacked and sent scampering down the dipping forest road. Sunbright and Greenwillow passed them, running the other way. The barbarian yelped, "Wait! They're defenseless! This makes no sense!"

"No, it's the way! The city is sanctuary! Once inside the walls, the prey is safe, and the hunters won't bother with helpless prey. They'll attack us fighters! That's a challenge; that's their game."

Nocking on the run, they now formed a rear guard as Dorlas and the other bodyguards got off the road and under cover. Even panicked, Sunbright counted his foes, studied their tactics. There were seven, four on flying disks and three on mechanical animals. The disks were golden, an armspan wide, and those riding them seemed to have nothing to cling to, neither stirrups nor reins, though the hunters stood as easily as if on a flat rock. The barbarian's analytical mind even assessed the flying beasts. They, too, were golden, set with jewels for eyes and decoration, the size of horses with wings as wide as a condor's, two like dragons and one like a splay-tailed bird.

Yet unlike birds or dragons, the clockwork animals didn't flap their wings. So the "dragons" were probably of the same material as the disks, and enchanted by the same means. And no doubt the leaders of the Hunt got the more gorgeous mounts and long lances, while the disk-foes were hired huntsmen or bodyguards with long cavalry flails and spears. That knowledge might come in handy, if he survived long enough to exploit it.

The four disk riders had split into pairs to flank the fleeing party—and so were already ahead and behind the barbarian and half-elf, for they moved like the wind. Oncoming were the three dragon riders. That suited Sunbright. He drew to his cheek, tracked the middle rider, and loosed. The speeding arrow missed as the Neth banked. He'd held his nock too long, signaled his target. Greenwillow, too, had shot, but Sunbright didn't see the strike.

He reached for his last arrow, but was suddenly shoved aside hard enough to bank off a tree.

A crackle and a sizzle of lightning struck the branch just above his head. The wood split with a steamy explosion. Leaves were blasted to flinders. A dark streak marked the bark as the lightning sought ground. Sunbright blinked at the thought of that charge hitting his head, coursing down his body. . . .

"Come!" shouted Greenwillow, who'd shoved him to safety.

The three dragons had flitted overhead. Sunbright saw their tails pointed at him, as stiff and straight as golden arrowheads. Far ahead, the hunters pursued Dorlas and the rest. "What was that?"

"Their rules allow only hand weapons and bows! And lances with minor magics: lightning and cold blast or fire. Anything else is unsporting, not the game."

"Game? Killing the humans that support them? That makes no sense! It's madness!"

"Aye, madness is a way of life for the Neth! They saw off the limbs that support them. Tell me how long their cruel culture will survive their cannibalizing themselves."

They saved their breath for running, though they ran toward a trap. Ahead, amidst the trees where the land folded, jutted an outcrop of granite like a big house studded with scraggly cedar trees and some thick green vines. Hunted, the dwarf had steered instinctively for stone. Sunbright could just see the bodyguards' heads amidst the jumble of rocks and leaves. Above, he saw the four huntsmen on disks whizzing around the outcrop like bees around a hive. Higher above, hovering, the three dragon riders had tilted up their masks to converse, no doubt planning a strategy.

If they're that high, they can take damage from arrows, noted the warrior. And the faces behind the masks were human enough, even if Neth. Their armor was fantastically fluted and gilt, and painted in every color of the rainbow, so they looked like monstrous hummingbirds. The masks were horrific, wolves or lions or such, but no more frightening than the masks shamans wore in Sunbright's tribe, and ones he himself might wear, if he lived so long.

He and Greenwillow paused for breath under the wide arms of an oak. Various plans rippled through their minds, and they both talked at once.

"Better to stay out here, strike from two sides. . . . No, they'll close and we'll need strength in numbers. . . . Hide until dark. . . . The dragons have some magic, can sniff us out. . . . Can't fire the forest to keep them high, it's too dry. . . . Only three arrows between us. . . ."

But something else was bothering Sunbright, and now he discovered what. His hand against the tree touched fresh gashes such as he'd seen back beside the road. The lower end of gashes, actually, for they extended above his head higher than he could reach with his bow. "Look! We've got—"

"Dorlas signals! Let's go!"

Like a deer breaking cover, the elf maid charged into the open, loosed an arrow at the back of a circling huntsman, then sped on toward the frantically waving dwarf. Sunbright ran after her, pausing to shoot side-on at a disk rider. He didn't wait for the hit but kept going. Evidently he missed, for as he reached the first vine-covered rocks, an ebony flail hissed by his head, ticking the pommel of Harvester slung at his back. At the same time, Dorlas reared just in front of him, leveled a crossbow, and shot. An encouraging grunt revealed a hit. Then Sunbright was climbing, grabbing vines and thorns and tumbling into the semi-trough of a rock split by water and ice action.

"They'll die as good as us!" pronounced the dwarf in satisfaction. "By the Rocks of the Reaver, I knew I should have demanded more pay up front!"

"You may get paid in full," gasped Sunbright. He glanced around to note their surroundings. This side of the three-quarters round outcrop didn't have any proper caves or even crevices. What they hunkered in was a simple gap shielded by a split boulder, though it was hard to tell under the dense, interlaced trees and creepers. Oddly, the sun-warmed cedars sent a thrill of nostalgia through Sunbright. It was amidst such trees that he and other children had played hide-and-seek on one of the tribe's yearly rounds though a cedar forest to hunt pheasant. He shook that happy memory away, for today's game was a deadlier one. The two were alone, Greenwillow having pressed on to beef up defenses elsewhere. "We might have an ally here somewhere, for there's a cave—"

"I knew that from the lay of the land!" The dwarf fussed with his crossbow, lining a bolt as straight as possible in its groove. "Don't tell a rock-eater how to read rocks!"

"I mean there's a bear's den somewhere nearby. Smell it? Bear shit stinks as bad as a human's!" Sunbright tracked the hunters, who circled and circled but didn't press. One worked to wrench Greenwillow's arrow from his thigh armor, though whether the barb had bitten flesh or only padding wasn't clear. Under the heavy armor, even their sex was unclear, though it appeared two of the dragon riders were women. Evidently the huntsmen awaited orders from those above. Sunbright saw one of the dragon riders tilt a wineskin and drink, and a pang of thirst stabbed him. He'd enjoy killing those bloodthirsty bastards when the time came; this was just a jaunt in the park for them.

"I don't smell nothing but cedar resin. And a bear can't hurt us," the dwarf growled, looking to his right.

"This one might. It's big. Gashes on the tree where it sharpened its claws stand higher than a rearing horse."

"Wonderful," groused Dorlas. "Just what we need. But maybe it's out hunting— Here they come!"

Clapping down their visors, the dragon riders banked their metal mounts and swept in to the attack. At the same time, two of the huntsmen skittered their disks close, then abandoned them. Hopping to the rocks, the two armored men descended on Dorlas and Sunbright. As if we were rabbits, thought the barbarian, to be flushed into the open and killed by the masters.

One hunter had a spear with a long barbed head, the other a flail, and they worked as a team. Whirling a whizzing wall of wood, one picked down the rocks and vines while the other poised, the spear ready.

"Split!" Dorlas refused to play their way. Clambering one-handed, he scrambled like a brown spider to the left. Sunbright propped his bow—he was out of arrows—drew Harvester, and swung right.

The Neth paused at such canny prey. In that second, Dorlas leveled his crossbow from six feet away and pulled the trigger. His eye was good. The bolt slammed the spear wielder just below the hip at a juncture of the armor plates. A squeak rewarded him; he'd hit flesh.

At the same time, Sunbright flummoxed the whirling flail by simply thrusting Harvester straight out. Steel screaked a protest as the flail's chain wrapped around and around the harder sword blade. Then came a grim tug-of-war, as the huntsman leaned to yank back on the long flail handle. Sunbright let him haul, then helped him out by stepping sideways and lashing out with an iron-reinforced boot. The armored man, already unsteady on hidden rocks and crushed leaves, let go of the flail to grab for balance. He caught only the tip of a cedar, which bent like a lily, and he pitched to crash on his side. Sunbright jumped after him, took careful aim for another armor chink, and stabbed down with Harvester . . .

. . . but leaped backward as a golden flash blotted the sunlight.

A hiss like an iceberg dropping into the sea roared by his hand. As the barbarian crunched amidst fragrant leaves and lumpy rocks, a searing blast of cold scorched the ground. Vines, a tree, the legs of the fallen huntsman, all were blasted a harsh, glistening white. Then the dragon rider with his deadly lance had swept on. Sunbright clambered up to strike at the Neth, but he levered himself off the rocks with his hands—his legs couldn't move—and tumbled headlong down a rock face to crash like a crate of dishes ten feet below.

Dorlas grappled with the spear wielder. He'd dropped his crossbow, crowded inside, locked the spear in his armpit, and now hammered with a stony hand on the end of the bolt to drive it deeper. The plagued huntsman strove to push the dwarf aside and dodge his punishing hand and was still backing off when Sunbright tripped close, took a short chop, and slammed Harvester's blade at the base of the Neth's helmet. The sword came away bloody, and the huntsman dropped.

But there was no time for congratulations. "Jump, boy!"

Without looking, Sunbright jumped as a fire flashed in the spot where they'd stood. The flying bird hovered not seven feet high, its rider's lance lipping flames like a water pipe. The barbarian landed, sprawling against the same rock face where the half-frozen huntsman lay. The Neth raised a hand, either for succor or attack, Sunbright didn't try to divine which. Slinging Harvester, he stabbed the man's armpit, shearing chain mail and knocking him flat. There was no time for a second blow, for a dragon rider swept at him. The rabbits had indeed been flushed, at the cost of two huntsmen.

Pelting over slippery rocks and ducking cedars, arms pumping, Sunbright raced around the ledge, flames kissing vegetation just behind him. Ahead he saw a long-limbed oak that leaned far enough to almost touch the rocks, and he dove headlong for the space underneath it. Flames licked his legs as he bounced into the tree's shadow, but he knew he was safe: the dragon rider couldn't follow here.

Spinning, he looked and listened for his companions, wondered how short-legged Dorlas fared. He hoped the dwarf had fled to the left.

Continuing right, under the brief shelter of the trees, Sunbright mounted the rocks, then paused, sniffing. The fuggy, wet-dog stink of a bear came to him. Above a narrow shelf, he saw the cave. It was not too high, though he'd have to duck double to enter, so perhaps the bear wasn't that big. He debated gathering the others and sheltering inside, then dismissed the idea. With those lances, the dragon riders could squirt fire and lightning and cold inside and roast, crisp, and freeze them all at the same time. And the humid odor of bear was strong; the animal might still be inside, despite a fine day for hunting.

And from above came the clash of steel. He bypassed the cave, grabbed vines, and climbed.

It looked bad.

Near the top of the outcrop was an abrupt shelf a dozen feet square. Somehow Greenwillow and two other bodyguards had been herded onto it by the paired huntsmen. Probably the elf had risen naturally, since high ground was always valuable, making it hard for the enemy to strike you, easier for you to cut down on them. But with enemies that swooped from the sky, it was a disastrous choice. Even as Sunbright climbed, he saw a bird-mount drop like a stone, halt nine feet up, and then its rider stabbed with a lance. One of the bodyguards was shocked with lightning and dropped her sword. The cracking lance pinned her through the gut like a butterfly, hoisted her a dozen feet, and dropped her down with a force sufficient to break her legs.

Greenwillow cut and thrust at a huntsman, trying to get past, to descend and escape, but the lackey simply flickered his flail in and out like a lizard's tongue to keep the elf back: the master would make the kill. Cut off, the other bodyguard was wounded by a spear wielder and dropped to his knees. The other two dragon riders hovered nearby to get in their shots.

Briefly, Sunbright wondered where the other bodyguards had gone, but decided they'd either hidden or hightailed it through the woods. He couldn't blame them: to stay was to die. Still, he hoisted Harvester, topped the rise on slipping boots, and charged with a barbarian war cry.

He didn't bother to slash at the armored flailer besieging Greenwillow. He hit the Neth with something bigger and heavier: himself. Shoulder first, he cannoned into the huntsman, who hadn't been expecting a rear attack. The flail flipped and rattled as the huntsman grabbed air. Greenwillow drove her cattail-slender sword into the eyehole of the man's wolfish visor. Blood spurted as a scream—a woman's—rang inside the mask. She toppled backward and slammed hard, skidding in the vines.

Sunbright watched the dragon riders, who crowded one another to fly at him on the shelf. The last bodyguard had been frost-blasted and lay huddled and still. He had no idea where Dorlas was. "Come on! Get down and under the trees!" But it was too late.

The sole huntsman braced his spear sideways to cut them off on the left, and a dragon rider hovered to the right like a giant bumblebee. The dragon and bird mounts flashed in the sunlight centermost, hovering slowly backward. Sunbright saw their plan: taking turns, they were backing for a slicing run.

"Take the bird; I'll take the dragon!" he shouted.

A shocking laugh sounded. Greenwillow's nose dripped blood that she spit off her lips. "You must be human to be that dumb! Might as well throw rocks! But let's make a good account!"

Yet the aspiring shaman never heard the last, for something was rumbling under his feet—or in his mind. A wave of fur-fug filled his nostrils, a brown hulk his vision. He blinked, trying to shake his eyes clear, but it persisted. What . . . ?

Here came the first dragon rider, zooming in like a golden dart. But she never arrived.

With a growl like thunder, a bear as big as a cloud

reared up past the lip of the shelf. The swooping Neth barely veered aside in time. As it was, the mechanical dragon's wing bounced off the bear's shaggy hump. The other dragon rider blocking their right never had a chance.

The bear was even grander than Sunbright had imagined. It must have been lazy, or crippled, to only scratch so high on the neighboring trees. It was almost twenty feet long, easily dwarfing a horse, and the barbarian could have walked under its belly while crouching. A relic of earlier times, it looked old, with gray shot through its thick red-brown fur and around its muzzle. But it had the power of a fourspan of oxen, and was angry at being disturbed. It lashed out at every moving target to crush it flat and eat at leisure.

The dragon rider whipped her lance sideways, but the bear was already too close. She hauled on the reins to gain altitude, but a paw as big as a bushel basket studded with knives slashed the air. The paw crumpled a dragon wing and capsized the mount. With a squawk, the rider was dumped to crash on her neck and shoulder. The bear threw its weight into its front paws and thumped down on her like a dog on a squirrel. A fearful crunching of bones sounded, and a screechy raking of claws through metal. The flier flipped upside down and crunched on rock.

The rearmost flier, the bird man, had dodged past the dragon rider to blast the bear with hoarfrost. But the creature's thick coat merely turned white. The bear never slowed, and the fliers had to spin away or be batted flat.

That left Sunbright and Greenwillow, cowering against the rock wall.

Blood on its claws, the great cave bear wheeled

from its first victim seeking a next. The huge paws
gripped the shelf preparatory to sweeping it clean.
Greenwillow spread her feet, pointed her sword, and
braced one hand on the wall behind her to thrust forward into the bear's face. But Sunbright slapped
hard and knocked her sword point down. Harvester
hung slack in his own left hand. The elf shot him a
quizzical demand, but the shaman-to-be ignored her.

Friend! he thought at the rearing beast, whose
head was as big as his torso. *Friend! Do not kill!*

There was no reaction, it seemed. The bear opened
its great mouth to latch on to their arms or legs, or to
crush their ribs. Sunbright saw long strings of saliva
connect teeth like knives of white flint. Beside him,
Greenwillow struggled to free the wrist of her sword
arm from his grip.

Friend! He hammered the thought at the bear.
What could make it understand? *We mean you no
harm!*

A gurgle sounded deep inside the beast, and it
seemed as if they could see all the way to its stomach. Greenwillow gasped, but the gaping maw
snapped shut. The bear cocked one eye at Sunbright,
puzzled. Something tickled in the barbarian's mind,
a buzz like a bee's trapped in his head. Was it the
bear's thought? Had he, in a blind panic, managed to
somehow communicate with an animal? He tried to
snatch the buzzing and pin it down. *We are friends.
We will go now. You go, too.*

More puzzled looks came from the round black eyes
under the coarse fur. The huge black nose snuffled,
seemingly tasting their scent. The barbarian and elf
held their breath. Would they be considered game,
or . . . ? Abruptly, the bear wheeled, saw the dead,
punctured, and frost-blasted bodyguards, and with
awesome paws swept the bodies from the ledge to

drag to its cave below.

By then the barbarian and elf were gone.

* * * * *

"What was *that?*" Greenwillow skipped as nimbly as a goat down the slope, in bounds longer than Sunbright could make.

Headlong, the barbarian jumped from rock to rock, any second expecting a magic blast, an icy lance through his spine, or a broken ankle from slipping on the loose scree. "Just . . . lucky! The gods favor . . . humans today, and not . . . the Neth!" No need to tell his secret, animal-speaking, if that's what he'd done. Someday he might be a shaman after all, and the thought made his spirit and feet fly. "Huh!"

He yelped as Dorlas popped up like a fat rabbit. The dwarf aimed his crossbow and fired an inch over the barbarian's shoulder. A *clank* answered; then all three were sheltered in the coolness of an oak forest.

Hands shaking, Sunbright wiped his brow. That was his first close-hand bout of animal-speaking, and it had rattled him worse than the buzzing dragon riders. Too much too soon, he reflected, and he'd be thinking like a bear and find himself naked in the woods, on his knees rolling rotted logs for grubs.

He tried to croak to his companions, but was too dry. His waterskin hung on a horse. Briefly he wondered if the merchants had gained the castle yet. Hawking phlegm, he yelled, "Which way?"

Dorlas clawed sweat out of his eyes. He'd lost his round helmet, and his short red braids flopped around his head, adorned with bright scarlet from a scalp wound. He grabbed wildly at his back quiver, found no more quarrels, and slung his crossbow back there. Straightening his pack, he rasped low, "To the city. To Dalekeva. It's the only safety. The Neth must abide by their own rules, even if we've killed members of their party."

"Why not hide in the woods until dark?"

"Because," hissed Greenwillow, "the mounts have magic to sniff—"

A sizzle erased her words. Lightning charred leaves over their head, leaving a hole through which flashed gold and gems. At another pass, fire outlined the hole, set fire to dead leaves and branches underfoot.

The three were far off by then, running flat out.

The deadly game of hide-and-seek lasted the afternoon, and threatened to haunt Sunbright's dreams for life. It was one thing to attack an enemy in the field, to clash and crash and live or die. It took another kind of courage to keep a cool head and calm stomach while hunted from tree to tree like a rabbit dodging a wolf. One of the three remaining defenders would circle a tree, glance, dive, see fire or frost or lightning strike. Then another would pop up, distract the fliers, and the first could hop up or crawl headlong.

There was at least no trouble with direction, for they descended into the valley, bounding in great leaps down shallow and steep slopes. Then the forest ended, and they lurked under the trees, soaked with sweat, gasping and rasping too badly even to curse.

Ahead lay the city, and sanctuary. But it was a mile across open country: orchards, plowed fields, and a rutting, curving road lined with stone walls. A mile to the gates.

"I don't see much for it," croaked the dwarf. "We run, is all."

Neither Greenwillow nor Sunbright commented

on the dwarf's stumpy legs. The elf asked the barbarian, "Can you run?"

"My other name is Steelshanks. Fastest runner in my tribe. You?"

A snot- and blood-bubbly sniff answered. "Together, or spread out?"

"Together," replied the males.

"Singly, we'll be picked off. Together, we can at least slash back," added Dorlas.

"Wait—or go now?"

The tree they stood under exploded into flame. All three ran, catty-corner across a field for the road. The fields were thigh-deep in crops or else fresh-plowed for winter, too difficult to run through. The orchards offered scant cover, for the branches were thin and wiry, and too low to scoot under. So it was the hard-packed road, stone walls and ruts and all.

They struck the road and headed for the gates. Attacks came immediately. Sunbright listened, looked, and yelled, "Down!"

A flier hissed overhead; fire spilled and ignited grass by the stone barrier. The rider had overshot, but would fire sooner the next time.

On they pelted, gulping air, an eighth of a mile, a quarter. A half. Twice, they had to scatter and dive. Once Sunbright had his hair catch fire and Green-willow beat it out. Once she screamed as lightning scorched her sheathed sword and stung her hip.

Then, as they'd expected all along, Dorlas, lagging behind, suffered. The dwarf had finally thrown off his pack, and there was no blast of warning this time.

The two in front heard a keen of rising air, then a shrill hunting cry, and a grunt. Whirling, they saw Dorlas had turned to face his enemy—and his death.

The lance had punctured his guts on the left side.

The bloody point, bowed by his weight, pointed almost straight down. Above, the male bird rider strained to withdraw the point, or lift the dwarf. But the dying Dorlas was too heavy to lift, and he had a death grip on the shaft of the lance piercing him. The female dragon rider, seeing her companion in difficulty, wheeled and swooped to strip the dwarf from the lance.

"Dorlas!" shrilled Greenwillow.

"Go!" grunted the dwarf. "Go! Do not help, unless you want my death curse upon you!"

The elf burst into tears, crying in her own language, but Sunbright grabbed her hand. "Don't waste his sacrifice!"

Spinning, he yanked her toward the castle.

Later, they learned why they'd made it the last quarter mile. Dorlas, they were told, had hung on to the lance. The rider, reluctant to lose his only weapon, clung too. And so he, not the dwarf, died first. For leaning low, he saw Dorlas jerk himself upward, driving the shaft deeper through his own body. And with his free hand, the dwarf swung his warhammer and crushed the wolf mask and skull of the bird rider, so man and mount and dwarf crashed in the road, the golden wreck a monument to a brave fighter.

Panting, near death themselves, Sunbright and Greenwillow blundered flat out for the gates, which swung open to admit them. The cityfolk, the guards and populace, dared not rush out to their aid lest they bring the wrath of the Neth onto their home. But they hurled words of encouragement to the runners—and bets to one another—as the two pounded for the gate.

Then the walls were stretching above their darkened vision. "Drop your sword!" yelled Greenwillow.

She put on a burst of speed.

"Never!" gargled Sunbright. He thought he heard a keen of wind behind him, but he couldn't turn or he'd fall, and he had no strength left to fight.

But he did draw his sword. And as Greenwillow sprinted into the tiny slot between the massive yellow gates, and a rising keen sounded behind him, the barbarian flung his sword after her. The rider might kill him, but she would not win his sword for a trophy.

Then the keening whisked overhead and sheared away, for he was too close to the gates for the skyrider to spear, and Sunbright stumbled through the gates into a sea of helping hands.

But even they couldn't hold him upright. His legs caved in, and he dropped. He heard Greenwillow ask about Dorlas. He himself croaked, "Where's my sword?"

Then the crowd of citizens and guards ducked as the mechanical dragon flashed over the wall and their heads. A hysterical laugh shrilled, and words were flung down: "Well run! Until next time!"

Then the hunter was gone, a golden dragonfly glittering in the setting sun.

Chapter 7

If Sunbright and Greenwillow expected a heroes' welcome, they were soon disappointed. The citizenry might cheer them on and the guards applaud their gallant fight, but before they'd even gotten their breath back, they were bracketed by eight palace guards and marched through the streets to be taken before the city council.

"You'd think we were criminals!" groused Greenwillow. She mopped at her nose and, finding crusted blood, asked the captain of the guards if she might wash at a fountain. When the man refused, she shoved through the phalanx and stepped to a fountain anyway.

The guards, helmeted with steel and hung with yellow-and-blue tabards decorated with a painted sunfish, the city colors and emblem, fidgeted while idlers who'd trailed them watched.

"Hurry, if you please," the captain urged.

The pair ignored them as they drank quarts of water, scrubbed their faces, combed their hair, and knocked the worst of the grime off their clothing. Sunbright discovered the back of his calves were blistered and weeping from scorching, and there was a crease alongside his neck he couldn't account for. Greenwillow continued to grumble, but Sunbright said philosophically, "No matter what they do to us, it can't be worse than what those Netherese hunters planned."

The half-elf snorted and resettled her tackle. "You've a lot to learn about city politics, country boy."

The two were "escorted" toward the center of the yellow-stone city. Greenwillow stumped along grumpily, obviously rehearsing some blistering speech. Sunbright sauntered, tired but glad to be alive, eager to see the strange sights of this southern burg. The houses were three or four stories tall, square and sheer, with thick walls of yellow stone or painted plaster picked out with blue and red. The streets were straight and regular, flagged with lumpy cobblestones that were hard on the soles.

The city obviously backed on the river, and as they threaded the streets filled with end-of-the-day shoppers dragging one-wheeled ricks, porters toting loads on their backs, sedan chairs hoisted by twos or fours, workers in dusty aprons and dangling tools, and more, they began to see signs of the waterfront: baskets of goggle-eyed whiskery catfish and freshwater oysters, bowlegged sailors in striped shirts who sang as they strode along arm-in-arm, piles of shavings dumped from planed masts. A curious sort, Sunbright found it all fun and exciting, and his happiness seemed to pique Greenwillow further. When the barbarian exclaimed about a new sight, a shaggy beast with droopy jowls and a single high hump, the

elf, who'd traveled widely in her long years, only
snorted, "Camels!"

Their guard turned away from the combined
palace and city hall, which had a circular island of
green grass all to itself, to a duller building opposite.
Past more guards they wended, then up clumping
wooden steps to a big second-story hall that echoed
to shouts and squabbles. Here the city council sat at
a long table, facing benches that filled the rest of the
room, while clerks with thick books and quills and
inkwells scribbled at a table to one side.

Here were the flushed and frantic traders whom
Dorlas had shooed toward the city just before midday—which seemed like years ago to the barbarian.
Thoughts of the dead dwarf and his noble sacrifice
banished his euphoria, and a grinding gloom lingered. Sitting on a bench, Sunbright was suddenly
dead tired and starving and shaky-legged.

Not so the traders, who'd had a chance to rest and
recharge their energy for their favorite and only
sport: bickering. The lot of them gestured and
shouted and harangued at the city council, who
yelled for order and threatened to cast them into the
street if they didn't quiet down. Their noise mattered
no more than the others'. Seizing the opportunity,
Sunbright lay back on the bench and dozed. Harvester made a lumpy mattress, but at least no one
could steal it.

At one point, the barbarian dreamed he was
falling from a great height. A giant sea gull had
plucked him from a stony beach and hoisted him in
the air to drop and shatter him like a clam. Flapping
his arms wildly, Sunbright watched the ground rush
up at him, braced his stomach and buttocks for the
impact . . .

. . . and landed with a clatter and crash on the

wooden floor of the council meeting room.

Instantly he was up, dragging Harvester from its sheath, but Greenwillow's voice ordered, "Cease. Leave off your pigsticker." She'd kicked over his bench to wake him, but wisely skipped back.

Sunbright rubbed his face. He must have been exhausted not to wake at someone's approach. The council room was dim, with only a few copper-backed candles lit at the clerks' table, where the scribbling continued. Otherwise the room was deserted. "Where is everybody?"

"Home. They'll continue the debate tomorrow, for what it's worth."

"What is it worth? What's the upshot?"

"That they're not continuing on to Tinnainen."

"What?" He rubbed his face harder, straightened his baldric. "But the Neth ordered it so!"

"They'll risk it. Don't let's stand here arguing. I'm so hungry I could kill the next fellow that passes and eat his liver."

Greenwillow passed into shadows and down the stairs without a noise. Sunbright in iron-ringed, hobnailed boots clumped along behind her. He said, "I didn't get to say anything."

"What could you tell them?"

"I could sing of Dorlas's bravery and sacrifice."

A delicate snort came from the dark. "Of that, they could care less. The lost horses were more valuable than the dwarf. Much more, for unless the dwarf's family returns, they won't have to muster his pay or offer blood money."

"What? That's not honorable!"

Now a sigh. "Oh, my poor yak herder. You've so much to learn."

True, he agreed mentally, but he was tired of hearing her say it.

Exiting the door past sleepy guards, Greenwillow swung unerringly toward the palace and river. "Do you know where you're going?" asked Sunbright.

"Not in particular. But fare and goods are usually simpler and cheaper the closer you get to the docks." They could see at least, for this far south, the late evening sky was luminous orange. The yellow moon showed gray blotches like distant mountain ranges. Sunbright had never seen it look so big. Lovers slipped by, kissing and giggling, and families strolled, and children played tag in the shadows. Prostitutes with red lanterns whistled to sailors, and watchmen called all was well. Greenwillow steered for a street lit by more torches above the doors than most.

"I expected more," the barbarian mused. "I thought the traders might be grateful we got them home safely, most of them at least. That their families would celebrate that they'd returned after so long, and we might be invited to recount some of the stories of how we saved their lives."

Greenwillow spat. "They'll remember only the bad, that several of their fellows died despite our efforts. We'll be lucky to get paid, and will probably have to camp on someone's doorstep to get anything at all." She peered over a bunch of revelers blocking a door. The tavern sign above showed a mighty arm clutching an axe. The elf sniffed and moved on.

Sunbright's stomach had growled at the smell of mutton and ale that wafted out in steamy clouds. "What was wrong with that place?"

"I prefer bars frequented by farmers or sailors, if I've a choice, but not one with a mix of patrons. Bring together carters and soldiers and sailors and porters and the insults fly and there's a fight and someone stumbles against your table and spills your broth and you have to break their heads before they'll buy you a new bowl. Trouble. Ah!"

In a short side street they found a place that held only six small tables and a short bar crowded with men and women in black robes with red and blue and yellow stripes around the sleeves. Sunbright found them oddly familiar, and Greenwillow explained, "Lawyers and clerks. They fight with words. And look you, decent women serving, which means none will be grabbed by the arse. Sit."

Although they collected curious glances, no one accosted them. Serving girls fetched them bowls of water and clean rags to wash their hands, then stale bread and ale to assuage their hunger until stew could be served. The warriors broke the bread and dunked it in their mugs. Sunbright relaxed so much he unslung his baldric and propped Harvester against the table. The clerks edged farther down the bar, but the barbarian didn't notice as he wolfed down his food. "So tell me again . . ."

"The short story is," recited Greenwillow, "that they cocked up, as Dorlas would put it. The delegation went to ask the Neth to stop the empire-building of the One King in Tinnainen. Which was stupid, you'll recall. That's like asking a lion to come amidst your flock and kill wolves. Since the Neth don't give a rat's ass whether groundling Dalekeva lives or dies, they fobbed the job back at the delegates, told them to go see the One King and order him to cease his depredations. Might as well stick your head in a noose and kick the bucket.

"Having limped back here and informed the council, the delegates whined that their job was done, they'd been through more than enough, and someone else should journey on to Tinnainen to bell the cat— see the One King and tell him to forget his dreams of empire. Naturally the council bounced it back, ordered the delegates to rest and continue on, but they refused, and no other fools volunteered, because no one wants to be transformed into a newt.

"So no one's going on this fool's errand. Everyone in this city will just keep his head down and pray to his gods that the One King invades somewhere else or chokes on a chicken bone and that the Neth forget they ever issued the order in the first place. Which they probably will. So everyone wasted his time running to Delia for help. Instead, as Dorlas said, they should have cooperated and declared martial law and drafted every healthy man into a city militia and raised taxes to support them and purchased arms and practiced them and beefed up the city's defenses and burned outlying farms and gathered in the crops and so on.

"Instead, when the One King arrives outside these walls, if he's got more than a thousand able men, I reckon he'll own the city within a day. Not by ramming down the doors, by the way, but because the same delegates will negotiate a surrender that allows the invaders to pillage some and rape a little and kill a few underlings. Such is history, more often than not. Fabled cities that fought invaders to the bitter end usually end up as ruins, of which I've seen a few. Fortunately, I won't be here to see the city fall."

Sunbright sliced mutton with his knife and gulped a hunk that would choke a wolf. "Where will you be?"

"Somewhere on the other side of the One King's army."

"Why?"

The elf slowed in carving meat with her dagger. Sunbright liked the way her slim hands worked, capable and strong but delicate. Now she sighed again. "I must journey to the court of the One King. I carry a missive for him from the court of the High Elves of Cormanthyr, who are distant cousins. My own fool's errand."

"Hunh." Sunbright munched, talking with his mouth full. "What does the missive say?"

She pointed her slim dagger. Her eyes were gray-green by candlelight, like deep-hued animate jewels. "I'll tell you what I told the council. My missive directs the One King to cease his empire-building, or else."

The barbarian didn't ask, Or else what? Instead, he swallowed and pronounced, "I'll go with you."

"You will?" Greenwillow was so surprised she dropped a chunk of meat. It landed in her bowl and splashed gravy on her chest. "Why should you? It'll be dangerous enough for me, but I'm an appointed emissary of a high court. You're just a freebooter. You might end up a . . . target."

Sunbright shrugged. His life was dangerous and had always been so. Distant threats didn't worry him. "We've fought together as comrades-in-arms. I can hardly let you continue alone after we've shared blood."

The elven warrior sat, hands poised, a softening expression on her exotic face until she looked almost like any simple woman alone in the world and far from home. "Well . . . That's very generous of you."

Missing her change of voice, Sunbright waved a hand. "It's nothing. A point of honor. Besides, I must journey to the One King's court myself, to gain information for Chandler back in Augerbend."

"Oh. Oh, I see." Greenwillow ducked her head and sawed her meat.

Finally, with typical male denseness, Sunbright sensed the frost in her voice. But of course it was too late to mend it, so they finished their meal in silence.

By the time they left the Bursting Book, the sky was fully dark. There were stars but no moon. Sunbright traced constellations with his finger. "There. The Panther rises. The time is right." He marched back toward the center of town.

Despite her coolness, Greenwillow fell in beside him. "For what?"

"I need to retrieve Dorlas's body before the wolves get it. Though I'll admit I don't know how to treat his carcass, whether to bury or burn it."

"You needn't do everything yourself, you know." In the darkness, he could see the pale shine of her face, but couldn't read her emotions. And too, they both had to watch their footing on the sometimes slimy cobblestones. "A city this size will have a fighters' guild. Part of their function is to see freebooters buried, their goods returned to their families if possible. They'll probably ask other dwarves to handle the funeral."

Sunbright mulled that over. If he'd died today, who would have buried him properly, who would have sent his effects home to his tribe wandering the tundra? He'd be lucky if anyone prayed his name as flames turned his muscle to smoke.

At the great locked gates leading to the farmlands, the guards were dubious about opening the night door. It existed to admit after-hours travelers, who were forced to walk a tight, long corridor where they would be subject to a rain of stones and quarrels. They feared the lone Netherese hunter on the golden dragon machine might still lurk in the woods. A group of Neth huntsmen had flown in earlier and retrieved the dead hunter and metal mount.

Greenwillow said, "They'll be gone. They have their own twisted honor. Once the quarry reaches the city, the game is over."

The guards waffled, for it was known that the city wanted to retrieve the gallant dwarf's body for a hero's funeral—once the coast was clear and the sun well up in the sky.

"We'll go now and save you the trip," Sunbright told them, and that clinched the argument.

By starlight and the ghostly glow of the dusty road, the two crept forth. Sunbright trod silently awhile, wary of ambush, but the elf, who had cat's eyes, told him there was no one about. So they talked.

Greenwillow asked, "What did you call that constellation you steered by?"

The barbarian pointed. "The Panther. There's her head, and there's her tail."

"My people call it the Bell."

"Ah." Having quarreled earlier, albeit silently, they were now overly formal. "I suppose it matters not, as long as we can see it. I doubt the stars care what mortals name them."

A sniff sounded, but the elf added, "That's poetic for a barbarian."

"Who better to know poetry?" Sunbright returned. "I know lowlanders call us savages because we don't read. We carry our tribe's lore in our heads. Give me enough liquor, and I could recite stories and sing songs the night long, and never repeat one. And I'm no storyteller, just a warrior. Our storytellers could talk you deaf with weeks of lore and song!"

Greenwillow said nothing, only marched along the road they'd run during the day. His boasting was pointless, in a way, for even in her short years, thrice those of any human, she'd learned thousands of stories and songs and forgotten more of them than a mere man or woman could know. But Sunbright paid himself a compliment by valuing his people's history and glory. Neither his head nor his heart were empty, she had to admit.

A grumbling snarl sounded ahead. Sunbright hissed, "Scat!" and two fat shapes waddled away. A short, dark outline in the road marked the dead dwarf, and the two were glad they couldn't see his face after raccoons had worried it.

The barbarian gave a short epitaph like a prayer. "Come, friend. Your work is done and the day gone. Let us hie you home, where many will sing your praises." Neither spoke as Sunbright hoisted the stocky body to his shoulder. It was surprisingly light from having lost so much blood. "Get his warhammer. We don't want . . ."

"I've got it."

They turned back toward the gates. To distract them from what he carried, Sunbright mused, "I wonder how the farm folk and harvesters knew to flee inside the walls. How could they know the Neth would come hunting?"

"Probably some other Neth sent the city elders a warning. I'd like to think that not all Netherese approve of hunting humans. But with their penchant for intrigue, it could merely have been a spoilsport scaring off a rival's game."

The young man stumped along with his burden, shifting it to the other shoulder. "How do you know so much about the Hunt?"

The silence was long. "The hunting rules the Neth abide by were adopted from my cousins, the High Elves of Cormanthyr, who have hunted humans for centuries." She added in defense, "As usual, the human mages have perverted the original purpose, which is lost in ancient times. Believe it or not, the High Elves hunting humans was a compliment, for it marked the ascendancy of mankind and the eventual decline of elves."

Silence implied the human didn't consider being hunted a compliment, so Greenwillow tossed out her own question. "How did you turn that great cave bear from attacking us?"

Sunbright waved his free hand, realized she couldn't see it—though she could—and said, "Oh, I just told him we were friends. I work to be a—" He stopped the word "shaman" before it escaped. "A friend to animals. Which reminds me. We'll buy a goat and tether it near the bear's den. You should thank anyone who gives you a gift, and my life is my most prized possession."

"Mine too."

For a second, the barbarian thought Greenwillow meant his life was precious to her. Then he realized that, of course, she meant her own.

So the three companions, two living, one dead, trudged silently back to the city they'd spent almost two seasons trying to reach.

* * * * *

In the end, Dorlas was neither buried nor burned. Three dwarves had taken custody of the body and worked the night through to plane and hammer a coffin that was only partly watertight. At dawn, as the sun rose rimmed in blood, the three carried the short coffin on their shoulders to the edge of the river. A quiet word had passed to the city elders that there would be no ornate state funeral. The only observers to the ceremony were Sunbright and Greenwillow, who argued they had been friends of the dead man, or at least comrades.

The dwarves eased the coffin down on the pebbly shingle. Each bent to pluck a handful of gravel that was then sprinkled over the wooden box. The rattling was loud enough to startle sleeping ducks from the cattails on the other side of the river. When invited, Sunbright and Dorlas also stepped forward and sprinkled handfuls of soil on the coffin.

The dwarf in charge of the funeral, Mondar, explained, "These stones will cover him as he begins his journey to his homeland." Dorlas, they'd been told, was originally from a tribe called the Sons of Baltar in the Iron Mountains far to the south. Since the river wended that way, the leaky coffin would be consigned to it. Somewhere along the way it would surely sink, but the idea was that the dead Dorlas could travel the rest of the way underground once he reached the riverbed. Together, the five participants pushed the coffin into the quiet water. It bobbed and tipped, then straightened side-on to the current and sailed southward. Mondar called, "Go, brother, and lead the way!"

Dorlas's warrior tackle had been stripped from his body, for it was thought there was no fighting in the afterlife, only simple pleasures and fulfilling work. Solemnly, Mondar held up the dead man's knife, and asked, "Who will take this knife, that it might work well and honor its master's name?" A dwarf held out his hand and received it. So went the crossbow and quarrels, baldric, even his file and fishhooks and compass. The dwarves were all workmen in the city and could find a use for the tools. At the last, Mondar held up the fearsome warhammer, frowning at it, for with its long narrow head and sharp parrot's beak on the back face, it would make a poor tool for blacksmith or cobbler or silversmith. At the ritual question "Who will take this warhammer, that it might work well and honor its master's name?" no one extended his hand.

In the awkward silence, Sunbright surprised himself and everyone else by saying, "I will."

The dwarves squinted in the bright light of dawn. Needing to explain, Sunbright said, "I have more battles ahead, and can do honor to Dorlas's name. But I promise that someday I will return the hammer to his family in the Iron Mountains. I'll tell them how he died and saved our lives."

"It is not necessary." Mondar frowned. "We know of his dying. Word will pass to his relatives."

"Good. For if I'm killed, I won't be able to relate the tale. But if I live, I will make that journey. I owe him that much." Behind him Greenwillow sniffed, but this time to hold back tears.

Without a word, Mondar laid the cold, heavy warhammer in the young man's hand. Sunbright slid it in his belt, felt it nestle beneath his ribs. He wasn't sure why he'd taken it or made that vow. Perhaps he was only being selfish, and hoped that when he was killed, someone would make an effort to see that his family knew. But whatever the reason, he was glad.

* * * * *

Barbarian and elf had slept for a few short hours in a soldiers' hostel where the women were separated from the men. Over a breakfast of bread and ale and cheese served at long tables in a surprisingly quiet throng, Sunbright suggested, "Since this is my first time in a city, you'd best lead the way. What do we do?"

Greenwillow used her crust to sop up the last of her ale and stuffed it in her mouth. "First we collect our wages, before anyone forgets they owe us. Let's go." Getting up from the table, she dropped her mug in a tub by the door and strode into the sunshine.

Unerringly, she marched to the left and up the center of the street. Sunbright had no idea where they were bound, or what their destination was, so he simply trotted along at her side like a child. Housewives and masons and fishmongers and schoolchildren watched them curiously as they passed.

Thinking aloud, Greenwillow said, "We bodyguarded them for six months, give or take. One hundred eighty days . . . at two silver crowns a day . . . with two of us . . . is seven hundred twenty crowns. The traders who survived were fourteen, so that's . . . fifty-odd apiece they owe us. Cheap enough for saving their lives, and they don't have to pay Dorlas or the other dead bodyguards. Still, I imagine they'll squeal like trapped pigs. We could go to the piepowder court for our wages, but that would take forever. There's one!"

Sunbright was flummoxed by her ciphering. He'd been fuzzy on the whole idea of being paid in coins, anyway. In his tribe, you bargained for the completion of a job, usually for supplies. So what she was doing was a mystery. But he recognized the flag over the shop door. It was a bluebird on a yellow circle, symbol of the house of Sunadram, a middle-aged trader with a yellow beard.

Sunadram was in his shop, which was heaped high on all sides with fabrics in every color. He held an account book, jabbing a finger repeatedly, demanding of his cringing clerks why the figures didn't add up. Greenwillow had to shout his name several times to get his attention.

When she did, Sunadram slammed the book shut and rubbed his face. "Oh, you two. What do you want?"

Sunbright didn't like his tone of voice, and would have punched the man for his insolence, but Greenwillow only spread her feet, planted her hands on her hips, and stated simply, "Our wages for bodyguarding. We kept you alive, so we'll take fifty silver crowns, if you please."

Already the fabric seller was shaking his head. "No, no, no. I pay no bills without a proper invoice. You'll need to write up your request, then have it notarized by the city clerk. I'll consider it then, but you'll have to wait. My shop is in chaos because of my long absence. These idiots can't add two and two without slipping three into their pockets. Now, I'm busy, so good day."

Greenwillow only nodded, which Sunbright found astonishing. The man, who'd bargained fairly at the beginning of the journey, now reneged. By barbarian code, the two fighters could cut him down, chop off his head, then take their pay in money or goods, or else enslave some of these clerks, though they were puny specimens. But Greenwillow only turned for the door.

"Wait!" Sunbright whirled after her, tackle jingling. "What about our—"

"Hush!" She stepped through the door into the morning bustle, then pointed to the doorjamb. "Stand there and be quiet. And sharpen your sword; it must need it."

"It does not! I hone it every night—" But a glare told him to belt up.

Bemused, the barbarian slid Harvester from its scabbard, put his back to the doorjamb, and worked to hone the edge with a fine stone, though he could have shaved with it already. Greenwillow waited, fuming. Inside the shop, Sunadram and the clerks watched and whispered.

It wasn't long before they learned what was to transpire. An elderly woman was brought near the door in a sedan chair toted by two sweating porters. Holding her skirts high, the woman stepped into the mucky street, careful not to dirty her red slippers. A pair of maids who'd walked behind flanked her. The lady glanced at Greenwillow, expecting the elf-maid to step aside, but the warrior instead barred the door with her arm. "Sorry, milady, but Sunadram can't see you. He's putting his shop in order."

"But—" The lady frowned with wrinkled lips. "I need fabric! I need a gown fashioned for Baroness Missos's ball!"

"Sorry. He's too busy," was the stoic reply.

From inside the shop came a gasp as Sunadram ran up, all afluster and abluster. But when Sunbright, still holding his naked great sword, turned curiously, the trader quailed. Greenwillow flipped her nose at the lady, who huffed and reboarded her sedan.

"Gods above!" Sunadram wailed. "You'll ruin me! Do you know who that is? That's—"

"A lost customer," Greenwillow stared him down. "The first of many. If you can't pay your help, you can't do business."

"I'll call the city guard! They'll throw you in prison or chain you in a galley to toil your lives away at the oars!"

Greenwillow shrugged. "You'd have to bribe them to tackle us, two doughty fighters. It would cost more than you owe us."

"So?" the merchant demanded. "Will you spend a month at my door just to get your money?"

"We've naught else to do," Greenwillow replied sweetly. "You can't do much in a city without coin!"

With a groan, the fabric seller hurried back into the shop, knocking clerks aside, and dug around under his counter, counting frantically. Momentarily, he hurried up and counted out five stacks of worn silver coins into Greenwillow's hand. "There! Take your damned wages and get away from here! If I see you again, I'll . . . I'll . . ."

"Thank us for escorting you home? I didn't think so. Come, Sunbright. And put your fool sword away."

Befuddled as ever, the barbarian slid his sword home in its sheath. "What was that all about? What was he afraid of?"

Greenwillow chuckled. "It was business, and he was afraid of losing money. Come on. We've got thirteen more merchants to pester."

They repeated the process up and down the street, making for a long morning. But while Greenwillow groused about the constant quibbling, Sunbright took it all with the patience of a herdsman and hunter, and his mellow strength and gentle joshing helped pass the hours. The merchants must have spread the word over the midday meal, for the afternoon's collecting passed more quickly. Some merchants gave the asked-for amount, some dickered to give only their share less what they'd need to collect from their dead colleague's estates, and one, late in the day, even gave them a bonus, an amphora of sunny southern wine and her hearty thanks.

So they got less than they wanted, but not much less, and ended happily, sharing the amphora with curious clerks and lawyers at the Bursting Book where they took their meals. But there was a lot of wine, and the others had gone home before it was finished, so the elf and barbarian, not wishing to waste such a bounty, tried to drink it all. As a result, they got louder and sillier.

Even the serving girls had gone to bed by the time Greenwillow said, "You know, you could almost pass for an elf. In bad light. If you were skinnier."

"Oh?" Sunbright made to throw his booted foot up

on the table, but missed and dropped it with a crash. " 'S slippery. No, elveses is handsome, and I'm all scar . . . scarey . . . scarredy . . . chewed up."

"Battle scars don't count," chuckled Greenwillow. She pointed a wavering finger. "Some elf-maids find 'em sexy. Like to nibble on 'em, see where they go."

"Go where?"

"Scars go. And you sing too. Like a bird. Not much for a hu-human man, but like a crow. Or a bug."

"Bugs sing?" Sunbright peered at the ceiling, as if to ask a nearby spider its opinion.

"Sing like birds! 'Cept if they make too much noise, birds eat 'em. Must taste yuckly, yicky, yucky." She stuck out her tongue.

Pointing again, she pronounced, "You respect nature too. Not many whatsits do that." She focused blearily at the bottom of her cup, tilted it up and splashed her chin. "Oops!"

"Oh, your lizard skin! So beau'ful!" Sunbright leaned over the table, knocking her cup crashing, and pawed at the front of her armor to wipe off the wine. Belatedly he saw where his hands stroked, and whipped back. He hit his head on the wall, but didn't feel it.

Greenwillow doubled over laughing, so weak she could only wheeze. " 'S funny! You're so funny, make me laugh! First time in . . . long time. Elves're too dour! Do it again!"

"A' right!" Sunbright brought his head forward, then snapped it back against the wall with a thump. He still didn't feel it.

"Noooooo!" The elf covered her mouth and laughed so hard she fell out of her chair onto her knees. "Not your head, your hands!"

"Hands?" The man frowned at his hands, found nothing unusual. "Are they dirty?"

"No, warm! Not there, here!" She pointed at her chest, more or less. Sunbright reached for her and toppled from the chair, landing atop her. The amphora rolled off the table and crashed, spilling the dregs of the wine.

"Ooh, mustn't waste!" Sopping her hand in the spilled wine, Greenwillow stuffed her fingers into her mouth, then Sunbright's. Unclear on the concept, the barbarian bit her fingers. "Not bite!" she yelped. "Gentle."

The half-elf used both hands to grab his ears, tugged him close, and bit his nose gently. Their wine-misted breath mingled. "Help me . . . up!"

Holding one another and the furniture, they clambered to their feet, kicking cups and chairs every which way. Greenwillow towed Sunbright by his jerkin out the door into the cool of very early morning. "Come on. We can go to the women's barracks. 'S a'right if we're quiet."

Blundering against a wall, she stepped on an errant cat that squalled hideously. With a gasp, she leaped into Sunbright's arms, and they both landed squashily in the mucky street. Greenwillow, in his lap, caressed his hair. "You like elf-maids?"

"Oh, yes!" the barbarian assured her as his mouth found hers. "I want . . . Hey!"

The empty streets were very quiet, and even a soft footfall made enough noise to be noticed. Sunbright jerked as he pointed wildly. "Look! Look, 's her!"

Greenwillow peered down the narrow street, saw nothing, then was unceremoniously dumped on her rump as the man scrambled up. Traveling sideways as much as forward, he rebounded off the nearby shop walls and charged into an even narrower street beyond. Cursing, the elf clambered up and trotted after him.

"Ruellana!" the barbarian hollered, his voice incredibly loud in the sleeping city. "Ruellana, stop!"

Ahead, in deeper shadow, a slender white figure in a simple, short shift flitted away. Calling, pleading, swearing, the man blundered after, his war tackle rattling, his boots clumping. Behind him, Greenwillow called out that it was a trap, but he didn't hear.

The ghost-girl paused and turned, and Sunbright got his first good look at her. It was Ruellana; he'd swear it, for her hair was like living fire. She'd mysteriously appeared at his campfire half a world away, then disappeared to haunt his dreams, and here she was again.

She held out both arms enticingly, then flickered sideways into a dark doorway. Sunbright didn't notice the shops on this street had no signs hanging above the doors, and the windows were either shuttered or boarded over. He crashed down the street, calling her name, pivoted wildly, and plunged through the door into blackness.

And fell a dozen feet. The crash onto rubble crumpled his legs beneath him, stunning him. Blinking, he cast about, but could see nothing but pitch-blackness and, high overhead, the grayish outline of the doorway.

Then there came a hiss like that of a pit of disturbed snakes, and around him rose a wreath like black fog.

With an oath, he watched the smoke coalesce and harden. Within seconds, he was peering up at a black-cloaked monster with flaming red eyes and hair.

Chapter 8

Horrified he might have been, but it was an automatic gesture for Sunbright to haul Harvester from its sheath scabbard. The leather-wrapped pommel felt warm and comforting in his hands. The long steel shank stood up before his face, sturdy as a tree. But inwardly his guts felt pierced by a thousand icy knives, and it was all he could do not to throw the sword away and run in blind terror. Of all the legends of the tundra, the stories of undead monsters who sucked the life from men—and yet left them undead to do the same—were the most fearsome. And here Sunbright, exhausted and drunk but rapidly sobering, was trapped in a death pit with an undead fiend.

The thing provided its own hideous light. A wreath of flame enveloped its head, and empty eye sockets flickered with flames as if through a slot in an iron door. The rest was indistinct in the wavering light, but Sunbright thought he wouldn't see it well under any conditions. According to folklore, wraiths and wights and ghasts were not entirely of this world, but wafted between the seen and unseen planes, so there might be only a portion of the monster visible, or it might be seen as thinner than it really was. So its shape flowed and folded like shadows on a rippling blanket. And here in the dark, it was master of its element.

Still, whether the creature was dead or undead, a shaft of hardened steel could still dispatch it from this world to the next—or to none—if one could strike hard and fast without shirking.

But his assault started out badly.

His head still reeling, Sunbright kicked himself upright and dropped back to brace for a long swing . . . and stepped on open air.

His iron-ringed boot jingled across torn rock; then his knee banged excruciatingly on a jagged edge of stone. Yet the misstep might have saved him, for the writhing wraith hooked a taloned hand at him, like a net of fishhooks, but barely grazed the front of his bearskin jerkin.

Gasping in pain, the barbarian dragged back his shorn knee. His long shirt was sopping wet, not with wine this time, and the clammy touch of it chilled his skin like glacier runoff. Shoving the sword straight at the beast to fend it off, he gingerly tested his leg, found that it wasn't sprained, only smarting. Afraid to fumble another step and cripple himself, he whipped his head around to study the trap.

By rippling hell-flame, he'd first thought the walls were coal, square-cut, and faintly glistening, or else somehow painted black. But neither idea made any sense for a simple cellar in the abandoned part of town. Wary of the advancing ghost-thing, he swished his sword right and left at the glistening walls, but touched nothing.

Frantic, he stabbed far to his left. Still nothing. Yet a glance overhead showed he was almost underneath the threshold he'd tumbled over. So either this cellar undercut the street tremendously, and the threshold sat on nothing, or else . . .

. . . or else he'd blundered into another world, another type of space altogether.

A world where wraiths stood triumphant.

The monster undulated like a hovering snake and snatched at his scalp with one hand, then the other, testing. A jab, a poke, and the slashes were turned. But for how long?

Chills raced down Sunbright's spine, raised hackles on his arms and neck and legs. If this were some other vacuous world, he might stumble into any kind of pit, fall down any slope, become lost in a world of blackness and death.

Or something worse than death.

"Sunbright!" Greenwillow's shrill brought him back from the edge of fear, back to life. The elf-maid hunched in the doorway, one hand on the jamb, the other dangling her slim sword blade. She's going to jump, the barbarian thought in terror.

"Don't!" His voice was unnaturally high. "Don't come down here! It's not real! It's somewhere else!" He was blathering, spouting nonsense that conveyed no information. "Stay there!"

He had to twist in a half-circle as the wraith circled him, as a fox would circle a caged bird. He tracked the thing, which mimicked his turnings. Sunbright had about screwed himself as far around as possible without moving his feet, when the ghost swooped in.

A clawed hand as wide as a pitchfork grabbed for the barbarian's shoulder, the other his face. Twisting, Sunbright ripped a figure eight in the air, a pure defense. But somehow a hand got through, raked his cheek, twitched upward for his eye, and Sunbright almost snapped his neck jerking backward. Then he fell in a tangle.

His feet clumped on something solid, but his left elbow disappeared into a hole with a downward-sucking roar that must have vanished into the earth. Rolling in terror from the awful depths suggested, the barbarian found a bigger crevice yawning on his right, one wide enough to swallow his shoulders. Freezing stock-still, he tried desperately to think.

What was the floor made of? His jumbling thoughts couldn't form a picture. Was he standing on the tops of flat rocks with cracks between? Or poised at the lip of some curvy cliff like a broken-backed snake? Or something else, a terrain the human mind couldn't map?

Whatever, he had to get up. Rocking forward, he slapped his hands down, found solid footing, and planted his hobnails on it. But where . . . ?

Icy hands like ice picks latched on to his neck from behind. Ten pricks broke skin, brought forth red blood that steamed against the alien claws. A half-inch, an inch into his neck muscles, plunged the nails. Any more, and he'd have his head severed like a chicken's.

But his feet were secure, so he could strike. With a stomach-wrenching grunt, he slashed his great sword Harvester overhead and down. A satisfying *chunk* answered him, and the pricking nails retreated. Yet the chilly horror of them lingered and kept his spine crawling, his back muscles spasming.

He had to get out of here, somehow, anyhow. But to panic would be to die, or be lost.

"Sunbright!" Greenwillow shrilled again. She'd been screaming at him steadily, he guessed, but he heard little. It was as if the pit sucked up sound as well as life. "Lead it over here! My sword is silver and ensorceled!"

But so is mine, he thought. Chandler poured an enchanting potion over the steel. It lets me wound shielded creatures. Yet assessing the blow he'd struck, he couldn't be sure if he'd wounded the wraith or simply knocked it back.

Stooping, feeling the ground with one hand, he swung blindly behind him with his sword and crept a couple of paces forward. His left toes were suspended over a pit. How could that be?

And why was he dizzy? He'd thought the effects of the wine gone by now, sweated out in buckets of terror. This was more a weakness, a sapping, as if he'd swum too long in icy water and developed chills. But perhaps that was a function of this nightmarish notworld.

Swinging behind him again, he eased to the right, felt solid ground, took a step. Greenwillow was above him, but seemed higher up now. She'd lain flat on her stomach, hanging her arms and sword inside, yet he couldn't have touched her sword with his own. Was the ground sinking farther? Would it continue to drop, like water behind a leaking dam, until he'd sunk to the bowels of . . . hell? No, not hell, for that place was warm. This was home to ice worms and ghasts.

And here the flaming beast returned, now outside sword range. So he *had* hurt it! He hawked to spit and throw it a challenge, but his throat was dry and his voice a pipsqueak. Never mind the bravado, he thought. Escape.

With no sound, the thing rushed. Red flames filled Sunbright's vision. How had he ever mistaken *this* for Ruellana? Swinging wildly from his left hip, he carved frigid air and forced the wraith to veer, but it only swooped low, fastening needle fingers on his leg.

Down he smashed with the pommel onto the thing's back, at the ring of fire, its head. But it ignored the blows. Like some northern shark intent only on prey, it fastened deeper into his flesh, freezing muscle to the bone, chilling the marrow. Desperate, the warrior sliced Harvester hard and fast inside, close enough to shave hair off his own leg. The cold blade thrummed on the skinny black arms, chipped flesh like ice. The wraith let go, and Sunbright felt blood pulse through his leg, and out of it.

But the thing slid under his defenses and clawed for his face. He'd never slash this close . . .

Above, Greenwillow called, and a caw answered. A tremendous flapping exploded in Sunbright's face— and the wraith's. A croaking rasp whipsawed the air.

A raven, thought the barbarian dully. The raven, the one that talked! It pecked and bated and shrilled, and the wraith backed off. Frenzied wings riffled the fire around the black head, and the ghast fell even farther back.

"Here!" called a voice from above, and Sunbright looked up. Greenwillow was closer again, almost within touching range. Had the broken earth heaved? Had the raven yanked it up as if on a string? The elven warrior trailed her sturdy black belt into the pit.

Unable to slash at the wraith for fear of striking the raven, Sunbright fumbled his way toward the belt, his free hand in front of his boots to feel for holes. Twice he had to stop, cut back, and sidestep. But then—glory be!—his hand clamped on to the warm loop of leather.

Surprisingly, he had no strength to haul himself up, despite his terror. He could barely retain his grip on the sword. In the anthracite-lined pit, the raven flew tight circles around the wraith, which shadow-boxed away from it. Then Greenwillow's warm hands, immensely strong, grabbed Sunbright's hand, then wrist. Grunting, he was dragged belly-first over the rough stone threshold and into the mucky street of Dalekeva.

"You're safe! Safe!" The elf-woman wept openly, pulling him facedown across her lap, dragging his boots across the threshold.

"Yes," he whispered. "Glad to be . . . with you. But I don't . . . feel well."

Those were his last thoughts.

* * * * *

Sunbright opened his eyes to sunshine, billowing curtains, and Greenwillow's face hovering above him. Others were in the room as well, he realized. Dimly he recognized the fat woman by the door: one of the merchant delegates, the only one to pay them a bonus and add thanks.

The elf saw his gaze and said, "Mistress Keenid was the only one I could think of. Out of the kindness of her heart, she's taken us in, hired nurses and a cleric to tend you."

Sunbright tried to joke, to say, "We owe her a bonus," to show them he was fine, in good spirits. But all that came from his mouth was a ghostly sough. The weakness, the hollowness of it, terrified him. What was wrong with him?

Greenwillow touched his lips. "Hush. Sister Fjord will explain."

A dark-skinned woman with long braided tresses came to his bedside. She wore an unadorned blue gown, the uniform of some sect popular in the city. Sunbright hadn't bothered to sort them out; he had his own gods. But they failed you, a voice added. But then, he'd left this world behind, hadn't he?

As if reading his thoughts, Sister Fjord said, "You're both an unfortunate and fortunate young man. Unfortunate to stumble into a pit of the Underdark. It's an old curse laid against the city's founders, according to legend. Like a volcano or hot springs, eruptions sometimes split the surface. In the abandoned quarters, they can go unnoticed and grow. Exorcism and barrowloads of rock plug them, but sometimes . . ." She shrugged with a cleric's detachment.

"Girl?" That one word hurt to gasp out, as if Sunbright had swallowed fire.

Greenwillow's voice was flat. "He means, did a red-headed girl stumble into the pit too?"

Sister Fjord shook her head. "No, we searched to see if others were trapped. There was no one."

Sunbright closed his eyes for a second, and upon opening them, he found it dark outside. Night noises, of owls and watchmen, rustled along with the curtains. He sat up with a start, feeling lost and alone. At his cry, Greenwillow appeared as if by magic. And so he slept again. And woke. And slept.

Most times he was dead to the world. But drifting in and out, he saw the red-haired Ruellana, smiling, laughing. Then her face would char and blacken, her hair ignite, and she'd try to claw his face off, laughing all the while.

* * * * *

Sunbright was up and tottering around in a few days, but he knew part of his essence had been left in that pit. Inside he felt hollow, and he was subject to queer dizzy spells that made him stagger to grab a solid surface. He was sore in several places, especially the back of his neck where the wraith had punctured him and ten fat, black-centered lumps still lingered. But finally he could dress himself and strap Harvester across his back, and shove Dorlas's warhammer in his belt, though both felt as heavy as anvils.

Three women were there to see him leave: Mistress Keenid, owner of the house; Sister Fjord, the cleric and healer; and Greenwillow, who seemed a stranger and sister to him at the same time.

Motherly Sister Fjord felt his forehead, looked in his mouth, slipped her hand into his armpit to tell his body temperature. "Your stamina saved you. Only the iron in your muscle helped you fight off the lifedrain. But eat lots of meat and eggs, drink red port, and you'll grow robust in a few weeks. But . . . you had magical abilities before, didn't you?"

Sunbright disliked that word "before." "I was . . . have . . . I think of myself as a shaman in training, on a spiritual journey of sorts. My father was a great medicine-healer, and my mother said I had the Sight. But all my people have some abilities with animals and nature and the edges of the world."

The woman nodded even as she frowned. "But those abilities come from the soul, the *ka*, or essence, whatever you call it. Yours has been shrunk, shriveled, crippled, I would wager. The . . . thing that attacked"—she would not say the word "wraith" lest she invoke one—"was only partly of this sphere. Had it wasted you away, you would have moved to that plane. Some of your essence did, and it's lost. I can't explain it all, or promise anything, but know that, if your heart remains pure and your vision true, your essence may heal. Meditate, observe your rituals religiously, look inward and outward, and continue your quest. No matter what, you'll be a stronger person for this ordeal, in spirit and in body. So do the gods test us, and prove us worthy or find us wanting."

Numbly, Sunbright nodded. Her words at least gave him hope that this debilitating weakness—internal and external—would someday end. Lacking any other way to thank her, he leaned forward and kissed her dark cheek, then that of Mistress Keenid, who cried. But when he turned to Greenwillow, she stepped outside ahead of him. And so, like a boy sent off to school by his aunts, Sunbright returned to the world.

He was glad to get outside, for having lived his life in the wilderness, he was never comfortable under a roof. Yet the sun overhead seemed watery, the cries of fishmongers and children muted and whispery, the rich, mingled smells of the city—privies and spices and fish and manure and perfume—seemed as thin as dust in an old cave. A pair of fork-tailed swallows jigging overhead were just birds; they could tell him nothing. Briefly Sunbright wondered how much of him pulsed in the Underdark and its sinister nothingness. Then he shook his head and dizzied himself.

"Where . . . where are we bound?" he asked Greenwillow.

The elf strode along ahead of him, and he struggled to keep up with her. Without turning, she called, "We're off to see the city council. They've requested an audience when you're available."

"Requested?" gasped Sunbright. But that was all he could say, and so he plodded after Greenwillow's stiff back.

They waited on a bench in the council hall for hours as endless piddling business and squabbling went back and forth. Before, Sunbright was able to ignore it; now he could barely endure the bickering, for his head throbbed and he wanted to scream at them to shut up. Greenwillow never said a word, which confused him. Hadn't she stood by him in battle with the wraith, and then nursed him through his sickness with tears in her eyes? Why, then, was she so angry and cold?

Finally a clerk called their names, and they stepped before the council's table. Sunbright, tired and still a bit weak, tried not to sway like some errant drunk.

The speaker for the council barely looked at them before reading from notes chalked on a slate. "Greenwillow. After much deliberation, the council has decided. You may continue your journey to the One King in Tinnainen. We are aware this king may be affronted by your missive from the High Elves of Cormanthyr, yet there is, we calculate, little chance he will unleash his fury at Dalekeva, since you are an elf and not of our city. We will enter our own negotiations with the One King, and so will neither hinder you nor send you succor. We wish you good luck."

Stupefied by this garble of pomposity, dismissal, treachery, and outright cowardice, Sunbright merely stared in openmouthed wonder. Then dust motes swirled in a shaft of sunlight by his side. He was alone. Without a word, Greenwillow had quitted the council hall.

The heavy-footed barbarian caught up as she marched toward the river. "Can you believe that lot?" he jabbered. "Saying they don't care if you go to be skinned alive, that you don't matter because you're an elf? They're negotiating with this butcher to save their own hides. And they won't hinder us, won't prevent us from leaving?"

"What did you expect, country boy?" She neither slowed her stride nor turned to look at him. "That they'd pick up swords and march east, keening battle songs while tripping over their gowns? They're businessmen who believe everything has a price, including freedom and safety. And you don't have to go, just I."

"Yes, I do." Sunbright stumbled over a cobblestone and almost fell. Wilt-legged, he ran to catch up again. He felt like a child striding alongside his father so many years ago, and found himself wishing Greenwillow would be more of a friend, and not such a stern master. "I said I'd accompany you, and I shall."

"Go or stay; I don't care. But don't whine about the ways of the world. It's tiresome."

Stunned, Sunbright stayed silent and followed her meekly.

Grim-lipped, Greenwillow bustled through the marketplace garnering supplies for their journey: rations of meat and dried fruit and hardtack and burlap satchels to carry them in, skins filled with water and wine, long arrows, extra blankets for the highland nights, waxed tinder, a new bow for Sunbright, small coins for the smaller villages. Hurried, she didn't haggle overlong, and the vendors' good fortune made them garrulous and curious. Yet when they asked the travelers' destination and were told, they quieted. One said, "Tinnainen? Where the One King's made his headquarters? You should know patrols of orcs and men scour the countryside east of here. Mixed groups, I mean, men and orcs traveling together!"

Another offered, "Aye, farmers across the river have lost sheep, cows, you name it. 'Course they say there's a red dragon been seen in the eastern skies around sunset."

"There's an ill omen, the worst kind. Or else the dragon was in Tinnainen already, and the One King drove it out. Or else it's struck a deal with him."

Still another said, "And these councilors. They'll sell us all into slavery once the army arrives. Right now they've got clerics and mages up on the top of Crying Tower, slaughtering goats and pigs and what-all in hopes of driving the dragon off or bribing it. I don't know which."

"Some say the council plans to raise taxes on us, maybe sweep the jails and drive the criminals out into the open for dragon fodder."

"We should be mustering an army, and the council's bickering about who to blame. But that's politicians for you."

And so it went. All had something to say . . . and none of it boded well.

* * * * *

Late that afternoon, Greenwillow stepped off a ferry onto the eastern side of the river. Sunbright, laden, as was the elf, with satchels and weapons, leaned into his burdens and faced east. Past rocky farmland there arose tree-covered hills and a broad flat road, for in better times Dalekeva and Tinnainen had traded mutton and beef and hides and ironware for dried fish and silver and grain. Sunbright looked at the hills and couldn't resist saying, "Perhaps we should camp for the night and think this through. We'll need a strategy for moving through enemy territory if we're to reach Tinnainen alive."

Greenwillow, eyes hot and brows puckered, rounded on him. "Whining again? Know this, mortal man. Perhaps I do go to throw my life away! It's no matter. I've been ordered to go, and I shall—alone, if need be! To cast defiance into the One King's face will teach him that there are those who oppose him, *real* fighters, not coin-counters!

"As for you," she added, "stop dragging your feet! I

remember a man who strode boldly down the roads and disdained all danger. Now I'm saddled with a carping cripple! Obviously the wraith drew more than strength from you; it ripped out your heart as well! If you wish to continue your 'spiritual journey'—as much as humans can have spirits—you'd best get on with it! Hiding behind stone walls will not restore your strength or spunk. Choose that, if you will. Choose to fail! But don't whine at me about your losses! I've lost more than you'll ever have!"

Stunned by this tirade, Sunbright could only stand as the elf marched down the road, nose high. He hadn't whined at all. Had he? And he hadn't suggested they not go. She was being obstinate and heaping blame on him for nothing. With his dizzy thoughts and aching back and clumsy feet, he didn't know what transpired, or even what he was anymore.

Nor did he know what Greenwillow was. She was an elf, which was mystery enough, and a woman, so doubly mysterious.

He could only go on and hope for the best. If he died, then perhaps that's what the gods intended for him. He wouldn't linger, or whine.

He did, however, curse a great deal, and that made him feel somewhat better.

* * * * *

That night, thinking that orcs preferred open reaches, they made a cold camp in the woods. Greenwillow had shot two fat rabbits, but they dared not light a fire, so Sunbright sliced the tough meat very thin, and they chewed it raw.

The elf agreed to take first watch, sitting against a tree, arms across her knees. Sunbright, who was exhausted, folded his blanket, pinned it shut with splinters, and flopped on his back. His throbbing head had whirled the day long, and finally he'd realized he lacked one thing: information. So, fighting fatigue and sleep, he asked quietly as the late sun set, "Greenwillow, why?"

For a long time there was silence. Then a soft sob choked her. Arching his neck, the man saw a tear course down her pale cheek. Sniffing, she whispered, "I was drunk, I'll admit. Elves tend to hold their emotions close, especially around humans. And it works against us sometimes, for too much wine or too much magic or too much fighting can make us lose our heads, go berserk or lust-mad. But I liked you and was lonely, and wanted to share myself with you.

"But in an eye-blink you pushed me away and chased another. I was forgotten, but I shan't forget.

"We can march side by side, fight shoulder to shoulder as comrades-in-arms. But that is *all* we'll be."

* * * * *

Day by day, as summer aged to autumn and the highland woods were tinged with red and yellow and orange, they pressed on. The lands of greater Dalekeva ended not far into the hills, and there were miles and miles of unsettled hinterlands. They made good time, even though they slid through the forest parallel to the road, never traveling on it. Out in the open, eating well, drinking pure springwater, tramping steadily and sleeping deeply, Sunbright found his strength of limb and leg returning, though an ache deep inside lingered. At the end of a day's march he swore if he thumped his chest it would ring hollowly, like a cracked bell. But the lack inside would heal, the cleric had promised, so he waited patiently.

With Greenwillow he talked once again, but only of incidentals. Which trail to follow, whether they might flush quail from a thicket, whether footprints they came across were those of men or orcs, or both. But they said nothing of the heart and shared no stories. Their evening camps were quiet enough that they could hear squirrels scrambling amidst their acorn harvests, and owls on tufted wings beating the night air to seek scurrying mice.

Eventually they passed into the realm of Tinnainen, though the city was still miles off. First was an isolated cabin, empty, with the door ajar. Then a stronghold cabin, two stories of logs with arrow slits on the second floor, not burned, but abandoned. Then late one afternoon they topped a rise and saw, curving below, a long, narrow valley. There were farms at the bottom, the fields harvested, the granaries full, the livestock corralled for the night, the chickens and geese penned. The road to Tinnainen cut straight across, due east.

"Looks quiet enough, for an occupied territory," hissed Greenwillow. Neither had spoken loudly since leaving the river.

"Even conquerors must eat," the barbarian whispered back. "You can't feed an army on rape and loot. Better to threaten the peasants into farming their hardest and leave them to it."

Greenwillow scooted forward and peered north and south. Both could see the valley ran for miles. "It's either walk miles out of our way to keep to the woods or wait until night." To never cross open land by day was an ingrained rule of the wilderness.

Without speaking, they decided to wait. They found a hollow spot, propped their baggage as pillows, and napped. Cool night air filling the hollow woke them, and they strapped on their packs and weapons in the dark.

Down the slope, slipping from tree trunk to tree trunk, they made their way. They paused a long time at the edge of the woods, tiptoed out to peer at the road, and listened. Finally they set out, hands free, wary. Sunbright hissed at the first field, for his heavy feet crunched grain stubble. Greenwillow moved with no more noise than fog.

They passed downwind of a large farm, but something roused the dogs, and they set up a ferocious barking.

Hard after came a long, low whistle from the woods ahead.

Sunbright locked his feet even as Greenwillow grabbed his arm. "Look!"

The elf's eyes had picked out what roused the dog. Straining, Sunbright saw it too.

A patrol of soldiers: hunched, knotty-armed, bow-legged. The two turned to discover another patrol coming up behind them. They were caught.

In the past, Sunbright Steelshanks would have put down his head and outrun them. But his old strength was gone, and he'd marched the entire day. Quietly he shed his baggage and drew Harvester, the leather-steel heft a comfort in his hands.

"Run. I'll hold them."

But Greenwillow, too, dropped her burdens and drew her slim ornate sword with a silvery shiver. "Comrades we are and shall remain."

Back to back, the two leveled their weapons and awaited the oncoming enemy.

Chapter 9

Many strange things had happened to Sunbright since he first fled his tribe, but what happened next was the strangest of all.

Taking a fresh grip on Harvester, he was judging in which direction to swing first when a growly or-cish voice sounded in the still night. "Good evening. Would you care to break bread?"

"What?" the barbarian gasped aloud. Break heads, he must have said. Behind him, Greenwillow squeaked.

The patrol fanned out as if to attack, but halted a dozen feet away. The barbarian saw now that there were men scattered amidst the orcs, confirming the rumors they'd heard in the marketplace. These were the same sort of orcs that had attacked him a year ago in the Barren Mountains: Thousand Fist orcs with neat gray tunics embellished with a red splayed hand. There were six of them, with obsidian-studded clubs or short swords, and three humans. The men wore the same uniforms, and all three had shaved their heads, probably because the tunics came infested with lice and fleas. Sunbright would expect to find only the lowest sort of lazy scoundrels mingling with orcs, but these seemed average sorts, if quiet. Lack of bathing had turned their skin grayish in the manner of orcs, however. Their eyes roved over the half-elf.

Over his shoulder, Sunbright hissed, "What have you?"

Her rump bumping his, Greenwillow reported three orcs and two men. She added, "Do we cut and run?"

"Come, come." The orcish commander was framed in darkness. "There is no need to fight. We shall make our small fire here and invite you to join us."

Safe in their own territory, the war party tramped to the road and dropped their packs and satchels. One soldier dumped wood while another sparked a fire. A third toted a blackened kettle toward the farm for well water, sending the dogs into a frenzy of barking.

The orcish commander waved a gray hand at the tiny camp. "Come. We'll have tea. You'll learn much besides." Then he walked toward his men.

"Learn much?" Sunbright asked the night air. "I've already seen wonders no storyteller could concoct."

Greenwillow nodded numbly. Far behind them, the owner of the farm—a human—opened a thick door and whistled in her dogs, then shut it with a thump. "That humans could live peaceably so close by . . ." The elf shivered.

"And an orc offer a tea party like some merchant luring customers into his shop . . ." added Sunbright.

"We've no choice. Should they will it, they can slay

us on the spot." But Greenwillow trembled uncontrollably, and Sunbright remembered that, of all the speaking races, elves hated orcs the most. Perhaps because, ran the rumors, elves and orcs were two sides of the same coin, opposites, and so were linked in some light-against-dark fashion. Still, it was the elf who picked up her bundles and edged toward the fire first.

"Glad to have you with us. Sit, please," growled the commander. Sunbright and Greenwillow squatted on their heels in the road and studied their erstwhile foes, who steadfastly ignored them. Some, seasoned veterans, pillowed their heads on bundles and dozed in the lull. Some gnawed dark jerked meat while waiting for the herb tea to boil. One honed a bronze sword until the commander ordered him to sheathe it.

The commander intrigued Sunbright. He had a gray pallor, a pug nose, pointed teeth, and bushy eyebrows as thick as caterpillars. But he was tall and held his head up, without the characteristic hunch of Thousand Fist orcs. With a shock, Sunbright realized he was only half-orc and the rest man. A product of rape, no doubt, yet with an oddly noble quality. Certainly he seemed suited to command, as much as one could command slovenly orcs.

The commander unwrapped an oilskin pouch and withdrew jerky, grinning wolfishly when Sunbright and Greenwillow refused. They had no idea what— or who—the meat had been originally. For something to do, they dug out their own jerky and chewed.

"The One King means to harm no one," said the commander abruptly. "He merely wishes to bring order to the chaos raging across our lands."

"Chaos?" Greenwillow was shocked into speech. "People farm the land and trade! Rarely do they fight, and there are no plagues that I've heard of!"

"The chaos of the heart and mind, then," continued the commander. Most of his soldiers didn't listen. Obviously they'd heard this speech before, many times. But a couple of the men followed the arguments as if memorizing them. "And the chaos wrought by the Neth."

"The Neth? You'd challenge the *Neth?*" asked Greenwillow. Sunbright elbowed her sharply, a signal not to antagonize their host.

"Aye, we would. The day has come for a new order, a new way of doing things—especially about the Netherese. But this new order can be achieved only through the imposition of a strong authority, a wise but absolute ruler. A broad broom cleanses the land. See what the One King has wrought already: orcs and men and even elves sitting and discoursing peaceably by a fire."

The last was pure moose dung, thought the barbarian. If he and the elf had their way, they'd have topped three hills by now. Only the threat of superior numbers kept them still. And any argument founded on a lie, he knew, would just form a bigger heap of lies.

But to keep the man-orc talking, Greenwillow asked, "Please, tell us more about this One King."

As if she'd plucked her finger from a dam, a torrent of words spilled forth from the zealous commander. The One King was all-wise, for he could see into the past and future, and into other parts of the world. He knew the minds of men and orcs and elves and Netherese. He'd lived a long time, studying in his youth, suffering to seek knowledge in the far reaches of the world, meditating on high, rocky crags until the snow came to his chin, questioning the wisest of the wise. And, learning at last all there was to learn, he'd come to understand the world and how its ills might be corrected . . . once he gained the cooperation of every living thing.

Cooperation! The barbarian wanted to spit. More, he wanted to leap up and smite off this smug bastard's head. How could anyone be so dense as to surrender himself to a tyrant who'd either have your "cooperation" or else boil you alive? It was madness! But a frightening madness, if this king's rantings could inspire such fervent loyalty in a pack of hideous orcs that they bypassed fat human farms and camped by night in the open road lest their campfire ignite the fields. This One King must be as persuasive as Selûne, She Who Guides. Or more so.

Seething, disputing everything in his head, though wisely not aloud, Sunbright bore the twisted arguments like someone staked on an anthill. And eventually the orcish commander ran out of steam, yawned, and excused himself. Unrolling his blanket, he insisted Greenwillow and Sunbright pass the night here, "safe," for he would post a guard. Quietly, the two agreed and unfurled their blankets.

But in the bustle, Sunbright hissed, "How could you stand to debate that lunkhead? He's as loony as a moon maid!"

"Hush!" snapped Greenwillow. "Any fact about the One King is another arrow in my quiver. You can never know too much about an enemy. I'll take first watch."

"Agreed." The camp would have two posted guards and one unposted one, for the barbarian and half-elf would keep surreptitious watch themselves. As he settled down, Sunbright eased Harvester into his blanket alongside him. He did that every night anyway, but this night, he drew the naked blade and slept against that.

And dreamed of orcs and elves and humans dancing around a maypole. They were singing gaily, naked except for garlands of flowers around their necks and brows. Impaled atop the pole was Sunbright's head, eyes staring in disbelief.

* * * * *

Candlemas scratched the back of his left hand, which had finally healed, although it itched as if fiends cavorted under the skin. He then scratched his neck, which was confined in a high stock of red leather that gouged the underside of his chin. He hated fine clothes and parties, for both were invariably uncomfortable. And the room was hot from hundreds of bodies and a thousand candles.

The whole mansion, in fact, was lit with candles from one end to another, and the mage reckoned only powerful shield spells kept the place from igniting. There was not a spot anywhere that wasn't decorated with triple-thick gilt or bright paint or some mural of great deeds and fantastic beasts and sorrowful romances. There were layers of curtains, tapestries, and paintings, as well as crystal and silver chandeliers, stuffed beasts and monsters, and items and oddities from the world over. And this fantastic palace, he reminded himself, was only one of several owned by his host, Tyralhorn the Archmage, who was in turn only one of several in this city of Anauria, a High City second only to Most-High Karsus. Lady Polaris herself owned two palaces here and others elsewhere, as well as her "country cottage," what she sometimes called the vast floating castle of Delia, where Candlemas was steward. The highest archmages of Netheril pursued mainly magics and excitement, but somehow wealth and property seemed to stick to their fingers in their search.

And the entirety of this mansion—every candlestick and bauble and self-emptying golden chamber pot—existed to impress other archmages, in a vast unending quest of competition to be the largest, richest, and gaudiest.

Sometimes Candlemas found himself wondering why the archmages sought to surround themselves with ever more gewgaws and gadgets. Yet he knew, if he had the chance to do the same . . .

" 'Mas, you came! How wonderful!"

Breezing toward him came Sysquemalyn. She wore a vast flowing gown in all the colors of the rainbow, yards of silken material that sprouted from her shoulders and trailed behind her, even sweeping in an arch behind her head of piled and bejeweled red hair, yet managing somehow to leave both breasts nearly bare. Oohing and ahhing, she circled Candlemas and twitted him about his fine clothes, a short brocade toga that crossed one shoulder and hung behind him and breeches of silk, hand-painted with interlaced flowers, and worn with red leather shoes. "My, my. You won't want to mix your stinky potions in those clothes! Were they to catch fire, you'd be days getting the flaming remnants off! And look at your lovely hand! So much nicer than the last one!"

Giggling, she caught his left hand and kissed the hairy back, but Candlemas yanked it away. He'd had a serving girl grind powder and mix makeup to disguise the lighter color of the new skin, hoping no one would notice, for if they did, the knowledge that Sysquemalyn had shorn off his arm would get around. One thing all the bored archmages collected avidly was gossip.

"Don't mock me," the mage growled. "This hand keeps me awake nights for itching. And you cheated in removing it, I'll remind you. Just as you cheated siccing that Hunt on my barbarian! He's supposed to survive tests of strength, but that was outside the rules!"

"Oh, come now!" Sysquemalyn, smiling at a young mage who pranced behind a jutting green codpiece and little else, patted her hair into place. "We all know that the only rule about magic is that there *are* no rules."

"But there are wagers, and honest bets require honest players. But you—"

"*Honest?*" The mage objected loudly. "You had him escort a traveling party of delegates! And sent him a raven for a familiar!"

"The merest buffer because I knew you'd cheat!"

"So," countered Sysquemalyn, "we're left wondering who cheated first. Which just adds to the game and makes it more diverting. We never know what will happen next. I haven't had this much fun in years, so let's not quit now. I've got something absolutely devilish planned for your barbarian. But excuse me, dear 'Mas, I must prepare for my entertainment. The Great White Cow—excuse me, Lady Polaris—commands, and I obey. Ta ta!"

Grumbling, Candlemas realized it was probably Sysquemalyn who had dragged him here. Somehow the chamberlain had offered Lady Polaris an entertainment, and her ladyship had accepted, then commanded Candlemas also to attend. Why, he didn't know. But as he sweated in the heavy clothes and simpered and smiled at his superiors—which included nearly everyone present—he wished he were home in his workshop.

There were entertainments going on everywhere, in gardens, drawing rooms, the front lawn, and even on the roof. Some were wrestling contests or fights to the death between slaves hoping to win their freedom, some were ancient plays and some were new ones, anything to keep the bored archmages diverted for even a moment. But Sysquemalyn's entertainment was rumored to be something spectacular, something new, and everyone buzzed about what it might be. So even Candlemas joined the throng jamming the largest drawing room, though he stood at the back wall as befit his station.

Lady Polaris swept onto a low dais at the front of the room, white hair and dress glistening in the reflected crystalline light. To polite applause, she announced she had commissioned one of her cleverer charges to produce a work that she herself had dreamed up. The archmage bragged about her cleverness; then she sat in the front row to see just what she'd commissioned.

Without any sign of Sysquemalyn, her entertainment began.

There was neither curtain nor light bank, but somehow the room went dark. Then, about head-height on the dais, a window into nothing opened, dropped, and became a door. From the door stepped a handsome man, as naked as a baby. Sketching with his hands, the man described more circles, and each opened into another window. From one he drew cloth to wrap himself. From another, a shining sword. A third window opened onto a sylvan glade, complete with waterfall, and this window the man tugged open until the water of the pool spilled over the lip and gushed onto the dais, then the floor, only to disappear. At this trick, the company of archmages oohed like children watching fireworks.

In the glade, the man met a woman, equally naked. He retrieved for her a bolt of cloth and wrapped it about her slender form. Arm in arm, they crossed the stage and stepped into a sunny desert. The audience could feel the warm wind and scent of cactus blossoms waft over them, and oohed again.

At the rear, Candlemas found himself oohing and aahing along with the rest. Then he shook his head, wondering how Sysquemalyn had contrived these tricks. Typical entertainments were a blend of illusion, sleight-of-hand, distant events viewed magically, and performances by hired actors. Certainly all these elements mingled here, but there was much more magic involved, and he was piqued that he could identify little of it.

As he'd guessed it might, the story soon turned tragic. An archmage entered the story, took a fancy to the beautiful woman, and demanded her. The hero resisted, so the girl was spirited away. Journeying through ever-increasing settings—twisted tubes of stone, empty expanses like black glass, tangled forests where the trees attacked, and so on—the hero suffered fear and sorrow, then gained a boon companion only to lose him tragically. The girl, who spurned the archmage's advances, was brutally tortured, both physically and then spiritually, tricked into thinking she'd killed her lover when he entered her room by night. Soon the girl died and spiraled into a pit of hells, each more fearsome than the other. Despairing, the hero killed himself, then flickered through his own hells, drawing gasps and guffaws from the jaded audience. In the end, the lovers were united only to be incinerated in a pit. But the archmage, taking pity on the misguided and headstrong humans, resurrected them as two ash trees at opposite ends of the sylvan glade, yearning to interlink branches, but never quite achieving it.

Finally, the scenes were whisked away, and only Lady Polaris was left standing there to bask as the audience roared and cheered and applauded. They demanded she take a bow, which she did, smile gleaming. But Candlemas did not linger. Mopping his brow and yanking at his collar, he staggered past servants and spectators until he reached fresh air at a back door.

Of course, he told himself, the moral was clear: mere humans must never defy the whim of an archmage, lest they be racked in every hell imaginable. The audience of archmages had, naturally, loved it.

But *where*, Candlemas asked himself over and over, had Sysquemalyn gotten those magics? And how had she manipulated them?

And most importantly, could she really control them?

* * * * *

In the morning, which Sunbright was moderately surprised to see, the orcish commander took pains to paint a smeary red hand on a curl of birch bark, with his own mark, a tiny red spider, in the corner. This, he explained, would be a safe-conduct to get them past later patrols as they approached Tinnainen. "And fortunate you will be to gain audience with the One King, honored be his name. Once you listen to him speak, you will throw off your doubts and join our glorious cause. Maybe soon, I'll see the two of you commanding patrols!" With a gurgly laugh, he waved them along the road and up into the next reach of forest.

Barely had they passed the first few trees, though, before Sunbright flung the red-painted pass by the side of the road and scanned the woods to either hand. "I reckon the south side will—"

Greenwillow cut him off. "What are you doing? Are

you mad?" She bent and retrieved the pass, blowing chaff off the wet paint.

"What?" Sunbright snapped back. "*Me* mad? You don't believe that chip of bark will protect us, do you?"

"Of course I do! That orc might be starry-eyed and dense as an oak tree, but he's honest enough. And he's empowered to issue passes, and now we've got one! So we don't need to skulk through the woods anymore, and so lose time. We can hie straight to Tinnainen."

"Listen to yourself!" Sunbright waved his hands in frustration. "An honest orc? Orcs can't be trusted, starry-eyed or not! Nor can most 'civilized' men, for that matter."

"Nor any men at all, say the elves. Think, frost-brain! We failed to slip past an orc patrol this far from Tinnainen. The closer we get, the thicker the patrols! We can't skulk any farther through the woods. Furthermore, if we tried and got caught, we'd likely be executed as spies. So we have no choice but to march down the middle of the road—as we've every right to do, after all—with this pass pinned to my breast."

"Save yourself the trouble!" Sunbright grabbed his hair, pulling on his topknot. "Just prop your sword in the road and put *that* against your breast! Better to fall on your own sword than go down to a dozen hacks from bloodthirsty orcs."

"I won't argue." And with that, Greenwillow spun about and tramped off down the road. Sunbright called after her, then yelled, then swore, and finally trotted to catch up.

He waved his hands at the openness above and to either side of them. "I still say this is stupid."

"Save your breath for walking, human."

* * * * *

Their new status as legal delegates to the One King was tested about noon. Climbing a steep road, they ran into a patrol of orcs coming down the ruts. Human and elf froze and waited nervously, Greenwillow's hand clearly showing the pass.

The five orcs pulled abreast of them, then shuffled around until Sunbright felt the hair on his neck and arms rise. He anticipated his last sensation would be the back of his skull caving in. But one of the orcs snatched up the chip of bark, studied the spider mark, then gruffly handed it back. Snarling at the others, they passed on without a word.

Sunbright let out a long breath.

"*Now* do you believe me?" Greenwillow glared with gray-green eyes.

"Yes. You were right and I was wrong. But glory to Garagos, being a diplomat is harder than being a fighter!"

And so they traveled for two more days. They slept two nights in the woods and, when closer to the city, spent one night at an inn. The place looked perfectly normal, for all that orcs and orcish men hung around outside sipping weak ale and bragging crudely of their conquests, sexual, battlefield, and otherwise. Inside, the human proprietor and his wife maintained business as usual. Too usual, in fact. They conspicuously acted as if nothing were wrong and there weren't a horde of orcs within spitting distance. Attempts to draw them into conversation went nowhere, and all the time they displayed smiles so tight Sunbright thought their faces would crack. But the elf and barbarian bought a passable meal and good brown ale, the harvest having just passed, and slept on pallets on the common room floor.

So it was that, finally, they came within sight of Tinnainen. It occupied a high plane almost devoid of trees, and the rocky road wended right to its front gates. Another road crossed the main one, and past the city steeper foothills gave way to distant mountains. In this direction, Tinnainen was the first or last city along the road, a fairish size but tiny compared to Dalekeva, yet it served as a market for whole communities scattered through the mountain range. Again, there was a small town surrounding the gray-walled city, which by fresh paint and new stonework showed it had been reinforced for defense, with catapults and ballistae on the largest flat-roofed building.

In the distance, crofters' homes were scattered in fertile pockets, but there was no farmland to speak of, for the land was stony and broken. It was sheep and goat country, and the smell of the pens by the roadside swept Sunbright up in a wave of nostalgia that almost smothered him. Too, the weather reminded him of home, for it had turned colder at this higher elevation, and clouds meshed and clashed over the mountains, churning the sky first blue and then gray. A shrill wind came and went, sucking around his bare legs. He couldn't help think that Talos, god of the tempests, was telling him to go back, go back.

The gates stood open and were thronged by orcs who largely ignored the traffic. In such a small city, everyone would know everyone, even the occupiers knowing the occupied. But the guards perked up quickly enough when the two strangers approached. Greenwillow showed her pass, explaining she desired an audience with the One King. Sunbright watched the traffic, which consisted mostly of humans going about their business. The people of Tinnainen, as in many small communities, resembled one another in sporting narrow, pointed jaws and beetling brows. But they seemed content enough with the orcish army occupation, buying and selling and gossiping. From a tavern Sunbright heard the sound of men singing, and occasionally a woman's voice joining in. It can't be too cursed a place, he found himself thinking, but he would still have liked to question one of the locals for a few minutes in a quiet corner.

An orc captain took Greenwillow's pass and detached two soldiers to escort her somewhere. The orcs spoke among themselves in a grunting, gargling language that sounded like someone choking. Sunbright watched Greenwillow's eyes. He'd neglected to ask her if she spoke the language, but read in her face that she did, for she followed the exchanges with feigned indifference. So the ignorant barbarian took his cues from her and stayed close on her left side, for she fought right-handed.

Tramping through the crowded streets, Sunbright looked for signs of oppression and found none. Whatever the One King's plans, he'd kept a rein on pillage and rape. They soon arrived at what Sunbright thought of as the city palace, entered a small side door, and squeezed into a room barely larger than an alcove.

The guards left them to a human clerk, and Sunbright breathed easily again. But soon he found himself missing the orcs. The clerk was a fussy, irascible woman who questioned them endlessly as to their mission.

"I told you thrice now," Greenwillow finally snapped, "I'm a delegate from the High Elves of Cormanthyr, here to see the One King!"

"And I've told you, elf, the king is a busy man! He

doesn't admit every saucy snippet that marches in here! Give me the missive to read, and *I'll* decide if it warrants the king's attention!"

Greenwillow cursed under her breath in elven, but handed over the missive, which Sunbright now saw for the first time. It was a wide and lumpy sheet of old parchment, much scraped and curled, folded thrice and sealed with blue wax with a simple sigil. With no pomp whatsoever, the clerk jerked her thumb under the wax and snapped the seal, uncrinkled the parchment, and read for a long time.

Finally she reread a section, then folded the missive shut. "I see. Wait here." She heaved her massive butt off a bench and passed through a wooden door.

" 'Kings think they rule, while clerks really do,' is a saying at court." Greenwillow sighed and studied the ceiling, reaching up and fingering dust along a beam.

Sunbright drummed his fingers idly, went to a shuttered window in the wall, and peeked between the slats. "What if the king . . . Garagos!"

His shout was drowned by an inrushing wave of orcs. They carried not studded clubs but hardwood batons, and wore red-and-black tunics and steel helmets and breastplates and greaves. There seemed to be a hundred of them, and they stampeded into the tiny room like a herd of mad buffalo. Before Sunbright or Greenwillow could even draw steel, the wave smashed into them, plowed them into a wall, drove them under feet and greaves and pounding batons. Sunbright was literally smothered under a ton of gray flesh and bright steel, and blows crashed, like an avalanche, on his head. He heard Greenwillow shriek just once. Then the lights went out.

* * * * *

Sunbright awoke abruptly and, remembering the attack, reached out to stop the invading orcs, lost his balance, and toppled off a bunk onto the floor.

Groggy, he crouched on hands and knees, listened and smelled and peered around.

He was in a room no bigger than a hayrick. A wooden door studded with iron spikes filled one wall; a tiny, barred window marked another. A wooden bunk with straw-stuffed ticking and a bucket were the room's only furnishings. Light from the window bounced off fresh whitewash.

A jail cell. The words came to him from tales he'd heard, for he'd never seen one. Indeed, he hadn't been in nine different buildings in his entire life. He'd spent almost every day outdoors.

Then he recalled what jails were for. With a choked cry, he scrambled up and pushed at the door, for he couldn't pull it open; there was no handle. Heedless, he threw his shoulder against the door until the iron spikes were tipped with blood. Failing there, he ran to the bars, grabbed and yanked and pulled. But the bars were thicker than his wrists. The view outside showed only another wall.

Howling, he grabbed the bunk and used it as a ram to batter first the door, then the window bars. But the crude bed was made of lightweight pine and soon cracked. Heedless, he smashed it to splinters that lodged in his hands.

Confined for the first time in his life, Sunbright, child of the tundra and the steppes, went berserk. He screamed and ranted and banged on doors and windows and walls until the whitewash was spattered with blood. And still he pounded and shrieked, all through the afternoon and long into the night.

Chapter 10

Orc and human guards found the barbarian lying on the floor of his cell. Punctures and scrapes and crusted blood covered him from head to toe, and for a moment they feared he'd killed himself. An orc guard rolled back the human's eyelid, jammed his thumb into the eye, and felt the prisoner squirm. Grunting, four soldiers lugged him upstairs.

Sunbright came to when dropped into a tub of scalding hot water. Blubbering, lashing out, he was restrained by firm hands and gentle reassurances. Opening his sore eyes, he found himself in the grip of two dark servingwomen dressed in damp linen shifts that clung to their bodies. The shifts each had a small red hand painted on the front.

Sunbright lay half in and half out of a small bathtub. "I . . . I don't understand." His voice was raspy and raw from screaming.

"Rest, good sir. Be at ease. Let us attend you, and

soon the One King will explain all."

Dizzy, groggy, still not at full strength, Sunbright gave himself up to their ministrations. Gently they washed and dried him, combing his golden hair and pulling it back into a topknot. Then they bandaged his hurts, most of which were self-inflicted, and fed him cakes and ale. They dressed him in a soft smock of light blue, painted with a red hand on the front, and slippers. Lastly, gingerly, they insisted he don silvery manacles. The barbarian refused, and argued, and finally pleaded in a way that amazed and shamed him, but the servingwomen were firm: he couldn't appear before the One King unless shackled.

"The One King? I'm to meet him?" Solemn nods answered.

Only the king could get him out of this mess—whatever it was—so, reluctantly, he extended his arms. The handcuffs and chain were cold, and glistened. With a shock, the barbarian realized they were silver, not steel. "Curious, this king's customs," he muttered.

Bidding the servants thanks, Sunbright gave himself over to the castle guards. These were unusually tall and upright orcs and a smattering of men, all in the steel soup-bowl helmets and breastplates and greaves and tunics of black edged with red. None of them spoke as Sunbright was escorted down wide stairs to the main hall.

The barbarian peered over steel helms; the guards were tall, but he was taller. The palace's main hall had plain stone walls, like those of many keeps, but banners and streamers of red and black hung where normally there would be the banners and pennants of enemies defeated in battles. As far as Sunbright knew, the One King had yet to conquer anything except this one tiny city. Courtiers lined the walls, city people and orcs and women dressed to kill, the oddest mix the barbarian had ever seen. There were more folks, guards and clerks and even a few dancing girls, seated along benches and tables flanking the throne. The throne itself was carved from ebony wood, and sported a pennant above it of a red splayed hand. The king looked like a bearded, black-haired man carved from wax. Sunbright waited a long time as the king attended business, making decisions and issuing commands in a flat drone.

Abruptly, the king stood and began to address the crowd. He began, "Fellow Tinnainens, citizens of the First World. Know that by doing my bidding, you cause the wonders of man to increase."

The proud and empty words rolled on for what seemed like hours. It was all fluff as far as Sunbright was concerned. The message was that the people, by obeying every order of the One King implicitly, would be part of some vague new order when he conquered the world. Independent, trained to think for himself—for only the alert survived on the tundra—Sunbright resisted the pettish arguments, but saw the city-born courtiers nodding in unison, as if hypnotized. Perhaps, the barbarian thought, if one listened to this mishmash of fact and fancy long enough, it would make sense.

At last, a plump, grayish man in a gray gown consulted a list, took command of the barbarian, and led him to yet another table staffed by clerks in an alcove at the back of the room.

The man was of middling size, stoop-shouldered, and distracted by his duties. If not for his average size and pompous nature, he would have been imposing with his grayish skin, pouchy jowls, black, burning eyes, and dark hair that formed a deep widow's peak.

In an unctuous voice he proclaimed himself to be

Angriman, the One King's chief minister, which Sunbright interpreted as chief clerk. He apologized for the rough treatment Sunbright had suffered, then asked the barbarian's mission. Simple and direct, Sunbright told the truth: he had accompanied Greenwillow on her mission, and was seeking information on the One King for his employer, who fretted about grain prices.

Angriman frowned, twitched his jowls, pondered, then shook his head and pronounced, "Thank you. The king has already concerned himself with Greenwillow. Sadly, her missive from the High Elves is one of defiance, which is not permitted. She will be held for punishment. You are free to go. We shall return your—"

"Go? Punishment?" Sunbright bristled so his silver chain clittered. Angriman stepped back; orcish guards moved forward. The barbarian's voice rose. "I'm not going anywhere without Greenwillow! And I don't see why she should be punished. She's only the messenger! If you've a quarrel, take it up with the High Elves, wherever the hell they are."

Angriman's jowls quivered as he signaled frantically for the guards, but the barbarian whirled and swung his chains to keep them back. Before they could circle, he trotted into the clear—right down the middle of the hall toward the king's throne.

Now people closed in from all over: clerks, guards, courtiers. But Sunbright yelled over their protests. "Sire! King! You will release my friend Greenwillow if you are a just man! She's done you no harm—" He hissed, for guards clutched his hair and ground the ends of their hardwood batons into his kidneys, all surreptitiously. But they ceased, and the crowd parted, when the king raised his hand, beckoning the tall barbarian forward.

Up close, Sunbright got his first good look at the

king. He appeared to be middle-aged, was unusually tall with handsome features, black hair and beard, and wore a gaudy crown of platinum set with red and black gems and bewinged with silver. The only jarring feature was the monarch's pale, almost sallow skin, which made him stand out amidst his courtiers, who were either sun-dark or gray-skinned.

There was no expression whatsoever on the king's face. No human warmth, no anger at Sunbright's presumption, no sympathy. With his yellow cast, black hair, and deadly calm manner, he reminded Sunbright of a giant hornet transformed into a man, an apt image, since hornets were easily roused and carried deadly stings.

Yet before the king could speak, something flickered at one side of the throne. A beautiful woman with the arching eyebrows and pointed ears of an elf rose from a wooden bench. She wore a garment of rainbow silk that shimmered like mackerel scales. Slim golden chains on thin wrists shackled her to the piece of heavy oak furniture. She smiled at him sadly, but held herself tall and proud. Sunbright blinked, rubbed his eyes with hands bound by clanking chains, and blurted, "Greenwillow?"

Then, from the opposite side, there came another shimmer. A beautiful woman with hair the color of flames, dressed in a gown of the same shade, sat close to the throne, her legs crossed saucily, her red mouth smiling slyly. Sunbright was even more boggled by this vision, but managed to keep from saying aloud the name that burst into his mind. Ruellana? *Here?*

The king spoke, his tone of voice as flat as his face. "You too, underling, now give offense. Such is not permitted in the lands of the One King—"

"Sire," interrupted the barbarian. The king was so surprised he sat back on his throne, hands on its intricately carved ebony arms. Sunbright was flummoxed to find the two women he cherished most here and was nervous about addressing the king in such a fashion, but he pressed on, regardless. After all, they could only behead him once. "If I might interrupt, sire. Greenwillow came only to deliver a message from her superiors. You yourself must send forth messengers throughout the lands, and you would be upset if they came to harm. Kings must communicate with lesser beings to preserve civilization."

That was almost a direct quote from the king's earlier speech. Sunbright had never spoken in public before, not even at the tribal council, but he had a good memory and could spin arguments as well as any man. "If you free her, I will see that she leaves your kingdom immediately. Or, if we have offended you, perhaps you might give us a chance to do penance. A task you need completed, perhaps, or an errand to run. We are both capable and strong."

With the innate drama of a storyteller, the barbarian crossed his arms before him as if saluting the king, then snapped them sideways. His silver shackles shattered in three places. In the crowd of silent courtiers, the *plink* of silver links on flagstones sounded loudly.

"At the very least," Sunbright finished to a rapt audience, "let me suffer the same punishment as the elf-maid. Return us to our cells together." His voice almost broke as he said the last, and his knees trembled, for the fearsome memory of confinement haunted him. He prayed his quivering stomach wouldn't puke up his meager breakfast at the king's feet. Yet he failed to notice that the crowd discerned the truth: this wild man feared imprisonment over death.

The One King, as he had proclaimed himself, sat a long time on his cold throne, staring without blinking,

and again Sunbright thought of a hornet and not a
man. Finally the king signaled for the barbarian to
move backward, and Angriman to come forward. Low
tones conveyed orders, and guards led Sunbright away.

Whirling around, the barbarian glimpsed Greenwillow looking after him with a proud smile. But too,
he saw Ruellana lick her lips and drop a sly wink.

Then he was hustled from the hall.

* * * * *

. This time he was incarcerated, not in a white-
washed jail cell, but in a luxurious suite of rooms on
the top floor of the castle. Couches with pillows filled
the place, painted murals lined the walls, and a bed
heaped high with fluffy pillows invited sleep. While
guards blocked the door and removed his trailing
manacles, serving girls minced in and out, covering a
low table with jugs of wine and silver platters of food.
Sunbright went immediately to the window to stick
his head out and thumped it on some invisible shield.
So this was a cell too, despite the luxury and fine view
of the city of Tinnainen and the mountains beyond.
The door was just as solid as the one in the dungeon.

It took all Sunbright's courage not to batter his raw
fists and sore shoulders against the door and walls and
window shields. But he'd tried that last night for hours,
for naught. If, he argued to himself, he and Greenwillow were to get out of this place alive, he had to restrain
himself, harbor his strength, and think his way clear.

So, semi-resigned, he sat on a couch, tore a wing
off a chicken, buttered black bread, and ate and
drank ravenously.

Until a slim pair of hands dropped over his eyes,
and a familiar voice giggled, "Guess who?"

Reacting as if to an attack, the barbarian grabbed

both hands and yanked. A slender female form catapulted over his head and crashed onto the table, scattering crockery and silverware and wine. The young
man let go of the slender wrists in astonishment.
"Ruellana?"

"Ooh," the girl groaned. Rubbing her back, which
arched her breasts nicely, she wiggled off the table,
then slipped cool arms around Sunbright's shoulders. "I mean, oooh, you're so strong!"

"Ruellana . . . how . . . where . . . ?" He couldn't
even frame a coherent question. "How in the name of
Mystryl did you get—"

"Hush, love." She planted red lips on his, chewed
at his mouth hungrily.

No, Sunbright thought, this wasn't real. It was
trouble. Whatever Ruellana was, she wasn't a simple
farm girl who'd gotten lost in the forest a hundred
leagues from here. To travel that distance and be
here in Tinnainen, she would have to either have
magic or be a magical creature. She was a mage, or
succubus, or witch, or nymph—not to mention the
One King's consort in the One King's castle.

With a groan, he pushed her away. "Wait! Ruellana,
how did you get here? Tell me, before I go mad!"

"Oh, but I'm mad too," she breathed warmly into
his face. Her green eyes shimmered before him like
spinning jade orbs of enchantment. "Mad for you!
I've worried so, Sunbright! I'm so glad you came to
rescue me!" Her tongue tickled his lips. Still he
spluttered, but she only smiled. "You don't like
kisses there? How about . . ."

A warning clanged in the young man's mind, a
premonition that should have sent him running in a
blind panic. But he was helpless as she plastered her
warm curves against him and his body responded in
the ultimate betrayal.

Well, he thought philosophically, he'd survived the last time.

* * * * *

After an afternoon with Ruellana, Sunbright found himself reluctant to leave the comfort of the bed. Ruellana brushed her hair in front of a bronze mirror, then blew him a kiss. "I'll be back quick as I can."

Rising, he snagged her arm. "Wait. I must have answers. It's not possible you're here. I mean, it is, obviously, but—"

"Silly!" she chided. "I came through a secret panel." A touch to a painted mural made a wooden wall inset swing inward. A black staircase descended from the opening. Sunbright gaped while the girl slipped inside. "Later, love. Be good!" Then, before he could grab her, she pulled the tiny door shut in his face.

Growling with frustration, the barbarian inspected the panel from every angle, tugging at the edges until he chipped the paint, banging on it lightly at first, then harder.

Curiosity warred with caution, but finally the former won. Plying a carving knife, he dug away at the corner of the mural, destroying a pond painted with placid swans, until he could insert his finger into the hole. An inch inside, he felt rough stone. Wondering, he gouged away a knight's black chest in the middle of the panel. He found rough stone behind it, too.

No staircase.

Ruellana had slipped through solid stone.

* * * * *

Sunbright was napping when the door rattled and four guards came to escort him away. Again he was taken to the rear of the throne room and made to wait. Though sundown was near, the One King still sat at his throne dispensing wisdom and justice. It was eerie, Sunbright thought, the man's icy calm. He wanted to ask the guards if the king ever left his throne to eat or piss, but decided against it.

Another speech came and went; then Angriman took charge and escorted the barbarian into the presence of the king. Again Greenwillow gave him a brave smile, but it quickly turned into a frown as he was distracted by a simpering, red-clad Ruellana.

Without preamble, the One King proclaimed, "I have a task for you. Fulfill it, and you and the elf Greenwillow may depart unmolested." Muck up and die, Sunbright mentally finished. "There lies a cave south of here. Within dwells the dread red wyrm Wrathburn. In the wyrm's possession is a great book crowned with a ruby and laden with great and arcane lore. Fetch the book."

Wyrm? Sunbright's brain numbed at the word. Dimly he heard Greenwillow gasp. Did the king mean . . .

As Angriman towed him to the back of the hall, the barbarian followed like a wooden doll dragged by one arm. *Wyrm?* Did he mean . . .

"You're a lucky man," Angriman told him at the rear alcove. "You, like your unfortunate friend the elf, offered the king defiance, which is not tolerated in this kingdom. But the king cherishes forthright virtues such as honesty and bravery and loyalty, even misguided loyalty to a comrade. You're very lucky."

"When he said wyrm," Sunbright finally got out, "did he mean . . ."

"Dragon, yes. Wrathburn is the great red dragon that's recently made a home in the Windswept Mountains. He's known to be unusually cruel, rapacious, and powerful, which is why no one's challenged him yet, though he's accumulated a vast hoard. The opening to his cavern is not far from here. That's how the king, who is himself a mighty mage, learned of this book. He could sense its mystic aura even at this distance. The tome holds the collected wisdom of an ancient, vanished race who predate humans. The king wishes that knowledge and has chosen you to fetch it for him. You're a very, very lucky young man. And if you can fight as well as you talk, you'll succeed."

Sunbright managed a weak "Thank you," before the guards escorted him upstairs. They largely dragged him, for his legs had suddenly failed.

* * * * *

That night the barbarian lay abed, nowhere near asleep. He tried to sort out events in his mind and figure out how he'd come to this pass. He didn't know much about kings, but it didn't seem fair that this One King could order him hither and thither at a whim. But then, he'd learned early that life wasn't fair.

There came a tiny click. He sat up, thrust out his hand, and felt a warm form covered by thin cloth.

Ruellana giggled and creaked onto the bed, running hot hands over his chest and downward. "You're so clever, Sunbright. You'll escape and make the king look a perfect fool! But we'll be long gone by then."

"Hunh?" Sunbright had a thousand questions to ask her—about secret panels and if she was truly the king's consort and exactly *what* she was—but it was hard to think when she was touching him so. "What are you talking about? Escape? I'll walk out of here a free man!"

Her roving hands suddenly stilled. "You and I, *we* escape! I'll meet you down the road. There's an inn . . ."

"But I have to fight a dragon!"

Nearly invisible in the darkness, she drew back, touching no part of him. "That's madness. Surely you agreed to pursue this book only to get out of the castle alive!"

"No, I agreed to seek the book to save—"

"Greenwillow?" Her voice dripped frost. Maybe Ruellana was a real woman after all, the man reflected. "That elf is useless, thin as a rake and cold as a fish. Elves don't mate with humans. They toy with them or hunt them. Surely even you know that. And no man of any stripe can battle a dragon. That's the stuff of fables. The reality is you'll go into that cave and never come out, except as a pile of steaming dragon shit."

Sunbright held his head and tried to ignore the image. It was true; he'd pictured that and worse the night long. Only enchanted knights with magic lances and mighty war-horses battled dragons. He didn't even own a shield. Of all the monsters, dragons were the worst. Even tiny wyverns no bigger than squirrels could burn your hand off, it was said. And of all dragons, red ones were the most wicked. But . . .

He tried to explain. "I've no choice. Greenwillow and I are bonded by blood. Even if I survived by leaving her to be executed, I could never call myself a warrior again, or even a fighter. I'd be nothing, have nothing."

"You'd have me, every day and every night." Ruellana *tsked* in the dark. "There are times when even the greatest of warriors must turn his back on foolish bravery."

Flopping back against the headboard, exhausted and confused, he replied, "This is not one of those times."

Suddenly his arms were full of warm, nearly naked woman. "Oh, please run away with me!" she pleaded. "You've no idea how horrid my life is! The king is a fiend, a monster in disguise! He beats and starves me, lashes me with a whip until the blood flows! I've waited so long, and only you—"

Dazzled by all this woman-flesh, Sunbright's hands roamed from her smooth shoulders to the inviting curve of her buttocks. But his nearly forgotten brain had been dragged into the fight now, and he mused, "Funny, your back is as smooth as a cat's. No scars, no scabs . . ."

Abruptly the woman tore away. The pleading stopped. Coolly, she asked, "You'd choose Greenwillow over me?"

Part of him growled, part pleaded. "It's not that. I said I'd enter the dragon's cave, and I shall. What happens then lies in the hands of the gods."

One thing Sunbright knew about heroes: they were simple. Leaving mysteries to others, they made decisions, then acted on them. They never waffled or backed down.

Of course, often they died.

"Have it your way," Ruellana said simply. Before Sunbright could grab her in the dark, she slipped away. Seconds later he heard the secret door—that was not a secret door—click shut.

* * * * *

Three days later, in a cold drizzle, an orc commander squinted and pointed at a narrow split in a monstrous boulder, then higher to a distant ledge marking a cave. There were nine stout fighters here, orcs and men, but the commander kept his voice low. "This cleft marks the beginning of a trail up to the cave mouth. You'll enter here. In a while we expect to see you reach that ledge and pass within. If you don't, we'll come hunting you, and then you'll crawl inside with both knees hamstrung. Is that clear?"

Sunbright nodded glumly. This squad had "escorted" him through the southern foothills and up the Windswept Mountains to see he didn't run off. It had not been an unpleasant trip, but its purpose made for uncomfortable silences. On one hand, the soldiers admired his stoic bravery; on the other, they thanked their gods that it was Sunbright who went and not them. Now the commander's short tusks creased his lips in a smile of gallows humor. "Good luck."

"Thank you." And shifting his scabbard at his back, Sunbright entered the cleft and climbed.

Grabbing with hands and sliding feet, he found the wet trail so steep it was like climbing drizzle into the roiling sky. He wore his own clothes and gear, more or less: a new linen shirt the color of a pale sky, bearskin jerkin with the fur shorn even, leather baldric, and iron-ringed and strapped boots with sturdy hobnail soles. He carried Dorlas's warhammer in a new holster on his belt, a waterskin, and haversack. But only Harvester was slung at his back, for no one in the castle thought he needed a bow and arrows. He knew they were right. This would be sword work or nothing.

Probably nothing, echoed an errant thought.

In short order, he reached a lip, which he crawled over, and a smell hit him like a slap in the face. A raw, reeking, eye-watering stink that took his breath away. Ducking his head first to catch a breath, he hoisted himself high enough to see.

Only slightly higher, twenty feet or more, was the shelf and cave. Here below the shelf were great, heaped mounds of brown-black gunk that reeked of sulfur and sewage. By luck, rain had dampened the odor, or it probably would have poisoned him.

"Well," grunted the barbarian, "bears don't dung up their caves. Why should dragons?"

Holding his nose, breathing shallowly, he cast about to the right and left and finally found a crack he could follow up to the shelf. He was actually in a hurry, he thought ruefully. Anything to escape this stink. A random thought intruded: now he knew why dragons moved their caves occasionally. Too bad he'd probably never tell anyone.

Picking over an older pile of dung bleached tan by wind and rain, he saw something glitter amidst the dried clumps. Kicking with his foot, he overturned a fluted helmet—with a brown-stained skull still inside. Ruellana's words about leaving the cave only as dragon shit came to mind and wouldn't go away.

Still, he had no choice but to persevere, ignoring the idiocy of what he was about to do. On shaky legs and trembling hands, Sunbright crawled up the crack and reached the fabled shelf.

And the yawning cave behind.

The cave mouth was tall enough to take a ship under full sail, wide enough to admit spread wings. After about twenty feet, the interior grew dark. From inside came twin smells, nauseating as they tried to overpower one another: a hot, brassy stink like rust burning off an iron pan, and the sweet, cloying, throat-gagging odor of rotting flesh. Holding his breath, the barbarian detected the faintest tiny hint of a sound, as of wood being sawed: snoring.

Shaking all over, Sunbright nearly sliced off his own ear clumsily drawing Harvester from its back scabbard. He took a step, then remembered to turn and wave at the puny orcs and men in the middle distance. They waved once, and hurried away.

Crouching in the icy rain, Sunbright admitted the cave would at least be warm and dry. Funny though, how the old legends never mentioned the heroes were afraid. Perhaps, then, he'd never become a legend. Just another skull in a heap of dragon dung.

And with those cheery thoughts, he walked in.

Advancing a short inch at a time, Sunbright had too much time to think. As a wilderness-trained hunter, he knew he could sneak through territory so not even foxes would scent him. But dragons were said to have acute senses, could even read minds. Supposedly they could hear a potential thief just *thinking* of robbery at fifty leagues. He didn't believe it, but that in itself wasn't much help.

Of course, he rattled in his head, he needn't actually *slay* the dragon. He had only to enter its cave and retrieve—steal—a big book with a ruby in the cover and get away safely.

Even if the dragon was asleep, the chances of his sneaking in successfully were remote at best. So . . . if he couldn't sneak in, or leave without the orcs hunting him down and flinging him back inside crippled, or kill the beast, what was left?

Not much.

He stopped, and waited, and wondered what to do. To advance and die seemed the only option.

So, how to die? Creeping like a rat? Or charging with sword outthrust and a battle cry ringing loud?

Would he be burned to a crisp, bitten in half, or simply be crushed by a scaled claw, like a demented mouse rushing a cat?

Then a rustle sounded behind him. And a voice.

"Sunbright! Wait!"

Chapter 11

The barbarian turned and squinted up to where something fluttered in the round, gray rim of outlined sky.

"Oh, it's you."

The raven cocked its feet, folded its wings, plunked to a landing, and clacked its black beak. "Stinks. Where are you bound?"

"Why should I tell you?" Sunbright's emotions were churning inside him, and anger boiled up. "Who failed to tell me when bandits were about to attack my party and ended up killing three of us?"

The bird tipped its head to present first one, then the other beady eye. "I can't know everything."

"You flew right over the road! You could have warned me!"

"I told you where to find that four-prong buck in the birches, did I not?"

The barbarian piffed. "A hunting dog could have

done that! I expect a magic raven to reveal more than the weather!"

Ignoring the criticism, the bird pointed its beak toward the back of the cave. "Why?"

Sunbright sighed, anger winking out, despair returning. He related the story of the One King holding Greenwillow.

Oddly, the raven commented on what was, to Sunbright, an inconsequential thing. "A book? You're to retrieve a book? With a ruby set in the cover?"

"So what? All the treasure of the world might be in there, for all the good it will do me. What color are rubies, anyway?"

The bird muttered something that sounded to the barbarian like "damsys" then croaked, "Red. What do you know of this dragon, Wrathburn?"

"It's a big red dragon packed to the eyeballs with dung." And armor and bones, he added mentally. The young man cast a nervous glance over his shoulder, but heard only a tick in the snoring. At least the stink was lessening, or else he was adjusting to it. He'd probably smell like death and dragon till the day he died.

"Wrathburn . . ." The raven hopped, nailed a cockroach from the stone floor, and gulped it down with his head back. "Very strong, devilishly wicked, inordinately vain, as I recall. And not too bright."

"Bright? You mean its scales?"

"No, its intellect!" groused the raven. "You're an apt match for it."

"What?" Sunbright warily watched the darkness for hints of advancing dragon. With his luck, he'd get stomped on without ever being seen. "That doesn't sound very helpful. How about a soft spot, you know, a white scale where a knitting needle would penetrate? Near his tail, perhaps?"

The raven shook his beak. "Sorry, no. But Wrathburn

does have a reputation for being vain. In a man, that's usually the most damning quality. More men have lost kingdoms to vanity than to any other vice. Remember the lesson you learned on the road from Dalekeva."

In a burst of feathers, the raven hopped into the air and plunged away, out the yawning cave mouth into the drizzle.

"Hey, wait! What lesson . . . ?"

Sunbright clamped a hand over his mouth. Here he was shouting like an idiot in the marketplace while, within spitting distance, a dragon slept.

Or . . .

Silent, hardly breathing, he listened.

The snoring had stopped.

Desperately, Sunbright tried to think. The road from Dalekeva? Walking to Tinnainen? It had been a long road with many minor adventures. The only true danger he'd faced was when he and Greenwillow had bumped into patrols of orcs. Of course, he'd wanted to skulk through unseen, but she'd insisted the quick and sensible way was just to clutch their pass and march down the middle of the road. . . .

A while later, Sunbright came swinging down a slope, sword at his shoulder, whistling jauntily. The floor of the cave was smooth from a dragon dragging its iron-hard belly scutes along the floor. The barbarian was guided by the flickering flame that welled from the nostrils of the dragon as it slept—or pretended to—and by the reflected light from the monstrous pile of gold, silver, gemstones, and other precious artifacts that made up the dragon's bed. Sunbright couldn't guess the treasure's value, but the hoard rose above his head in some places. The cave sprawled in many directions, the distances lost, but the treasure pile had been scooped out in the middle to make a resting place for the dragon, like a kitten in a pile of mittens.

The dragon was immense. Its head was longer than a rowboat, frilled with horns like stalactites, its neck like a stone bridge, its back like a low hill. Details were indistinct, but its scales seemed as big as a man's hand, overlaid so tightly they bristled outward. The beast's pointed ears drooped at the tips, and its nostrils were flame-blackened around the edges. Sunbright stopped and planted himself right in front of those nostrils and tried not to think about how hot they were.

His whistling trailed off, like birdsong fading into the forest. He bit down on his quivering stomach and willed his legs to stay steady. His bravado had almost failed him as he entered this vast cavern, for he'd passed the rotted remains of a dozen corpses of all sizes, including endless fragments wedged in cracks to rot to nothingness. But at least he'd gotten this far, which was farther than those unfortunates. And he had a ghost of a plan, which was something.

Still, those nostrils were as big as caldrons, and the flame that winked within hotter than any forge. He could feel the heat a dozen feet back. He hated to see the flames well out of that awesome nose, but on the other hand, when the dragon breathed in, the cave became pitch-black, which was even more disconcerting.

Then the slanted yellow eyes opened, and Sunbright knew what it was to be a mouse being stared down by a cat. The dragon's black pupils were bigger than his head.

Yet he held his ground and boldly called "Good day," his voice a bit shrill.

Without lifting its head, the dragon opened jaws that could swallow a man whole. "You pick a painful but noteworthy suicide, fleshy morsel." The rumble of Wrathburn's voice, like a stone boat over a wooden bridge, made Sunbright's breastbone tingle.

"I've been sent by the One King to slay you!" he announced in what he hoped were cheerful tones.

The dragon moved like a glacier, rearing upward to tower over Sunbright and better aim his nostrils. The barbarian heard plinks and clatters as jewels and coins cascaded from the beast's scaly hide in a precious rain. The dragon inhaled deeply, like a blast furnace being stoked.

"But after seeing you, I cannot even imagine harming such a beautiful creature!"

Wrathburn gulped as he swallowed fire. "Beautiful?"

"Truly!" Sunbright assured him. "Unparalleled beauty and unspeakable magnificence! Never have I beheld such a wonder, and never could I lay a hand on such a fearsome, awe-inspiring being! You are truly the most marvelous creature in all of Toril! Why, you take my breath away!"

Confused, the dragon mulled over the compliments. He wasn't used to flattery. Screaming, begging, crying, whining, yes, but not compliments.

Still alive, neither flinders nor cinders, the barbarian dropped his sword dramatically and slathered on the praise with a trowel. "As long as I live I shall sing the praises of this most magnificent sight, the glory and grandeur of the king of all skies, the noblest creature in creation, who looks down upon the world with his fearsome gaze, knowing every being to be his inferior!"

Summoning every scrap of story and song he'd ever heard, the young man waxed eloquent for what seemed like hours, until his voice began to creak and his tongue grew numb and stumbled. And repeated itself, at which point Wrathburn grew restless and began to swish his tail back and forth amid the gems and gold. He wanted new praise, an endless stream of it. But Sunbright knew eventually he'd run out of words and then be dinner. So, drawing a mental breath, the barbarian took a leap into unknown territory.

"But oh, the perfidy of the One King!" Sunbright threw his arm across his eyes in mock horror. "To think, to think!"

"Think?" rumbled Wrathburn. He twitched his tail harder, flattening a suit of silver armor. He didn't want to hear about some king, but about himself. "You mentioned this king before. What about him?"

"To think he would send me to slay *you!*" wailed Sunbright. "How could one man be so heartless as to think of assaulting something so proud, so famous! Why, better to command that I put out the sun than cause the world to lose the glory of Wrathburn the Magnificent! I would become the most hated man in existence! And yet . . ."

"Yet *what?*" Flames flickered all around the dragon's snout, throwing black shadows across the crags of his face.

"Why, the One King must be jealous! That's it! He's sat too long on his throne, accumulated too much power, and has come to think he's the equal of Wrathburn. Consumed as this petty man is with jealousy, he's sent me, the most insignificant of warriors, to slay the light of the world! How cruel, how callous, how blind of this lowly beast-man, to challenge the might, the divine right of rule inherent in the noble breast of All-High Wrathburn. . . ." The barbarian trailed off, panting. He would have killed for a slug of ale; his tongue was practically hanging out.

Fortunately, Wrathburn took his cue. Pointing a long, whiskery snout at the distant cave mouth, he asked, "Where lives this One King?"

Sunbright pounced. "I can point the way!"

"Then do." Picking up a foot as large as the One

King's throne, the dragon crushed coins and made the cavern shake, jarring Sunbright's bones.

Scurrying out of the way, the young man took one last gasp and called, "There is one more little thing, if it please your greatness?"

The head swiveled to aim nostrils like matched volcanoes at the human. "Yes?"

"A book."

* * * * *

Eyes closed, Sunbright gasped for breath and hung on with all his might. He didn't look down.

Hurricane winds tore at his face, yanked his topknot, whistled in his ears, and pressed his tackle so hard against his body it dented his skin. By the time they landed, he'd be blind, deaf, and bald. If his arms didn't fall off first. As long as he lived—which at this point he figured might be a little past sunset—he'd never even climb to the second story of a building.

For he was miles in the air, soaring faster than the wind. He perched standing on Wrathburn's neck, which was as slippery as sleet-slick flagstones. Both arms were wrapped tight around one of the horns rimming the dragon's frill. After careful consideration, he'd chosen this one for the craggy folds in the scaly skin at the base of the horn. These handholds, such as they were, had seemed adequate at the time. Now his fingernails ripped from his flesh as he tried to hang on, he pressed his face into the crook of his elbow to breathe, and he tensed his legs to the breaking point to remain in one spot. If he slid an inch, he thought, even a half-inch, he'd be flung into space like straw from a barn swallow's beak. And the last—and only—time he'd dared to look, the mountains below looked like gray smudges in a tablecloth.

Sunbright hadn't meant to be here. He'd hoped to "point the way" to Tinnainen, then run like hell over hill and dale to get back to what remained of the city. Trotting and walking without stopping to sleep, resting only occasionally, he had reckoned it would take a long day. But the dragon had a different idea about what "pointing the way" meant.

Wrathburn had been gracious enough to allow this poor mortal to ride his neck into battle. Never before, in the eons of his existence, had the dragon allowed such a thing. Usually, he explained, he dealt with average men by biting them in half. Troublesome types, knights and paladins and such, he often swallowed whole, armor and all, that they might awake in his churning stomach and so die slowly, proving their folly. Sunbright had smiled tightly and marveled aloud at the dragon's creativity, brilliance, and droll sense of humor, as befit a godlike being. Then, as commanded, he'd hastily grabbed a handhold, felt a rippling run like an earthquake, and watched the earth—and his lunch—recede until the mountain was a mere pinhead below him.

And the blasted dragon didn't even *fly* well! He didn't swoop like a hawk or glide like an albatross or soar like an eagle. He pumped his short red wings up and down like a drunk in a saw pit, like a demented duck, like a lopsided windmill. Dragons weren't meant to fly at all, the human judged. They were an anomaly in the air, just as bats were winged mice who flailed the air just to stay aloft. And all this flying must be giving the beast a tremendous appetite.

But he might never know. Chilled to the marrow and fatigued beyond endurance, Sunbright felt his numb fingers slipping. He'd reach earth before the dragon ever did. It might be worth it to get out of this damnable roaring wind.

Then the air was warmer, rushing upward. Sunbright erred by opening his eyes and saw a square lump like a child's sand castle. Then the dragon struck the earth with a gut-wrenching wallop that shook both of them. The barbarian unclawed his hands and crashed onto the rocks with his shoulder. For a moment, he hurt so much all over he didn't care if the dragon trod on him. Then he realized the great ruby-studded book was wedged against his back, grinding his kidneys, and he recalled his mission.

He'd done it. Maybe he'd be a legend after all.

Staring upward while willing life and warmth into his frozen muscles, he saw the sky suddenly occluded by a whiskered, horned head. The dragon peered down into his face, so close Sunbright breathed sulfur but dared not cough.

"Uh, thank you for the thrilling ride, O wise and beautiful Wrathburn!

"How looks this One King?" The earth shivered under Sunbright. "Humans appear much alike to me."

"He is tall and yellow-faced and wears a long robe and that wondrous crown I spoke of." Wrathburn had listened intently when Sunbright talked of the platinum and gem-studded masterpiece. "He is usually to be found in the biggest room in the largest building in the city." The barbarian levered himself to one elbow, inadvertently banging Wrathburn's snout with the other. "You can see the roof of the building above that wall!"

Yellow eyes pinned Sunbright like a butterfly. "You do me great service to warn me of this viper so close to my bosom. You will wait here to accompany me back to my cave for your reward. Look forward, lucky human, to a long and illustrious career as songsinger for Wrathburn the All-High!"

Sunbright's face split into a grin like that of a dried skull. "Joy!"

Then the dragon tromped off, tail dragging a furrow, like a ship come aground in a hurricane.

Rolling upright, Sunbright wiped his face with both hands and took what seemed his first breath of the day. He watched as the dragon thundered toward Tinnainen. The beast had landed on a flat stretch of lichen-covered rocks and tufted grass not far from the road. Sheep and goat pens lined the road on both sides, and the animals sent up a pitiful bleating at the sight and smell of the giant predator. From the small town surrounding the city, terrified homeowners either fled down the road, into the hills, or toward the gates of the city, shoving orcish and human guards aside to gain sanctuary. The frightened guards tottered like puppets, some fleeing, some fainting, some dropping to their knees to pray. And all along the gray city walls, Sunbright saw heads pop up to see the dragon, then disappear, only to pop up again. The smart folks, he decided, were seeking the deepest cellars to burrow into.

Whistling as he watched—the dragon's back was as high as the walls—Sunbright hoped the beast would merely take his quarrel to the One King and leave the city unharmed. He hated to think he might be responsible for the deaths of dozens if—

That hope evaporated along with a score of sheep and goats. As Wrathburn passed the pens, he snuffled and blew a firestorm of flame that slaughtered the livestock. Charred, smoking lumps were all that remained, except for an occasional bleating goat, its skin scorched half away. Even the battered corral stakes burned. The barbarian didn't know if Wrathburn was simply being destructive in a mean-spirited way, or if he cooked the animals to eat later. Either way, it seemed Tinnainen was going to pay for harboring the One King, occupied willingly or not. A wail of terror from the folk along the city wall echoed the thought.

But Sunbright had his own worries, his own tasks. Drawing Harvester, he trotted wide behind the dragon to keep out of the beast's line of vision. He had women to rescue, and scores to settle.

There were only three guards at the gates now, two orcs and a human. Trembling, they lifted their pikes as the dragon approached and called, "Halt in the name of the One—"

Wrathburn wheezed, and flames shot from his nostrils. The stone gateposts blackened, the wooden doors ignited, even the granite threshold blistered. The guards shriveled to charred twists dotted with molten metal. Screams sounded inside the gates as people's clothing and the thatch on houses ignited. Terror had come to Tinnainen.

Wrathburn ducked to peer through the gates, his head as high as the stone lintel painted with a red splayed hand. Inserting his snout, the beast lifted. With a groan of grinding stone, the lintel pulled loose of the supporting gateposts. The small flanking towers crumpled like sugar cones. Blocks as big as bushel baskets bounced off the dragon's scaly head, but except for blinking, Wrathburn didn't seem to notice. Growling, the dragon jerked his nose clear, and the whole gate structure collapsed onto the smoldering mess that remained of the One King's guards. More screams sounded within, but they were fading as the people fled out the city's smaller gates.

Sunbright had to get into the city, and his chance came as Wrathburn slowly turned and paced along the city wall. The dragon arched a neck armored with red scales and peered over the barrier, sending more blocks cascading into the muddled streets. At one point he huffed and puffed a jet of flame that billowed high. Obviously someone had offered resistance, or perhaps simply a tempting target.

Sunbright skipped nimbly over the rubble and wreckage of the main gates. At one point his hobnails skidded down a blood-slick surface. The stumble saved his life, for just before him crashed a huge stone block that could have snuffed him like a candle. With a hasty glance upward, he dashed through the crumbling walls into the city proper.

Chaos, not the One King, reigned. Townsfolk were largely gone, having fled to leave the fighting to the soldiers, but here and there ran fat traders who'd rescued their strongboxes and fathers who dragged children. A scorched dog ran between Sunbright's feet, howling. A dozen thatched roofs burned, flinging flaming tendrils of straw and reeds into the sky and swirling into the street. Blocks from the city wall had smashed in roofs, crushed a well, sent market stalls tumbling like dominoes. Like rats spilled from an upset grain sack, looters yanked stalls apart to grab unguarded goods. One thief slashed a knife at a merchant shielding his wife, demanding the man's purse. Loping past, Sunbright kissed the thief across the back of one knee with Harvester's keen blade. Hamstrung, the would-be robber collapsed. "Run for the hills!" yelled the barbarian over his shoulder as he sped on.

The king's palace was a madhouse. Three stories tall and flat-roofed, it was one story higher than the city wall, and this third story was reinforced along that side with ramparts and stations for ballistae and catapults. An orcish general waved his arms and shouted frantically for soldiers to arm a ballista, a giant crossbow. The oncoming Wrathburn watched the activity with bored detachment, as a boy might study ants. At a shout, the ballista's restrainer was cut. A tremendous *pung-clack* resounded, and an arrow nine feet long slashed the air, glanced off Wrathburn's shoulder, and plunged half its length into stony soil.

Hissing, the dragon reared upright like a bear, planted giant talons on the ramparts of the third story, scattering the defenders like teacups, and blasted hellfire in one sweep across the roof.

Sunbright watched all this while peering around the corner of a house that was still standing, for he didn't want Wrathburn to glimpse him. There wasn't even a scream or whimper from the palace roof. If that had been the king's main defense, the battle was over. People and soldiers raced and shoved their way out of the wide doors of the palace, and Sunbright had to wait until the flood stemmed. Sword cocked over his shoulder, the barbarian slipped inside.

Compared to the chaotic streets, the interior of the castle was quiet, most of the defenders on the roof dead. Someone must have left a trapdoor open, for the stink of scorched death wafted down the stairs as Sunbright ran up.

The second floor held the main hall and throne room. As always, the One King occupied the throne. Sunbright wondered if it would be burned from under him. The king calmly addressed a tiny knot of sweating courtiers and orc commanders. Behind the throne, Sunbright glimpsed the rainbow shimmer of a familiar gown.

On his left hand, Sunbright heard a rustling of papers from a clerks' alcove, where Angriman gathered paper and parchment to his bosom as if they'd form a shield against an angry dragon. Sunbright padded into the room as silent as a leopard, yet the minister whirled. Gray-faced and pouchy, he demanded, "What have you done? *What have you done?*"

"Brought you something," said the barbarian evenly. Reaching behind his back, he snapped the rawhide whangs that tied a bundle to his scabbard. Onto the table he tossed a thick book crammed with lumpy vellum pages. It landed with a thump. The ancient, cracked cover sported a ruby as big and evil as a dragon's eye. He added, "Though it's more of a trade, really. Wrathburn wants the king's crown— with his head mounted inside."

The angry man shook all over, spilling papers. "You weren't to bring the dragon here!"

"The king commanded I enter the dragon's lair and retrieve the book. So I have. So I shall take Greenwillow and go." And Ruellana, he added mentally. "Now stand aside or die."

"You'll destroy the dream! You'll leave the world to wallow in chaos and disharmony!"

This was blather taken from the king's speech, and could go on for days. Unwilling to kill an unarmed man, Sunbright edged the minister aside with his sword and strode toward the throne. Courtiers and soldiers parted, some hurrying to the door. Ruellana was not in sight, but Greenwillow rose from her bench, golden shackles still chained to it, and smiled when she saw him. The barbarian nodded formally, both a greeting and a command to wait.

The One King also rose and, for the first time, departed his throne to step onto the flagstones and block the barbarian's path. He was taller than Sunbright had reckoned, especially with his heavy, gaudy crown with backswept wings of silver.

The barbarian held his sword by the pommel and blade. "I fetched your book; now free Greenwillow." And be quick, he thought. Grinding, tearing, stone-rending noises were increasing by the second. The dragon was ripping through the castle as if it were a stale cake, and this was his destination.

Calm as a pillar of ice, the monarch proclaimed, "None may command the One King. Your offense must be punished."

"A real king honors his bargains," spat Sunbright. "Defend yourself!"

The king stood still, hands by his side.

Sunbright didn't know what to think. He hated to kill an unarmed man, but the king had access to any number of weapons in the hands of the nearby courtiers who watched the contest of wills. And Sunbright had given more than fair warning, been overly generous with this oath-breaking snake.

Rearing back, slinging his sword behind him, Sunbright sucked wind, gave a mighty battle cry, and slashed Harvester in a great, glittering arc at the king's neck.

The sharp sword with the arched and hooked tip slammed to a halt against the king's cheek and bounced off, as if Sunbright had hacked at an iron-wood tree.

Hurled off balance by the force of his blow, the barbarian staggered, shuffled his feet, and brought Harvester up in automatic defense. Aghast, Sunbright prayed. What in the name of Mystryl's mysteries . . . ?

The One King had barely moved. No blood appeared at the long cut on his cheek. Instead, dark gray smoke flowed outward.

Courtiers gasped. Soldiers dropped swords.

In the dragged-out silence, with only the rending and booming of falling stone in the background, there came a slow, soft chuckle, as dry as last year's dead leaves.

For the first time, the One King exhibited emotion.

He was laughing. But not properly, head back and shaking, but with the same deadly calm as always. The mouth was like a black slit from which issued the slithering chuckles.

Then, more horror. The king reached strong, corded hands to his face, and dug thick fingernails into his eyebrows below the shining crown. Smoke swirled faster from the wound that was not a wound. People groaned involuntarily as the monarch tugged, then tore the skin from his own face.

Shreds of false skin hung limp from his hands like taffy. But no one noticed, for they stared, pop-eyed, at the smoke-wreathed face.

It was dark gray, shriveled like an old leaf, with wrinkled pits for eyes and mouth, and only slits for a nose . . . and a parchment-wrapped skull.

"Lich!" grunted an orc.

"Lord of the undead!" rasped another.

Fiend, monster, Sunbright's mind reeled off the names. And master trickster and schemer, plying the patience of the dead to work its evil ways amid living men.

Gripped by terror, Sunbright backed involuntarily, his feet clumsy and heavy. Harvester's tip dragged on black marble to strike sparks. There seemed to be only one thought in his mind, and that was to run, hard and fast.

Then all present turned as the rear wall of the castle broke and crumbled. Great blocks of stone crashed down into the hall or fell to clatter outside. Weak sunlight illuminated the room.

Then it was blocked completely by a scaly face and glaring yellow eyes. Smoke spilled from Wrathburn's nostrils as he rumbled, "King! I want *you!*"

Chapter 12

Sunbright backed farther away from the lich king. Fearsome as it was, the threat of the dragon receded. The beast could only destroy his body. A lord of the undead could destroy him utterly, body and soul and being.

The lich that had been the One King seemed to revel in the humans' terror. It raised healthy-looking hands above its hideous, rotted visage and shrilled a mad, screeching laugh. Smoke continued to dribble from the deep cut in the parchment skin of its cheek, but a single swipe of the man-hand sealed the wound.

This was nothing he could fight, Sunbright knew. There was no way to kill something undead. And a lich was the most powerful undead thing of all, it was rumored, an indomitable spirit wedded to an indestructible body, centuries or eons old, perhaps once a true and mighty sorcerer-king in the dim, distant past.

Whatever, attacking the lich would have the same result as attacking the dragon: a senseless and painful death, or worse. In the superstitious turmoil of the barbarian's mind, he feared the lich might simply will him to death with sheer terror.

And the dragon was rumbling, hissing, the lich keening some weird cry or incantation like nails on a slate.

More of the walls collapsed until, looking up, Sunbright saw portions of the apartment he'd occupied above. Plaster and blocks fell like lethal rain. The courtiers and soldiers had finally had enough and raced for the far doors. Seeking only to free Greenwillow and flee, the barbarian bulled his way through them.

The elf threw out her chained hand, shouted something Sunbright couldn't hear over the crash of masonry. Whatever it was, he thought, it would wait until he'd gotten her out.

A strap whisked past his nose, snugged around his throat, and tightened like steel. His wind was cut off, his lungs empty. At his ear, the minister Angriman hissed, "You'd destroy the dream, so I'll destroy you!" He gave the thick leather belt around Sunbright's throat a savage twist.

Backing, Sunbright lashed out with his elbow to ram the man's gut, then stomped to crush the minister's instep under a hobnailed heel. But dumpy, pouchy Angriman must have been a soldier at one time, a good one, and was still tough as oak. Dodging the wild swings, he jerked the barbarian backward until he crashed into the side of the ebony throne. By the time Sunbright thought to stab overhead with his sword, the minister had ducked behind the massive structure. He could strangle his victim without being stabbed.

Sunbright would be out of the fight in a moment anyway, for his vision was blackening like storm clouds. He flailed and kicked, but only managed to shoot a foot from under himself. He fell, hung by the throat. He had his sword but precious little good it would do him. His last image was of Greenwillow, thirty feet away, hopping up and down and making a chopping motion. His eyes must be deceiving him.

How humiliating, to survive a dragon and a lich, only to be killed by a crazed clerk.

Then he got it.

He tried to suck a deep breath and got nothing, gave up, arched his back, aimed as best he could through the red, swirling air, and flung Harvester hard.

Spinning like a birch leaf in autumn, the heavy sword sliced the air and thudded point-first into the heavy oak bench to which Greenwillow was chained. He'd hoped to get the weapon close enough for her to sever the chain's links, but his aim was better than he imagined. Harvester's heavy nose slammed through the links as if they were paper, and Greenwillow was free.

That was all Sunbright saw as the world flooded red and black. Maybe the dragon had finally coughed and blistered him into another world. . . .

Dimly he heard an elven shriek, and the pressure on his throat disappeared. Gagging, he sank onto the floor, found it wet with blood not his own. Immediately a cool hand was tugging him back up. Through a roar like the ocean he heard Greenwillow shout his name. Lumbering to his feet, he draped an arm around her shoulder. He croaked, "Harvest—"

"I've got it!" She hauled him along bodily while her severed chains clanked and his boots dragged. Slowly vision returned, and he could see to walk.

Or run. Greenwillow dashed to the wall the dragon had almost leveled. Sunbright could have reached out and touched the creature's smoking nostrils. Wrathburn rumbled at the lich in a guttural language while the lich shrilled and waggled its arms like a skeleton outraged at being dead. They were arguing, but about what? Possession of the crown? Was that why Wrathburn had, so far, withheld his wrath and burn?

Possibly, for as the two staggered for the far doors, the dragon stopped arguing, snuffled, and filled the room with fire. Smoke and flame exploded around them, and Sunbright threw the unprotected Greenwillow, who wore only a thin silk dress, ahead of him, then landed on her. Over his shoulder he glimpsed the lich, reduced to a true skeleton that slowly collapsed. Angriman, wounded in the head by Greenwillow, was reaching for his master and his dream when his skin turned black and ignited. Then burning paint, wood, cloth, plaster, and everything else in the room gave off such smoke it blew clouds out every exit.

Retching, crawling, Sunbright collected Greenwillow in one arm and clutched her to his chest, while she dragged Harvester between his legs. Together they half fell down the stairs, then tumbled outside as hot smoke gushed all around them.

Shielding his eyes, Sunbright looked up at the palace. It was completely engulfed in flames. Fire licked through the windows and flared through the roof. Pressed flat by the leaden sky, smoke roiled from above and spilled out holes to writhe, like giant snakes, in the streets.

Sunbright ran down the side of the palace, along the front and down another side. Greenwillow had hiked her skirts to show long legs flashing as she pelted with him. Her chains jingled. "What are you doing? Where are you going?"

"Ruellana! She might still be inside!" Heat and flame drove him back from the small door they'd entered upon first reaching the city. "She must be on the third floor!"

"There *is* no more third floor!" hollered the elf. "Stop trying to be a martyr! She would have gotten out early; she knows to take care of herself first!"

Even in fire and battle, he thought, Greenwillow found time to be catty. But she must be right. No one would stay in a castle while a dragon was peeling off the roof. The two trotted back to the street where a crowd stood well back and watched the palace burn.

Sunbright stared, squinting. "That's the end of the One King, I'd say."

"True." Greenwillow rubbed a smudge on her nose, chains clinking at her wrists. "If he walks out of there, maybe he deserves to take over the world."

"No, he's gone," said a woman's voice behind them. "Imagine being so taken in by his mad dreams. We must have been mesmerized."

The pair spun about to find Ruellana standing behind them. Her bright red hair was raked straight and streaked with soot, and stripes marked her throat. She wore a queer costume: a red leather vest and silk shirt, red-striped trousers with flop-top boots, and a white baldric with a basket-hilt sword. It looked like a dancing girl's idea of traveling togs, or perhaps the costume of an actor playing pirate. She held up a bundle of dark green, black straps, and an ornate sword: Greenwillow's clothes and tackle.

The elf didn't hesitate, but shucked her thin, shimmery dress to stand mother-naked in the street. Sunbright felt his eyes bulge, for it was the first time he'd seen all of Greenwillow, who was lithe as a whippet but had womanly curves aplenty. Unconcerned, the elf donned her fine elven clothes, yanked her hair back into a fine black ponytail, and borrowed Harvester to pry off her manacles.

Sunbright had seen Ruellana do many odd things, so this latest conjuring trick didn't rock him. But he asked anyway, "How did you . . . ?"

"I saw the dragon coming through the window and knew the king was doomed. So I donned my fighter's garb and grabbed Greenwillow's from a chest. Not bad for a simple country girl, eh?"

She was hardly that, Sunbright knew, but he didn't comment. Instead he tilted his head at a familiar sound coming from down the street, faint above the crackling of the burning building and other houses, but rising. Shouts, calls, cheers. "What's . . . ?"

Down the street ran a trio of orcs, weaponless, protecting the backs of their heads with gray hands. Behind them rushed a mob of citizens hurling stones, bricks, and crockery. Some stopped to snatch up fallen swords or pikes. A dazed orc who staggered around a corner with a head wound was tripped and kicked, then stabbed in the belly by a balding man in a freighter's smock.

"The citizens," mumbled Sunbright. "Their city was occupied by the One King's army, and now they're revolting!"

The citizens who'd been standing around gaping at the fire joyfully took up the shouts of resistance, then scrambled away to find weapons and hunt down orcs and the king's men.

"Shall we go?" asked Ruellana.

"Go?" Human and elf stared at her. "Go where?"

Ruellana plunked her fists onto her hips, tilted

jauntily so her sword rode at an angle. "Wherever you like! You've won the day, survived a bout with a dragon and a lich, killed an evil minister, freed a city, retrieved a magic book, and started a legend. Go where you will!"

"Actually," Sunbright pointed to the flaming palace, "I think the book's been burned up."

Ruellana snapped her fingers and dragged from behind her a white haversack the other two hadn't noticed. Lifting the flap, she displayed the ancient book with the ruby-studded cover. Smiling, she tipped up her shapely nose. "Shall we go?"

Sunbright and Greenwillow mutely spread their hands, then trotted after Ruellana through the rubble-strewn, ash-smudged, blood-dripping, smoke-streaked—but free—streets of Tinnainen.

* * * * *

Escape didn't prove that easy. The city had gone mad, and those caught in the turmoil had better duck their heads until the fever had run its course.

Trotting around a corner, sniffing and hacking in the thick smoke, they rounded one corner only to find a trio of orcs charging toward them. The creatures wore the red-edged black tunics of palace guards and carried red-hilted swords. One had a head wound streaming blood, another a shorn hand. Whether they were fleeing a crowd or pursued some private business wasn't clear. But at the rubble-strewn intersection of two streets where the houses were going up in flames, the leader pointed a long gray arm that dripped blood at Sunbright and growled, "He slew the king!" Howling, they rushed.

Sunbright had no quarrel with these orcs or anyone else. He wanted only to rest a moment and drink water until he floated. An afternoon in dragon smoke and now a city afire had scorched his throat so badly his tongue felt swollen. Certainly he'd had enough fighting to last a lifetime. But if he hoped to get any older, he had to defend himself. He hoisted Harvester, though the sword seemed as heavy as a dozen crowbars, in arms that sagged like lead.

The orc captain charged and slashed overhand, anger and fanaticism lending it strength. Two-handed, Sunbright parried cross-body in automatic defense, and kicked for the orc's knees barbarian-style with his heavy boots. But the knotty-armed orc leaped above the kicks, banging again and again on the barbarian's sword blade. Finally, timing the blows, Sunbright simply stepped out of the way. When the orc blundered past, he'd cut it across the kidneys or neck, following with a chop to the back of its leg to sever an artery and end this fight.

But he snapped alert and learned why the orc was a captain. The creature had been anticipating the sidestep and plunged past the end of Harvester, but abruptly stamped to a halt and threw its shoulder into Sunbright. Bulling the barbarian forward and sideways, the orc swung its sword in a short, vicious arc to slash at the human's kidneys.

For lack of a better defense, Sunbright shot out his legs and landed square on his butt, jarring his spine to the top of his skull. But the orc's slash passed overhead, just ticking the human's topknot.

Flopping onto his back, the barbarian thrust overhand and overhead. Harvester's fat tip slid into the orc's side and guts, then under its rib cage and nicked its heart. Twisting to sink the hook and enlarge the wound, Sunbright yanked back and brought a red rain onto his head and arms. The orc collapsed like a pricked balloon.

Keeping clear of the stricken orc—even dying warriors could strike back—the barbarian levered himself to his feet, spit blood off his lips, and automatically cast about for his comrades.

Greenwillow was fencing with another orc that already bled from several wounds. Snarling, the creature curled gray lips and lunged again, slashing mightily with its sword. But it was careful to keep the sword before it as a whirling shield. Greenwillow shuffled, ducked, aimed, stabbed, and whipped her hand back, then repeated the pattern, so the orc now bled from four spots on its forearms. A few more such surgical pinks, Sunbright knew, and the orc would be too tired to fight or else hamstrung. Then it would feel steel in its throat.

And Ruellana?

Again she surprised him, for she was fighting magnificently, dancing death around the orc. This was a monster, the biggest of the lot, but Ruellana laughed as she skipped.

As the orc slashed, like a man swatting a bumblebee, Ruellana trilled a snatch of song and her hand flickered. The bright tip of her blade sliced the orc's pug nose sideways below the bridge. So sharp was the blade the beast-man barely felt it, but blood ran down its lips and fangs. It jumped and slashed again, but its sword struck stone, for Ruellana had danced away.

The next time she pricked the orc in the buttocks through his black tunic. As it turned in outrage, she sliced its ear almost through, so the gray point dangled by a flap of skin and flopped against its neck. Ruellana pouted at her misstroke, skipped dangerously close, and whisked the ear off. As the beast roared, she sliced again, downward, so the orc's nose was split vertically into four even chunks.

Tired and disgusted, Sunbright felt his stomach churn. He'd seen battle and killing, knew it was often a necessity, but Ruellana was enjoying this tremendously. She was killing the orc a piece at a time, slicing it like a ham for a feast. The barbarian shouted for her to stop, to dispatch the orc quickly, but a merry trill was her only response. Tripping in close, Ruellana jabbed and split the orc's eye. Roaring and leaking blood, the creature hacked a fast, hard circle in which to trap Ruellana. She laughed, teasing, and drew the orc's attention. As it whirled to squint, one-eyed, at her, she poked the other eye.

Magic, Sunbright thought. She had to be using magic to move so lithely, so fluidly, anticipating her enemy's every blow. But then, he'd known she possessed magic, he'd just avoided dwelling on it.

Sickened, the barbarian turned away, so he didn't see Ruellana level her blade so that the orc might charge onto it. The beast's throat split and gushed blood, but she only hopped far enough back to avoid the spray. She'd deliberately withheld the death blow. As the orc dropped to hands and knees, Ruellana leaned in. Chuckling, she pricked the orc's back and neck a dozen times before it collapsed and died.

Sunbright stood with Greenwillow, who'd ended her opponent's life neatly and cleanly. The pair watched Ruellana rake back her red hair and laugh as if at a party. The observers shivered as she waved her bloody sword toward the city gates.

Distracted as he was by the cruelty revealed in his former lover, Sunbright nevertheless managed to observe the streets and the sky at the same time. Any moment they might blunder into more orcs or even blood-crazed citizens not ripe for listening. Still back at the palace, he hoped, was Wrathburn. The dragon had come for the crown, and to scotch the king. He had lost the crown, which had been melted to slag by his own fire, but had removed the king from the face of the land. The question now was, would that satisfy the dragon's temper, or would he seek to level the city that had harbored the king? If so, the place to be was elsewhere, for there was no way to stop the monster.

And too, Wrathburn had told Sunbright to stay put so they might both return to the cave, where the barbarian would be lifelong bard to sing the praises of Wrathburn the All-High.

But as if in answer, Ruellana called out and pointed up. Through smoke and haze, they saw a slender shape beat stubby wings as Wrathburn thrashed homeward. "He's had enough," Sunbright breathed. "And he must have forgotten all about me. The raven said he wasn't too bright."

* * * * *

Half a mile down the road, away from the smoke and noise, having slaked their thirst and mopped off soot and sweat at a creek, the three studied the sky and debated how long to walk before sunset, which was not far off. Sunbright reflected to himself how just this morning he'd walked into a dragon's cave. It felt good to be haggling over a camping spot and thinking about shaving a bow and fletching arrows, so he might shoot game on the trek to Dalekeva. And they'd have to watch for orcish patrols, lest the creatures hadn't heard their master was dead—or if they had, and reverted to their old habits of loot and rape.

Man and elf walked ahead on the narrow road, Ruellana trailing behind them. She sang gaily, a lengthy epic of love and sorrow and loss and more love, a tune designed to entertain a court on long winter nights. Sunbright walked beside Greenwillow, studying her surreptitiously.

What now? he wondered. He had his comrade-in-arms and his sometime-lover both on his hands. Greenwillow, he hoped, cared for him deeply. But her heart had been wounded when he'd run off to pursue the phantom Ruellana. Yet how much love could there be between human and elf?

And who—what—was Ruellana? Definitely not a simple country girl, not quite a succubus either, but definitely a bloodthirsty bitch when aroused. Little chance of long-term romance there. For all her exotic, cool facade, Greenwillow was the more uncomplicated of the two, while Ruellana, who pretended innocence, was some complex creation he couldn't begin to comprehend. But she smoldered sexually and loved as hard as she laughed and fought, which counted for a lot when his groin and his heart warred. Still, Greenwillow's lithe form would fit well under his hands. . . .

A scream—"Sunbright!"—jerked both fighters around.

There in the road shimmered a gilt-edged portal like a ring around the sun. Swooping from the middle came a huge yellow glob only vaguely man-shaped, with arms and head. The jellyfish arms had enfolded Ruellana and were dragging her toward the shimmering portal. She fought valiantly, but striking the blob only resulted in her hands and arms sinking into it, entrapping her.

"Sunbright!" she screamed. "Stay away! Save yourself—" Yellow fingers clamped down over her mouth. Headfirst, she was yanked into the shrinking portal.

Unsheathing Harvester as he ran, Sunbright dove and grabbed and latched on to Ruellana's boot with his free hand. He might as well have grabbed the reins of a double team of plow horses. Smothered in yellow ectoplasm, the woman was hauled steadily into the glittering portal.

Hanging on doggedly to Ruellana's slippery boot, Sunbright stabbed along the length of the woman's struggling body, frantic not to jab her accidentally. But Harvester's fine point slid into the mass without striking anything, and the blade came out clean.

Greenwillow ran to the barbarian's side, grabbed his arm, and tugged. Most of Ruellana, kicking and writhing, had slid inside the blob, so only her legs below the knees remained.

"Let go!" the elf shrilled. "You can't help her!"

"I can go with her!"

"No! Don't! We'll find another way to rescue her!" There was fear in Greenwillow's voice.

"I can't . . . desert her now!" Sunbright grunted. "I didn't desert . . . you!"

"But she's not what she seems!" the elf wailed. "Please, don't—"

"Get to Dalekeva!" Sunbright roared. "I'll meet you!"

Then, hanging on to only a foot, he lunged head-first at the portal, now no bigger than his hips.

With a twinkle of golden light on his hobnailed boots, he was gone.

And Greenwillow was shrieking his name to empty air.

* * * * *

With the rough cloth of his sleeve, Candlemas polished the palantir again and again. "Unbelievable! How could she? It's unbelievable!"

High in his tower workshop, he pressed his nose against the black glass, but there was nothing to see except Greenwillow circling one spot, crying Sunbright's name, alone on the road near a city shedding smoke.

Moments earlier, the mage had chuckled in triumph, for he'd finally won. As the final bet, he'd wagered Sunbright could stand up to the One King, who was known to be as crazy as a bedbug and as unpredictable, and come away unscathed. Sunbright had not only faced down the king, but also destroyed him, or at least helped.

And inadvertently, Candlemas had penetrated the blank spot on his map. It turned out that the One King had set up wards to prevent scrying, so no one might learn he was undead. Clever, but more clever was Candlemas who, through his agent the barbarian, had made the One King bobble his wards. A red dragon dropping in tended to distract a body, alive or otherwise.

So Candlemas had killed two birds with one stone: he'd finally beaten Sysquemalyn *and* increased his knowledge. And knowledge, every mage knew, was the only lasting power.

But suddenly, out of nowhere, a shimmering portal had snatched away Sysquemalyn and his barbarian. "Unbelievable!"

"Like my little surprise?" came a laughing query.

The mage whirled to see Sysquemalyn, still dressed in her faux-pirate's garb, stride jauntily into his workshop with a thick book cradled in her arms. The woman raked back her red hair, which complemented her flushed cheeks, and wiggled her hips as she walked, making her sword harness jingle.

"I'm brilliant, am I not? And a fine actress! And even though your meaty barbarian is still alive, *I've* gotten the book the Big White Boar sought. So I win this round—"

"Shut up! Shut up! Stop jabbering! How did you get away?"

"Get away?" The woman blinked at his rudeness and confusion. "From what? Oh, the blob? I commanded it to yank me through the portal so what's-his-name would follow me! I made the fiend, silly. It's my servant."

"*Made* it? Your *servant?*"

"Don't mock me, Candlemas." Green eyes flashed beneath red brows. "I'll concede you won the second test, or whichever number this is, but now we're even again, so we'll defer our crude gratifications. Neither of us wants to be flayed alive, after all. So I've initiated another test, and the game continues—"

"Game?" Candlemas jammed his finger against the palantir. "You'd play a game *there?* I've never seen a portal like that, but I've read of them! It looks as if you opened a doorway into the Nine Hells! Is that true?"

The redheaded wizard replied with a *tsk* and a wave of the hand. "You're being petulant and picky. I think you're jealous!"

"So it's true." breathed the mage. "I can't believe even you could be that mad!"

"And I can't believe you're that boring. I'm leaving." She minced for the door, sword swinging in time to her red-striped hips. But she stopped and leveled a red-nailed finger at him. "Ken this, hedge-hopper! I know perfectly well what I'm doing. I'm in complete control. And with what I'm learning, I'll soon be way beyond you, running an empire with the Dead White Fish emptying my chamber pots while you're still here dosing sick cows or whatever you— What?"

Seeing the horror on his face, she peered behind her.

A shimmering portal had opened in the workshop. From it flowed a giant that resembled a jaundiced genie. Its head was anvil-shaped, its mouth a gaping gash lined with jagged teeth, its eyes black holes like tears in a blanket. It was bright yellow.

One, two, then nine hooked arms rippled and wrapped around the quailing Sysquemalyn. In seconds, she was being dragged into the portal.

Face twisted in terror, she fought by both rattling off protection spells and grabbing at furniture, then by clawing for a hold in the cracks in the floor when she fell and struck her chin. The nine hooked hands mauled her, shredding leather and clothes and skin until blood spurted and hair tore.

Candlemas wanted to dive in to save her, or to utter a spell, or hurl a magical weapon. But he stood frozen by some unseen, unknown force and couldn't even blink.

Then the bleeding, sobbing Sysquemalyn was dragged through the portal, her red hair disappearing last. Her screams were cut off as the portal winked out.

Candlemas could move again, and the first thing he did was grab the table's edge to support his shaking legs. But even that comfort soured, for something flickered on its surface: the palantir.

Bidden to scry out sources of magic, the black glass globe now revealed a rocky field wherein another portal flickered open. Candlemas guessed the area was somewhere north of Tinnainen. But what magic was working there?

He bit his lip as the portal widened, disgorging a rolling ball of fire that splayed open like flaming oil. But this flame ran uphill, swarming over rocks and up a scrawny tree, igniting it like a torch. The flame continued onward, slithering around rocks and, upon touching a pool of water, evaporated it.

Hellfire, he thought. The real thing. But how . . . ?

The globe flickered, revealing another magic source. Here was a field of rye, and above it, another portal. This one widened by hundreds of feet, then disgorged thousands of writhing maggots and grubs that spilled onto the field.

Another flicker, and a ghoulish arm poked from a portal, only to be sheared off as the spasming orifice winked shut. Another flicker, and the sea boiled to steam as more hellfire appeared underwater. Then another, and another, and another.

Never had Candlemas seen so much magic occur in so many different places at once. Toril—the whole world—had sprung hundreds of leaks.

Leaks from the Nine Hells.

Then a face materialized, a female mage whom Candlemas had met in the past, but whose name he'd forgotten. She shrilled, "If anyone can hear, in the name of the gods, send help! My caverns are overrun with trolls by the thousands! They're—" Her face disappeared. Moments later, a lesser mage flickered in, yelled Candlemas's name, and begged him to contact Lady Polaris and inform her that purple slime ran in rivers inside his manor, originating in his workshop.

There were more reports crackling over the ether, more fiendish invasions, more eruptions in the fabric of magic. Some deaths, many losses, boundless destruction.

"May the gods help us all," Candlemas breathed. "Sysquemalyn's cracked the wall to the Nine Hells. The fool, in her blind trifling she's endangered Netheril itself!"

A shriek interrupted his dread thoughts. Running to the door of his workshop, he shouted down a corridor, then froze. A gigantic black bat pursued a screaming maid. More spun up the stairwells, forcing him to slam the door shut. Dashing to the window, he saw thousands more fluttering around Delia, attacking anything that moved for its blood.

The horror had come home.

Candlemas beat his forehead in terror and frustration. Only the greatest archmages of Netheril had ever dared to challenge the Nine Hells, and most of them had never returned. Sysquemalyn had been sucked into its maw, and her and Candlemas's home, indeed their entire world, was under attack. The high mages of the Netherese would come soon to investigate, and they would trace the trail to here.

Their punishment for Sysquemalyn, and himself for not stopping her, was too awful to think about.

He had only one choice.

Standing still, he raised both hands over his head, first and fourth fingers extended.

And raised a high, wailing keen.

And disappeared.

Chapter 13

In growing dimness, Greenwillow sat on a stone wall and stared at the space where Sunbright had disappeared. Perhaps, wherever he'd gone, he'd find a way to escape and come back to her. She doubted it, but didn't know what else to do.

A cool evening wind swirled from the mountains and kissed her cheek, whispering in her ear seductively. Elves weren't supposed to fall in love with humans, the message seemed to remind her. The two races stood apart for good reasons. And all along on this benighted quest, her doomed mission to deliver condemnation from a haughty elven council to an undead king, she'd fought to stay aloof, reserved, cool. She'd battled against love harder than any mortal enemy she'd ever fought. In vain. She Who Shapes All had laid the path before Greenwillow's feet, and the half-elf could but walk it.

Until now, when the one she loved had catapulted

after a temptress, a trollop, a . . .

Without any tickle to her keen elven senses, a man stood by her side.

Instinctively she shot up, laid a hand to her sword's pommel, and slid the weapon from its sheath a hair. Certainly there was magic about the human, for he hadn't walked to this spot. That she knew. But too, he looked vaguely familiar, was podgy, bald, and bearded, dressed in a plain linen smock. Then she recalled.

"You . . . talked to Sunbright that day just before he joined our party of merchants. In the village of Augerbend, it was."

"Did I? Oh, yes, yes." Candlemas was distracted. A lot had happened since then. He stepped across the road to where the portal had materialized.

"But who are you?" demanded the elf. "Sunbright said you were steward of the castle, but that was untrue."

"Hmmm?" The mage studied the wreckage of Tinnainen, the gaps pounded in the walls, the trickles of smoke in a dozen places, the collapsed roofs and gutted palace. He shook his head in wonder at what he and Sysquemalyn had stirred up—all for a silly wager, or was it something more? Now the air reeked with the residue of mighty magics, of dragons and liches and others, power only a Neth could master. But at least that battle was over, the fires out, Wrathburn departed. Within days, Tinnainen would be a backwater again—unless the Nine Hells erupted nearby.

He frowned at the sky. Was his eyesight fading? No, he'd just come so far east the sun had already set here. He felt old, was all. Constant intrigue and tension ground a body down.

"I asked," Greenwillow said, jerking her sword from its scabbard with a steel whisper, "who are you?"

He turned to look at her. Despite smudges and nicks, she was more lovely in real life than when seen through a palantir. Always swayed by feminine beauty, the mage spoke formally. "I'm sorry, my dear. I am a steward, but of another castle, uh, higher up. I'm a friend."

Frowning again, the mage knelt stiffly and ran his fingers over the soil. Still warm. Then he flinched as something black fluttered near his face. But it was only the raven, which said nothing.

Greenwillow did, though. "You're a friend to the raven, too?"

"Eh?" Candlemas craned to see her face. "Oh, ah . . . What do you know of the bird?"

"That it talks. I followed Sunbright a few times, just to—" Now she hesitated, even blushed. "Just to watch him. He didn't see me, but I saw him converse with the raven. Did you send it?"

Candlemas nodded absently. Lifting his hand palm up, he felt for the exact spot where the portal had been. Waving his hand slowly, he traced the outline: the rift in the fabric of reality. "Good, good. Or very bad. For me anyway."

Rising, extending his hands with fingers spread, he keened again, a long, loud wail.

The portal winked into being. Nothing showed inside it, just a view of the stone wall.

With a cry, Greenwillow jumped up, slapped her sword home, and started to push past Candlemas. But the mage swept her back with a thick arm. "Stand back, young woman. There's nothing you can do."

Sighing, he hiked his skirts and stepped through the portal. The golden shimmer tingled around his legs, then his body, as if he crept into lightning-charged water.

The mage paid no notice to Greenwillow. For too long had Candlemas been steward of a castle, where his orders were obeyed immediately without question.

Greenwillow didn't question him either. She just shadowed the bulky man, hovering inches behind him, and held her breath.

Seconds later, the portal winked out, and the road to Tinnainen stood empty.

*   *   *   *   *

Candlemas stepped onto a platform of black glass. Not much wider than a public fountain, it curved up all around, so he slid toward its center. The mage didn't recognize the conveyance, but it resembled the bottom of a palantir, as if he stood inside. Perhaps he did.

Around the platform was nothingness, a blank limbo like fog. Candlemas didn't dare touch it.

Sprawled like a rag doll on the glass platform lay Sunbright, his sword under him. The barbarian was dirty and scraped up, but alive and breathing. For now.

A cry sounded. With mild annoyance, the mage found the half-elf Greenwillow had followed despite his orders. She stooped to gather Sunbright in her arms, smothering his face with fervent kisses. That brought the barbarian around better than a bucket of water.

His first words were accusatory, aimed at the mage. "Chandler! What are you doing here?"

Single-minded, barbarians were, Candlemas thought. If humans were dumb brutes, as Sysquemalyn argued, the tundra people were no smarter than their reindeer. This young hide-wearer leaped to battle instead of waging love on the elven beauty. The mage sighed, "I'm not a simple steward. I'm more than that."

Clutching his throbbing head, Sunbright clambered up from Greenwillow's embrace. To her questions, he rasped, "That yellow fiend that grabbed Ruellana. It saw me following somehow, and crushed me with a hand like a hayrick. I don't know where it went from there."

Still groggy, he slid a pace on the glass platform and almost pitched over the side—if there was a side. No noise or feel or smell came from the foggy limbo. They might have been bugs in a bottle, Candlemas thought, and perhaps were.

Sunbright leveled a scarred arm and calloused finger at the older man. "You're a filthy mage, aren't you?"

A tiny shrug. "A mage. My name isn't Chandler, by the way. It's Candlemas. A chandler makes candles, see?" His rueful smile was not returned.

"So everything you told me was a lie?"

"Not everything." Candlemas scanned their surroundings, which were the blankest he'd ever seen. How could he entice the barbarian to penetrate the not-fog? "About half, well, much of what I said was true."

"You used me!" A finger stabbed downward. "Even that damned raven is yours, isn't it?"

Candlemas blinked at the platform and saw the raven. Funny, he hadn't seen it enter the portal.

The raven cocked its head as if also confused as to how it had gotten there. It croaked, "Sorry. That's how the egg breaks."

"The raven is an avatar," Candlemas explained. "A shade of mine sent to watch over you. Like a homunculus, only more reliable."

Sunbright rubbed his throbbing temples. He snarled, "I don't want any more of your damned magic near me! Wait, you sent Ruellana, too, didn't you?"

"Ah, no." The chunky mage cast about again, then

settled creaking onto his hams, which slipped down the glass toward the middle where Sunbright stood. He had to drag his hands to stop his slide. "Ruellana is an avatar—no, a persona—of another mage named Sysquemalyn. She's chamberlain while I'm steward of, uh, a castle. She got us into this current pickle. And I'd have to say that, while I've used you somewhat—but kept you from harm repeatedly—she's used you worse and meant you harm. Of course, you probably don't believe anything I say. I understand. But the latest round involved sending you after that book, and she arranged it! No doubt she whispered in the One King's ear that he needed the book, so he dispatched the next able warrior who strode into his court to fetch it before—"

The mage stopped himself, but Sunbright caught the implication. The barbarian's eyes were as hard and cold as glacial ice. "Before you could send me, correct?"

Candlemas shrugged. He hoped the young man wouldn't attack him here. Magic shields would be dicey in a spot like this. They might do anything from protect Candlemas to crush him like a cockroach.

But Sunbright's native curiosity overcame his thirst for vengeance—for the moment. "So Ruellana is a lousy mage too. I should have suspected all along. I was too blind to see. But what was that thing that grabbed her, and where have they gone?"

Candlemas bit his lip as he thought of the manner in which Sysquemalyn had left his workshop. "Good questions."

Sliding Harvester home in its scabbard, Sunbright suddenly whirled on Greenwillow. "And you? What are you, really? And who's your master? And what do you get out of . . . attending me?"

Shocked, the half-elf's conflicting emotions warred on her expressive face. Combining sorrow and rage, she flared, "I'm not anything but what I appear to be! I've been your comrade and friend and . . . that's all. I don't want anything from you. You chose to accompany me to Tinnainen, remember?"

"I know only that I've been used, prodded, steered, and cheated by everyone I've met since leaving the tundra!" roared Sunbright. "But no more! I'm stuffed to the eyes with lying lowlanders, and I'm going home as soon as I can. I'll take my chances at being killed by friends and relatives over skulking, lying fiends the day long."

Greenwillow shrilled once, *"Nooooo!"*

But Sunbright had hunched at the edge of the platform, stuck his head into the limbo-fog, then planted his hands on the surface and vaulted into the void. There was nothing left to indicate he'd ever stood on the black glass bowl.

Greenwillow blazed hatred at the mage. "This is all your fault! Your backstabbing, traitorous, lying, sneaking, thieving magic ways! I hope you rot in the deepest pit of the Nine Hells until the sun falls from the sky!"

So saying, she leaned over the platform, sprang outward, and was gone.

"That's the problem," Candlemas sighed to the raven. "We just might."

The raven pecked at the black glass, hopped up and down, and clacked its beak at its master. "That's the way the egg breaks."

It squawked as Candlemas booted it off the platform.

Sighing, skidding to his feet, Candlemas leaned gingerly into the fog, then rolled over the edge as if tumbling from a boat.

* * * * *

Greenwillow ghosted through fog that was not solid under her feet, but neither did she plummet. If anything, she swam through the air in slow motion, but that didn't describe it either. She tried to steer for the route Sunbright had taken, but had no real sense of direction.

After a few seconds—or hours—her feet plunked on stone. Two steps broke her free of the fog, which clung in shreds that she brushed off like spiderwebs.

Immediately, she called, "Sunbright?" There was no answer, and without thinking she drew her slim, elegant sword.

She'd landed on flagstones the color of pale moss. Before her was a half-wall of the same material. Behind her was a taller, similar wall. Arching overhead, a bowshot high, was a distant ceiling of green flagstones as wide as rooftops. There were more low walls and tall ones, all marching into the distance. Even the light seemed green, though she couldn't find a source.

There was nothing else in sight.

"Sunbright?"

She'd expected her voice to echo in this cavern, but it seemed to travel a distance and then stop. Hesitant, she laid her hand on the low wall. The stones were as smooth as river rocks and were warm like the back of a lizard lying in the sun. The floor was also warm, despite the shadows.

"Sunbright!"

Movement behind her made her whirl, sword leveled.

But what she saw was herself, reflected in stone.

Wonderingly, she advanced. Her image crept toward her. It was fragmented by cracks and wavy from imperfections in the stone. And hardly natural. She could tell it was magic, for the stones couldn't reflect like mirrors.

And her face was ugly.

Her brows were straight across, almost a bar, not arched like an elf's. Her nose was wide, with flaring nostrils, and stippled with blemishes. Her mouth was fat-lipped and pendulous, her hair thatchy and uneven above rounded ears. Even her slim elven figure had coarsened to thick hips and fleshy arms and huge feet.

With a shock, she realized she looked not like an elf, but like a human.

Horror-stricken, Greenwillow ran her hands over her face, felt her nose and lips. But all were numb, and she couldn't tell if the reflection were true or not.

What was this? she wanted to cry. Had some curse turned her human? Was this a hell for elves, to be degraded to an inferior race? She looked down at her legs and feet, but a mist in her eyes—incipient human blindness?—clouded her vision. Even her hand before her eyes was a blur. Yet the reflection stayed as sharp as before.

A trick, her mind replied calmly. A passing madness in this fragment of hell or whatever it was. Yet her eyes contradicted her thoughts, until she wanted to cry out and beat her brain into submission, or blind herself and spare the misery.

Turning away with a gasp, she banged into the low wall, which had somehow crept up on her right. She hadn't shifted, she was positive: the wall had. But perhaps it sought to engulf her, like a trapdoor spider. Whirling, she jumped for the open space, stubbed her toes on a raised step that hadn't been there just a moment ago.

More flickers to her left. The reflection now had

gray hair. The face was wrinkled, the scrawny arm too weak to hold up the sword.

Age, she thought. Humans age too quickly and die, like dandelions living a single season. Was this happening to her? Desperately she ripped at her ponytail, dragged it before her, but the increasing self-blindness prevented her from seeing if her hair were black or gray.

Blindly, she groped along the wall, but the image followed. Between two high walls she saw twin reflections, like ghosts who sought to drive her mad. Her reflected back was now hunched, her legs trembling.

"Love of Mystryl," she prayed, "if Sunbright saw me like this, he'd—"

He'd what? Reject her? Never love her? He didn't love her now, did he? Or she him?

Suddenly she didn't know anything. Could she love a human? A sweaty, garlic-stinking, sour half-beast that would age almost overnight into a decrepit wreck? Was this her curse, to feel affection for a human and so to become one? Many of her fellows would say loving a human was like marrying an animal. Humans were no better than orcs, equally without worth or honor or use, a plague loosed on the earth by malicious gods to chastise the true folk, the elves.

"No!" she called aloud. Her reflection showed a caved-in mouth empty of teeth.

Then two reflections. No, herself and . . .

Sunbright, no longer human.

His bright blond topknot was normal, and his rugged, tanned, lean face. But his light eyebrows pulled upward at the ends to almost touch his scalp, and his eyes were slanted, his ears pointed. He looked lean as a whippet, with thin but powerful arms. His tapering torso showed no chest hair.

He was an elf!

How had this transformation occurred? And why now, when she'd been made human . . . or had she? Did the gods hate them so much that now Sunbright would be acceptable to her people as a lover and husband, yet she'd been reduced to the gutter-level of faded, hairy, grotesque humans? Could any gods be so cruel?

And how much of this was real? Was it her own guilt at loving a human that plagued her? Did she punish herself worst of all?

Something was happening in their reflections. The elf-made Sunbright caught the skinny, saggy arm of the hunched, aged, too-human Greenwillow. The ugly crone tried to turn away, to hide her face, but the elf-man saw her wrinkled, toothless mouth, warts, and chin hairs. Repulsed with horror, the elf-Sunbright staggered back and turned, crying, from the vision.

Shrieking, Greenwillow, too, dashed away from the horrid image. But a low wall rammed her knee and sent her tumbling. Her sword clattered to the green stones, and her clumsy hands seemed too crabbed and numb to grab it.

Below her, more images roiled in the stone. Fascinated, hypnotized like a bird by a snake, the elven-or-human woman watched.

Touching her from underneath, equally on all fours, was another Greenwillow, still human but younger and naked, with a swollen belly showing she carried a child. Her white skin was stretched as tight as a drumhead and enflamed with coarse blue veins, so she looked like a fat-uddered cow too long unmilked. Did she carry the elf-Sunbright's child, a baby half-elf? Would her child be hated by both races? Would the child hate her for birthing it? Would the elven Sunbright desert her for becoming human? Would she die alone and unloved in some empty wasteland?

Crying openly, Greenwillow crawled to her feet. Before her loomed another wall with yet another reflection. A deadly pale, naked Greenwillow staggered as her belly was punched from within. Gory red goblinlike arms split her skin, ripped her open so blood ran in rivers. She was birthing a monster and dying in the process.

Shrieking, she whirled and ran. Another wall had been erected behind her, forming an arch. Running full-tilt, half-blind with tears, she ducked to dash under it.

The arch lowered as she came. Lights exploded in her dark mind as her head slammed stone.

* * * * *

Sunbright floated and swam through fog, dropping slowly until his hobnailed boots chuffed in what he guessed to be dirt. Fog swirled around his shoulders, but a quick shake dissipated it.

Instinctively casting about for the lay of the land, Sunbright concluded this place, wherever it was, didn't seem dangerous, just a tunnel cut through dirt. But instinctively he found Harvester in his hand, for the tunnel hadn't been cut by humans.

Giant earthworms, more likely. No part of the tunnel floor was smooth, but every step was ridged, rippled like the bottom of a shallow stream—or something else. Then he got it. It resembled the guts of a reindeer, tubes ringed with muscles, and he was caught inside like a tapeworm. Nor was any stretch straight, but twisted every inch. Ahead the tunnel rose gradually, then so abruptly he couldn't have climbed the walls. Another sloping branch from an acute angle turned suddenly downward, then leveled again.

His judgment, his decision to jump from the black glass platform, had been foolish and hasty. He might follow turns to dead ends and backtrack for days and never find his way clear to whatever was above ground. He was underground, and yet he could see. Light didn't come from any one source, but seemed to hang in the air, if that made any sense. And the fog he'd dropped from was gone.

Seeking courage, he pronounced aloud, "Well, I can't stand still forever." But the tunnels of guts sucked up the sound of his voice.

Too, they sucked at his courage, like wading in icy water sucked body heat, until all that was left was coldness inside. Sunbright shook his head, but couldn't shake the sensation of dread. Time and again he flicked a glance over his shoulder, trying to catch whatever crept up on him.

Coward, the tunnels seemed to whisper. *Gutless. You're afraid of your own shadow, a child frightened of the dark.*

Frowning, grip on his sword sweaty, Sunbright turned right and went up the slope. Upward would be his strategy for the nonce. But the trail didn't go up for long; it only flowed over a hump and back down again. He cursed. "What now? Back or ahead?"

Cursing more, he turned back. Perhaps if he returned in the direction from whence came the fog, he'd go "up," since he'd dropped "down." Or had he?

But that, too, failed. He counted as he walked forty paces back, but he couldn't find the fork. Any fork. Just more wavering tunnel.

Now the grip on Sunbright's sword made the weapon slippery. If the tunnels could change when he turned his back, he'd never get out. He'd be lost until he died of thirst and his body rotted to bones.

Despite years of wilderness training and lore, Sunbright panicked and ran. Cursing, gasping, fighting not to cry out in fear, he plunged through the tunnels headlong. Clambering up with clawed hands, sliding down slopes steep enough to break legs, choosing directions willy-nilly, he charged—until he ran out of wind and dropped.

Heaving, retching on air, he fought for control. Perhaps this was good, he thought. Perhaps getting the panic over would leave him cool-headed. Certainly he was ashamed, not that anyone would ever know he'd panicked. Only himself.

And certainly he could blame himself for leaping off the platform and leaving Greenwillow, a boon companion, if an enigmatic one. The feeling of dread turned to bitter sorrow when he thought of her. Surely abandoning her was the worst mistake he'd ever made. He'd die unhappy knowing . . .

He rapped his skull with the heel of his hand. Flogging himself wouldn't help. Better not to think at all. Stumbling to his feet, the barbarian forced himself to walk, not run, and to try to think his way out of this dilemma. If only he had a landmark to work from, he might . . .

As if the maze had read his thoughts, a stretch of rippled wall turned dark and craggy. The giant earthworms had cut through something jagged and splintered like a midden of broken brown glass. While some frightened childlike portion of himself wanted to run screaming, his native curiosity made him pause. Perhaps it would provide a clue, point the way out. He studied the lumps overhead and underfoot and at either hand.

They were bones, so old and buried so long they'd taken the color of the earth. Thick, many of them, with knobby joints like those of a lion or bear. A flattened claw was long and hooked like an eagle's talon.

And on one wall was a huge brown beak, much bigger than any eagle's could be, larger than Sunbright's head.

Bears with beaks?

Something stirred in his memory. Hadn't someone somewhere once routed a valley of—what were they called?—owlbears? These people had slaughtered hundreds of them to gain the valley, which held gold or copper or other riches. A few of the creatures had survived, but not many, left to wander the deeper forests, seeking prey and never dying.

Idly he felt the walls. How had owlbear carcasses come to be here? Was this the bottom of a huge kettle, a natural cavity in the forest gouged by a glacier? If he chopped at the ceiling, would he see daylight? Or must he hack through thousands of bones only to find more dirt? If he could find freedom, could he win back Greenwillow? But with her name came the crushing doubt again and heartbreaking sorrow. What was wrong with him?

Under his fingers, something tingled. Snatching back his hand, he found frost crusting his fingernails. What . . . ?

With a splintering, clattering roar, an owlbear broke free of the wall.

Rearing higher than Sunbright, the monster raised long claws like brown glass and slashed at the barbarian. A fearsome beak, like obsidian, clacked and clashed for his face. Yet it wasn't a proper owlbear. The skull was only partly clad in dusty fur. Its coat sported huge rents through which could be seen brittle brown bones. The gaping eye sockets glared empty, and its breath was as musty as an old grave.

Undead. Superstitions overwhelming him, Sunbright's head swam. Lying uneasy, the bones steeped in ghosts had needed only a living touch to come alive and wreak vengeance. The fiend had sucked life-force from his hand, and now it would destroy him and gain company, the living joining the dead.

All these thoughts occurred in seconds; then Sunbright swung. Panic gave him strength, and Harvester chopped deep into the owlbear's side below the powerful forelegs. But he might as well have used a stick to beat a rug. A puff of stone dust rushed around his hands, choked and gagged him.

Backing, clutching his sword as if it were a lifeline, he tried again. Two-handed, he swung high and chopped low, putting all the might of his shoulders into the blow. He aimed for the lower leg, hoping to cut deep and knock the underpinning from the monster.

The sword chuffed into fur, then bone, but failed to bite, for the bone was ancient and as hard as ironwood. Skipping, the barbarian danced aside, sawed the great parrot-beak arc over the creature's tough limb, and twisted to hook Harvester's crook behind its knee. With a gasp, he yanked on the sword hard enough to rip an oak tree up by the roots.

The hook simply skidded off. Flailing, Sunbright staggered and crashed on his back. Glassy bones and beaks and claws clattered at his elbow. The undead owlbear swung like a juggernaut and slashed the air above him.

Dread returned in a wave. He'd die here, he was sure of it. Sunbright fought an overpowering urge to throw away his sword and run or crawl off into the tunnel, gibbering in fear. No one would know his cowardice, came the whispers.

Yet, clambering to his feet, he couldn't even run. The undead beast had felt nothing of his blows, had never even paused. A maggot-eaten paw swung claws like a fistful of knives. Sunbright dodged and hurled his sword blade at the thing's head. The blade thunked in dry fur, sheared to a dry skull. Did nothing.

Then the fiend's claws scored. Like a giant's pitch-fork, the razor talons ripped down Sunbright's arm, ripping meat and arteries and shredding them from his bone.

Red blood spurted on bone-thick walls as the barbarian stumbled. The owlbear's other paw sliced up under his stunned, hopeless defense and raked his side. Sunbright backed away, tripping over his heels, looking frantically for escape, a chance to run for his life. But his spine slammed the rounded wall as the owlbear's paws trapped him on either side. Its claws raked down fragments of comrades that clittered to the dirt around Sunbright's feet.

Gasping, growling like a bear himself, Sunbright managed to jerk his sword up and shove it into the beast's body. He felt only tough skin part; then the blade waggled in emptiness. Desperate to escape, he bashed his forehead against the brute's beak.

It might have driven back a live owl or even a bear. It did nothing to the dead owlbear. Claws from both sides rasped into his sides, splitting skin, shedding blood, seeking his vitals. He felt guts tear deep inside.

He'd never survive now. He was dead but still standing upright. What should be his death song, and where would his body lie? Would he feed grass or worms, or simply rot into shreds of dusty bones like those around him?

Too weak to even sag, Sunbright watched the awful dark glass beak snap. He saw only darkness inside.

The beak swallowed his head whole. The last thing he felt were the points piercing his neck and his forehead. Pressure and pain crashed upon him like a falling tree.

A grinding like an earthquake told him his skull was being crushed. Then nothing.

Chapter 14

Candlemas shivered as he hopped along, as clumsy as a crippled frog. For company, he cursed himself and Sysquemalyn and everyone else he could think of. Especially Lady Polaris, though she'd done nothing especial lately.

He missed a step, slid, dropped his foot into a gap with ankle-wrenching agony, teetered, and flopped on his side. His bald head struck hard, so a clotted gash cracked anew. Cursing, almost weeping, he rubbed blood from the sore spot, then levered himself up. Immediately he slipped and fell again, smacking the same spot.

Bleary-eyed and gloomy, he studied his unchanging surroundings. The floors and walls and low ceiling resembled a sea of giant glass marbles in all directions. Every surface was a half-sphere an armspan wide. Between them were gaps perversely as wide as his sandaled feet. The cloudy marbles were slippery and could roll in place, yet the only way to traverse them was by hopping from one to another. Often he stumbled, sliding in between them, twisting his ankles and banging his knees. He knew he'd shattered and ground his ankle bones to paste by now, but magic kept them firm and the pain low. So far. His magic could last only so long, and the dull ache was rising. Soon he'd be distracted by it, then tortured.

Grabbing a marble with bloody hands, he climbed atop it and gingerly skidded toward a wall. But just before he reached it, it swung away like flotsam on a sea wave. He tumbled and cracked his knee, losing skin to stone. The low glassy ceiling, he'd learned, could dip unexpectedly, and he'd rapped his bald head many times.

Cursing feebly, the mage squatted atop a marble and tried to think how to escape. Slowly the marble turned over, and he had to squinch his backside to stay atop. He'd get no rest in this cold hole.

Too, he was flummoxed, his thoughts murky. The only thing he could concentrate on was blame and doubt: overwhelming blame for others and himself, doubt of everything. This anti-confidence was a curse too, more magic he was sure, but knowing that didn't banish it any better than ignoring a toothache would make the pain go away. If he hadn't wagered with Sysquemalyn . . . If he hadn't attended Lady Polaris . . . If he hadn't manipulated the barbarian . . .

Hissing, he bit his lip, shook his head until his brain rattled in its pan. He had to think. There was something he'd learned once, a way out, but he couldn't recall it. If only he were smarter. If only . . .

A flap and squawk, and the raven skittered from above to perch on a nearby marble. Preening its wings, it tugged loose a shed feather. The black pinfeather slid down a marble surface and vanished into the crevices between the orbs. Candlemas tried not to imagine what might lay underneath.

"Tough sledding," croaked the bird.

"Never mind that," snapped the mage. His breath fogged, for the temperature was chilly. Cold also made him clumsy. "What have you found?"

A jog of the humped beak. "Only more of this. The glass balls move, too. I hit walls twice."

Candlemas stifled a sigh. "How far does it extend, you lopsided menace?"

"Farther than I can fly without hitting a wall." The raven turned its tail to him, cocking its head to peer at the ceiling.

Candlemas cursed. He was like a cockroach trapped in a rolling jar of marbles. If only he'd brought his potions, or his grimoire, he might have . . .

No. "If only" led to sorrow and madness. It had killed more than one dream, and dreamer.

Hissing at rasped skin, the mage continued to crawl from marble to marble, like a pigeon hopping from fencepost to fencepost. But his palms were raw and slippery with blood, and when his hands betrayed him he careened and smacked his cheek into another cold marble. The hand, slipping into the crevice, was chilled to the bone. If not for his magic shields, he'd have been frozen solid by now. If only he'd worn a cape.

The bird waggled its tail, then leaped into the air. Candlemas yelled, "Hey! Come back! I need a direction—"

But he'd reached out unconsciously. The marble underneath him shifted and rolled. The surface from below was frigid, almost paralyzing, and he jumped to get away.

Everything whirled, and his head was flying toward another marble. He stabbed out with numb hands to halt his fall, felt his finger snap as he rolled helplessly.

He'd never catch himself in time, came a doubt. Then he recalled with a shock . . .

. . . There *was* a way out.

He'd seen it before. In the palace of Tyralhorn the Archmage, in Anauria, at Sysquemalyn's "entertainment." The benighted human hero had suffered in a hellhole like this too. And he'd won free by doing . . . what? Something about cutting saplings, tying them under his arms to support himself? No, there was more to it.

But at that point in the story Candlemas had been distracted, wondering what Sysquemalyn intended, reckoning how he might get the upper hand and defeat her without harming himself.

If only he'd paid better attention.

These black thoughts came in a flash, then exploded to black as his forehead crashed on glass.

Groggy, Candlemas snorted and pushed at something brushing his face. His clumsy hand banged against stone.

Sitting up with a start, he bumped his nose on more rock. He could see nothing but darkness. If stone lay all around, he must have been buried in an avalanche. With the thought came panic, and he bashed his knuckles and hands on more stone that was oddly warm. Then he realized his hands were free, after a fashion.

The stone before his eyes slipped down, away, and he could see. Though not everywhere, for a searing, blue-white light filled the center of the chamber, and he had to avert his eyes.

He saw that the stone prison moved on its own,

like snakes of living rock. Then he saw fingers and knew they were stone arms. Moving, passing over and down his body, trapping him. He could stick his arms through gaps, but then sliding stone arms would force them down again, pinning him like a fox in a trap.

"Awake, dear?" cackled a woman's voice. "I'm so glad! I've much to tell you!"

Oh, yes, Candlemas recalled, I'm in the Nine Hells. Animate stone beings were to be expected where madness reigned. And there would be no waking from the nightmare. Or rather, only waking as he'd just done, plunging him afresh into new nightmares.

This one was worse than most.

The stone arms were only part of the phenomenon. The walls in this large chamber rippled and convulsed in all directions, so a body grew seasick watching them. Corpses of animate stone formed the walls. Humans, elves, orcs, dwarves, and other races that Candlemas couldn't identify had been turned to stone and fused together like madcap building blocks. Yet some life or unlife still remained in them, for the carcasses heaved and twitched and groped until the walls seemed thick with gray, crawling beetles. A head would bob up, roll blind eyes, then be submerged as a hand or leg or buttock shoved it back and down and another lost soul writhed to the surface. Arms, fingers, toes, breasts, shoulders, bobbed on the sea of living stone like drowning folk struggling for air.

And perhaps they were. Candlemas couldn't imagine a much worse torment than being turned to stone—to live forever frozen—then being cast into an ocean of like-damned sinners, to struggle for purchase, for air, for a chance to see light, only to be dragged back down into black death. The mage, who'd seen many awful things in his years of magic-making, shuddered uncontrollably at the fiendishness of it.

But there was more to see. He was pinned by groping arms and legs that somehow had been stimulated to entrap him. So, too, was Greenwillow, who hung, upside down, on the far side of the chamber. The doughty elf struggled against her stone bonds whenever she got a hand or leg loose, but she only succeeded in winning herself more scrapes and bruises. Still, Candlemas had to admit she was trying to win free, and he wasn't. But then, he knew better how small their chances of survival really were.

Here, too, was the raven. The flustered bird hopped and flew a dozen times a minute as it vainly sought a spot to alight that didn't writhe or bear thorns. It had little luck and squawked unhappily. Some of its discomfiture communicated itself to Candlemas, its master, pity heaped on sorrow. Much of his own making, his own fault.

There was still more to take in, for at the center of the chamber was a huge, twisted ball, like a giant snarl of yarn. Yet the strings were metal branches studded with wicked thorns. Suspended in the thorns, punctured in a dozen places, was the still-unconscious Sunbright. The silvery metal glittered in the eye-smarting, blue-white brilliance that emanated from deep within the center of the loose snarl. Candlemas couldn't comprehend the source of the light, but guessed they would all have been blinded by it if not for the thicket of thorns. What could shed that much light?

"Do you like it? I fetched you all here to admire it!" Striding over writhing stone bodies came Sysquemalyn, raking her red hair back in her vainglorious fashion. She still wore her Ruellana garb, with the rips and claw marks from the fiend that had dragged her off. For that matter, some of the wounds still dripped blood. But the female mage didn't seem to notice as she wiped her nose and left a red streak. From her scraped hand trailed Sunbright's heavy-nosed sword, Harvester of Blood.

"This is my *finest* creation!" The mage waved her arm and sword at the hideous chamber. The blue white light cast her shadow dozens of feet tall, eclipsing the lost souls in their perpetual struggle. "It's not what you think, not the Nine Hells, but my very own unique construct for the delight of my friends and enemies!"

"You're mad." The whisper slipped from Candlemas unintentionally, but it didn't matter, he supposed.

"What?" The woman peered up at him like an adult puzzled by a child's odd question. "Did you say *mad?*"

"Insane. Moonstruck. Addled. Crackpated. Buzzy-brained. Pickle-witted." Candlemas had to pause as a stone arm slid past his nose, brushing his beard. He resumed, strangely calm, in the voice of a tired man ready for death. "Funny I never spotted it, working with you all these years. But such is dementia. It creeps up slowly, and no one notices, until one day the loon lashes out and kills folks, and then it's too late."

The red-haired mage lifted the sword to where Candlemas hung pinned and prodded his toe, drawing blood. "I don't like to be called mad."

"No, I imagine not. Nor do ugly people like to be called ugly, nor cruel folk cruel, nor fat nor slow, and so on. But anyone who would meddle with the Nine

Hells . . ."

"This is *not* the Nine Hells!" Petulant, Sysquemalyn jabbed at his foot, missed, and bounced the point
off a stone orc's head. "I made this place, I tell you!
You're just jealous." Angry, she batted at a stone finger and only dinged Harvester's edge.

"By the Silver Lady!" Candlemas shook his head,
thumping his ear on a stone nose. "You don't know
what you're dealing with. It's *impossible* you made
this place. Look around! There are thousands of
trapped spirits here. Where did they come from? You
couldn't have conjured them all from thin air. Most
gods couldn't do that. And these tunnels, endless
numbers of them, all dipping deep into the very bowels of hell. Can you honestly believe you've plugged
them all? And what about that yellow fiend that
dragged you here? You're still dripping blood from the
wounds, yet you claim to have crafted it? You've
tapped the wrong portals. You don't have the strength
to cope with the Nine Hells!"

To his horror, Sysquemalyn only laughed with delight. "Ah, yes! Did you like my fiend? True, it was a
little rough when it came to fetch me, but that's just
the merest bump to hammer flat. And your 'wrong
portals.' Piffle! I'll admit I drew certain grace notes
from the Nine Hells—I studied them long enough—
but this is a creation all my own! My presentation,
my 'entertainment' at Tyralhorn's party, was merely
a rough draft, the most preliminary sketch. *This* is
the perfection! Let's see the Snorting White Sow top
this!"

There lies the explanation, Candlemas sighed in
his mind. Unknown to him, Sysquemalyn had spent
too much time studying the Nine Hells. And watching madness, mulling it, dipping and drinking it, had
infected her mind. Like a missionary amid lepers,

she'd become what she sought to conquer.

"I won't argue—much. But whatever you did, and no matter how clever you think yourself, you've released lesser horrors from the pits all over Netheril. After you were dragged off, my palantir suddenly rattled with reports of hellfire and trolls, plagues of maggots, and rampaging ghouls. Delia was beset by giant black bats lusting for the blood of your chambermaids!"

For the first time, doubt flickered over Sysquemalyn's face. Her red lips pouted; her brow clouded in thought. Then the storm passed as she reverted to her self-centered fantasy. "Oh, valiant effort, dear 'Mas! Nice try! But you won't talk your way out of this. I won, and you lost. But yes, let's sound the finale of our little symphony."

Sword trailing and clittering on stone heads and limbs, Sysquemalyn pranced to the thicket of silver thorns. With a snap of her fingers, Sunbright jerked, shook his head, then immediately froze as he felt sharp points prick him.

"How's the head?" called the mage. "I saw the owlbear eat it, but it looks sturdy enough now. That's the beauty of my private hell: I can torture someone to death, make them feel every agony, then resurrect them to suffer anew! A dozen times a day, if I wish!"

Carefully, Sunbright opened his eyes, flicked them over the surroundings, then focused on Sysquemalyn.

"Ruellana," he spat without moving. "You've deceived me yet again."

"Oh, I've done much worse than that," chided the mage. "And my name is Sysquemalyn. Reins of Shar, but you're a dense child! I show you a goddess aborning and you see a randy barmaid. As low-minded as humans are, I don't think you even qualify as one.

I've taught dogs tricks more quickly. You're hopeless!" Her *tsk* made Sunbright writhe in his barbed bonds.

Dismissing the youth from her mind, Sysquemalyn returned to gloat before the podgy Candlemas. "Old friend and partner, I've reconsidered my concession of your win, whenever that was. I'd rather win. So your precious barbarian will not, after all, survive his sojourn to Tinnainen. Or rather, he won't after I drop him through that portal I've opened into the core of a star."

From high on the opposite wall, Greenwillow gave a shriek, then returned to struggling her way free. She reckoned that if she timed the groping stone arms correctly, she might slither free without breaking a limb. What she'd do after that, though . . .

"Star?" Candlemas groaned. "Is there nothing you won't tamper with? You're like a child with a hammer set loose in a potter's shop. You'll destroy the universe on a whim! Please, Sys, listen. Let the mud man go. The game has gone too far. It never should have begun. Call it a draw if you like, or say you've won, but we must quit this foolishness! Let me go, and perhaps together we can patch the holes you've rent in the fabric, before the gods themselves stride down from on high and snuff every one of us like candles."

"No, dear 'Mas. No." Bright-eyed, the mage waggled a finger tipped with a broken red nail. "If I let the groundling go, you'll just change the rules. No, I've already decided the forfeit for the final game, which you've just lost. You shall spend a year here, exploring all the reaches of my custom-made hell, experiencing the ultimate in torment hour by hour. I think it a small enough punishment for opposing me all this time, when you knew you couldn't win. I'm just too powerful for you. Look around yourself! Having harnessed a shadow of the Nine Hells, am I not more powerful than the Malodorous White Maggot? So . . . where was I? Ah, yes!"

Skipping like a child, the preening goddess-to-be approached Sunbright, who hung on hooks like a rabbit ready for the pot. Smiling, she called, "Thanks for the fun, dear boy!"

With a grimy finger, she drew a small circle in the air that encompassed Sunbright, then swirled the spell toward the fiery heart of the pulsing star beyond the portal.

The barbarian hissed as the metal thorns twisted, curled, parted, coiled. Still entrapped, he saw one side of the thicket part to reveal the distant blue-white light. He averted his eyes rather than be blinded, fought to slide a hand or even a foot loose so he might hang on. But, as one by one the barbed strands sprang free, he was nudged from behind by hundreds more, making it impossible to retreat or dodge aside.

As the last thorn was plucked from ravaged skin, he was hurled headlong as if shot from a catapult.

Cursing, grabbing madly for any purchase, Sunbright spun head over heels. Whirling, a cool nothingness enfolded him even as the heat of the star made his skin prickle with violent burns. He sucked air to make a final effort to fight, somehow, but was stunned to find there was no air to breathe.

He was falling through nothingness into a star. What a legend this would make. Too bad he'd never hear it.

His lungs ached, crushing him from within. His heart pounded like a war drum. Even his eardrums and eyeballs threatened to explode. And all the while, the blue-white light cooked him as if it were a bonfire.

The heat built intolerably. Soon he'd scream out the last of his air, fly shrieking to his flaming death.

Then, just as his lungs swelled to bursting, he disappeared.

Squinting, Sysquemalyn pouted red lips. It was hard to see into the fearsome blue-white brilliance, but . . .

" 'Mas, dear, did you see that? The manling just vanished. But how? I didn't do that!"

Pinned by stone-snake arms, Candlemas groaned. No matter how bad things got, he'd often noted, they could always get worse. And just had.

"I think," he growled at Sysquemalyn, "you've finally attracted the attention of . . ."

He, too, vanished.

* * * * *

Sunbright landed with a crunch on his shoulder, fetching his head a solid crack that made it sing.

Grunting, he flopped on his back. But he was unfettered and alive, though he couldn't guess how, and so he snatched Dorlas's warhammer from his belt and crouched to bash his way to freedom if possible.

In an eye-blink, three people flickered onto the stony ledge where he stood: Greenwillow, Sysquemalyn, Candlemas. The raven appeared a moment after.

The podgy, bald mage finished his sentence. " . . . someone big."

Sunbright attacked.

He didn't sound a battle cry, for while it may have startled his foe, it also would have warned her. He simply leaped and swung the warhammer from the end of his arm.

The long tapered head, five pounds of hardened steel, struck Sysquemalyn at the juncture of neck and shoulder. The weapon would have crushed her skull or snapped her neck if the light weren't so bad or the footing so uneven. As it was, the warhammer shattered her shoulder to flinders, for her shield spell was down or magically drained. The *thud* of the blow and *crunch* of bone made Greenwillow and Candlemas grunt.

Sunbright didn't pause. Still charging, aiming for the wall behind her, he kicked Sysquemalyn in the throat with heavy boots as she pitched forward in agony. The jolt knocked her into the wall, bounced her skull off stone. Bleeding red into red hair from a scalp wound, she collapsed into a heap.

Sunbright let her fall and scooched for his sword, which she had brought with her. Once he gained his weapon, he'd see if she needed another blow to kill or incapacitate her. Furious as he was for her callous use of him, her betrayal, and the attempt on his life for no reason whatsoever, he wouldn't kill her unless she were still too dangerous to control. Their party might need her to escape wherever they were. So far he'd glimpsed only dark stone strewn with ashes.

And too, some part of his heart lingered with the traitorous mage. Some part of him still felt love and lust and longing for the sweet Ruellana who had never really existed. But Sunbright would stop her from using her magic first, for he was no lovesick fool.

Though it lay only inches away, he never reached his sword.

A swirling, like a miniature tornado, erupted from near his feet. Sunbright flinched and backed away, but within seconds the tornado turned green-brown and gray, then tightened around him. The spinning mist took the form of serpents, longer than horses and as thick as Sunbright's arm, hissing and twisting and clenching tightly to enwrap him like iron bands. Four or five fanged heads ducked and bobbed against his torso, and he heard more hissing behind him. Round black eyes that glistened fixed him with an intelligent, hypnotic glare.

With a gasp, Sunbright filled his lungs to prevent their collapsing his chest and concentrated to free his hands and wrists that he might pry the beasts off. His mind warred with his body, curiosity with fright with ferocity. On one hand, he didn't fear these serpents much, for snakes were rarely dangerous and he could wriggle free soon. On the other hand, they'd appeared magically and so couldn't be natural beasts. Or could they, only magically summoned? Either way, he wouldn't think overmuch, but fight to get free and deal with abstractions later.

He never got the chance. With a grunt, he was hoisted into the air so his feet dangled a yard off the ground. The serpents consolidated their grips and quieted. Just below Sunbright, Sysquemalyn lay sprawled and moaning against the rock wall, one shoulder crumpled lower than the other. But it was the astonished gaping of Greenwillow and Candlemas and even the raven that finally arrested Sunbright's attention and made him crane to see.

Worse than any nightmare, was his first thought.

The humans and elf were perched on a sharp promontory that jutted over a vast subterranean amphitheater. Harsh red light flickered as jets of gas along the stone walls billowed smoke and flame. The bottom of the amphitheater was a pool of glimmering lava that bubbled and boiled and gave off a sickening, long-dead, stomach-churning stench. Ringed around the amphitheater on craggy terraces were wave upon wave of monsters: skeletal warriors clad in rags, jaundiced yellow genies with anvil-heads, twitching imps studded with horns and spikes, blobs that roiled and seethed with their own internal fire, and many more loathsome creatures of the cursed planes. The obscuring dimness and smoke were a blessing, a protection against screaming madness.

For worst of all was their master, a hideous giant who hunched on a round bluff rising above its monstrous ranks. Three times the height of a man, it was covered, from its blocky head to great splayed clawed feet, with corrugated red skin. Bright yellow tusks curled its lips below eyes as black as jet. Wings of blood-red skin curled half around its mighty shoulders.

Though the twisted tusks dragged its mouth out of shape, there was no doubt from any of the watchers that the pit fiend regarded them with the greatest amusement.

Like new toys.

"Sysquemalyn!" boomed a voice that crashed like thunder in the vast chamber. "Sysquemalyn of Netheril, arise and meet your fate! You've been very naughty, human. Tsk, tsk! Plagiarizing the Nine Hells!"

The black-eyed pit fiend waited for a second, but not seeing Sysquemalyn put in an appearance, gestured. Gasping in pain, the female mage was jerked upright, her shattered shoulder bones ground to splinters in her tortured flesh. She was hoisted off her feet to hang above the promontory like Sunbright. Yet she hung as limp as a rag doll.

When she didn't answer, the fiend made a two-handed gesture as if straightening a straw and, with a crinkly snap, Sysquemalyn's shoulder was fixed, healed as good as new. The redheaded mage reached out and touched her shoulder tentatively, marveling that the pain had vanished.

Then from below came a dry chortle, like rocks grinding together. Both of Sysquemalyn's shoulders snapped as if from invisible blows. The mage screamed until her voice cracked. And just as abruptly, the shoulders reset, and she hung limp, dripping with sweat.

"Better?" crashed the voice from below. A saggy smile rippled around the tusks in the great red face. "Don't fuss about such little pain, human. 'Tis the merest warmup for things to come. You've earned special attention. Never before has anyone been so foolish as to usurp my corner of hell. Such presumption!"

"I . . . I didn't usurp your realm." Still hanging like a dead goose, Sysquemalyn hunched her shoulders in dreaded anticipation of more abuse. The fear haunted her worse than any pain. Her voice was tiny, quavery, like that of a chastised child. Her pride had melted in pain like sugar in the rain. "I . . . built this place on my own, made it myself."

A vast gobble was laughter. The fiend's wings twitched to the shaking of shoulders as broad as a ship. "Brave of you to lie when I can remove your organs one by one yet keep you alive. You did no such thing! You thought to borrow our power and not pay interest and then pretend surprise. Your little amusement has opened new portals into our realm, as a shovel shears through an anthill. Many new rents you've cut, through which we can issue to muster new strength for our war against the vile tanar'ri. Your people will pay the price of your presumption in blood, and fire, and rape, and endless pain, and bitter death. As will you."

The awful gaze of black eyes, like pits themselves,

turned on Sunbright. His soul felt seared by the gaze, even as his skin had been seared red by the blue-white star. The snake-bonds trapping him suddenly hissed anew, heads twitching and tongues flicking. Then the snakes dropped away, coiled a few times, and returned to the mist from whence they'd come. Released from their clutches unexpectedly, the barbarian dropped three feet to crash painfully on his knees. He was raw and chapped and slashed and burned from head to toe, and this callous dumping made his temper flare. But there was little—nothing—he could do to the pit fiend or whatever this monster was.

"On your feet!" boomed the great voice. Aching, Sunbright stood. Not back against the stone wall, as did Candlemas and Greenwillow, the sensible ones, but at the very edge of the promontory, before the gaze of the fiend and its fellows. Let them see how a brave man dies, Sunbright thought. At least he could die well.

Movement caught his eye. From the ashes, his great sword Harvester levitated, spun, and came toward his hand. He almost hesitated to catch it for fear of bewitchment and contamination, but when the sweat-stained leather fit his palm, he knew the sword was all right. His father had borne it into battle, and now his son carried it, and would triumph. Or go down fighting.

The pit fiend curled its lips around its tusks and seemed to ruminate like a cow. Then it pronounced, "You, manling, have this ludicrous creature to thank for your current predicament and that of your friends. I grant you a chance to take back a bit of your own. Strike off her head, so it might get an early start at eternal torment. Schemers fear separating mind and body above all. So strike hard and true. Show us the might of a barbarian's arm."

As Sunbright weighed his great sword, Sysquemalyn was magically turned sideways in midair as if by invisible hands, until her head floated above an imaginary block, arms pinned at her sides. Her glorious red hair hung so long it brushed the ashes of the promontory.

Sunbright stood unmoving, pondering. His thoughts were overwhelmed by the depth of Sysquemalyn's treachery. To kill her a hundred times would barely sate his barbarian thirst for revenge. Now, through vanity and foolishness, she'd endangered the whole world, all Sunbright had ever known and a thousand times that. Perhaps her death would alleviate some of the suffering, both past and future.

Unconsciously, he found himself raising his sword and taking aim.

"Don't hesitate, mud man." Exhausted and discouraged, Sysquemalyn hung, unresisting. "Strike, and get it over with."

The great sword bobbed in the air as if it were alive and thirsty. Harvester of Blood was its name, but Sunbright hadn't named it. Vaguely he wondered what he would have named the blade, given the chance. But that was a thought for another time.

The barbarian backed away from the shivering mage, dropping the curved sword tip to touch stone.

"No."

Chapter 15

"What?"

The pit fiend was not used to being disobeyed. Its tusked mouth fell open like a cavern, and fire and smoke gushed on its breath. The lesser fiends ducked their heads. A pair of erinyes perched on an outcrop were blasted from the wall, feathered wings afire, to spiral and plunge into the roiling lava below.

Standing foremost on the promontory, Sunbright felt the heat of the pit fiend's fury, felt his skin and eyeballs dry, his hair tingle as if about to ignite. Too, the roiling, sulfurous smoke sickened him, made his stomach churn, until he'd have given a year of his life for one breath of pure tundra air. The barbarian fought to keep his knees from shaking. To fight berserk in battle was one thing, for a man was busy then. But to stand up to a fiend and pretend calm was quite another. It gave a body too much time to think of the awful consequences. Still, a warrior's wit must be a weapon too, as his people said.

So he hollered down, "I mean, no, not without some other reward!"

This gave the pit fiend pause. The idea of bargaining—especially when it could easily renege—was familiar and diverting. Scratching its lower lip with a claw like a slate shingle, it rumbled, "Other reward? You dicker from a precarious perch, manling. Here in my high hall I hold the whip. I offer you revenge, and you demand else. What would you offer in return?"

"If I do this thing—behead Ruellana, or Sysquemalyn, as she's called—will you let me and my friends go?"

The pit fiend frowned as it pretended to ponder, then grinned tuskily. "To turn a human phrase, hell, no!" It gobbled at its own wit, and the ranks of underlings below its feet hooted and chortled and applauded.

Sunbright waited, impassive, and let them laugh. He wasn't sure what he bargained for except time. Perhaps the two mages behind him would wave their wands and pull a rabbit from a hat like some medicine-show mime in the marketplace. Perhaps they could rip open a portal for escape. Perhaps Greenwillow would spot a bolt hole and get away. Any delay could be valuable.

Still chuckling, the pit fiend asked, "What else, mortal?"

"Consider this," offered Sunbright. "I'll execute this mage and stay on as your headsman for one year if you release my friends."

He nodded over his shoulder, risking a glance at the others. Through yellow-gray smoke he saw Greenwillow standing against the back wall, off to one side where she could watch the pit fiend. Her hands were empty, but her thumbs rested on her

hips, ready to draw steel in a second. Candlemas—
whom Sunbright still thought of as Chandler, and
not exactly a friend— stood upright, podgy and bald
and bearded but solid-looking. His arms crossed his
chest, and for a second Sunbright was irritated at
the man's feigned casualness. Then he realized the
mage could demonstrate non-aggression only by
folding his arms: free hands in any position might be
generating a spell. The raven pecked at rock, either
oblivious or stupid or posing.

The pit fiend wobbled its great horned head and
flapped its leather wings erratically, like a sea gull
battered by storm winds. It addressed not just Sunbright, but also all its followers as it bellowed, "You
misunderstand, insect! Here, I reign supreme! There
are no quibbles, no bargains, no repeals. You bargain
whether to sever this upstart's head or not, but I say
you'll do as ordered. Whether you become a headsman or lemure or black pudding or shoe leather is up
to me and me alone. And so, I *command* you, strike
off her head and kick it down here!"

Well, it was worth a shot, Sunbright thought
philosophically. He hadn't really expected compassion or honor from a fiend any more than he would
from a tax collector. And he could think of nothing
else to do to stall for time.

So he spit over the promontory into the lake of
lava and took a fresh grip on Harvester. He shouted
loudly enough for all to hear, "No, I won't do it!
Whatever this creature—be she Ruellana or Sysquemalyn or some other—has done to me, she is still
closer to me than you and yours! I will not harm one
of us for the amusement of such as you."

So saying, the barbarian stepped back a pace to
raise Harvester high behind his shoulder, as if he'd
lop off the head of the pit fiend itself. Then he bobbed

his chin. "Bring on the fiends of the Nine Hells! Sunbright Steelshanks, son of Sevenhaunt and Monkberry, child of the Raven Clan of the Rengarth tribe, bids you battle the Harvester of Blood!"

Enraged at the human's presumption, the pit fiend raised long arms, howled some ancient oath, and pointed broken claws at the single man on the high ledge. "*Attack!*"

In a flash, Greenwillow was at Sunbright's side, calling, "Swing hard but spare me!" She added a bright, star-eyed smile, then turned to the grim work to come—their last battle, they both knew.

First to attack were the winged erinyes. A dozen or more, naked but for wings, flapped and swooped at them. Clutched in both hands were chunks of broken stalactites like flint daggers.

Sunbright waited, timing the attack, then swept Harvester like a long-bladed scythe. The sword sheared through a wrist, hacked toes from a foot, lopped off a wing. Out of control, one erinyes flipped over onto its back in midair, then plummeted toward the lava pool, keening like a hog at slaughter. Another, beating its wings at Sunbright's head, had its belly sliced so a loop of guts spurted loose. A third, creased across the forehead, flipped backward and crashed before Greenwillow's feet. Between jabs, the elf kicked the creature over the edge.

The yellow-haunted sky was a sea of skin and wings and slashing daggers. Up close, Sunbright could see that the erinyes had complexions as chalk-white as those of a corpse, and their wings were not lustrous and sharp like a live bird's, but dusty and ragged. Nor did they bleed when struck; it was as if he'd sliced leather. Sunbright didn't strike to kill, in case he fetched Harvester up in a gut or bone, but conserved his strength and slashed to keep them back, for even this attack might buy them precious time to retreat—if there were any place to retreat. The erinyes were not hard to kill, for they were clumsy and crowded one another in the small space before the promontory. But they were so many, a dozen at least, with more flying from holes in the cavern walls, a sky-filling flock of them. Had they worked together and simply dived and plowed into the humans, their prey would have been smothered in seconds. As it was, Sunbright could only wade into the assault swinging his great sword.

Elven blade flashing, Greenwillow stayed close enough to the barbarian to keep them from being separated, yet out of range of the awful scything power of Harvester. With her slim true-steel blade, she aimed surgical stabs: throat, eye, breadbasket, groin. Stricken monster-angels would shrill and drop or fall back or flutter away, for they could feel pain, especially from her blade, which contained elements of silver. Yet never was there a pause in the furious, feathered attack. Always there were more and more targets above, before, below, to the side. Hale and hearty as she was, Greenwillow knew her arm would grow weary long before the beasts' numbers were exhausted. Before long, she had been nicked on the forearm by a flint knife, sliced across the back of her hand, pinked on the shoulder before she shoved back the attacker with a blade tip jammed into its mouth. Overhead, the black raven flashed amidst the white monsters, striking and pecking at eyes and fingers. But even it lost black feathers that pinwheeled to ignite in the lava far below.

Dancing back a pace for room, Greenwillow saw that Sunbright already bled in four places, including the side of his head below his topknot. Yet he ignored the wounds and watched his enemy, swiping at them so hard that his sword hissed in the air. But he was already grunting with the effort.

From the corner of her eye, Greenwillow saw Candlemas hammering on Sysquemalyn's chest. Thinking he'd gone mad, she shrilled, "Leave off your stupid feud and fight!"

"I am!" returned the bald mage. "I seek to shatter her mystic bonds!"

Abruptly, the feathered beings fluttered backward. Sunbright's sword, in one last swipe, ticked only an errant white foot, shearing toes. Immediately the barbarian dropped the tip of Harvester to the stone to rest and panted in great gulps of the hot, fetid air. Greenwillow wiped sweat from her face with her wrist, hissing as the salt burned in a long slash. Both warriors watched the leader of the fiends below.

The mighty pit fiend rolled its lips around its tusks as if tasting something foul. With a wave of clawed hands and a huge puff of wind, it blew the erinyes to either side of the cavern. Many, exhausted and wounded, crumpled like dust balls on the jagged stones and plummeted to crunch on dark rock, or plunged, sizzling, into the lava pit.

Then, glaring at its foes with blazing hatred, the archfiend jerked its hands as if snapping a stick.

The world dropped from beneath the humans' feet.

Sunbright had only a vague notion of what happened next.

A grinding, crashing, rumbling roar drowned out all sound. Rocks as big as huts were crushed to powder, splintered and shattered on more stones. The cavern walls lurched sickeningly, and fiends of every sort jumped and scampered to get away. The raven squawked and beat the air to gain height.

Only for a second did Sunbright fall; then a giant, invisible cushion blossomed under his rump and back. It vanished just as abruptly, and he crashed painfully, wracking his elbows and butt and head.

Amidst a roiling cloud of ashes and dust, he saw he'd landed on broken rubble. Cracks big enough to trap and snap his leg ran everywhere. Groggily he realized that the pit fiend had reached out with magic hands and yanked down the promontory they'd fought on. The fractured stone lay beneath them in a mound of boulders and gravel, and from under it leaked yellow blood such as Sunbright had never seen before.

But if he and Greenwillow had fallen half a hundred feet onto rock, how had they survived?

"Rouse, rouse!" barked Candlemas. "There'll be another wave!"

The podgy mage helped a shaken Sysquemalyn to her feet. Her invisible bonds had been broken, Sunbright noted, probably in the shock of the promontory collapsing. And if Candlemas, or Chandler, were on his feet, he must have triggered the spell that had cushioned their fall.

Now they lay at the bottom of the great cavern. Only the pit of boiling lava at its center was deeper, and Sunbright saw a yellow-red jet of it flung higher than the lip, burst, and drop like fiery rain. In the distance, seen through heat waves shimmering over the pit, hunched the pit fiend, shouting and waving and pointing—straight at them.

All around them, the sides of the cavern rose, somehow looking larger from below than from above. And just as populous. The yellow blobs were thicker than fleas. Skeletal warriors toted ancient pitted bronze swords, and spiked imps capered to attack while the surviving erinyes flapped clumsily overhead.

All this Sunbright took in with a glance, though

there was much more he couldn't see, either because the hellish red light flickered too wildly, or because the craggy fissures in the cavern walls sucked up any glow while spilling shadows. That Candlemas could conjure at all was encouraging, for it meant—perhaps—that they were not entirely unprotected from magic.

Then the next wave arrived.

Sunbright heard the word "Lemures!" escape Greenwillow. He had time only to pick a platform—a raised rock fairly flat with gaps all around to slow the enemy—then they were fighting anew.

To Sunbright's eye, the lemures were pale yellow and half-melted, like badly dipped tallow candles. Vaguely human-shaped, their faces were naught but big black eyes like glass globes and sagging string-strung mouths. Folds of their skin hung in runnels, and long globs dangled from their outspread arms.

And there were hundreds of them.

The first to spill up the rubble mound Sunbright dispatched with his sword. Or so he thought. Aiming high, he smashed Harvester deep into the skull of a lemure to test its mettle. The sword's heavy nose penetrated deep, popping a black eye to spill gore, knocking the lemure to the ground with a split head. But the wound only spilled a yellow ichorlike pus before it snapped closed . . .

. . . and healed.

Quick as thought, Sunbright "killed" another five. He rammed the sword point straight into the mouth of a wretch, twisted to set the hook, and ripped. The lemure sank to blobby knees. A questing hand from the right, the barbarian sheared off at the armpit, so it landed squishily at his feet and flapped like a grounded fish. He slung wide to the right and bowled over another with a half-severed neck, slung left and chopped the leg from another so it toppled on its fellow, rammed again to drive Harvester's point through one head and pierce another crowding in from behind.

But the first lemure he'd killed had heaved itself up to its hands and knees, shrugged off its fallen comrades, and now stood upright again. The yellow pus had run off its skull; Sunbright could still see a white line from the wound. And the lemure was shorter, having used its own body to rebuild. But it attacked anew. So did another that lacked an arm, but was growing a new one.

And more were coming. The cavern was carpeted in yellow as lemures poured from holes in the ground, caves, or thin air, summoned by the howling pit fiend above the lava pit. Erinyes took to the air to avoid the pustular flood, and skeletal warriors and imps clattered out of the way or were trodden under.

Hundreds, perhaps thousands, of lemures deluged Sunbright, and none could be killed. His heart almost failed within him. "Staff of Garagos! We'll never stop these things!"

Surprisingly, a voice sounded by his ear. "Correct! They can regenerate indefinitely! Only a blessed blade can destroy them!"

It was Candlemas, who'd crooked first and fourth fingers to wield some spell from just behind the warrior's protection.

Sunbright stabbed, hacked, stabbed again. "You enchanted my blade! That day, by the river, with magic potion!"

"That was a lie! You needed confidence!"

Sunbright swung hard enough to almost tag Candlemas. "I need to kill you when we get out of here!"

"I'd be glad to die anywhere outside the Nine Hells!" retorted the mage. Then he hollered, "Duck!"

Hollering *"Volhm!"* the mage slapped his finger-extended hands together.

Sunbright scooched low, but still a clap of thunder almost bowled him into the mass of lemures pressing him. He was blinded as a lightning bolt scorched the air.

Like the breath of a god, a hole appeared in the packed ranks of fiends. Scores of shuffling, dripping lemures were obliterated, blown to fragments and steam by the fearsome bolt. Yellow glop sprayed in the air and fell like hot rain. The ground itself was charred and streaked, and the acidic stink of burned, undead flesh hit the humans and half-elf like a hammer across the nose. Greenwillow and Sunbright gagged, and even the protected mages covered their faces. The air, already thick with yellow smoke, grew foul enough to cut. Stunned, the nearest lemures paused in their attack. But the hordes behind merely tramped on, climbing over their insensate fellows. More pus was crushed from yellow bodies, until it ran in rivers and spilled into the lava pit, where it hissed and steamed and stank abominably.

In the brief pause before the next wave, Sunbright felt a cool hand on his scraped arm. Sysquemalyn pushed alongside him, hair bedraggled, eyes red, nose running. Over the thud of feet and the wailing of the pit fiend, she yelled, "Keep them back! You too, 'Mas, and you, elf! I think I can gate us out of here!"

"Why should we trust you?" retorted Sunbright. The wave of lemures was only a dozen feet away, and he frowned as he inspected his befouled blade's edge. It was dull from hacking through flesh and not-flesh. "You've done nothing but lie from the start!"

"That's the beauty of a crisis! You have no choice!" Despite her begrimed state, Sysquemalyn chuckled, delighting in conflict. Sunbright couldn't reconcile her with the soul-dead loser whose head he'd almost removed. She meant to say more, but suddenly pushed him forward. "Stop them!"

The hordes of lemures faded from Sunbright's vision as he beheld a new menace urged on by the screaming pit fiend. Bounding from the very feet of the monster came four or five imps or . . . Words failed the barbarian. They looked like armored knights, if the armor were made of dried leather, and were studded with tall spiral horns, high arching bat wings, and spikes along their arms and legs. The wings obviously were vestigial, for the fiends jumped in great bounds like manic grasshoppers. Where they landed they crushed lemures by the handful, so yellow gore marked their taloned feet.

All five had been thrown into the battle against the sole living beings in the chamber. Sunbright had time only to shout, "Greenwillow, back to back!" before they were involved in the fight of their lives.

The lemures never fell back, and more were crushed as the imps crashed upon them almost at Sunbright's feet. Two attacked immediately.

The monsters used no finesse, just brute strength in a headlong charge. Huge brown leather hands studded on the back with bony spikes opened to tear off the barbarian's head. Resisting the urge to fall back, Sunbright countered with an equally brutal assault. He'd wrapped both hands around Harvester's haft and tucked it under his right armpit. Now he lunged, straight and true, praying his hobnails didn't slip in the sea of yellow ooze upon which they battled.

Up close, the imp's face was a blank mask of leather stippled with spikes no longer than a fingernail. The eyes were blank holes, and when it opened its mouth, the black cavity showed nothing, as if the head were hollow. Sunbright intended to find out. Crowding the monster, he felt the horny hands brush his topknot and clasp shut. But he'd struck.

Harvester's widened point jammed into the beast's gaping mouth, struck leather on the far side, and split it. Cranking the pommel, grunting with the effort, the barbarian felt the hook tear as he yanked back toward his gut. Harvester's barb jerked loose, snagging on the creature's lower jaw where a lip would have been.

By now, Sunbright was taking punishment from a score of spikes. One leather-clad arm raked across his shoulder, splitting skin with jagged spikes like the teeth of a giant garfish. The other arm slammed him alongside the neck, and he had to hoick his head to the left to keep his windpipe from being shredded.

But at the same time, he twisted Harvester again and pushed, straining sideways. With the hook in the jaw acting as anchor, he scored a deep gash from the imp's slash of a mouth halfway around its neck. With a heave, he sliced its head half off.

Barging in so close he felt white bone spikes ping his chest, the barbarian shoved to drive his sword down the thing's throat, then levered the opposite way.

Like gutting a deer, he peeled the imp's head off.

Only a flap of leathery skin remained at one side of the neck, and the heavy horned head toppled down behind its shoulder. A dry stink like shorn metal welled up from within the fiend, and Sunbright wondered if that represented its spirit, if beings here had them.

Headless, blinded, the imp staggered, stepped back, piled up questing lemures against the back of its knees, and crumpled atop them.

"Sunbright, help!"

He'd almost forgotten Greenwillow guarding his back. He found her on her knees, pressed down by the sheer weight of an imp she'd skewered through the chest. The hilt of her slim sword was wedged between spikes, but the fiend simply flailed at her with horned hands like hard-swung morning stars.

"You have to tear them open!" Sunbright yelled. Unable to dive past the whirling arms, he opted to lunge. Harvester's spread tip rammed through the leather hide directly beside the shank of Greenwillow's sword. "Cut the other way!"

Veteran of a hundred battles, Greenwillow understood instinctively. Bracing with her knees, she put her slim muscles behind the bright edge of the keen blade. Sunbright plied his heavy hand-forged blade—fine quality, but no match for elven true-steel—to yank away from the elf's cut.

Neat as sawing a tree, the imp came apart in the center. The same brassy stink gushed out as its top half toppled behind its rear end. The tall horns struck sparks from the stone floor.

Yet three more imps crowded in, smashing lemures aside to kill the human and elf. Sunbright stifled a groan of exhaustion and despair. Already, his hands and arms and legs were trembling. Blood ran down his forearms and dripped to the ashy ground. More wet redness ran down his shirt from his aching neck where spikes had gouged a furrow in his shoulder. He was torn in a dozen other places, and Greenwillow, always pale, was almost as white as the bony creatures around them. Worn to the nub, they'd surely lose when these charging imps reached them.

Yet he fought on as an imp darted forward to grab him. Showing intelligence, this creature reached in low and tried to snag its target's ankle to pull it out from under him. The barbarian slammed Harvester straight down like a crowbar into the armored, studded arm. But perhaps the imp had considered that. By the ghastly red light and infernal smoke, Sunbright saw the free hand snatch at him—and found that Harvester was fetched up in the thing's other arm. The blade was suffering the same as its master, and even the hook's inside edge, usually as keen as a fish knife, had worn dull. As Sunbright tugged to rip the edge through tough leather, the studded hand closed on his calf and yanked.

The world whirled as Sunbright flipped and crashed on his back. Only his thick topknot saved his head, but he received a solid crack. And even before he could shake his head to clear it, the armored fiend jumped on him.

The barbarian's breath shot from his lungs as giant, heavy studded feet thumped his chest. He smelled a whiff of dust and musty-bear odor as his vest was crushed to him. He fought for air as the imp wrapped two leathery hands around his throat and squeezed and pulled. The thing even smelled of hot leather, like horsehide gloves hung near a fire to dry. It was a question whether he'd be choked or have his head torn off. Flailing with his right hand, he managed only to whap Harvester against the beast's thick hide. He couldn't get purchase to strike. The world went dark and spinning, and he knew his time was running out.

In a desperate burst of fury, he curled and convulsed into a ball, managing to hook a foot in the fiend's crotch. It had no genitals to break, but the toehold would do. Straining until he thought his heart and head would burst, Sunbright braced his back and kicked straight up.

He was lucky, he knew, for the imp had been overbalanced. His throat and chin suffered as the leathery hands were dragged off forcibly. Then the imp toppled onto its head, half-wedged in a crack, and Sunbright could painfully crawl away—not that there was any safety to crawl to.

Wheezing, rubbing his raw throat, Sunbright glimpsed Sysquemalyn and Candlemas standing together a dozen feet off, eyes closed, right hands raised and touching. He thought that queer behavior for a battleground, but supposed it to be some secret mental communication between wizards. And so it proved, for within a few seconds they jumped apart and clapped their hands together.

Meanwhile, a studded imp clawed at Greenwillow. Lurching, still gulping rank air, Sunbright fended it back with the point of Harvester . . .

. . . and a studded arm snugged around his throat. Another imp had seen a weak spot and copied the first. Black wings fluttered as the raven, swooping in from on high, bated the imp's face, without effect.

Throttled, fishhook-sharp barbs lodged against his throat, the barbarian fought panic as he kicked away from one imp to drive back the other. But the hold on his neck only tightened, until he thought the spikes would puncture the underside of his jaw. Greenwillow screamed once, then higher, near panic. Kicking and jumping to keep close and relieve the pressure, Sunbright snapped Harvester over his head, trying to slash the fiend's face. A bony-encrusted arm as hard as a barnacled bollard beat Harvester aside. Desperate, the barbarian switched positions and shoved the sword down between his own legs, praying he could chop a leg from the imp. But he only succeeded in slicing himself.

He wouldn't escape this choke hold.

"By M'dhal's sansevil!" roared a voice. "Protect this man, the living from the dead!"

With a tearing wrench, the imp was ripped loose from Sunbright and bowled backward. The barbarian fell, choking, rubbing blood from his shorn throat. Greenwillow, also bleeding in a dozen places, crawled toward them. Vaguely, Sunbright had the sense that some magic had knocked the fiends back. And through a red haze, he noticed an invisible circle surrounding them, as if a tornado had erupted, blowing away their enemies but sparing them.

Protecting them was Candlemas, who didn't look like a funny fat man anymore, for his upraised hands crackled, and lightning coursed down both sides of his body, so that his beard bristled and his clothes were as fuzzed as a scared cat's back. He bellowed again, not to the barbarian and elf, but to the gods and sources of magic. "Karsus, grant me strength! Foul things, feel the bite of Tolodine's killing wind!"

Instantly, a howling, shrieking, keening, whirling song of death ripped the air, left them breathless, made the pit fiend in the distance howl in rage. Lemures, imps, skeletal warriors, all were churned, battered, shoved hither and thither. Some blew one way, some the other, so they collided and collapsed and thumped together, as if sixteen errant winds fought to wipe them from the earth. Fiends tumbled like grass before a hurricane. But up on the bluff, the pit fiend was conjuring too. A red mist was rising around it and blowing contrary to all the winds to envelop them. The fiends it touched were tinged red as if dipped in blood. Sunbright didn't care to imagine what it would do to the living.

But before the awful red wind could reach them, Sysquemalyn shrieked, "By Quantol! By Smolyn! By Gwynn the Vampire and Hersent's Sigil! Trebbe, heed me! I command you—move us!" And she clapped her hands like a god.

Cavern, monsters, smoke, pit fiend. Before Sunbright's eyes, all vanished.

Within an eye-blink, the barbarian was sprawled on a dirt floor surrounded by dirt walls. There were only humans and the elf here, no fiends in sight.

He scrambled to his feet, instinctively making sure of his grip on Harvester, then groaned as he cast about.

"That was no escape! This is hopeless!"

Chapter 16

Sunbright waved his free hand and sword.

"This is still the Nine Hells! I was trapped in here before! These tunnels change as soon as you turn your back! There's no escape this way!"

"Hush, fool!" Sysquemalyn was up, though shaky-legged, and she pulled at Candlemas's sleeve to rouse him. The podgy mage rolled clumsily, as if drunk. "This is as far as I could gate us!"

"What's wrong with him?" Greenwillow gave up wiping blood from her wounds and helped. Her clothes were more red than green and black.

"He suffers from conjuring in a foreign land," the red-haired mage snapped. She looked tired and wretched, her eyes sunken and encircled, her proud red hair lank and lifeless. "We're too far from the reservoir of dweomer amassed by our patron, Lady Polaris." It was a sign of her desperation that she eschewed any insults for the lady. "We're drawing magic from afar. The local magic is corrupt, the wrong color. . . . Never mind! Why explain to ignorant groundlings? Help me move this bucket of lard."

Groaning, the halt helping the lame, human and elf got Candlemas to his feet. The bedraggled raven, its tail feathers charred along the ends, limped and hopped along, as exhausted as its master. Sunbright levered his shoulder under the mage's arm. Sysquemalyn left them to it, then snapped fire on her fingers to better light their way. "Follow me. I think I can get us out. I built this place, after all."

"No, dear, you didn't." Candlemas was awake and coherent. Despite his fatigue, he argued with his old rival. "The pit fiend said no, and it ought to know. You simply plagiarized—"

"Belt up, Candy-Ass!" snapped the mage. "All right, if I didn't exactly build it, at least I know what I stole and where it leads!"

But waving her flaming hand around, she hesitated, searching both ways. In one direction the tunnel curved up to a hump, then probably dropped. The other direction curved, so she led that way. But when they'd plodded a hundred feet, the dirt floor dropped away abruptly.

Looking backward, they saw that the tunnel now curved up as steep as a chimney. Greenwillow sighed. "I was in a place that shifted every minute too."

Sunbright still propped a sagging Candlemas on his shoulder. "Perhaps we should rest here," the barbarian suggested.

"Aye," groaned the mage. And collapsed.

All together, like four children frightened in the woods, they huddled against one cold wall of the tunnel, feet stretched straight out in front of them. Sunbright propped Harvester across his lap, ready to fight if need be, but he had to fight his own urge to nod off. To keep busy, he dug a whetstone from a pouch and honed his blade. The edge was as dull as a butter knife from chopping bodies as if they were cordwood. Too, he straightened his clothing and tackle as best he could, but everything was so crusted and stiff with dried blood it was like one great mass. Oddly, he still wore his bearskin vest, and his body stank sharply within it, but despite the heat he couldn't divest himself of it, for he needed its scant protection as armor.

Greenwillow tested her sword's edge, found it to be as sharp as ever, so she only scrubbed the blood and ichor from it. She croaked, "Can either of you mighty mages conjure us some water?" The very word made Sunbright's throat constrict as if he'd swallowed desert sand. He'd had a waterskin once, long ago, but had lost it somewhere.

"One definition of hell is eternal thirst," groaned Candlemas. "But I'll see if I can locate any."

Holding his head in both hands, the tired mage muttered under his breath. Sunbright heard the name "Zahn" repeated. But nothing happened, and after a while Candlemas sat back against the wall. "There's none to be found. I'll have to transmute some."

"That'll cost us dearly," put in Sysquemalyn.

"If we're to squabble, we'll need wet tongues." Even tired, the bearded man could joke about their foolish rivalry. "Now . . . Mistress Elf, if I might borrow your breastplate?"

Wondering, Greenwillow loosened the straps to shuck her black boiled-leather armor. The act brought a whiff of her natural fragrance to Sunbright. Like himself, he knew she was sweaty and rank as a hard-ridden mare, but he drank in her scent as if she smelled of wildflowers.

Candlemas laid the breastplate facedown, scraped sand and dust from the tunnel floor and trickled it into a pile, like a child playing in a sandbox. He muttered half to himself, "Funny, at home I could conjure an ice storm with one hand. But let's see if Proctiv's the arch-mage he was rumored to be."

And laying his hands on the sandpile, he whispered a rhyming enchantment that went on and on. Sweat came to his dirty brow, and his head began to swing a slow circle. When his revolving had made him dizzy, he made a final call, bent his head swiftly, and spat on the sand.

It turned into water.

Greenwillow gave a chirp of delight, Sunbright whooped, and even Sysquemalyn snorted approval. One by one, careful not to spill, they put their lips to the water and slurped. Conjured in hell with impure magic, it was brackish and bitter and scanty, but never had Sunbright tasted anything better, not from all the rushing waterfalls in the highlands. Even the raven croaked in appreciation as it pecked up the last drops with a knobby purple tongue.

"So magic's good for something." Greenwillow rubbed her dry face and tried to smooth her filthy hair. "I wish we had a barrel of it to wash in."

"You're lovely even when dirty," quipped Sunbright. Then he was acutely embarrassed by the blush that overcame him and the elf-maid.

With a sigh, Candlemas changed the topic. "Magic's done us more harm than good lately. If I hadn't agreed to this foolish wager with Sys, none of this would have happened."

"It was my fault," replied the red-haired mage. "I kept trying to top you—and the Whiny White Weasel, may I someday peel her putrid face from her skull—

and things got out of hand. There are wards I could have set, protections I should have triggered to warn me, but I didn't bother. And you've all suffered for it."

"The *world* suffers for it," Candlemas corrected. "You forget that up above—or outside or wherever—all of Toril and the Netherese Empire is beset by the vile spawn of these Nine Hells. I reckon that pit fiend could conjure a thousand times that number of creatures to beset us, except most are currently running amok through field and forest. Perhaps this twisted tunnel is the safest place to be these days. Who knows but the world and empire are doomed."

"Everyone makes mistakes."

Three people turned to stare at the fourth: Sunbright, who'd made the strange pronouncement. The barbarian was surprised himself.

"I should think you would be the most enraged," replied Candlemas.

"Aye," added Sysquemalyn in a low voice. "You've been deceived frightfully. I've . . . many of us have . . ."

She didn't need to finish, for they all knew. Sunbright had been tricked into a dragon's lair, lured with lust and love by the false Ruellana, confronted by a lich, and cast into hell. But he dismissed it all with a shrug.

"It's just simple truth. People questing for something higher, whether greater magic or just to be a shaman, make mistakes along the way. Sometimes the gods smile and excuse them. Other times, they pay dearly. Certainly I've made my share of blunders on this adventure. If I'm forgiven, then I need to forgive others their errors. And so far our mistakes haven't killed us."

Sysquemalyn raked at her dust-clotted hair. "I've certainly learned a lot about mud men. I judged you wrong, manling. Very wrong."

The barbarian only nodded. "Apology accepted."

Greenwillow's eyes were suspiciously bright. "You're wise beyond your years, Sunbright. You will return to your people someday and be a wise and mighty shaman."

The barbarian didn't know how to answer that, so he only leaned over and kissed her dirty cheek.

"I'll say one thing," Sysquemalyn added. "I'm done with wagering. I've learned my lesson."

"Good enough. Now if we can survive this one to not collect." Groaning, Candlemas pushed to his feet. "I don't reckon any yard of hell can be safe for long, so I suggest we move on. If this plane has been torn open, and maggots and hellfire and vampire bats can invade the world, then sooner or later we'll find a crack to slide through."

Refreshed and with a glimmer of hope, the party clambered to their feet. Sysquemalyn snapped her fingers alight, and they pressed on, for the tunnels had again shifted, and a flat stretch presented itself.

But for all Sysquemalyn's bravado, they didn't get far. Sunbright glimpsed a shimmer in the corridor ahead, a rippling of the dirt walls. The tunnel suddenly looked much longer, as if it extended for hundreds of feet.

Candlemas grunted. Greenwillow gasped. Sunbright swore.

The far end of the tunnel was blocked by a single giant eye. An eye as wet as shiny slate. As the eye blinked at them, they saw the massive eyelid bore patchy red skin.

"Watch out!" yelled Sysquemalyn. "The tunnel's 'witched! Run . . . Ow!"

In the lead, Sysquemalyn had bumped her head where only seconds before they'd had plenty of room. Rocked by the blow, she halted and grabbed at the low ceiling.

Sunbright's heavy, scarred boots suddenly tilted under him. The floor was sloping toward the giant eye at the far end.

"The other way!" shouted Candlemas. Climbing uphill, he shoved past Sunbright and Greenwillow.

Lurching, clinging to crumbling dirt walls, the party turned. But now another giant eye blocked that path. And the floor tilted in that direction as well.

"This makes no sense!" Sunbright cursed. "You can't fall two ways at once!"

No one heard. Sysquemalyn shrilled a spell. Greenwillow grabbed Sunbright's shoulder for support. Candlemas called for his raven to fly.

Then the tunnel upended as if they were mice trapped in a box.

Floor and ceiling became walls as the party plummeted straight down. Reaching for a handhold of any kind, careful to keep tight hold of Harvester, Sunbright only ticked his fingernails on dirt. All four howled as they dropped toward the great black eye at the bottom.

Falling from the mouth of the tunnel, they passed through open, smoggy air, then landed hard on a stone floor that rattled their teeth. Cradling Harvester, Sunbright banged his left shoulder frightfully before rolling against a jumble of rocks.

No, not rocks. Through spinning smoke he beheld the ugly leer of the pit fiend, still on the bluff above the lava pit. Above them. It was the creature's rockhard splayed toes Sunbright had fetched up against. All around them gibbered ghouls and ghasts and imps, hideous monsters of every type.

The pit fiend squinted with eyes like wet slate, opened a mouth that drooled acid from yellow tusks.

"Welcome back. Now, where were we? Ah, yes! Hordes, *attack!*"

Moments later, Sunbright was glad he'd honed his sword to a fine edge, for he killed a dozen fiends in as many minutes, until they were heaped around him like a makeshift barricade, until they had to clamber over their own dead to reach him. He was spattered with blood and pus and gore from topknot to boots, and scorched besides, for the anvil-headed genies snorted blue fire. Yet he fought on, and still the monsters charged.

He didn't battle alone, but as part of a team of four who stood back to back in an impenetrable square. Sysquemalyn waved her hands and spouted arcane curses at his right elbow, Candlemas at his left. The mages hurled every spell they knew, and they were powerful, for this chamberlain and steward to Lady Polaris were not far from being archmages themselves. He heard the name Anglin, and a searing wall of hissing, multihued light drove back a clot of fiends. The name Valdick was invoked, and a section of the stone floor dropped away, carrying a dozen clattering skeleton warriors with it. At the name Xanad and some unspoken howl, three imps were slapped back so hard their limbs became disjointed. Primidon was called on, and a burning cloud like a miniature thunderhead scorched lemures and sent up a sickening stench like charred garbage.

Too, Sunbright heard Greenwillow challenge the fiends, heard her cry out in exultation each time her elven blade struck home and dropped a foe. And he had the incongruous thought that such a fine, beautiful woman, so sleek and lovely, could be so hard and deadly in combat, like a tooled and tempered blade herself.

Even the raven above them fought, flapping and

pecking and clawing, and Sunbright wondered how Candlemas could control it and blend spells at the same time.

Yet there was some sphere of protection over or around them, for many of their enemies couldn't crowd close, or seemed to struggle to cross an invisible barrier. And too, when the mages had touched their shoulders with hot hands, he and Greenwillow had been lent superhuman strength and endurance, or else they would have collapsed long ago. In some ways Sunbright hoped they would, for it seemed all his previous life had been a dream, and this nightmare was the only reality, one that would endure forever, as if he'd already died and were being punished in Hell.

But they couldn't fight much longer, for they were being steadily beaten down. Mighty as the mages were, they'd been born in the material world, and this was Hell. Even Sunbright, who knew nothing of magic, sensed their magical energies running low. Their spells took longer to pronounce and had a smaller effect each time. The living party was succumbing to death here in the land of the undead, their strength melted away like a snowball dropped into a bonfire.

Too, their foes never diminished, but increased. The pit fiend had shuffled back, wings flapping uselessly, to watch its minions battle. Perhaps the fiend enjoyed the show. Howsoever, it would raise a broken-clawed hand and wave it toward them, and from fissures and caves and even the boiling lava itself came taller, more fearsome creatures. These, Sunbright suspected, were so fearsome even their leader couldn't completely control them. From a pit climbed bone monsters with scorpion tails and blinding-white limbs that made others shrink away. Barbed creatures ridged with spines wore burning skin that ignited lesser fiends. And tall brutes with dead-white skin and blind eyes simply tore with long clawed hands into anything that moved. Sunbright heard Candlemas ask what the last were, and Sysquemalyn gasped, ". . . amassed . . . ongoing war . . . rivals the tanar'ri of the Abyss!" Hints of horrors the barbarian didn't even want to ponder.

It was as the blind giants wreaked havoc that the party took their first casualty. The raven, fluttering madly, must have broken through whatever protection served them, for suddenly a rearing anvil-headed genie puffed flat cheeks. Blue fire, blinding even to see, seared the raven in midair so not even a feather tip remained, only a jot of smoke and a dusty stink.

Sunbright heard a groan and risked a glance. With the bird's death, some part of Candlemas had died also. The mage went pale, his eyes bleary, his hands trembling.

With Candlemas's affliction, their well of protection crumpled. Sysquemalyn shrieked and shot both hands in the air as the fiends redoubled their attack. Sunbright stepped over Candlemas to straddle him, while Greenwillow tumbled back against his shoulder.

A roar sounded above the clash and howl of the monsters. The pit fiend, impatient, bellowed, "Hurry and die!" Raising a huge foot, it stamped stamped stamped on the stone floor of the huge cavern.

Within seconds, cracks radiated from the stamped spot to splinter the stone floor in all directions. When the cracks reached the lip of the great lava pit, they fractured ten times as wide, then wider. Sunbright saw an edge crumble and disappear, taking a handful of the scorpion-tailed bone creatures with it and flinging a gout of red-hot lava almost to the ceiling. As the earthquake shocks reached the walls, stone rained down on the horde, crushing scores to yellow and gray and red pulp. The barbarian couldn't comprehend the senseless violence of it. The pit fiend had no compassion whatsoever for those it commanded. But perhaps that was hell too, to be toyed with by unknowable monsters.

Then Sunbright was busy watching his own feet, for the cracks under him widened. Deep inside, they glimmered with lava and fire.

Hanging on to Candlemas and Harvester, he scuffed his boots first this way, then that to avoid gaps that could easily swallow him. Heat rose around him; he felt it under his long shirt and on his face. Frantic, he was holding the mage, fending off fiends, minding he didn't bump Sysquemalyn or Greenwillow into a crack, and worrying. If the gaps widened . . .

They did. As if made of glass, the floor continued to splinter, fragment, fracture. Soon Sunbright had only a cracked patch as big as a tabletop to stand on. He clutched Harvester and Candlemas in the same hand so he could hang on to the collar of Greenwillow's shirt with the other. Fiends no longer beset them, for many were fighting to keep their own footing. To his right, an imp tried to bound clear only to bang into a fellow and disappear down a jagged slot. One of the blind giants charged until its big feet sheared off an edge. The monster dropped to its waist in a gap, screaming in agony as its feet were seared by white-hot flames. It lashed out with long-clawed hands for support, rending lemures to yellow putty. Then the crack split anew, and the giant sank into the fire.

"Greenwillow! We need a place to stand . . . What?"

He gave a shout as Candlemas rose in the air. At first he thought the mage had been seized by the erinyes. But nothing held him aloft save magic. Sysquemalyn, lank red hair like dead snakes rattling around her head, had levitated herself and her comrade off the floor. She hung, tilted, a dozen feet up, crooking her fingers to bring Candlemas to her. But Sunbright clung to the man's rope belt and wouldn't let go.

"Release him!" Sysquemalyn shrilled over the noise of grinding earth and shrieking fiends. "I need him!"

"I need him too!" shouted the warrior. "Levitate us all!"

"I can't! I've not enough dweomer! I'm using 'Mas's to levitate him. Let go! We'll call for help!"

"You lie!" Sunbright was enraged but fought to control his temper at the thought of more treachery. Perhaps she spoke true. Certainly the two mages looked as wrung out as rag dolls. "Forget me and just levitate Greenwillow then! She's light!"

"I . . . can't!" And clenching both fists, Sysquemalyn hoicked Candlemas into the air so hard he was wrenched from Sunbright's grip. "Fight on! Help is coming!"

Sunbright glimpsed Candlemas stir as Sysquemalyn slapped his face hard three times. She shook him violently and shouted in his ear. The podgy mage nodded groggily, but Sunbright couldn't hear their scheming, and had to turn his attention back to his own situation.

The tabletop they'd occupied had shrunk to the size of a chair, and Greenwillow and Sunbright teetered on it precariously, as if balanced atop a stone column. With the elf pressed to his chest, her dark hair tickling his nose, the barbarian cast about

for a direction in which to jump. The light was more
hellish than ever, yellow flames splitting the floors
and spilling black smoke. The chasm below them
glowed red some distance down: twenty feet or a
hundred, there was no way of telling. Not far off, perhaps six feet, was a shaky-looking promontory, with
staggering lemures beyond. Sunbright made a fast
decision.

"I'm closest. I'll leap across, turn around, and lie
flat to catch you when you jump. If I don't make it,
you'll know it's not safe."

But the elf wasn't listening. She wrapped both
arms around his chest and hugged him tight. Almost
as tall as he was, she pressed her head against his
ravaged neck. Despite the heat and smoke, he felt
her wet tears spill down his skin, tickling his chest
under his bearskin vest and shirt.

"Sunbright, I . . ." Greenwillow hesitated, afraid
to say the words that were in her heart.

"I know," Clumsily, the barbarian cradled her slim
back and patted her dark hair. "I feel the same, but
there isn't time now. We must go."

Giving him a final hug, then tearing free, Greenwillow stuck her sword in her belt—it was too crusted
with filth to fit in her scabbard—and pointed. "Yes,
go. I'll follow."

But Sunbright couldn't just run off, not if both of
them were to die then and there. Grabbing her slim
chin, he planted his salt-crusted lips on hers, found
them as cool and delicious as a draught of springwater.
Then he shoved Harvester in his belt and turned.

The promontory beckoned from six feet off, barely
his own length, a moderate jump given full strength
and a running start. He had neither. Making do, he
squatted low on his toes, poised, sucked wind, and
leaped into space.

In the short time he was airborne, he had the thought he'd never make it, that he was falling short. But something gave an added boost to his rump and heels, and he crashed to his knees on solid stone, only his ankles and heavy boots dangling over the edge of the fearsome pit. Harvester ground into his side, dead weight he probably should have discarded.

Greenwillow, he thought. She'd shoved him with all her strength to carry him across. Without her help, exhausted as he was, he'd have surely fallen in. He had to get her across quickly.

Spinning about on bleeding knees, he flopped on his belly and stuck his arms over the edge to catch her. Peering through smoke and flame, he shouted, "Come on, Green—"

She was gone.

Stupefied, horror-struck, Sunbright at first wouldn't believe it.

No, he thought. It couldn't be true. She couldn't have . . .

Down he stared into the fiery caldron that raged in the gaps. If Greenwillow had fallen . . .

Then it hit him.

She'd sacrificed herself to save his life. She'd known he couldn't jump the whole distance, had hunkered low and shoved him off. That's why she hadn't attended his instructions, because she'd known she'd never make the jump. Heaving his weight had cost her the precarious perch, and she'd toppled off, fallen to her . . .

. . . death.

"Noooooo!"

Blind with rage and horror and sorrow, Sunbright came to all fours. Harvester dragged on stone, and in fury he ripped the sword from his belt, prepared to throw it down into the burning chasm and himself after it. If he hadn't worn his heavy sword, perhaps she needn't have pushed him. If he'd thrown it first . . . If she'd only told him, he could have hurled her first.

If only, the death of dreams.

Frantic, he scrambled to the very edge, leaning out and craning his neck to see. But roaring heat seared his eyeballs and curled his sweat-damp hair. If only she'd landed on some outcropping. If only . . .

Something tugged at his boot, and he spun in place. Blind rage was creeping up on him, an urge to kill and smash and destroy. It was a curse of his people, he knew, the berserker's rage that made a man or woman charge into battle and kill and kill until he or she was cut down and hacked to ribbons.

And the one who'd tugged his boot was Sysquemalyn, the source of all this trouble.

Howling like a banshee, the barbarian locked both hands on the mage's throat, raised her in the air, and shook her so savagely her teeth rattled and her neck almost snapped. He screamed, "You! You did this! You killed her! Your scheming and plotting and desire for power . . ."

Hoisted as high as a chicken at slaughter, Sysquemalyn struggled, kicked, raked the back of his hands with chipped red nails. Only her personal shield kept her alive, for the barbarian's strength was awe-inspiring. This man could snap her neck like a straw.

Hammering and drumming on his arms and chest, she still tried reason. "Yes, it's my fault! But don't kill me, or you'll never get out of here alive! You still need magic—"

"I don't *care* if I die!" Spittle flew from Sunbright's lips. His face was a gargoyle's leer, his mouth dragged down and distorted, his eyes flaming red. For the first time, Sysquemalyn was truly frightened of him. This "mud man" was suddenly the most dangerous being in this corner of hell. "I'll see you dead first!"

"Greenwillow . . . wouldn't . . . want that!" the mage gasped. Despite her shield, her throat was constricted, and she gagged on a snarl. "Don't waste her sacrifice, fool. She kept you alive to live and fight. Help is on the way. Now fight! For her!"

The command to attack penetrated Sunbright's grief-stricken mind and he snatched up his sword. Running across the cracked floor, the first thing he encountered was one of the blind giants, presently mauling an imp with both fists. The human roared and attacked both. Flinging Harvester behind him with no attempt to parry or shield, he swung so hard he cut clean through the imp's horned head and deep into the thigh of the giant. When it turned, as dead-white as a rotten fish, as strong as an oak tree, he slung the sword directly overhead. The bending giant felt the sword strike it square between its eyes, smack in the forehead, and the awesome blow stunned even this insensate thing. It collapsed full out, but by then Sunbright had attacked elsewhere.

Right, left, whirling behind him, the berserker lashed out at everything that moved, as mindless and hostile as the blind giants themselves. He saw nothing but a red haze and moving shapes, and he struck, again and again. From far off he heard voices: the pit fiend's howl, Candlemas calling his name, Sysquemalyn screaming spells. But nothing penetrated, except the fact that Greenwillow was dead and had died to save his worthless hide. So on and on he fought, intent on killing until he was killed.

But gradually, the red haze gave way to white. Bright whiteness, brighter than that of the bone creatures, brighter than sun on snow or the biggest star. The white light pulsed and flared, flooding the dark chamber with brightness never seen in these depths before. Even Sunbright, berserk and raging, couldn't face the white light, and he had to turn away, looking for more enemies.

But there were none to be found. They'd retreated, hundreds of them. Gibbering in dismay, whole rivers of fiends jumped gaps and chasms in the floor to race for fissures and caves and other exits. Leaning from the white light high above the lava pool, the pit fiend roared at them, even kicked and crushed its followers to stop them. But it couldn't stem the retreating tide any more than it could extinguish that blinding light.

Finally, bathed in fearsome light, Sunbright let Harvester's bloodied nose fall. Candlemas and Sysquemalyn waited, all the embattled humans squinting, unable to stare at the light.

But the two mages wore expressions of dead weariness blended with relief. Candlemas breathed, "Thank all the gods we know and those we don't. It worked."

Then the white light spoke.

Chapter 17

The blazing white light slowly spiraled inward, waning, until there stood in the air above the chamber a woman Sunbright had never seen before. Her hair was glossy white, though she was young, her skin pale and smooth, her gown a simple long black robe chased in silver down the front and around the hem and sleeves.

Mostly it was her manner that stunned the barbarian: she was as cool as a glacier, confident in her immense power. There was nothing in this room she couldn't grind under with one step, her calm air suggested. And Sunbright, his mind cloudy with grief and hatred, wondered if she were indeed a rescuer, or a worse threat than these monsters.

"Lady Polaris!" sneered the tusked-faced pit fiend. Beside the glorious white-haired woman, the creature looked like some grub turned from under a rotten log. "You bitch! What do you mean invading my kingdom?"

Even the woman's voice was cool. "I shan't keep you long, Prinquis. I've come only to retrieve some of my possessions. I don't care to lose my most promising apprentices. Not even to their own folly."

Turning in midair, she located the filthy and bedraggled Candlemas and Sysquemalyn. A white-painted nail pointed. "There they are. I'll just fetch them along home."

"Not so!" The pit fiend roared in hatred. "You've overstepped yourself this time! Hordes, destroy her!"

That, thought Sunbright, would be difficult, considering she was suspended in the air. But the hounds of hell, commanded to fight and die and rise again and fight and die again, for all eternity, surged forward, pushed by the wave of hate flooding from the pit fiend. Imps bounded like crabbed grasshoppers, bouncing higher each time to grapple for the white-haired woman. Blind giants blundered forward, crushing lemures between their toes. And the few surviving erinyes, naked and dusty, plucked up their stalactite-daggers and flapped clumsily toward the shining woman.

None got closer than a dozen feet. Without even raising her hands, the archmage hurled a pulse of white light like an errant star. Sunbright grunted and wished he'd had a warning, for the brightness seared his eyeballs and left a purple dot centered in his vision that half blinded him.

When he could see again, he realized the blast had been more than light. Feathers and hide and horns littered the ground for scores of feet around Lady Polaris. But there weren't enough scraps to account for the attackers, and Sunbright had to reconstruct what had occurred from the burnt stench in the air. The first circle of erinyes and imps must have been simply obliterated, evaporated to not even dust. The second wave had been crisped as if by lightning, leaving only feathers and toenails and horns. Farther out, fiends were seared and scarred beyond belief. Some had lost faces, the skin burned down to skulls, yet they feebly clung to life and moaned and gibbered. Others had lost arms, skin, eyes, lips, and these poor wretches crawled backward to live and suffer or to die and find relief. And all the others, mostly unharmed, had learned their lesson, and cowered low and whimpered.

Most amazingly, Sunbright and Sysquemalyn and Candlemas had stood at the same distance as the third rank, and so should have been killed. But the destruction had circumvented them, while even the lemures behind them had been reduced to puddles. The barbarian marveled at this woman's power, so mighty yet so contained. If she represented just one of the archmages of the Netherese Empire, it must surely endure a thousand years or more.

The high mage waited, doing nothing but shaking back her frosty hair. Sunbright wondered that she could stay so cool in a such an inferno. It occurred to him then that she might *not* be here, that what he saw was some projection of her, like a candle-show mimed behind a sheet. Who could know anything of how these archmages worked? Sunbright could no more understand them than a beetle could comprehend a king.

Prinquis, the pit fiend, surveyed the casual destruction of its kingdom, and its fury mounted beyond reckoning. Rearing on its great splayed feet, pounding its chest with horny hands, it threw back its head and roared a battle challenge that made the walls ring and Sunbright cover both ears with his hands. Then the fiend spread its leather wings and launched itself at Lady Polaris, like a red mountain taking off.

It fared no better than its slaves, though this time the archmage did raise her hands, mildly, as if chiding a child. Sunbright saw her power more clearly now, for only a single cometlike pulse flared from her hands. It struck Prinquis square in the face and almost snapped the creature's neck. Slammed as if by a giant sledgehammer, the fiend was bowled head over heels to slam into the far wall. A wing crunched like kindling; then the beast crashed upon the bluff where it had previously stood, a red, charred heap.

A moment of silence hung breathless over the pit. Imps and lemures and skeletal men hunkered and scuttled like cockroaches exposed to the blinding flare of Lady Polaris and her power.

Then, a stir on the bluff. Shaken and battered, Prinquis rose anew.

Its broken wing trailed and dripped gore; its face was red-black and stippled with blood that spattered its tusks. With scabby hands it scrubbed its face, making a coarse rasping noise. Reaching behind it, the fiend straightened the broken wing, snapping it back into place with a shudder. Then, most amazing to Sunbright, the creature grinned around its tusks.

"First round to you, Polaris. But you won't get away from here. You don't have what it takes to best me, not in the long run. Your pulse couldn't kill me, so nothing can."

Strong again, the fiend touched the wall of the cavern behind it. Sunbright knew the barrier was solid rock, yet the creature inserted its hand into the cleft and made the granite crumble like cheese. Looking up at the white-haired mage, Prinquis called, "Shall I ply my strength now? How about I tear down these walls around us? Collapse this cavern so even a

snake couldn't wriggle through? Then you and I—
near-immortals that we are—can lie crushed in
darkness, trapped but alive, feeling yet unable to
move, smelling the dead around us rot to nothing.
Think of all we could discuss in a thousand years,
Polaris. Think what it would be like to miss the sunlight for a millennium. In such time, could you conjure a spell that could truly harm me, here in my
own abode?"

Sunbright reeled at the notion of being trapped in
blackness for generations. Yet Lady Polaris, on high
like a god, never even blinked. Her voice continued
coolly, "I didn't think I could harm you, Prinquis.
That's why I arranged a portal between here and the
only place you fear: the Abyss."

A wail rose from the assembled horde, and there
began a new scampering to get clear, to escape. The
pit fiend roared in rage and horror as Lady Polaris
flicked a finger at it, or rather behind it.

On the far wall of the chamber, a glowing line appeared, like the mark of a glowworm. The light was
white, the work of the archmage, and thickened and
spread. Then, as if it were a blanket being torn, the
wall split and peeled back. Rocks were smashed to
dust or spit out to bounce on the bluff and off the pit
fiend's thick hide. The whole wall was crushed aside,
leaving an opening big enough to admit Prinquis,
with wings spread.

But what erupted through the rent to the Abyss
were fiends larger and even more savage than Prinquis. Towering, bull-headed, bewinged, and horned,
the horde of balor rushed into the great chamber in a
vast, earth-shaking stampede. In their fearsome
claws were morning stars, flails, many-tailed whips,
and other instruments of cruelty. Flames wreathed
the monsters so they were difficult to see, but clear

enough were their cries of savage ecstacy.

Sunbright couldn't begin to guess how long this feud had been raging. He'd heard Sysquemalyn talk of Prinquis's never-ending war with bitter rivals, the tanar'ri of the Abyss. He supposed these creatures could wage feuds just as tribes of men and women did in the tundra and highlands and elsewhere. And he had to admire Lady Polaris, who coolly set one gang of fiends upon another so she could hover above and watch the senseless slaughter she'd engendered.

And as long as he lived, Sunbright would never forget the horror of the display. Balor killed for sheer joy. They grabbed imps by the arms and ripped them apart, even splitting the hollow leather bodies down the legs and torsos. With broad hooves, they stamped and stamped on skeletal fiends until only white dust remained, and they stamped yet on that. With great sweeps of their flails, they spattered lemures to gobbets, then punched down on the squirming mass to ignite it, so the lemures burned even as they reformed. The barbarian was sickened by the sight and wanted to cover his eyes to shut it out. This was ferocity on an unheard-of scale, and he knew it had raged for centuries and would continue for all time. From the glee these balor exhibited, he knew they would kill their rivals, crush them to flinders, burn them to ashes, and then resurrect them to do it all again.

Then he didn't have to see any more, for a cool voice cut through the chaos. "Children, come." Magically he was lifted off his feet, levitated along with Candlemas and Sysquemalyn to hover at the feet of Lady Polaris. With a single finger she'd lifted them, and now raised another digit to take them elsewhere.

The three of them, Sunbright thought. Not four.

Not Greenwillow, who was gone forever.

For a second, he wanted to stay and be killed, to see if he could find her in some afterlife.

Then a blinding white flare from a frosty fingernail engulfed him, and he could see and feel nothing.

* * * * *

"It was wise of you two to cooperate to summon me. Neither of you were strong enough, alone, to reach me from the Hells. You did well."

The party stood in bright sunlight that flooded through the windows of Candlemas's workshop in the floating castle of Delia, one of Lady Polaris's many homes. Sunbright stood unsteadily, marveling that they could travel from such a hell-hole to a bright and beautiful and peaceful place in an eyeblink. The sky beyond the windows was blue and clean, and red-tailed hawks with feathers like broad fingers banked on the fair winds. Through one window he could just glimpse a hilltop thick with trees, and knew he hung over the Great Forest.

Suddenly a great yearning to be there, down among the sturdy aromatic pines and dappled glades and cool, clear pools overwhelmed him, and Sunbright almost cried out. But he had to bide his time and keep a low profile, as if stalking game in dangerous territory. He was safe here, for the moment, as safe as he could be in the clutch of wizards. They'd lied to him and used him, and he had to be wary.

But he was almost too exhausted to stand, let alone think. In fact, he took the lead of the two lesser mages and sank to the floor, bracing his back against a sturdy table leg.

Graciously, Lady Polaris excused their weariness and allowed the three to sit in her presence. Gently, she queried Candlemas and Sysquemalyn as to how they'd found themselves in the Nine Hells, and the events that had led up to their being there. Sunbright marveled at Sysquemalyn's version of the story. The barbarian didn't know all of what had happened, but he knew that much of what the mage said was pure fabrication. Still, the archmage listened patiently, as if to a small child reciting an exciting dream. The red-haired mage finished with ". . . and so we thank you from the bottom of our hearts for our deliverance. We hope in serving you in the future, we can pay back in some small measure your magnificent and lordly rescue."

"You're very welcome," pronounced the lady. But Sunbright, a forgotten observer, thought he detected a hint of ice in her tone. More than anything, he thought, she looked like some great white cat who'd plucked a mouse from a hole and now contemplated what to do with it. "On the other hand, your pranks—both of yours—have caused considerable mischief. No doubt you're unaware that my fellow archmages have been compelled to step in to close the leaks you sprang in the Nine Hells, Sysquemalyn. In the last two days, we've all had to slave to correct your mistakes, and have labored harder than we have in the past hundred years. Many projects and games and plots had to be abandoned while we cleaned up this mess. You've no idea the total losses in revenues and lives. Even here in my own castle, I was required to pluck the body of a dead maid, entirely drained of blood, off my bed. Nor was I happy to be reminded constantly by the other archmages that it was one of *my* charges who had slipped her leash. Oh, no, I am not pleased."

Down had thumped the white paw onto the mouse, thought Sunbright, and he was glad to be temporarily overlooked. He froze, not even blinking, as someone else was raked over the coals. He prayed he wouldn't get a turn.

"Now, I believe there was something about a wager." Lady Polaris's eyes were bright, and Sunbright realized she enjoyed chastising her underlings.

Sysquemalyn's face was shiny with sweat, her eyes wide with fear, her mouth jerked into a rictus like a skull's. "Oh, the wager. Uh, that's been suspended. Candlemas and I called it off."

"Nonsense," corrected the lady. She took a step back and clasped her hands, as if readying to work. Candlemas, who'd been slumped near Sysquemalyn on the stone flags of his workshop, began to edge away as quietly as possible.

"Not at all," the archmage continued. "You played; you lost; you pay the forfeit. That's the way of the Netherese, and such you are, although of the very lowest, most common sort, barely above the beasts."

Sysquemalyn went pale, and her lower lip trembled. Covered with grime, her once-glorious red hair filthy and lank, she resembled something dumped on a garbage heap, while Lady Polaris, pronouncing sentence, loomed ever larger and more beautiful, like some god.

The archmage's even contralto droned on. "It's been instructive watching the two of you squabble. I expect that of children, for it's one way they learn. But you, dear Sysquemalyn, have expended too much time carrying tales about your lord and mistress. I've heard myself addressed as the Great White Cow, the Dead White Fish, the Whining White Weasel, and so on and so forth. You projected into the future, when you would be archmage and I your underling. You said I would have my nose slit and be the plaything of the palace guards and empty your chamber pots. All fascinating, enlightening stories. Some of it I discarded as the prattle of a child, but I'm afraid that now you've overstepped your bounds."

Caught in her scheming, stunned that her words had come back to haunt her, Sysquemalyn cried out in protest. Tears spilled down her cheeks, leaving streaks in the dirt. Lady Polaris's face was frozen in anger. Sunbright rolled his eyes to scan the windows and the only doorway out. If the archmage loosed her pulse of white light in here, it would be the last thing any of them ever saw.

"Remember you the terms of the bargain, dear Syssy?" Polaris went on. "This barbarian hulk here was to be given escalating tests, his only goal to survive. Bear witness: he's still alive. He's withstood every test you could connive, and now he's been to the Nine Hells and back. That's the ultimate test for a human, to my mind. So you, Sysquemalyn, have decidedly *lost* the contest. And what were the terms at the last?"

Sniffing back tears, Sysquemalyn mewled pitifully. Her dirty hands skittered on the floor as she backed away from her mistress, too terrified to speak. She flinched as Lady Polaris stepped forward and raised a hand, touching her brow.

Sunbright thought the archmage was being gentle, until the lady's hand suddenly jerked. There came a horrendous ripping noise that turned the barbarian's stomach, for he'd heard that sound before when he'd skinned game. He tried not to look, but his damnable curiosity made him.

With one yank, Lady Polaris ripped Sysquemalyn's skin and clothing from her body. The chamberlain's skin tore at the back of her head, along her spine, parted at the back of her arms and legs.

What was left was a quivering, writhing mass of red muscles over bright-white bones. Round, staring green eyes bulged from her head, and her teeth looked huge, exposed in red gums without any lips to mask them. Everything that had looked like Sysquemalyn hung like an empty sack from Lady Polaris's dainty hand.

Distastefully, Lady Polaris flung the skin to one side. It landed on the floor with a squishy plop. Calmly, she spoke to the skinned woman, who writhed at the pain and cold of being flayed alive, yet living magically. For the first time, the archmage spoke loudly, because Sysquemalyn had lost her outer ears with her skin and had only gaping holes above a toothy jaw. "Now, you'll no doubt be pleased to know that I've capitalized on your toy and stabilized this pocket universe of yours. It's still there, waiting."

Stepping back, she lifted a finger, and Sunbright saw a now-familiar white streak glow along one wall. Stone crumbled and bounced, and a slit not much wider than his shoulders gaped open. From within came the light of hellish red fires and a distant shouting and screaming. Did this pocket include the great chamber of the pit fiend Prinquis, and the hordes of fiends and rampaging balor?

As if in confirmation, suddenly from the pit swelled one of the anvil-headed genies. With a fanged mouth sagging in a grin, it swooped into the room like some elongated fish and wrapped two sturdy hands around Sysquemalyn's stripped ankles. She howled in pain at the hot touch on naked muscle.

Lady Polaris walked parallel as the flayed mage was hoicked off her naked buttocks and dragged along the floor, wailing in agony. "And do you know the most delicious part, Syssy? When someone imagines a hell, they conceive what they themselves fear! This will be the perfect place for you, your worst dreams come true, and you'll have a whole year to explore your own creation!"

She caroled the last, for Sysquemalyn, dragged on skinless fingers that left a bloody trail, had been dragged wholly into the slot.

With a pop, the portal snapped shut.

"Candlemas."

The podgy mage jumped as if jabbed with a spear, for all his mistress's quiet tones. Sweat ran off his bald head, trickled out of his beard. Off to one side, Sunbright wished he were somewhere—anywhere— else. At least he'd had a chance when fighting fiends.

"Don't fret, child. I'm not angry at you—*much*." The lady paced back and forth, from table to window and back, a sign she was already eager to move on to other pursuits. Perhaps the worst was over, the two men hoped. "No, I'm pleased with your performance, overall. You recovered the book from Wrathburn's hoard, and it pleases me."

Reaching into a black sleeve no larger than a sock, she extracted the massive book with the ruby-studded cover, the tome of ancient, magical lore of some lost race. Sunbright recalled *he'd* collected that book, but he kept the information to himself.

Casually she dropped the book on a window ledge, then continued pacing, the men tracking her movements with the sick fascination of a wounded bird watching a cat. "True, you were foolish enough to abet Sysquemalyn in her inane wager, but gambling is a curse of the Netherese, and we'll chalk you up as having been led into temptation. And you kept her from committing worse sins, I suppose, so we'll excuse your part. And besides, I can't expel both my chamberlain and steward, or there'll be no one to run my estate. So, as a reward, I'll forward you some scrolls and divinations that will let you exploit some higher resources previously denied you."

All this time, it seemed, Candlemas hadn't breathed. He sucked air now as if unable to believe his good fortune. Not only had he not been crushed like an insect, or worse, but he'd been rewarded with access to superior knowledge. Perhaps, if he absorbed it correctly, he could step up a level and become an archmage himself. It was more than he could have hoped for, and it made him dizzy . . . and wary of his dangerous, unpredictable mistress.

So his head jerked as she finished, "And please remember, dear 'Mas. A wise master—or mistress—treats his servitors well."

Candlemas had to swallow to get out the words, "Yes, mistress. I'll remember."

"Good." The archmage propped her hands on the windowsill and raised herself on tiptoes, like a little girl, to see around a tower of the castle. "Now get back to work, for there's much cleanup left. I believe there are at least a dozen dead bats littering the wine cellar and poisoning the well. And we've lost our chamberlain to her little dollhouse, so you'll have twice the work to keep you out of trouble. Go now, and attend your chores."

"Yes, mistress!" Scrambling off his fat backside, churning his chunky legs, the mage left dust spinning in the air as he ran for the doorway and down the corridor.

Lady Polaris sniffed, rubbed the end of her nose, then turned and gathered up the ancient tome. Hefting it as if for an evening's read, she started for the door, striding as elegantly as a deer.

Greatly daring, Sunbright cleared his throat.

Was it with a flash of irritation that Lady Polaris paused and regarded him? Certainly her voice was cool. "Oh, yes. What are we to do with you?"

Sunbright wasn't even sure the question was addressed to him, or if she were simply thinking aloud. But he spoke out boldly. "If you please, send me back to the surface. I've been too long below and above it."

A white eyebrow arched. "You wish no other reward?"

The barbarian almost sighed with exhaustion, both physical and mental. But he bit his tongue, careful to show nothing that could be conveyed as disrespect. Like an animal hunted to its lair, he could only beware and hope. "No, milady."

A shrug. "Done." The eyebrow arched in his direction.

The world spun for a second, a stone ceiling replaced by blue sky replaced by a mountaintop replaced by pine branches. Sunbright had thrown his hands to the side to grab hold and now clutched pine needles. Blinking, he sat up, making sure Harvester was safe at home in its sheath. If he had his sword, he had all he needed.

Except, upon finally finding himself alone and safe once more, he remembered the ache in his breast, as if his heart had been removed.

He was alone, because . . .

"Wait!" Suddenly his brain was clear and throbbing, and he shouted a name at the sky. "What about Greenwillow? Milady! Please, if you can, bring back Greenwillow! Please!"

Only echoes returned.

After a while, his voice cracking in grief, the barbarian collapsed and knew no more.

* * * * *

Far below human trouble, deep in the crust of Abeir-Toril in a cavern that had never known sunshine, a clutch of upright cones poised on stinger tails that were as hard as diamonds. The creatures were agitated and often whirled in place, as if eager to be away, somewhere, anywhere. That they could not go where they wished was their reason for gathering.

Lost. Two more of us, gone.

Dead forever.

And not even our magic can re-form them.

Magic is too much for humans to handle. They do not understand it and never will.

We must wipe them out before they spread too far.

I suggested that centuries ago, but no one listened.

We're listening now.

Too late.

Too late for us, then.

Returning to my suggestion . . .

That again?

Gentle beings, we've just witnessed the worst magic-storm in our history. It occurred far below the surface, farther than humans and other spined ilk have ventured before, and killed two of our tribe. Magic seeps downward, and the humans expend it like rainfall. Soon there will be no room for the phaerimm. We can perch here and bewail our fate, but words accomplish nothing. Nor has anyone offered a good suggestion.

Our lifedrain has weakened the humans' hold on the earth and generated instability. The lowest masses, the workers, will rise against their masters on the day the last loaf is eaten. Even the high Neth begin to grasp that. As pressures build from below, like a volcano, and resources grow shorter, the strain will tell in the upper levels of their society. Let us con-

tribute to that pressure rather than seek to avoid it, as we cannot. To undermine the Neth, to stir up their magics as tornadoes stir the atmosphere, will force them to expend more. Let them burn bright and hot, and extinguish that much quicker. Let us heap fuel on their fires!

Fight fire with fire, as humans say?

Yes, until the inferno overtakes them.

And we take what is left, which will be next to nothing?

We take what remains, true. But now even the earth is not our own.

I am in agreement.

I, too.

And I.

So say we all, then. Heap magic on their heads until it burns them.

Where do we start?

Chapter 18

"Sunbright!"

The barbarian whirled to peer at the darkness and aimed Harvester at the voice. This was no cave, but an old mine, cut square and pillared, but with a very low ceiling, scarcely the height of a dwarf. Sunbright didn't like the looming confinement, but he'd endured worse. The gray-square exit was no more than thirty feet behind him.

And before him . . .

"Greenwillow!"

The half-elf stood farther on in the darkness, her pale skin almost glowing in the dim, reflected light. She stood tall and proud, but with her arms held before her enticingly. Sunbright could see every feature plainly: her peaked eyebrows, slanted green eyes, pointed ears, slim neck. She wore only a thin sheath made of some clinging fabric the color of spring leaves. Her statuesque beauty and slim, curved body set the warrior's heart racing.

"Greenwillow!" He trotted forward a dozen steps, almost doubled under the low ceiling. One beam had slipped off its post and hung at an angle blocking the way, so he had to scoot underneath it. "How did you escape from the Nine Hells?"

Oddly, the elf didn't advance. She stood still, arms outstretched, hands reaching for him. "I yearned for you, Sunbright! I wanted you so badly, and I finally found you. Come to me, darling!"

Half under the obstructing beam, the barbarian paused. Something was wrong. Greenwillow had never called him "darling." But she'd been missing for several months now.

She took another step, her small bare feet sinking into the dust and clinkers scattered on the mine floor. Her movements were slinky, powerful but controlled. Her slim arms were inviting, and Sunbright longed to feel them around his neck.

Sliding under the beam, he crept toward her, now only a dozen feet away. Every step deeper into the mine meant less daylight, and his own huge shadow eclipsed Greenwillow's white form as she cried, "Come to me!"

The barbarian halted. What was wrong? A year or two ago, when he was younger and less experienced, he would gladly have run to the arms of any beautiful woman who beckoned him. But he'd learned to be wary in many things, and warning bells were sounding in his mind. "Come out here, Willow. Out into the light. We can't stay in this cave."

The elf suddenly wrapped her arms around herself. "I can't; you have to come in."

Almost alive in his fist, Harvester's wide tip bobbed in the air like a hound sensing danger. "Why can't you come out? Are you enspelled? Under a geas?"

Still hugging herself, the half-elf looked at the ground as though ashamed. "Yes, my love. They said I couldn't leave until rescued by a worthy man."

"Oh?" That sounded like a vague sort of curse. Slowly, Sunbright hunkered on his heels and scooched to one side to let more dim light fall on Greenwillow. Squatting helped him resist the pull, too. What exactly the pull was he couldn't say: lust, the scent of a woman, a lonely aching in his heart, the need for another's touch. His heart warred with his head to go on, go on.

But his head had powerful arguments that kept him rooted. Now that he had a moment to think, Greenwillow's state of undress disturbed him. He always pictured her dressed as she had been when he first met her, in a long green shirt and boiled black armor. In the court of the lich king, she'd worn a shimmery mackerel-scale gown, and later he'd seen her naked for a brief moment while she donned her traveling clothes and armor again.

So if she wore only a filmy sheath, whence had it come?

And why wouldn't she come closer to the light?

"Darling." The word rang foreign on his tongue, but then he hadn't used it much. "Tell me how I might free you."

"Oh, I'm so cold!" Hugging herself, she shivered, and Sunbright saw real gooseflesh. "Won't you just hold me while we talk?"

Sunbright shook his head, but found his thoughts growing increasingly murky. The smell of the mine seemed normal enough: cool earth, stale water somewhere, a tang of bat guano. Why then was he muzzy-headed? He'd heard some mines gave off poison air that was invisible and felled a man unawares. Perhaps that was the problem. He couldn't even see

Greenwillow clearly anymore. But if he were to rush forward and just grab her and run, then outside they could . . .

That's what was wrong.

Blinking, he peered at her, really sized her up for the first time. She stood erect, with her arms seductively wrapped around breasts and loins. A small smile showed under glowing green eyes. Sunbright found his own loins aching to join her, wanted to hold her tight and never let go.

Except . . . How could she stand upright when the cave was only dwarf-high? Greenwillow was nearly as tall as he was, but he couldn't straighten to more than a crouch. Either the cave opened up farther down, or this was some kind of illusion.

If it was an illusion, then it had a purpose.

A trap.

And if a trap, his first step backward would spring it.

Still, he hesitated, with his sword held out before him. He couldn't be sure this was a trap, or that this was or wasn't Greenwillow. The one truism he'd learned in his travels was that nothing was certain.

"Greenwillow." He talked quietly, thinking madly. "How did you get out of the Nine Hells?"

"I walked, darling." Her voice was assured, calming. "The caverns of hell are convoluted, true, but they have exits. You've seen them."

Had he? the barbarian wondered. For months now, he'd tracked rumors of openings into the Nine Hells, seeking a way in for himself or a passage out for Greenwillow. His heart thumped at the thought he'd finally found her. But she acted so queerly.

Breath tight in his lungs, stomach clenched hard, he asked, "The fire?"

"I fell through. The chasm opened below, and

though the flames spanned it, they were not deep. I passed through them, incurring only minor burns, and landed in a deep lake in another cavern. You know how the corridors twist. But I was lost and alone, and called your name for hours. You didn't come." Her voice turned pitiful, and tears spilled down her cheeks.

Now Sunbright's fingers clenched so hard on the tilted beam they dug splinters. It was possible that she'd fallen into yet another corner of hell. Anything was possible in that mad maelstrom. Yet he stayed put.

It might truly be Greenwillow, under some mind-clouding spell. How else could she know she'd fallen into fire? Yet . . .

"Take my hand." The warrior would compromise. He extended his left hand, Harvester clenched in his right. "Meet me halfway, and we'll leave together."

"I told you, I'm under a spell! If you won't rescue me, it means you don't love me."

Clinging to the beam like a drowning man, Sunbright extended his left hand until his shoulder creaked. "I do . . . love you. I think I always did. But we have to work together. Help me help you. You were a warrior!" Strangely he found himself speaking of her as part of the past.

"No! You're cruel and hateful. I'm going!" She spun around, showing a straight back and long legs.

"Don't go!" Sunbright stood up so fast he banged his topknot on rotted boards. Dirt speckled his shoulders. Releasing the beam, he took a step forward. How queerly she was acting, enspelled or not. "Come . . ."

Greenwillow whirled in place, the sheath clinging to her small breasts and flat belly. "You do love me!"

But her sudden turn had startled the befuddled

barbarian, and he stepped back, raising his sword.

And sprang the trap.

With a hissing snarl like that of a giant snake, Greenwillow was replaced by her opposite. Not pale skin, but skin so black it glistened violet. Not soft hair, but scruffy patches that stood up all around her head. Not yearning, outstretched hands, but hooked claws as black as chert. The face was all beaky nose and glaring round eyes, as red as embers in a dying fire.

The night hag snarled some curse or command that Sunbright couldn't understand. Then she pointed her palms at him, as if by doing so she could shove him backward.

And something did. The barbarian grunted as a punch like an invisible sling ball slammed his breast. His bearskin vest and tough muscles absorbed the blow, preventing his ribs from breaking, but he'd be bruised to the bone. And he flinched at the thought of being struck invisibly in the face.

Mind racing, he weighed the odds of a charge versus a retreat. It was no contest; to stay and fight a night hag was pointless. He'd run.

Harvester aimed straight at the creature, the warrior felt behind him as he hunkered to clamber under the tilted beam. It wasn't more than fifty feet to daylight, and he guessed the hag couldn't follow him into the sun. At the cost of thumping his head again, he moved free of the beam, backing steadily.

The hag came on, hands upraised and hooked. She paused at the beam, screaming and gibbering at him. More curses, but he dismissed them as he scuttled away, watching her warily.

Until he sensed something behind him.

A smashing blow, like that of a giant whip, slapped his leg, shot pain clear to the top of his head. At the same time, claws like red-hot nails sank into his neck. Strong arms leaned on the claws to shove him flat.

The whip came again, low, raking his knee. Sunbright squirmed to get under the claws without kneeling or being squashed on his belly, helpless. He couldn't swing Harvester behind him, nor free Dorlas's warhammer from his belt without dropping his sword, so he fought otherwise.

Sidestepping, he rammed his right elbow backward with all his strength. Something grunted and let go of his neck.

Slinging Harvester before him, Sunbright whirled and struck hard at whatever had attacked.

It was a black silhouette against distant daylight, but he recognized the pointed head, barbed spine and tail and knees. A barbed fiend, poised to strike.

But first came such a rush of fear that the barbarian paused for a near-fatal second. He didn't want to die, or suffer, to feel pain or be flayed alive or . . . Thoughts of death and mutilation rattled in his head, overwhelming him.

Yet part of him stayed cool, for he knew the fear to be induced by this creature. Another part recalled he'd fought these things by the dozens in the Nine Hells. One was not much threat.

Biting on his fear and swallowing it, still hampered by the low ceiling, he braced his off foot far back, took aim, and swung Harvester in a sizzling arc.

Overconfident with its spells and fearsome appearance, the barbed monstrosity was unprepared for an attack. Harvester's heavy tip slammed into the fiend's side directly below the armpit, where the heart would be in a human.

Sunbright didn't know if he struck the creature's

heart or not, or even if it had one, but he proceeded as if he had. Twisting Harvester in the deep wound, he set the hook in the fiend's armpit and yanked. He expected a shower of blood, but got instead a gout of reddish glop like lava. Still, it was bloody enough. Hopping sideways and shoving, he plied Harvester like a pry bar to thrust the creature down, then leaned with all his might. If he could, he'd puncture the thing, run it through until Harvester bit dust.

But instead he stumbled forward, crashed to his knees, and almost sliced his own forearm. The fiend had disappeared.

As he should. Without looking back, he turned to bolt for the exit.

Teeth sank into his upper arm from behind.

The fangs were cold, biting to the bone. He felt his heart jump at the frosty touch. He had to get free.

Jumping, he grazed a beam with his head and wrenched his arm loose, losing skin and muscle in the process. The night hag hissed in frustration. Spinning, he found her racing to claw out his eyes, his blood bright on her long fangs and pointed chin.

A new wave of emotion flooded him. Not fear, but anger. He didn't know if it were induced or not: madness to cloud his thinking. But something within him snapped. This monster had probed his mind to find his utmost desire, then perverted it to lure him close and feast on his blood and meat. It was no more deceptive than a fox giving a rabbit's cry, he knew, but still it enraged him to have his mind raped.

Howling, forgetting even his sword, he swung his left fist and smashed the hag in the face. He struck her long nose, and broke it, pounding it flat. Another punch bashed her upper lip, snapping a long fang loose. A third in the throat gagged her. Sunbright howled, cursed, and raged incoherently, months of pent-up anger flooding from him, driving his fist to smash again and again. He could barely see for a red mist before his eyes and knew he'd keep pounding until the hag was black pulp on the mine floor.

But suddenly his fist struck dirt, then again.

Shaking his head, cursing feebly, he cast about for the hag. All he saw was a dark gray mist low to the ground that slowly trickled back into the black depths of the mine.

Shivering with cold and blood loss and the aftermath of battle fury, the barbarian turned and dragged himself outside, toward the sunlight and realm of humankind.

He emerged, squinting, into dim sunlight, only to find a war party awaiting him.

Grimy and blood-spattered, the warrior hefted Harvester in one fist. The easy way he toted the weapon gave the war party pause. There were nine in all, six orcs and three men. Five wore gray tunics with a familiar red splayed hand painted on the breasts. The others wore red armbands on both arms.

The lead orc, with a red-hand placard on his rusty helmet, asked, "What do you in there?"

Sunbright hawked and spit dust. "I stabbed a barbed fiend and smashed in the face of a night hag. Now, *step aside.*"

They stepped aside.

Warrior's instinct on the alert, the barbarian didn't walk through them to invite a stab in the back. Rather, he stooped and picked up his blanket roll, satchel, and bow and quiver with one hand, then sidled around the party. A stream ran between the hills not far off, and he made his way toward it. This was climbing country east of Netheril, the farthest east he'd ever gone, discounting journeys to the netherworld. In eight months of searching, he'd quartered a goodly portion of the known lands, and some unknown. Only in these reaches, though, had he found a semblance of peace, for the hills reminded him of the foothills of the Barren Mountains above the Great Forest.

Stomping through yellow grass and buttercups—it was again late summer, with autumn's breath in the morning mists—he hopped to a rock to vault the small stream, set down his baggage, then placed Harvester flat on the grass close at hand. If the orcs and orc-men crossed the stream, he decided, he'd kill those he could and run. If they stayed on their own side, he'd leave them be. That they were nine and he one didn't bother him much: he'd faced bigger odds and survived. He'd remain wary but calm and in control.

It occurred to him, like a distant song, that as a lad he'd dreamed of returning to his tribe someday, a tall, scarred, confident warrior who feared nothing. Somewhere in his journeys, he'd become that man. And someday, he knew now, he would return, to settle old scores and rejoin his people.

After he found Greenwillow.

Scooching, not kneeling, he washed his hands and face and drank from his palms of the cold, clean water. Too, he watched the war party descend the slope, talking among themselves. They argued loudly, where conspirators would have whispered, so they probably were peaceful enough. But he didn't stray far from Harvester.

Keeping to their side of the stream, out of weapon's reach, they clustered behind their leader. Without preamble, the orc said, "One of us went inside and saw the tracks. You are a mighty warrior."

Two years back, Sunbright would have grinned

cockily. Now he just smoothed his hair through his topknot. He knew what he was, no matter what others thought.

"You should join us," continued the leader, a hunchbacked orc with a gray muzzle, old to be campaigning. The others were a mix of seasoned and green. Two of the men appeared to be father and son. The last had scars enough to be a warrior. "We journey to the camp of the Lich Lord to join his army. It will be the mightiest army ever formed and will conquer the world from sea to sea. Now is the time to join, to share the glory and receive a goodly portion of land and wealth in the aftermath of peace."

There was no fool like an old fool, Sunbright thought. Joining a madman's army to grow rich and retire. The barbarian had already guessed their purpose, since they'd painted themselves with smeary homemade renditions of the Red Hand banner. But as he scrubbed dirt from Harvester's blade, he said, "I've heard of the Lich Lord's army. Do you really think following an undead ghoul will lead to peace?"

"Truly." The old orc straightened its back as much as possible. "Wherever his army travels they find chaos, and wherever they conquer grows quiet."

Chaos because sensible folk flee before them, and no one's alive afterward, thought Sunbright disgustedly. But it had been a while since he'd talked to anyone, and his native curiosity won out. "I know men flock to the banner, but I fail to see why. This Lich Lord called himself the One King until his real identity was exposed. At the same time, a red dragon descended on his city and incinerated his army and him, or so I heard. So how can he—"

"Not true, not true," the old orc interrupted. It squatted painfully, balancing, getting comfortable for a bout of storytelling. The other orcs and men remained standing. Sunbright honed Harvester and listened. He was in no hurry.

"The great red dragon Wrathburn was sent to assassinate the One King by the conniving Netherese, who were jealous of his power. But the One King's bravery brought defeat to the dragon, which was slain. His ribs and spine have been erected in an arch leading to the gates of the city Tinnainen, and the king now wears a pair of dragon's teeth in his crown. After such a glorious and dire battle, he pronounced himself the Lich Lord so his followers might have a better picture of him and more easily see his great plan. Angriman is his loyal aide, the servitor of the king, and sees the Lich Lord's orders are carried out. Even now the One Lord's army pacifies the lands east of Cormanthyr, for he felt the land of the Netherese unworthy of his attentions and moved on to remove the threat of the elves, who are the enemy of men and plot their deaths in many forms.

"Some cowards went weak-kneed and watered their loincloths when they beheld their master's true form, and those were quickly dispersed to the six winds. But a greater form means greater power. Other, better men flock from all the corners of the kingdoms to join him. His ranks grow larger than ever, for these days the Lich Lord is less lenient with his foes, and his punishments ghastly to receive. But his victories are glorious, and we shall all reap the benefits."

Sunbright stifled a sigh as he laid Harvester back down on the grass. Pure, purest horseshit, he wanted to shout. He had been there to see the lich and black-browed Angriman blasted to ashes, had witnessed Wrathburn flying serenely away, the obvious victor. And how could any soldier be stupid enough to pledge himself to a dead fiend and an army that fled

Netheril for the hinterlands to attack the homelands of the elves? That was sticking one's head into a hornet's nest! Greenwillow had been the doughtiest fighter he'd ever met, barring the dwarf Dorlas, and . . .

Thoughts of Greenwillow set him drifting off. The mine still beckoned. He'd entered only because a shepherdess had told him of seeing light inside on rainy days. It wasn't much to go on, but neither had been a hundred other rumors.

But his thoughts were drifting like dandelion fluff, which was not a sound practice when faced with nine fanatical orcs and orc-friends.

Having decided, the barbarian stood, slid his sword home in its scabbard on his back, and picked up his belongings. Oddly, the fact he'd sheathed his sword made him look more dangerous than when the blade was naked. "That's all very well and good," he said politely to the orc, "but I've other fish to fry. Good luck on your quest to serve the Lich Lord. I hope you receive your just rewards."

The old orc frowned so its tusky teeth dented its lower lip. "Anyone not of the army will suffer when it arrives. You'll be sorry you turned us down."

Sunbright reflected that, like most fanatics, the orc had begun with a soft pitch and finished with a dire threat. "I've much to be sorry for now; one more thing won't be a burden. Good day."

And, tackle swinging around him, he swung off down the hill. He wasn't pursued, and hadn't expected to be.

* * * * *

Weeks later, Sunbright huddled under his blanket strung between four trees and nursed a small, damp fire. He hoped to get the fire hot enough to roast a brace of rabbits he'd shot earlier with his long arrows. So far he had a lot of smoke and precious little heat.

It had rained for three days, and everything he owned was either soaked or rusty. Further, winter was settling in, and he'd come far north in his quest—and hit the biggest dead end of all. For in topping a rise this afternoon, he'd seen a cleft mountain in the west and below it a tiny town split by a river. He'd forgotten the town's name, but remembered the place. It was the first town he'd encountered when dumped from Lady Polaris's high castle so many months ago. It had been in this town where he'd started his quest to track down all rumors of openings to the Nine Hells. For almost a year, he'd hoped and prayed to find a way to slip back inside those hellish tunnels, to find a way, somehow, to rescue Greenwillow. But each lead had proven false.

He'd persisted, even though, deep down, he knew Greenwillow was probably dead, that she had perished in hellfire or been killed by the fall onto stone. But part of him wouldn't accept it. It might be his native stubbornness, a flat-out refusal to believe anything until it was proven before his very eyes. Or perhaps he was simply becoming mush-brained.

And besides, if she were dead, wouldn't her spirit have visited him by now?

That would not be possible if she was still alive, and despite everything, he believed she was. Perhaps his shamanistic abilities, which came and went like dreams before sunrise, somehow were attuned to the half-elf, alive but trapped somewhere. Perhaps that signal, that siren's call, that promise led him on. Perhaps. Since he couldn't switch on his priestly powers like an ale tap, he could only wait for more to be revealed: in dreams, in campfire flames, in the murmurings of animals and the wind. Perhaps he shouldn't be using his legs to search, but his mind.

But he didn't know how.

He didn't know what he knew, except that his quest had ended in failure. Today he'd come full circle, back to his starting point, with winter crashing down, and no hope of searching through the snows. That hope was dashed, and there was nothing to take its place.

So what now?

"Ho, the camp!"

Instantly the barbarian located the source of the voice in the gathering gloom and located his weapons, sword and bow and warhammer. But too, he recognized the voice, a familiar one.

"Ho, Sunbright! May I enter your camp?"

Cursing inwardly, the barbarian kept his mouth shut. Although it was the worst of wilderness manners not to invite someone to his campfire, he bit his tongue. Perhaps the speaker, if ignored, would go away.

No such luck. The voice called, "I'm coming in! Don't shoot!"

From the dark shuffled a figure in a plain shepherd's smock, with a blanket cloak folded around his shoulders and head. The man squatted and duck-walked under Sunbright's sodden blanket. The hood was pulled back, revealing a shiny bald head. Candlemas eased to his knees and warmed his stubby hands by the fire.

Without speaking, Sunbright studied the mage. He looked older, his eyes more sunken and pouchy, his beard speckled with white. The barbarian had thought mages didn't age, or aged only slowly, but Candlemas looked like a grandfather after only a year. Some great strain must be pressing down on him, but the warrior felt no sympathy.

Rubbing his craggy hands, hissing as if from arthritis, the mage said, "I know you probably don't want to talk, but we should."

"Why?" The word was jerked from Sunbright, who hadn't talked to anyone in days. "Do you have more dirty work no sane man would tackle, so an innocent must be tricked?"

"I used you; I admit it." Candlemas didn't look at Sunbright, but at the tiny fire. "I can spark your fire higher, if you like."

"Leave it be. I'm done with magic."

"I always intended to reward you, you know." Candlemas ignored the barbarian's rudeness.

"Likely," Sunbright snorted. For something to do, he skinned his rabbits, which didn't take long. "I was nothing but a tool. If I didn't meet your expectations, you were willing to see me destroyed readily enough, and look elsewhere."

A casual shrug made the warrior grab the warhammer, so Candlemas sat still. The patter of rain in the oak forest and the constant drip of runoff from the blankets was a small music around them. "But you did live up to my expectations, them and more. You have the most amazing ability to survive I've ever seen or heard of."

Another snort. "A horse can climb a mountain if whipped hard enough. That means nothing."

"No, it's true. You survived where a dozen men would have died. And you bested your foes in a remarkable fashion: a dragon, a lich lord, fiends. I can't think it was luck or mere brawn or even fighting savvy. I think you possess something that even you don't suspect."

Despite his effort at disinterest, Sunbright paused

in slicing the rabbit. The mage's words were an echo of his own bleak thoughts of only moments ago. If his brawn couldn't find Greenwillow, perhaps it was time to try something else.

"Anyway, I always pay my debts," Candlemas droned on. "I would see you properly rewarded."

"What could you possibly give me? I need nothing."

Well, one thing he needed.

"Not true. I can give you, well, more than you can imagine. Training in magic, for one. I cannot make you the equal of a Netherese archmage; I haven't made that rank myself, yet. And I doubt you'd ever make much of a surface mage. Somehow I don't picture you scrying secrets for kings or fashioning magic jewelry boxes, or overseeing farms and orchards as I do. But I can point the way to some magics you'd find interesting. Magical devices and scrolls and potions that would make you the equal of any groundling wizard in your own field of study: the ways of animals and plants and rivers and trees and stone. I know these things matter to you, else why would you be here in a rainy, cold forest when you could be elsewhere in comfort?"

Sunbright didn't tell the wizard that, in contrast to living on the snow of the tundra, this rainy forest was paradise. Rather, he fought down the desire that swelled in his bosom, the desire to *know* natural things in the real sense, not just on the surface but down to their very core. His father Sevenhaunt had had that ability. That had been the source of his name, for he'd been haunted the seven days around by questions without answers. And Sunbright was his only son and, according to his mother's words, heir to that power—or curse.

"You're quiet." Candlemas cut into his thoughts.

"It's late. I'm tired," quipped the warrior. But his

hands hung idle while his mind raced.

The podgy mage hunkered close, one hand balled to a fist to contain his excitement. "Come with me, Sunbright. Work for me—with no more games, I promise. I'll make it worth your while. Every day you're with me, helping me find what I need, you'll learn more about yourself and how to get what you—"

"Can you bring back Greenwillow?"

A cloud crossed the worried face, and he shook his head. "No."

"Can Lady Polaris, or any of the high mages?"

Another denial.

Sunbright shook his own head, rejecting everything Candlemas had said. "Then what good is magic? I can't bear to think of her, trapped in that place because of me!"

"You've been trying to get back there." Candlemas didn't need to make it a question, for he already knew the answer. "The High Neth worked day and night for months to find and seal all Sysquemalyn's leaks from the Nine Hells. Things are largely back to normal. I knew you'd been searching for a way in. Did you ever find one?"

Sunbright debated whether to tell this man—who might be an enemy or might be a friend—the truth, then answered, "No. I came close a few times, got into depths that blistered my eyebrows and got me jumped by monsters from . . . But no, I never got close to the Nine Hells."

"Do you really think she'd want you to?" Candlemas saw the barbarian's eyes snap, but he didn't quail. "Greenwillow gave her life to save yours. As Sysquemalyn said, you mustn't throw away that gift, her sacrifice. You're meant for greater things. You need to find what they are."

Sunbright rejected talk of himself to cling to the

memory of Greenwillow. Talking of her lessened the ache within him. "Tell me something useful. Is there any way she can be saved?"

Candlemas blew out his breath, made the tiny blaze dance. "If she died there, as she must have, then no magic I know, or even suspect, can resurrect her to this plane. But her spirit may linger, trapped. With work, it might—*might*, I say—be set free."

"So." Sunbright picked up a stick and prodded the fire. "If I work for you, will we try to find a way?"

"I'll do what I can, if you will. That much I promise." If Candlemas felt any thrill at getting his way, he didn't show it. Mostly he sounded tired. "What I can't promise is results."

"No one can," replied the barbarian.

The two were quiet a long time. They listened to the drip of rain in the forest, the soft rustle of leaves overhead. Far off, a strange bird gave a plaintive cry like the ring of a cowbell. Sunbright didn't know that birdcall, but he'd learn it.

Abruptly he scooched onto his heels and caught the corner of the sodden blanket, tied off with a length of line. With nimble but cold fingers, the barbarian loosed the line and channeled the trapped water to splash on the fire and extinguish it.

Without the meager light, the forest loomed dark all around them. Candlemas, Sunbright knew, would be spooked by its damp, silent depths. But to the barbarian, it was an inviting home. And soon he'd know it even better, deeper. Truer.

And he'd show it to Greenwillow, somehow.

In the encroaching darkness, Sunbright's voice was as clear as that birdcall. "If you'll try, I'll go with you."